T0198912

# SCARLETT

# SCARLETT

HALEY MILNE

iUniverse, Inc.
Bloomington

# SCARLETT

iUniverse books may be ordered through booksellers or by contacting:

iUniverse
1663 Liberty Drive
Bloomington, IN 47403
www.iuniverse.com
1-800-Authors (1-800-288-4677)

Because of the dynamic nature of the Internet, any web addresses or links contained in this book may have changed since publication and may no longer be valid. The views expressed in this work are solely those of the author and do not necessarily reflect the views of the publisher, and the publisher hereby disclaims any responsibility for them.

Any people depicted in stock imagery provided by Thinkstock are models, and such images are being used for illustrative purposes only.
Certain stock imagery © Thinkstock.

ISBN: 978-1-4620-6195-2 (sc)
ISBN: 978-1-4620-6196-9 (ebk)

Printed in the United States of America

iUniverse rev. date: 10/14/2011

# Chapter 1

*L*IFE SURPRISES YOU IN THE greatest of ways sometimes. One minute, you think you're perfectly happy with the way you've always wanted everything to go and in the next fate shows up and slaps you right across the face. My advice to you is; embrace the unwanted things that come by and don't let any moment pass. You might just regret it in the long run and believe me; it will haunt you for the rest of your life. I don't care if you think that it's the wrong thing to do at the time, go with what your heart tells you and tell your head to just shut up.

I was born the only daughter of very rich and very well-known people. Our family never had problems with money and my two older brothers and I went to the top private school in the city. I was a privileged child, I'll admit, but my family is something I never quite fit into.

Holden recently turned eighteen years old and the greatest sports player to ever enter Beverly Hills Preparatory. He is a year older than Max and I and he runs the entire school. Everyone bends at his whim with a simple word out of his mouth. He's always been the more mellow, laid-back guy but when it came right down to it, he could take charge if anyone needed him to. He and I aren't very close but he's still my older brother and I love him. His girlfriend, Jessica Hamlin, happens to be my friend's older sister. She's the type of person that will ignore you, even if you pass her in the hall, if she thinks you are of no importance to her.

Max (real name is Maxwell) is my identical twin who's six whole minutes older than me. Even though we share the same deep auburn red hair and Cornflower blue eyes, he and I are nothing alike. Beside the fact that his face is littered with freckles while mine are just brushing under my eyes and across my nose, Max owns a 2007 Ford Mustang that he loves to race on the weekends. My dad bought it for him on our sixteenth birthday and he's been reckless with it ever since. Rich people are suckers for a good drag race and I'm afraid my brother is just the same. You can always tell when he has lost a race because he shuts himself up in his room for two days straight. I am normally the one who has to pull him out and drag him back to the real world. Don't get me wrong, I'm happy to do it but at some point in his life I won't be around to get him back on track.

My father, Benjamin Hera, has been the top lawyer in Southern California for nineteen years. He comes from a long line of legal aids and workaholics as well. My parent's marriage, at the moment, is on the rocks. It's not as if it was ever perfect but they did love each other, and I have to believe they still do somewhere deep inside. But the point is my father is still avoiding my mother at all costs to save his own hide from an argument.

Jane Hera is the best OB-GYN in the whole country. She is also and always will be my best friend in the whole world. My mom and I established a strong bond from the very start of my life. Part of me thinks that it's because I am her only daughter and the one she gets to unload all of her knowledge unto when I become a woman. We share every secret we keep from everyone else and a shoulder to cry on if it's ever needed. She's been distant from me recently and she won't talk to me about it and I'm beginning to worry that something's wrong.

Then, there's me . . . the odd ball of the family. I'm the type of girl who could spend hours in her room with a book and never be bored with it. I have always received straight A's in school and I hate to lose at anything. I quit dance after five months when Becca Price got the lead role as the Fairy queen, I don't play any sports, and I hate chess. Mainly because I had to learn by myself and I never figured out how to play, but that's beside the point.

You could say I'm a nerd but I wouldn't say it to my brothers. They've been known to beat up anyone who makes fun of their little sister. I suppose that's a good thing for me but they are guilty of the same crime they pummel other boys for.

I'm very high strung and assess everything before I do it. I love writing on my laptop and whoever tries to take it away from me (save for my parents) will be seriously injured quickly. The only boyfriend I've ever had was Carter Jenkins, a transfer student from London, England. He and I had a brief fling in 8th grade but nothing came out of it. Yes, we shared our first few kisses but anything after that was out of the question. And the worst part of it is . . . *my first name is Scarlett . . . as in a Scarlett woman*!

"Scarlett, can you come down here for a minute?"

My mom's voice rang out from the bottom of the staircase. I had been cleaning my room at the time and she had just interrupted me alphabetizing my books. Honestly, why can't she just come upstairs and talk to me in my room? This is part of her whole avoidance plan. I swear she can be so immature sometimes it's unreal. She can be worse than a child! But I did as she asked and ran down the stairs to meet her in the kitchen.

As I was running down the stairs, I heard my brother's watching a game with my dad on our big screen TV in the living room. The sounds of shouts and swear words echoed throughout the entire house and all I could do was laugh at their macho jock-ism. You'd think they'd have an aneurism with all that hollering like that.

The first thing I saw was her face, all red and blotchy and her eyes were puffy and bloodshot. She had been previously crying about something and I had a very bad feeling about this. I walked over to the island countertop and placed my right hand over the top of hers in comfort.

"Mom," I asked her cautiously. "What's wrong?"

She sniffed and tried to collect herself before replying, "Why don't we go for a little drive just the two of us, huh? Maybe get some ice cream or a burger perhaps?"

I didn't know what was going on but I agreed to accompany her. She obviously needed to talk and I was the only person to console her without judging.

We took her black Mini Cooper to the local café a couple miles from our house. She ordered a slice of chocolate cake while I got a vanilla milkshake but it was all in silence. She was on her last bite when she decided to finally start the conversation but by that time, I really didn't want to hear it. I mean she should know that she can say anything she wants to me and I won't be mad at her. Whatever it was it couldn't be that bad.

"I'm moving out . . . your father and I are getting a divorce."

OK, so I lied.

"What! How could you do that to us mom? You can just up and leave your children like that without a second thought?"

"Scarlett I think it's the best thing for all of us. And could you please lower your voice."

"Lower my voice?!" I repeated astonishment and sarcasm. "I have a right to yell mom! You're dropping this huge bomb on me right now and you expect me to 'lower my voice'. You have *got* to be kidding me!"

"Can you please talk to me about this? Daddy and I are just not happy with each other anymore and that's the plain truth."

"Stop talking to me like I'm some child mom! You know I grasp concepts pretty easily and I—"

"Alright, alright, we haven't told your brothers anything about this yet. I expected you to take it better than you are but I guess that was my mistake. I know this is a big deal for you, I know how you might think of me right now but you have to understand where I'm coming from."

"I know you and dad have your problems but can't you just go to couples counseling? I mean this can't be the real end, can it?"

"I'm afraid it is sweetie. There's nothing either of us can do or say to change our minds. I want your father to fight to keep me but he won't and I can't live with someone that doesn't have the same feelings anymore. It's just the way it turned out and I'm truly sorry we have to put you guys in the middle of this."

I don't know exactly what it was about what she said to me but whatever it was, it made me snap. My breaths came quick yet shallow and I could feel my face getting red with rage. Tears began to leak out of my eyes at the thought of my mom not being in our house anymore. Everything was going to change now.

"Oh honey, please don't cry—"

She tried to hold my hand to make me stop but I ripped it from her and stood up. I gave her the most hurt face I could before spitting out the words, "I hate you," and stomping out of the restaurant. I ripped the passenger's side door open and threw myself onto the seat, crossing my arms in the process. I pursed my lips in a thin line and stared in the window of the restaurant at my mom. She was looking straight back at me with sadness in her eyes. Good, I hope she is sad!

I watched her pay the bill and set the tip on the table before she walked outside. I turned my head away from her and kept my gaze locked at the window while she got in the car.

"I know it won't mean anything to you right now but I love you."

I shifted away from her even more when she said that too. That was how mad at her I was. She was tearing this family apart and she was expecting me to say 'I love you' back? She must be on medication or something because that's just reaching for the stars that is. I heard the ignition turn on and I crossed my arms but loosened my facial muscles. It hurt the jaw to be mad for this long.

We reached the stoplight right before the turnoff of our street when I started thinking about the whole situation. I should've seen this coming from a mile away. And it's not my mother's fault if she and dad are both unhappy in their relationship. Things just go wrong sometime and you can't do anything about them. I have to reluctantly admit, I overreacted about this.

"Mom." I whispered with my head still facing my window.

No answer.

"Mom," I repeated a bit louder so she could hear me.

I turned my head and saw the tears running silently down her face and knew they were from me. I heard screeching off in the distance but didn't think anything of it.

"I—"

A blinding light broke my sentence and then . . . nothing.

# Chapter 2

$S$ WIRLS OF MULTICOLORED LIGHT DANCED across pure blackness and I felt like I could just reach out and touch them. If it weren't for the searing pain traveling up my entire body, I would have assumed I was in Heaven. Seriously, it was the worst pain I have ever experience. It was like needles were stabbing my entire body and I couldn't even move to escape them.

I could hear my name being shouted far off but I couldn't tell who it was or even answer them back. I couldn't even move my fingers up and down or side to side. There was no doubt in my mind that I was dead now. And all I could think about was my English final I would never be able to take now. How sick and twisted is that?

"Scarlett! Scarlett sweetie, please you have to wake up. I can't lose you too . . . please!"

Someone was crying over me. I could feel their pressure against my hand that they were clutching for dear life. So I couldn't be dead, could I? Could the dead feel the living? This is such a confusing concept it's giving me a headache. And oh joy, more pain! This has got to stop or else because I can't take it for much longer. I tried one more time to move anything at all and to my surprise my eyes actually fluttered open. My dad's face was the first thing I saw.

He was sitting on a chair next to a hospital bed that I was currently residing in. Benjamin was hunched over and still holding onto my right hand like it was my lifeline. Who knows, it could have seemed that way to him. An intense jolt of pain shot up my legs and arms and my eyes clenched shut again. After all that work and I only received an inch of progress by opening my eyes.

"Dad?"

Was that me? Did I just croak out that word? Yes it was! My vocal cords work now! His head lifted from my wrist and looked at me with hope in his tear soaked eyes.

"Daddy, it hurts," I managed to say weakly.

He jumped off that chair like it was on fire and joined me at my side with concern and happiness stamped on his face. Well he was obviously happy that I was alive so I couldn't blame him. I knew I would act the same way if our positions were reversed.

"What hurts sweetie?" He asked me while gently brushing a strand of fallen hair out of my eyes. Even the slightest touch felt like he was stabbing me with a serrated knife.

"Everything."

He broke down into heavy sobs while wrapping me into a tight hug which, evidently, hurt me even more. I didn't interrupt him, however because this was his moment and I couldn't ruin it for him. Whether he and mom were getting a divorce or not.

"What happened?" I asked when he finally released me.

"A semi-truck didn't see your mom's car when he blazed through the intersection. He sideswiped you guys and flipped the car three times. You've been in a coma for two days now."

Thoughts cruised through my mind at the speed of light and the only one I was capable of isolating was the way I must look right now. Being through a car accident could only look so good on me and I didn't have a doubt in my mind that I looked pretty banged up after being in a coma for two days. So I asked my dad to ask the nurse for a compact mirror as one passed by. She handed me the compact and I took a long, deep breath to prepare myself for what I was about to see.

I let out a gasp when I took in the sight. My eyes were almost swollen shut and bruises and tiny cuts cluttered my entire face. I was stitched up in two different places, one streaking above and through my left eyebrow and one on the right crease where my lips met. I didn't even want to know what the rest of my body looked like. And if I looked like this, I couldn't imagine what my mother must look like. Speaking of which, where is she?

"Dad, where's mom?" I asked him while sitting up on my elbows the best I could.

His head hung low and the sobs returned with a vengeance. I tried to comfort him the best I could but I was still trying to wrap my head around the reason why he was crying like this.

"There—there was just nothing they could do. They tried—they tried their hardest to revive her but it was just no—no use. She was already gone."

I just laid there in silence. Seriously, I didn't do a single thing but sit there and stare. I didn't cry, scream, or bash in everything around me . . . not even crack a single emotion. Staring off into blank space seemed like a better concept than any other at the moment. And I didn't stop staring for two full weeks.

I was released from the hospital a week later but still had the stitches on my face. I also had four broken ribs that left thirty stitches on my sides, fourteen on my right and sixteen on my left. And I'd like to point out that my leg was ripped up and had more stitches than I could count running from my upper thigh to several inches above my knee. They told me that they had to pull about half the windshield out of that spot. I almost died from loss of blood and would have if the ambulance had gotten to the scene any later that they had. My left arm was broken in two different places and I had to have a splint on it for two weeks. But nothing on the outside could compare to the wounds occurring on the inside.

I had immediately tried to run up to my room when my brothers brought me home but it turned into more of a fast wobble. Facing them after what I had done to her didn't seem right in my eyes. If I told them what I said to her they'd hate me forever, just like she will probably do now. And my dad had to drop more bad news on me a week after my return.

My mom lived in Willow Creek, Montana before she started her medical school in Harvard. Her parents, my maternal grandparents, still live there. After hours and hours (who knows . . . maybe even days) of loud bickering on the phone between my dad and my grandma. She was begging him to let them bring my mother's body back home and bury her in the town cemetery. I didn't hear much of the conversation but I gathered that much out of it. And apparently, my grandma won the argument in the long run. We left for Montana three days after dad told us the news.

My habits didn't really change even when I was in Montana. I still stayed inside and read my books but every now and then I helped my grandma do some cleaning or cooking, whatever she needed help with. I was still deathly quiet but the good thing about my grandma is that she doesn't question things. Her opinion is that if someone has something bottled up inside and they don't want to share it; you shouldn't pry into their personal life just to see what's wrong. It's none of your business anyway. But there was a small part of me that wished she would pry. I know I need to talk to someone about this but I have no idea how to start a conversation like that.

She no doubt grew that opinion from forty-seven years of marriage to my grandfather. Truth be told, I don't even call him grandpa. Oliver Costarelli is the most reserved man I have ever met. Never have I seen someone so stubborn and opinionated like he is. Well, besides me that is. He still holds onto his old-fashioned views and he will most likely take them to the grave. I'd guess that he was just brought up this way. Oliver was born in Sicily, Italy to a farmer and a house wife. He was brought up with strong Italian outlooks and was expected to take over his father's farm when he passed but Oliver didn't want to. He then proceeded to move from Italy to little old America where he met his wife and ironically bought his own farm. They've lived in the same place for just as long as they've been married.

I rarely talked to him when we were there. He was locked up in a separate part of the barn all day long doing Lord knows what. Everyone else was bustling around the house trying to get the funeral prepared. My mom is gone forever now and she'll never hear my apology. How could I have said that to her over something so stupid? I couldn't even look myself in the eye with the guilt weighing down on my shoulders.

"Scarlett, everyone's ready to go," Max's voice came from the doorway of the guest room I was sleeping in.

I gathered myself up and looked in the mirror one last time to see if I was presentable. Instead of the normal black color like everyone else was wearing, I had on a soft pink, slightly below the knee length dress so no one would see my stitches. There was a reason for my rebellion however. My mom always told me that I looked good in this color and should wear it more so I thought I'd honor her memory by pleasing her wishes. I grabbed a dark brown and thick headband out of my suitcase and placed it on my head so my bangs were out of my face. You could imagine what she said about the hair in my eyes all the time.

I had a hard time walking in the church. Everyone kept staring at me and my dress and talking behind their hands. The pews were littered with men and women I've never met in my life and they were all gossiping about my appearance. And to make things worse, I was the last one of my family to walk up to her casket and pay my respects. In a way I kind of appreciated being last. This was going to take a lot of courage for me to muster up in order to look her in the face one last time. So I walked at the slowest pace I could behind my dad and hung my head so I didn't have to watch everyone say bad things about me.

I was next. My dad was right in front of me in the isle and he was just now walking up to the beautiful mahogany casket surrounded by white calla lilies and yellow roses. I could barely make out what he was saying to the dead body lying inside. And what I heard broke my heart.

"I'm so sorry Janey, I never meant for it to be this way. I should have been there to protect you. It should be me lying in this coffin instead of you. Please—please forgive me for avoiding you all those years. I love you so much sweetheart and I always will. Forever and ever . . . with my whole heart . . . no one can change that."

He placed a kiss on her snow white cheek and moved away for me. The room started spinning around me, making me hyperventilate and start to stumble back. For a moment, I swore I was about to faint in front of everyone at the funeral. But my feet had other plans. I turned around and bolted back down the aisle and shoved open the wooden door to get away from everyone. I heard my dad shout my name twice before disappearing outside. I had no clue where I was running to and I honestly didn't care. I wanted to get as far away as possible.

My feet gave way down the street and on the lawn of *Donna May's Beauty Salon*. Two ladies that worked at the salon ran out to see if I was alright but Holden reached me first. I told you, you can always count on him in a time of need.

"Scarlett, are you OK?"

I didn't answer him. I just lay perfectly still on my back staring up at the blue sky. How could it be so nice today when such a tragedy occurred? While resenting the sun for shining that day, I burst out into the first tears I've cried since the accident. Holden came and sat down next to me on the lawn. Pulling me up in a sitting position, he wrapped me in his arms and hugged me tightly to him as my tears streamed down like Niagara Falls.

"Shh, it's ok . . . it will be alright," he tried to reassure me.

But even he knew then that everything wouldn't be alright. At least not now that is. The sun shone down on my back with intense heat as if it were mocking me.

# Chapter 3

HOLDEN, MAX AND I ASSUMED we were going back to California the day after the funeral. Boy, were we surprised with the news my father gave us! He sat us all down one day after dinner for a "family meeting". We haven't had one of those since I was about eight. And that was to tell me that the family dog had just been hit by a car. Well this obviously can't be good.

"So, how do you guys like the town so far?" He began by asking.

Why was he starting off with this question?

"It's a bit small but it's kind of cozy. I've met some of the locals here and they all seem decently friendly." Holden answered.

"Why are you asking dad?" Max broke in.

I knew exactly why he was asking us this. I told you, I'm very bright for my age.

"Because he wants to move out here," I answered for him.

My brothers' mouths dropped open and looked at my dad for confirmation on something I already knew to be true. He wanted to be closer to mom whether she's in the ground now or not. But what was he going to do with his job if we move here? And what about all of our stuff? Will we go and pack up our life or just ship it all to Montana? So many questions running through my mind, so little time for answers.

My dad searched with the realtors out here for a week but he finally found a place. It was in a community of houses just outside of town and fifteen minutes away from our future school. Luckily it was summer and we didn't have to worry about that quite yet. The house is a beautiful two-story white house with light green shutters and a large yard out front and back. It had four rooms, we each received our own, and mine was the second biggest. I suppose it was my dad's way of saying he was sorry for everything I've gone through recently. But it didn't stop the guilt from passing through me. Not only of my mom's death but also of my eldest brother being suckered out of what should have been his. So I politely declined it and traded places with Holden. He seemed happy enough to receive it but I could tell he was still keeping an eye on me.

Since that day he had to coddle me in front of those people, he has been very cautious around me. It's as if he's expecting me to explode again at any minute. I try to reassure him as much as possible but he never seems to get that I'm done freaking out like that.

Anyway, back to the house. The living room and kitchen are huge and seems to be the complete opposite of our old one in Beverly Hills. Our garage fits two cars so Max will have to park his mustang outside. We have two bathrooms in the house, one being my dad's and the other being us kids'. And to top it all off, we have a pool with a conjoining hot tub in our backyard. Not the image of living you'd imagine in Montana but at least it's nice.

"Scarlett," my dad's voice came from downstairs.

I had been up in my room unpacking boxes when he called me. I ran to meet him in the living room. He had a wide smile on his face as if he were proud of something. I walked over to him and placed the back of my hand on his forehead to check if he was running a fever. This wasn't his normal behavior and he was up to something, I could tell. The question is; what exactly?

"I'm fine! But you need to come outside with me to see something I bought today." He said to me while pushing my hand away.

I did as he asked and followed him out the door and stood on the porch in my ratted jeans and Ramones t-shirt while he went into the garage. I don't know what he's up to but if he bought a new car for himself I'm going to slap him. There's no possible way we could fit another one of his cars around here. Just then, I saw the tail end of a blue truck bed peeking out from the side of the house. Oh crap! It was a large, dark blue 1976 Ford Bronco pickup truck with rust stains and the most ancient tires I have ever seen.

My dad put the truck in park and jumped out of the beast. He basically skipped toward me and I knew that I couldn't tell him how I really felt about the piece of junk.

"It's yours sweets! I bought it for you as an arrival present. Do you like it?"

I swallowed back the vomit that up heaved in my throat at the mere thought about driving that thing in public and nodded my head yes.

"Oh thank God, the man I bought it off of was worried about me purchasing it for my sixteen year old daughter. I'm so happy you like it. It was the best thing I could find in town."

Wow, doesn't say much about the town, does it?

"And I know where your first drive can be in it. You need to get new tires on it and if I gave you a piece of paper with the size and model of them could you go down to the hardware store and pick them up for me? They'll even install them in the back of the store for you."

"Umm, well dad I was kind of busy unpacking—"

"Oh . . . yeah . . . yeah I understand. That's OK; I can just drive over there later and get them myself. I just thought you'd enjoy seeing the town a little before you start school this fall."

"No dad, that's alright, I'll go."

"Really?" He asked me flabbergasted.

"Yeah, I needed a break anyway," I replied with a fake smile. I seem to be doing that a lot lately. Nobody seemed to notice so far so I guess that means I'm a good liar.

He took out a folded sheet of paper and shoved it in my face. He had already written out the design of tires and the size. My dad is so funny when he doesn't try to be. But I would never tell him that no matter what. He handed me the money and I was on my way into town.

Apparently, they were expecting me at the tire shop-thing. *You actually need and appointment to put tires on your truck!* Can you believe that? And it wasn't easy to find size 25 radial tires let me tell you. There were all sorts of brands and designs, ones for off-roading and paved street use. I eventually picked out the right ones, I think, and told the store clerk about putting the tires of for me.

"Pull your truck around back and I'll have Caleb change them for you," the clerk said.

I did as I was told and was met in the back of the store by a boy about my age. He was several inches taller than me (which isn't hard to accomplish), wearing Levi blue jeans with holes in them and grease stains everywhere and a plain, white tank top that were in the same condition as his pants. He would be semi-good looking if he weren't covered in all that gunk and motor oil.

I'm not one to like the dirt and grime . . . never have and never will. I did, however, notice his very big brown eyes. Yeah, that, I am a sucker for! And they were deep brown too, none of that golden or honey crap. Sort of like a dog's eyes. It actually made me consider what our children would look like for about five whole seconds. His skin tone was very tan and his hair was medium in length, swept to the side, pieces were in his eyes, and slightly messy. Honestly, he could pass as a Chase Crawford lookalike. It was a chocolate brown too, not very dark but not at all light.

"Hi . . . um, I have an appointment to get my tires changed. They told me to come back here and someone would change them for me."

He ignored me. Which I'm not going to lie, made me quite mad at him. You shouldn't ignore your customers like that, even if they are girls with no car experience at all. Instead, he pushed past me (gently) to reach the wall of tires that were apparently behind me. Go figure! I stomped quietly over to the opposite wall and crossed my arms over my chest to appear as angry as I felt and waited for him to finish with my truck.

OK so I have to admit, he looked rather good tightening those bolts on my tires. He had those biceps that tend to ripple during physical exertion if you must know. And even though he was covered in filth I couldn't help but drool a bit while my eyes stayed glued to his backside.

I couldn't help but notice a piece of paper sticking out of his back pocket. But hey, it was as clear as day and I was already looking there so why couldn't I try and read the paper too? It was an invasion of privacy, yes, but I don't know this guy and he doesn't know me. Surprisingly, I didn't feel an ounce of shame turning my head to read the wording.

"This Friday . . . Bring your own . . . all night long," were the only things I could read from it. I wasn't stupid, it was for a party this Friday night somewhere and it would last all night long. And I am just guessing that the "bring you own" part is talking about alcohol. I *am* a teenager and although I do not act like one most of the time, I know how they think. Teens and alcohol shouldn't mix, but try and part them, get ready to lose limbs.

"I'd prefer you don't read my things, thank you." The mechanics voice cut through my thoughts. My cheeks pinkened but I didn't say anything. I couldn't say anything because I was so embarrassed. So I kept my eyes straight forward and studied his greased up, black *Converse* shoes.

"Hasn't your mother ever told you not to stare?" He asked me not even once glancing in my direction. How did he know I was looking at him if he didn't look at me? This boy is *beyond* strange.

"My name is Caleb by the way, Caleb Darwin."

I was silent.

"This is the part where you tell me your name, princess."

"Just fix my car so I can leave please, thank you." I bit back at him. Mainly because I was still embarrassed, but also because I couldn't stand being around this guy any longer. I wanted to leave as soon as possible and I was in no mood to make small talk with some stranger. But he obviously wanted to talk to me, because the conversation didn't stop there. It turned into somewhat of a battle of wits too.

"What crawled up your behind and died?" He asked sarcastically.

"Probably the same thing that died on you. Have you ever heard of showering?" I counter argued.

"What? You don't like the natural, dirty boy look? Sorry to say toots, but most girls love it." He retorted, moving around my car and knocking into one of my feet in the process. I grimaced at him and stuck my tongue out when he turned around and glanced at me with a smile.

I wasn't about to be polite to a guy who didn't return the gesture back toward me. He may be a looker but I was brought up to appreciate a proper mind and good manners instead of relying solely on what a man's appearance is.

My old friend in California would find him downright scrumptious to look at. She is as shallow as a wading pool. You know the one with the sister who dated Holden? Yeah her. Sapphire Hamlin is as expensive as her name entails she might be. She was the apple of her parents' eye as far as I remember and as spoiled as ever let me tell you.

So, how did me and little Miss Prissy becomes friends you might be asking yourself? Well we met at the private school in freshman year and back then she wasn't like the way she turned out to be. Back then, she was just as lowly as I was with bad acne to boot. As soon as it cleared up and she started dying her pale blonde hair to a lighter tone, she became just as superficial as her sister had always been. She and I stayed friends after that but I never approved of how she acted around other people.

But this guy, this guy brought back some bad memories of her and parties where she left me in some corner while she was off making out with the quarterback of the football team.

My mind was brought back to the auto shop when I heard him slide the metal thing that he was laying on out from under my car. I don't even remember him getting on that thing much less witnessing him check out the underside of my car. But apparently there were some problems down there because he came back up with a used wrench. And he had the audacity to place his hands on other side of the table I was sitting on and hoisted himself up inches away from my face.

He was so close that I could taste the scent of his toothpaste he used previously. I could see flecks of green inside of his deep brown eyes and, if given the time, could most likely count all of the freckles on his face. His left hand had brushed lightly against my own and my breath caught in my throat. Who did this guy think he is to be fresh with me? Ugh! So I pushed him away from me and crossed my arms in annoyance at the cocky, young boy.

That guy, Caleb, was done with my car in a matter of minutes surprisingly. So I gave him ten dollars for his tip and stepped inside my car, only to be stopped by a strong hand holding my door open when I tried to close it. The audacity of this guy was astounding to me. What made him think that he had the right to touch *anything* that was mine?

"Let go of my door," I snapped at him with a bit more anger than I had anticipated.

"Not until you give me a name." He said with a smile. He had nice teeth by the way. They were very white and very straight, for your information. But that still didn't help the fact that he was bullying me into getting a name. So I decided to pull a little prank on the smug little boy instead.

"You want a name? Ok I'll give you a name . . . Vivien Leigh. That's your name."

He kept staring at me like I was insane but he finally let go of my door so I slammed it and drove off as soon as my ignition kicked in. The truck really was a piece of crap, I have to say. You see, Vivien Leigh is a famous actor from back in the day. She plays Scarlett O'Hara in the movie *Gone with the Wind*, so technically I was doing no harm to myself or him. If he was so smart, he would figure it out on his own.

When I arrived home, I was the only one in the house. My dad must have gone out while my brothers tried to look for summer jobs in town. Me, I had different things on my mind. Like completing my unpacking and arranging my room to my liking. I was such a clean freak but at least it's a bonus to live with me.

Cleaning out my suitcases was the easy job. It was moving everything from my bags to fit perfectly into place was the problem. I was so wrapped up in what I was doing that I didn't realize a faint howling coming from downstairs until it grew so loud that I swore it was a person. My instincts kicked in and I grabbed my brother's baseball bat from his room before creeping down the stairs as quiet as a mouse. Whoever it was, I was going to catch them in the act.

Peaking around the stairway and down the hall, I saw that the door was pushed wide open and a small summer breeze was rushing through it. Whoever this burglar was, he was just plain stupid. I mean who leaves the door to the house you're attempting to pilfer wide open? Honestly, some people are just so brainless! I didn't see anyone there so I continued further into the hallway and looked out the door to see if they might have left already. A scratching sound behind me told me that my assumption had been false. I slowly turned around with the bat still in my grip to see the intruder. I choked up on the bat while walking down the hallway and into the living room where I saw the break-in artist.

A full grown cat sat in the middle of the oriental, Ming Dynasty rug as plain as day. It wasn't even frightened to see me or anything. It just sat there as if it owned the place or something. It was all white save for two black streaks going along both sides of it. The cat was staring me in the eyes and if it weren't for my intellect, I'd swear it was staring into my soul. Instead of the normal cat-like green eyes, this one had pure blue. They were crystal clear . . . like looking into glass. It stood up from that spot and started to saunter its way over to me. While rubbing against my leg, I heard it purr louder than anything I've ever heard before.

My aunt Cassie (my mom's sister . . . full name is Cassiopeia) has a cat. She used to let me play with him whenever I would visit her house. Jinx was a small thing at the time and he loved to bat around a little blue ball hanging from string. Jinx is pure black and has a white splotch taking shape of an eye located in the center of his chest, just below his neck. But Jinx still had the same piercing blue eyes as did this cat.

My dad made us stop visiting her once she blurted out to everyone at Thanksgiving that she was psychic. My mom thought that we should be supportive about her mental illness, but he didn't think it was fitting. I think aunt Cassie's under the watchful eye of a very nice nurse now. She's still in her home but she's not allowed to leave unless the nurse comes with her. The point is . . . that cat is still alive.

I picked him up, after I determined that it was a male, and began looking for a collar or anything I could see that had an address on it. Nothing that I could see had anything on it, not even a name for the poor beast. But as I looked for identification I did notice something peculiar about his markings. They strangely resembled angel wings. And that's no exaggeration my friends. They were perfectly formed into two beautiful, feathery black wings on both sides of his body.

"Well then, Angel it is," I said to him quietly as I scratched his belly.

Even though a cat showed up in the house instead of a burglar, I still didn't grasp the reason as to why the door was ajar. I remembered specifically shutting it before I walked upstairs and unpacked. And Angel couldn't have accomplished turning the doorknob by himself, so why was it open?

# Chapter 4

ANGEL SLEPT WITH ME IN my bed for the next couple of nights. He has a bed that I bought him but he prefers lying on my second pillow, purring loudly in my face, instead of that thing. Not that I minded or anything but he does sleep like a person. He sleeps on his side and one of his paws is usually tucked behind his head. I can't really yell at him or push him off because, let's face it, he's downright adorable.

At first, my dad wasn't too keen on the idea of a cat staying in our house. You see, he's hated them ever since one of them attacked and ate his hamster back when he was five years old. Don't ask me why he still despises them with everything he has. It's quite funny to watch him around Angel though. He doesn't much like him too. He usually does his best to steer clear of my father as much as he can. Max was the one who helped me talk him into keeping the cat. We both reassure him that it was only until I found his owner and then he will be gone. I was sort of resenting that day, if it came.

I chose to make signs and ask businesses if I could post them up in the shops and all around town. You know, the old-fashioned way. So I took my truck and chugged along Main Street until every post and store was covered with signs carrying Angel's face on it. But I could have just been wasting ink because Angel followed me everywhere I went.

To me, the town was still mostly uncharted territory. I haven't had the guts to just go wandering around by myself to get to know it better and I was still afraid now. I mean, what if they still hate me for the funeral incident they all no doubt remember? I can sure make an impression on a town, can't I?

While I was in one of the convenience shops, a man told me about a bookstore just outside of here that I should put the signs up in as well. It gets a decent amount of business in the summer due to the fact of it being the only place to get a good cup of coffee around. So I did as the man offered and hauled my butt all the way to the edge of town and began looking for *The Eagle's Eye Books.*

This guy wasn't exaggerating when he said that it was a ways out. I literally had to drive fifteen more minutes just after the last house. It was located in front of a forest and right beside a small pond. It had that rustic vibe to it; you know . . . where the building looks like it has been hidden behind those trees for maybe 100 years or so. The store was completely made of wood and the roof was a black color. It had a porch wrapping around the entire front and chairs surrounded a wooden coffee table facing the pond. Is this really the bookstore? It resembles more of a house in my opinion but who am I to judge? A large red and white HELP WANTED sign hung from the window.

I parked my truck and let Angel jump from out of my door onto the ground before shutting and locking it. I was still used to living in Beverly Hills so locking it was just a precaution. Even though I can almost guarantee I won't need it. The inside of the store was ten times more beautiful than the outside. OK, so I say this because of all the books, but I can still appreciate perfection every now and again. It also had the coffee section, which I expected to check out later on, and another table exactly like the one outside with different, brown chairs surrounding it instead of white. A counter with a rack of post cards and a cash register sat in the front of the store.

Behind that counter stood a young, ghostly pale woman with medium brown hair tied neatly in a ponytail hanging on the base of her neck. Her brown shirt had the name of the store and its logo of an actual yellow eagle's eye in the dead center. She was no less an inch or two taller than me and she had a very pleasant presence about her.

"Good afternoon young lady, may I help you?"

When she spoke, it was as if her lips didn't even move. Her voice was velvety smooth yet had the undertones of motherhood and years of experience behind it. She had light, tea green eyes—yes, actual light tea green (look it up on Wikipedia if you don't believe it exists)—pulled out at the corners as if she was of Mexican decent. But if that were the case then she would be much, more tan than she is displaying herself as right now.

"Umm yes, you see I have recently found a cat hanging around my house," as I said that, Angel jumped up onto the counter. Instead of becoming angry like I expected her to be, however, the woman actually started to scratch Angel behind the ear. He began to purr loudly once more. "And I can't seem to find any identification on him. Would you happen to know anyone who's missing a cat lately?"

"No dear, I'm sorry but I can't say that I have. I'll be happy to put up one of your fliers in the shop if you'd like?"

How did she do that? I didn't even show her them yet? This town is weird!

"Alright, thank you so much."

I handed her a flier and grabbed Angel to walk out of the store when she stopped me a lot less forcefully as that boy had days earlier. In the softest voice I could ever imagine hearing she said to me, "You just moved here didn't you?"

"Yes ma'am, about two weeks ago to be exact."

"Well, are you looking for a summer job still or did someone already snatch you up?"

I'm not going to lie; I was downright amazed at how forward this woman was with me. They must not have had a lot of applicants in or something because you usually don't just ask the first person who comes in off the street if they would like a job in your shop. But I have to admit, it was a good opportunity. And besides, it was a book store for Heaven's sake and I do LOVE books. So what would it hurt to do a little interview and see how it goes? If my brothers can get jobs, then so can I.

"No, I don't have a job yet ma'am."

"Well, would you like one?" She asked me all sugar and sweetness.

Holden had just recently been called into work at the lumber yard in town. He has to haul logs around for about $8.50 an hour and every now and then makes a delivery out to Lord knows where. He told me that he picked that job to "get in shape" for football try-outs that are in August but I knew the truth. It was the only place that called him back. Now I know that's not a good piece of information to release about your brother but I'm being completely truthful in this little book so why start lying now? Oh, and he wants to show off for a pretty little thing that works right next door at a diner. He spotted her one day and claimed that he fell in love the moment he set eyes on her. He hasn't worked up the nerve to talk to her quite yet but I can guess that she will be sexually harassed by Holden in about another week. In a nice way, of course. So what happened with Jessica, I wonder?

Max, ironically, works with Caleb down at the Auto Shop. Lucky me, right? Yeah not exactly because Max has told me Caleb keeps asking about me and what my name is. I got to Max before Caleb had the chance to ask him that, however. The night after he received the job there, I begged him not to say a word about me.

"Who's Vivien?" The conversation started on Max's part.

"What?"

"Caleb keeps talking about my sister Vivien, but the last time I checked, I didn't have one."

"Oh Max, please tell me you didn't tell him what my name really is!"

His response was like a typical "older" brother's and he began to grill me if Caleb had done anything to hurt me yet. I thought about saying yes but decided against it in the end. I would prefer if no blood spilled on my brother's hands on my account. I mean I know Caleb's decently built but my brother could take him down in a heartbeat if ever provoked.

"Yes, that would be great ma'am!" I said to the lady behind the counter, trying to muster up that fake smile again. But I think it just looked like I was grimacing. I no doubt sounded excited to get the job, though.

"Oh, no 'ma'am' talk! Around here I go by Jackie and that's all. Would you like the tour before you start?"

"Now?" I asked in amusement.

"If you have the time that is. And would you mind starting tomorrow? We have been a little short handed as you might have guessed and it would mean the world to me if you did."

I nodded my head yes and followed her everywhere around the store. She showed me the storage closet, the bathrooms, the stock room, employee parking spots, and lastly gave me my instructions for tomorrow.

"Oh and by the way, you will be working with my little sister. Thought I'd warn you in advance, she's a bit of a handful."

I entered my truck (or as I nicknamed it THE BEAST) and before driving off with Angel sitting in the passenger's seat, I checked my cell phone to see if I missed anyone calling me. Surprisingly I did. It was only my father though, sort of a buzz kill if you ask me. The message said this:

"Hi honey, I was hoping that you could run over to the grocery store before you come home tonight. Your brother is making baked macaroni and cheese and needs a carton of eggs, butter, milk and elbow macaroni noodles. I would really appreciate it if you would. Call me back if you can't."

Yeah did I mention that Max likes to cook? Well actually he LOVES to cook just like I LOVE books. Who would have ever guessed a grease monkey who races cars for pleasure would find cooking enjoyable? And he is very good at it too! Anything with pasta he's a wizard at. I swear it's like eating at the fanciest, most delicious restaurant you've ever been to. The downside is, well, he doesn't much like to look in the cupboards before he starts planning and I'm usually the only one free to go and get it for him.

I wasn't going to make my dad do it when he got home from Legal Aid (where he worked) so I drove back into town one more time. The supermarket had everything you could want for a good home-cooked meal. The problem with that is, the place is huge and it's very hard to find anything easily in there. But I accomplished my grocery list and stood in line to check my things out and leave. Angel was still sitting in the truck after all. Too bad HE showed up right as I was walking through the sliding doors.

"Why did you give me a fake name?"

"Oh you found out about that did you?" I asked trying to play innocent and sweet.

"Yeah, after I made a fool of myself in front of your brother. I looked it up on Wikipedia and you know what it says? A bunch of crap relating to some movie star back in the1930's. Why didn't you just tell me your name?"

I tried not to look back at him, mainly because I couldn't handle seeing those chocolate brown eyes this close and not swooning. So I kept an eye on my truck as if it were my goal and clutched the brown, paper bag to my chest, quickening my steps in order to lose him. Yeah, didn't work out so well.

"And just what would you do with my name, huh?"

Now I was just taunting.

"Well for one, I'd like to stop begging your brother to give it to me," He answered with a very biting tone. But I couldn't help but snort and giggle at his little confession. He didn't think I knew this?

"If you must know, Mr. Nosy, its Scarlett," I said indignantly.

"Scarlett? But your brother said your last name was Hera?"

He scrunched up his nose and furrowed his eyebrows like most people tend to do when I tell them my name. Scarlett isn't really the name you hear everyday . . . unless you watch that movie again and again, which I do not. So I couldn't hate him fully when he made fun of my name. OK and he looked adorable when I caught a glimpse of his facial expression. He looked as if he just sucked on the sourest lemon he could find.

"Yes Scarlett," I answered while putting my grocery bag down on the floor of the passenger's seat where Angel was taking a little catnap in the sun spot.

"Are you pulling my leg again?" He asked.

"No, this time I'm serious."

"Well what kind of name is that?" Sour lemon again.

"A rich person's sick joke I suppose. Now can I please go home? I have milk and butter in that bag that I really can't leave out in the sun for very long. And you seem to be a very avid talker so I might as well be forward about it."

This made him lean back and take a good look at me. Yeah so I'm a girl with a brain . . . big deal! There's no need to be a jerk about it. So instead of just waiting for his answer, I climbed into the driver's side of THE BEAST and drove away. But not before hearing Caleb mumble, "And you, miss, are no lady!" And right in front of my open window too! Like I've never heard *that* before. Next time come up with something original. I've heard every euphemism you could imagine for my name and it's just not funny anymore.

It's not like the conversation was going anywhere anyhow. I really did him a favor if you think about it. Not too many people can handle my sarcasm for more than a couple of minutes. If I thought this was the right decision to make though, why do I feel so bad about leaving him there by himself? He wasn't speaking anymore and I have other things to do. Like informing my family of the job I got today, for example. What's so harmless in leaving a boy speechless, I ask of you? It's not like we have any chemistry together!

# Chapter 5

*I* ARRIVED AT WORK BRIGHT AND early the next morning in a pair of khaki jeans and a plain white tank top that I had to wear just until they ordered my shirt in. The door was unlocked when I pulled it open but I was expecting that. I was, after all, working with the owner's sister. But as soon as I entered, I really wished I hadn't!

Nothing disgusting was taking place mind you, but a girl about my age was doing yoga in the center of the room with stretch spandex and a purple and green fitting tank top. There was another, smaller girl sitting on the counter reading Jane Austen's *Sense and Sensibility*. I thought Jackie told me that I was only working with one sister today? But then again, these two certainly don't look like sisters.

The one doing yoga looked exactly like Jackie, medium brown hair that fell below her shoulders (over the top of her head at the moment) and a petite, pale white body. When she switched positions I noticed that she was the same height as me. She was wearing a permanent smile on her face and you could tell her teeth weren't as straight as, let's say, Caleb's. They were still a very pearly white and it was a nice smile but a little intimidating in my perspective.

I don't think she noticed me standing in the corner yet. What can I say, I prefer to observe rather than be the center of attention. She hopped up the first moment she spotted me though, rather too excitedly I might add.

"Ooo, the new girl!" She squealed.

She ran over to me and . . . no lie . . . hugged me as tightly as she could. Did I mention that this town is so weird!? Well it is, and not just the townsfolk obviously. I did catch a good glimpse of the girl's eyes. Unlike her sister's they were much like clover instead of tea green, but still classified as light. They still carried that Mexican look to them though.

25

"I'm Portia Valent—," The little girl at the counter gave a small cough, the first sign I've seen of life out of her yet. "I mean Portia Bennett.," She said in a chirpy tone.

"Oh, Portia . . . like *The Merchant of Venice*, right? Scarlett Hera," I offered up. It's a play by Shakespeare (one of my favorite authors of all time) in which Portia is a rich Heiress. It's a very good play and I recommend anyone read it.

"Oh I've already heard all about you from my sister. This is my niece Kate, by the way."

She pointed to the little girl sitting on the counter reading the book. How in the world is that possible? Kate had bright blonde hair with natural, caramel highlights shining off of it like a halo. Her eyes were of the tea variety which was the only trait that I could see inherited by her mom. They were also large but didn't pull out at the sides like the other two women I met. It makes me really want to see what her father looks like! I'd pin her at maybe . . . nine or ten years of age.

"So, do you like Willow Creek so far?" Still chipper as ever that one.

"Well, yeah I guess so. I haven't really been anywhere yet so I still don't know a lot of people."

There was a sucking sound from far off yet you could tell it was still in the store. It was as if someone was sucking their tongue against their teeth because they liked the sound. Or smacking their lips together . . . you know when you're hungry and something looks *really* good? Whatever it was, it was weird and creepy!

"Katie, it's time to go back home." Portia said to her niece.

"Why? I'm not doing anything to hurt anyone, am I?"

"But I think it'd be better if you just went somewhere else and read that book. The new girl and I have to work," she scolded.

"I have a name—" I tried to put in but I was ignored.

"Now go home or I'm calling your mom and telling her you're being disobedient," Portia finished.

Kate finally listened to her reluctantly but didn't disappear out the door until giving her aunt the dirtiest look she could muster up. Portia and I were finally alone and ready to work. Well, almost ready that is. She went in the back and before I could ask what she was doing, classical piano concerto music started to blare rather loudly from the speakers in the back room. CLASSICAL! Not that I have a problem with nice, soft music but Portia doesn't strike me as the girl who would jam to this in her room 24/7 like normal teenagers do with Rock or pop. But I'm not complaining so, oh well!

"So you were saying that you don't know many people yet?"

"Y-Yeah," I stammered out while I almost completely missed one of the stools behind the counter. She was standing so close to me it was making me nervous. "I haven't had the chance to socialize with the locals thus far. Not that I'm all too willing to do so. Meeting new people scares the living daylights out of me."

Why was I admitting all of this to her? And why was she breathing down my neck? What kind of sick and twisted family is this? Perhaps I had 'Look at me! The shy new girl with no spine whatsoever' tattooed onto my forehead or something? Whatever it was, I do not like the reaction I'm getting out of it at all. I heard a loud inhale coming from her. Reacting by reflex, I shifted my entire body away from her for my own protection. When I did so, however, my butt slid completely off the stool and I hit the floor with a very hard thud. She let out a little laugh before sticking her hand out to help me up.

"What were you doing?!" I shrieked out at her.

"Umm, nothing . . . just admiring your perfume. It's Scent Bent, vanilla right?"

I nodded my head but I still probably looked like I was freaking out. Well what do you expect when someone basically assaults you? Is this girl sweet on me or what? I'd hate to break a heart my first day but I don't swing for the other team and I'd want to make that perfectly clear.

"So listen, there's this party tonight up by Harrison. It's only a half an hour away; do you want to go?" She asked me.

I began to stutter again.

"P-Portia, I-I'm . . . I think y-you should know that I'm . . . . I'm not . . . well, I like men. A lot! Well, not a lot but do you get what I'm saying?"

She didn't act the way I was certain she would. Would you like to know what she did? She started to laugh at me. And not a small giggle, oh no this was a full out, side-splitting chuckle fest for her. A customer walked in too and even then she didn't lighten up or quiet her little fits. Boy was she being very rude right now!

"Scar-Scarlett, I didn't mean it . . . ha-ha, I didn't mean it like that. I thought you might want to go with me to meet new people. Almost everyone from my class and above will be there and I thought I'd show you who's cool and who's not!"

More laughter followed. She even checked out the guy's book that he was purchasing while trying to hold in her obnoxious sounds. But her laugh became infectious and I began doing the same. How could I have thought that this girl, as pretty as she is, would be hitting on me? Oh and that wasn't meant to be a slam on me. OK maybe a little but it wasn't my full point. My point is that I was ridiculous to make assumptions when I don't know anything about Portia. The man left and we both let out one last chortle before collecting ourselves.

"Actually, that sounds like fun. When is it?" I asked her.

"I'll pick you up at 9:00 and we'll make a fashionably late entrance. And we'll take my car. Showing up in that truck won't do spectacular things for your first impression. And besides, my car fits more people."

"Wait, just how many people are going with us?"

"My best friend from school and my brother will probably hang out with us after the party. Andrew and Gunnar are cool people; you'll like them for sure. Is that alright with you?"

"I suppose so," I answered her in an unsure tone.

Remember, I'm not so good with new people. Exhibit A would be how I just reacted when Portia was trying to identify my perfume. Let's just hope that tonight goes a bit smoother than today.

# Chapter 6

$\mathcal{P}$ORTIA WAS AT MY HOUSE promptly at 9:00. Not even a second out of place, right at the hour mark. I tried not to question this certain phenomena the best I could, but I'm a curious person.

The place where the party was held was at this huge farm outside of town. Two girls that I forgot the name of were throwing it for everyone in the school as a little start of summer party. While Portia was explaining this to me in her 2008 black SUV, I took in to account that she looked much better than me.

She was wearing a low-cut Abercrombie and Fitch jean skirt and a red halter top from Pacific Sun. Her shirt showed off her perfectly sculpted abdominals with a little silver chain surrounding her belly. No piercings as far as I could see though. She had a pure white American Eagle jacket resting on her shoulders because she said it was going to get colder.

Me, on the other hand? Well, I wasn't the vision of style. You see, I haven't worn shorts or a skirt since the accident. With that nasty looking scar covering up almost my entire leg, who could really blame me? So I wore my typical Hollister jeans with designer tears in them (no part of the scars were visible through the holes) and a simple light blue, spaghetti strap tank top that hugged my curves. Yeah, I had plenty of those compared to Portia . . . curves I mean. It was my favorite top because it made the blue in my eyes pop out. I ran back inside and grabbed an old coat that I always wore in the winter but thought it would provide the same type of service in the summer. It was a black, fake wool pea coat that came down to the start of my hips.

We arrived at the party no later than 9:20, and with the way she was driving I'm surprised we weren't there sooner. It was harder to find a parking spot than nailing pudding to a tree. There had to be at least one-hundred and fifty kids out there, if not more. And they were all parked in the same spot too. So we found one basically five miles away from the party (overly exaggerated for emphasis). We walked down to a table with drinks on them but I politely declined any alcoholic beverages for tonight.

I've only been drunk once in my life but it was enough to teach me a very important lesson in life. Alcohol and clumsy people just don't mix well together. Sapphire and I crashed a junior and senior party back when we were freshman and there were about three kegs in the middle of the room. My brother, Holden, was there but he didn't know I was. That is, until I had about ten beers and fell off of a table, passing out cold. Holden carried me out to his car and drove Sapphire and I home after that.

So I think I made the right decision to skip out on wearing the rose colored glasses tonight. Besides, I'm in a new town and people already think I'm a bad person, what, with wearing pink at my mother's funeral and all. So why give them any more of a reason to hate me? Portia grabbed two red, plastic cups, one containing beer and the other a Coca Cola and we started to walk around. Before we went three feet, two very attractive people of the male persuasion ran up to Portia and started to talk with her. They both gave her a large hug but one pecked her on the cheek.

The one that kissed her was quite a bit taller than the both of us with shaggy black hair sticking up everywhere. The sky still had that daylight tint to it and I could just barely make out that his eye color was piercingly light blue, strongly unlike the girls in his family. This was definitely Portia's brother! That kiss didn't look like anything too harmful, but you can never be too sure in these situations.

His shirt was plain white with the Hollister seagull in dark blue and his shorts were blue plaid and from Hollister too. He was very good looking but I was more interested in hearing their names so I could figure out just who the other one was.

"Oh, I'm sorry Scarlett. This is my older brother, Andrew Bennett," she cupped her palm against the shoulder of the black haired one, "And this is Gunnar Belwin. Guys this is Scarlett Hera."

"Au Chantey Mademoiselle," Gunnar said as he grabbed my hand and kissed the top of it, you know, like how you see it in French movies.

His curly, sun soaked blonde hair was short but still hung down in his clover green eyes (just like Portia's) and held that shaggy appearance. He was taller than me but shorter than Andrew and built rather skinny. But then again, I've been known to sway more to the skinny ones. When I looked Gunnar over, the first thing I noticed besides the sexy curly hair and pale complexion was his calf muscles. Gunnar was no doubt a runner for the track or cross country team. They were built for speed and agility and so muscular they became funny to look at if you kept on staring at them.

My favorite feature on him thus far would be his smile, though. Gunnar had those two little dimples that appear only when he gives you a bright smile. And when you catch a glimpse, it's impossible to look away.

Another guy ran up to Portia and picked her up by the waist, spinning her around and kissing her full on the mouth. Well he was *definitely* no relative of hers . . . at least I hope not.

"It's disgusting to watch, isn't it?" Gunnar whispered into my ear.

Something inside me let out a gut-wrenching scream when Gunnar got that close to me. I don't know what it was about and why it sounded as such, but it was as if warning bells were ringing in my ear right along with his voice. It was probably just because I wasn't used to being around guys still. I've only had one boyfriend my whole life, remember?

"Who is it?" I asked Gunnar.

I turned my face towards his to look into his eyes but I didn't anticipate just how close we were to each other. I could feel my breathe mingling with his own.

"Her boyfriend, David Jackson. He's a real tool if you ask me."

I watched as David set Portia back down on her feet and held her for just a bit longer. A sharp twinge passed through my heart unexpectedly while an image of Caleb floated around in my head. Now I know there must be something off on my 'good men radar'! There would be no possible way that I would pick someone like Caleb over someone like Gunnar. Granted, I didn't know either of them as well as I should before evaluating that decision but that's beside the point.

And this David guy *did* look like a tool. He was actually wearing a black t-shirt on with the logo, "tickets to the gun show is just a kiss away," and had two arrows pointing to his upper arms. He had so much gel in his brunette hair that you couldn't tell if the white flakes were dandruff or just the dried excess. His muscles were bulging out of his skin tight disgrace for a shirt and his pants looked like they were sucking the life right out of his legs. No doubt to show off what little male anatomy that he has. Guys like that should seriously be locked up in a zoo somewhere. What on Earth could Portia see in him?

She introduced him to me and he had the gall to actually wink in my direction as if I were some piece of meat. EWW! You could tell this boy was sure not faithful to Portia by just looking at him.

All five of us talked for about a half an hour in that exact same spot. The sun went down and I didn't even notice it until several minutes later. What made me realize this little fact was someone bumping into me rather drunkenly and making me spill my soda all down the front of my favorite shirt. My fingers brushed up against the hand of whoever this person was and I felt a jolt of electricity come off of my tips.

"Oh, excuse me," the voice said from behind me.

I knew who it was as soon as I heard the first word leave his lips. Turning around to confirm my assumption wasn't helping me either. Luckily it was too dark to see those eyes. And that was when I figured out just how dark it was around us. There was a fire burning a few feet away but the glow wasn't bright enough to reach us from where we were standing.

"Red!" He yelled out through slurred words and sloshed his drink when he threw up his arms to give me a sloppy hug. I shoved and shoved with all my might but I couldn't pry him off of me. Probably because it was all dead weight leaning against me. Max ran up to me and helped me peel the intoxicated Caleb off of me.

"Sorry Scarlett, I turned my back for two seconds and he was gone."

He had to hold Caleb up properly and I helped Max place him in a plastic, flimsy chair right next to us. He was still conscious but his head fell back and he just kept staring at the sky while mumbling to himself.

"So . . . who are your new friends here?"

I glanced at Max briefly and caught him looking only at Portia from the corner of his eye. Go figure he would only be interested in my new female friend. But he's a typical guy and I can't really blame him for looking. I did say that she was very pretty too. Max, however, wasn't getting the same reaction out of Portia. She was more along the lines of glaring at him with a scowl planted firmly on her lips. I wondered what was wrong with her.

"Everyone, this is my twin brother Max. Max this is," I went from the closest person next to me and to the right around the circle that we were all in. "Gunnar Belwin, David Jackson, Andrew and Portia Bennett."

"Bennett, huh? As in the movie, right?" He remarked toward Portia.

"No, Bennett as in the main character in the great Jane Austen's masterpiece *Pride and Prejudice*. Read a book every now and then you ignoramus!" She spit at him. Why was she so angry?

"There are pretty . . . hic . . . lights in the . . . hic . . . in the . . . hic . . . sky," Caleb babbled beside us.

"And this gorilla here must be my competition in the racing circuit this year. Caleb told me that you've never lost a race since you were sixteen. Well, that record has been shattered since the day I walked into your town."

"Max . . . don't," I tried to stop him from provoking David.

"Oh so you race do you? Well let's just see what you've got then, huh hotshot?" David asked in a confident voice.

I couldn't let my brother race anymore, not with what I've been through. He shouldn't be so stupid about it anymore too. But I guess he hasn't learned his lesson quite yet. He should know by now that racing under the influence isn't such a hot idea as well. His best friend (and previous racing partner) was paralyzed that way . . . how could he want to end up the same way? Or worse . . . I shudder to think!

"No, absolutely not! Not tonight!"

"Oh so you need your sister to fight your battles now do you? Maybe you should have her drive for you too." David kept taunting.

"I need no such thing to kick your sorry butt back to that hayloft where you were obviously born."

Everyone around us gasped. I hadn't noticed that we had a large audience listening in on this little exchange of words. Max couldn't do this! I don't want to lose another family member to the dangers of the road. Especially my twin brother!

"My tummy feels all funny," Caleb complained.

"I think you need to take him home Max. He doesn't look so go—"

Before I could get the word out, Caleb turned his head and bent down to the left. He painted the entire leg of the chair and the grass beneath it with his vomit. Everyone backed up and started to laugh while Caleb continued to empty his stomach contents of all that alcohol. Even though I strongly dislike the guy, I won't subjugate him to this kind of humiliation. Someone had to take care of him, right? So I ran to him and did my best to pick him up off the chair and wipe his mouth clean of everything he had just gotten rid of on the grass with a nearby napkin. He wrapped his arms around my waist to hold him up and rested his head on my shoulder when I had finished cleaning him off.

"You're comfy Scar . . . hic . . . Scarlett," He slurred.

"Please Max; can you help me take him to your car?"

I made my eyes wide and my other features soften to try and persuade him. Max could never really turn down my puppy dog face. I felt Caleb nestle his nose further into my neck and I could smell that awful breath of his. But it didn't replace the warm and fuzzy feeling in the pit of my own stomach when his lips grazed my collar bone. His hair tickled my neck and I actually shivered a bit. Am I turning into a ditzy little bimbo over this guy? Oh please, say it isn't so!

Max sensed my uncomfortableness and pushed aside his pride.

"Let's go then," he said with a droopy frown on his face.

I hated to crush his fun but I'd rather have my brother in one piece than seeing his pieces scattered all over the freeway. I was about to ask Portia if she wanted to come along but she was already by my side with both of our jackets in hand. And just what did we hear next?

"Bawk—Bawk—Bawk—Bawk!"

David was clucking at my brother . . . as in calling him a chicken. And there's one thing my brother can't stand to be called and that's a chicken. Surprisingly, he tried to ignore it and kept walking with one of Caleb's arms resting on his shoulder while I had the other. David had to do it louder though.

"Bawk—Bawk—Bawk—Bawk . . . Bawk!"

Oh, why me?!

Max flung Caleb's arm off of himself and pushed his body toward mine so I was left to try and not fall over with one-hundred and eighty pounds of dead weight lying against me. By this time, Caleb was passed out cold and snoring soundly against my chest. And yes, I do mean chest because by that point, he was too heavy for me to carry by myself and he began to slide down . . . evidently, pulling me along with him. Lucky for me Portia was around and noticed both of us falling and came to my rescue. She grabbed the other side of Caleb and propped him up until I could stand up straight and help her out.

Max was right in front of David and fighting with him in silence. You know, when boys stare each other down until one gives in? Yeah well it seems very immature if you ask me. I was never expecting both of them to break away and make a mad dash to each of their cars.

"Portia, do you think we can put Caleb in your car until I beat my brother into a bloody pulp?" I tried to ask her as quickly as I could because it seems like the boys weren't slowing down at any point.

"Yeah, it's fine."

But it was too late. I heard the sound of engines revving loudly on the strip of country road and I prayed to God that my brother wasn't *that* stupid.

# Chapter 7

"How could he do that to me?!"

"Calm down Scar', he won the race and no one was hurt. Stop worrying so much."

She was sitting behind the counter at the bookstore and I was pacing around with a pricing gun waving around in my hand while I spoke in an outrage. How she could have been so mellow about this was beyond me but I suppose she was just a calmer person than I. It was her boyfriend *too*, you know! Being around me today would be much better than last night though. When Max and I got home . . . I chewed him out for maybe an hour straight.

We had put Caleb on Max's bedroom floor with a pillow under his head and I turned on him.

"*What on Earth could you have been thinking Maxwell Robert Hera?! Do you know what seeing you racing in that car did to me? You almost gave me a heart attack you ignorant little jerk!*" I screamed.

Our dad was out of town for the weekend, attending a seminar that he had in Great Falls. Holden was out with a girl that he met that day (still hasn't asked that girl from the diner out yet) so we had the house all to ourselves. And it was perfect because it gave me no noise restriction.

"I needed to win that race Scarlett, you just don't understand," he mumbled while fiddling with something on his dresser.

"*Oh I don't understand? In case you've forgotten I was in a* car accident *not even two months ago and, oh yeah,* mom died in it! *How could you stand to hurt me like that Max?*"

"*And just how did I hurt you, Scarlett Evangeline?!*"

"*All I kept thinking was 'please, not my brother too'. I couldn't handle losing mom* and *you Max. Please don't make me.*"

"*You're not the only one that lost mom, OK?!*"

This conversation continued, like I said, for quite some time after that. And in very loud tones I might add. It was only interrupted when Caleb woke up and started to run out the door, no doubt to find the bathroom. Max followed him to make sure he tossed his cookies in the right place. Hearing Max say that I wasn't the only one to lose her was like a slap in the face to me. I knew my dad must have felt something over the loss but I never took into account to think of my brothers in all that aftermath. It had always been about my pain and no one else's. Was I that selfish?

"Porsh'," I whined. "My mom and I were in a car accident recently and she was killed. Max can't die like that too."

She was the first person I talked to about this ever. Portia just had this presence about her that made you spill your heart no matter what the consequences. And I have to admit, it did feel good to get some of this off my chest.

"Is that what those scars are from on your face?" She asked cautiously.

I nodded my head and turned so she could get a better look at them. I thought briefly about showing her the one on my leg but decided against it. No one will see that scar unless it's on my death bed. OK so not such a good choice of words, but you get my point. It was ugly and misshapen and I couldn't even think about letting anyone outside of my family see it. The bell attached to the door jingled behind us.

"What do *you* want?" I growled at the new body in the room.

"Can I please just apologize about what I did last night?"

His brown eyes looked sad and he seemed lower than usual. His attire was of the motor-oil-stained fashion. He had a smudge of grease on the side of his cheek and stubble aligned his jaw beautifully. He obviously was on his lunch break from work. Why did he take it to come and apologize to me? Well whatever the reason, I'm not accepting it.

"No," I plainly stated while walking behind the counter in a perturbed way.

"Please? I'd like to buy you lunch at the diner as a truce gift."

"Like a date?" I was growing angrier.

"No, no . . . just lunch. A friend lunch."

"I can't, I'm working," I answered back.

"She can take a break!" Portia yelled out a bit too enthusiastically.

"What?!"

Why in the world would Portia be helping out Caleb in a time like this? She knows I despise him, especially after last night. Well, I guess she doesn't have the best taste in men. Just look at her boyfriend! If she thinks there will be something coming out of this so called "lunch" that he has in store, she is sadly mistaken.

"Great, then it's settled." Caleb said with a wide smile on his face.

Before I could protest, he grabbed me by the elbow and started to drag me out of the store and to his truck. Ooo, I hate people so much! His vehicle was much, much better looking than mine. It was the new model of the Dodge Durango and it was black and shiny. It must have cost him a pretty penny to buy something as nice as that.

Part of me wanted to run away but the other part wanted to get to know one of the locals in town just a bit better. And if he was the one they were offering up then so be it. I climbed in the passenger's side of his truck, and I do mean climb, and rode in silence all the way to the opposite side of town. He liked to talk but surely knew how to keep his mouth shut at the most awkward of times. And he's quite the gentleman too, even if I would hate to admit it to him. He opened my car door for me and even the diner door when we were walking in.

Guess who our waitress was? And also, does Holden know her name is Kitty? Or maybe it's just a nickname. I could plainly see why he is convinced he's in love with her. She is a petite blonde with beautiful dark blue eyes and a voice that could melt butter if you put it to the test. Surprise, surprise too, she isn't a total witch!

"Hello, my name is Kitty. What can I get for you all today?"

It was then that her eyes looked up from the notepad in her hand and spotted something she did not like.

"We don't serve people like you," She gritted her teeth and glared at Caleb.

She began to walk in the other direction when Caleb's hand shot out and took hold of her elbow. Boy, does this guy have a touching problem or what? Certainly with girls, that is. Kitty and Caleb obviously have a history together otherwise she wouldn't act like this. Oh wow, I just realized how corny their names sound together. Kitty and Caleb . . . weird!

"Oh Kitty, come on, don't be like that! Please, just take our order and you won't have to come over here again until you give us our food and check."

See, right there! I'm not the only one to melt for Caleb's eyes! She gave the cheesiest smile she could and turned toward the table once more. I would never believe this if I hadn't seen it with my own two eyes. It made my stomach churn just by the mere thought of it. Caleb was a player . . . and a master one at that. Not many men can pull off keeping one girl around when he was on a date with the other. But this isn't a date so I guess it's not that big of a deal.

"I'll have a double cheeseburger and curly fries with a root beer," Caleb gave his order.

"And, do you still want it rare?"

She knew how he likes his burgers! This must have been pretty serious!

"Kill the cow and put it on the bun," he answered her.

Sick!

She turned to me and I gave her my order of a chili and cheese omelet with hash browns and a Coca Cola. I didn't think anything of my order until Caleb said something. And what he said really made me think.

"You're not like most girls, are you?"

"What do you mean?" I asked him taking a sip of my soda once Kitty brought us our drinks.

"Well, every girl I've taken on dates usually just get a salad and a diet Coke. You ordered an actual meal . . . I'm impressed."

"Thanks, I suppose."

"Why?"

"Most guys think that if a girl orders large then she's a porker. And then if she orders a salad she's apparently anorexic. I say, who cares what other people think about what you eat. Get what you enjoy and be happy with it."

"That's a good philosophy to have. You're a very smart girl, you know that?"

"I've been told."

I actually blushed! Who blushes when someone tells you you're smart? Especially when you already *knew* that you were! I mean, I've been told the same thing since I was five. Having it come from him shouldn't make me embarrassed about it. If I was going to be embarrassed, he is going to be too.

"So what was up with you and our waitress?"

"We dated for about five months last year," he confidently stated.

Oh come on!

"Oh really? What happened between the two of you? Why did you break up, I mean?"

OK so I was prying into his past, so what?! I told you I'm a curious person and I like to know things others don't. Even if it's about a single person, I don't care, I must know everything. It probably makes me sound like a brainy show-off . . . maybe that's what I am . . . but I'm not as bad to be around as the way I'm making it sound.

"I couldn't stay away from other girls," was his response.

I was right! He is a player and I should stay as far away from him as I possibly can! You know, if I wouldn't look like such a basket case, I would probably do a little victory dance right now. What can I say, I really like being right. So instead of dropping my mouth in shock, I just smiled a toothy smile and shook my head in disbelief while letting out a small giggle.

"What?" Caleb asked me.

"Nothing, nothing at all."

He let my cryptic smile go unanswered for the moment. Mainly because our food arrived and he was too busy shoving a whole masticated cow down his throat. Seriously, you could still see the blood dripping from the sandwich in his hands. It was truly a disgusting sight to witness. I almost tossed up my breakfast while watching him. But eventually I turned my eyes down and concentrated only on my food. The image of him eating his meal still haunted me when I was eating my omelet.

"You know," he said between bites, "that was the first time I've ever seen you smile. It's very pretty; you should do it more often."

He was right; it was the first genuine smile since the accident. Was I going insane or did this boy have some special powers over me or something. I mean he made me *smile* for Heaven's sake! Granted, I was laughing at his ill-fated attempts to stay faithful to one girl but it was still amazing. Why did it have to be him that pulled me out of my shell? Or at least he was trying to pull me out anyway. Well, I have news for him . . . it's not going to work! I'm the one who's going to stay locked up and his brain is going to be the one under the microscope.

"So, how old are you?" I asked him.

"I'll be eighteen in December. How old are you?"

"And how old is Kitty," I avoided his question. "She seems to be a bit older than you from my perspective."

He swallowed the last bite of bloody burger and took a drink from his soda before answering. "Kitty's already eighteen. She and I dated back when I was a sophomore and she was a junior. How many boyfriends have you had?"

"And just how much does Kitty know about you?" I continued to ignore his questioning and go on with my own.

"She knows my underwear size . . . if that's what you're asking."

"You mean her . . . and, and you . . . you—"

"Did laundry together . . . yes we have."

Ooo, he was so evil! But what business is that of mine to ask such a personal question? I don't even want to know that much about him and I'm asking him straight forward. Alright, now if I don't care what happened in his past, why do I want to ask what "doing laundry" actually meant? He isn't my boyfriend and I don't like him. Stop acting like some foolish little crusher Scarlett! Ahh, better!

"So just how many girlfriends have you had, Caleb?"

"I'm not answering any more questions until you answer some of mine, Red."

"Fine . . . I'm sixteen and I've only had one boyfriend. Now spill," I prodded.

"And what's your favorite band?"

This boy just won't let up! Insufferable little jerk!

"It's Maroon 5, now please answer my question."

"I feel it a bit odd that you want to know just how many girls I've been with. If I didn't know any better, I'd say that you actually do like me. Do you Red; do you honestly like me more than you let on?"

So I overreacted a bit with that question. I stood up from the table, called him insensitive and nosy, which I am well aware of the contradiction, and ran outside. But the images of my own past stopped me before I could even enter his truck. Was history about to repeat itself for me? Was I some kind of jinx that can get another person killed just by riding in the passenger's seat of their vehicle? And maybe I was acting childish at that moment but what happened to me was very scary, literally and figuratively.

My knees gave way and I fell to the ground in front of my door. Tears fell down my cheeks and I buried them in my hands to make sure no one saw that I was crying. I almost jumped out of my skin when a large hand was placed on my shoulder.

"Scarlett? Scarlett, what's wrong?" Caleb asked in a panicky voice.

I lifted my head to look him in the eyes and I watched his expression go from panic, to pity, right back to panic again. What do you expect? Caleb's a guy and guys don't really know how to handle it when girls cry. Luckily I'm no sob queen and never will be. Just seeing how worried for me he was made me see how stupid I had been. So I rubbed the salty streaks of water off my cheeks and out of my eyes and laughed a bit. I am just a regular sixteen year old girl after all! Who would have guessed it?

Caleb was shocked when I stood up on my own and brushed myself off and climbed into his truck. Oh he asked me if I wanted to go home instead of back to the book store, but I declined. It was just a small breakdown . . . nothing to worry over. Besides, I couldn't leave Portia there all by herself today. It was going to become busy there in about fifteen minutes due to the afternoon lunch rush and she wouldn't be able to handle it alone.

"So . . . how was the date?" Portia immediately asked when I walked in the door.

"It wasn't a date!"

"Did he pay for your meal?"

"Well, yeah but—"

"Then it was a date, missy," said Portia in mocking tones.

I didn't feel like arguing with anyone right then. I think I've gotten my fill of drama in the past twenty four hours and I don't want any more. And fighting with Portia doesn't seem that much fun to me. So I sat down on the stool beside her and we waited for the rush to begin. Angel came strutting through the room and hopped up on the counter. He does this quite often. He has the habit of getting out of the house and walking through town just to wriggle into the window a little to the right of the shop door. What can I say; he's about as attached to me as I am of him.

I was about to start a conversation on her boyfriend but something stopped me dead in my tracks.

"Portia, you're bleeding!" I shouted.

A small streak of blood lay visible on her wrist. I don't think she noticed it, or otherwise she forgot, because she was using that hand to pet Angel on the counter as plain as day. I've read about people cutting themselves to relieve pressure from the stress in their lives but I've never seen it. And most people hurt themselves badly from doing it. Portia tried to play it off as no big deal and wiped the blood off of her arm while saying, "Oh, I must have accidently gotten a paper cut when I was putting some books back." Do I look that stupid? Honestly, who would believe such a thing?

But what baffled me the most was that when all the blood was gone, there was no cut nor scratch anywhere on her arm. Not even one little scrape! Just untouched, smooth skin. Whatever that was, I *do not* want to know!

# Chapter 8

THE NEXT DAY, I TOOK the time to just relax and hang out with my brother and make four cheese stuffed shells. After berating him a bit more about the whole racing thing that happened at the party, we started to just relax and laugh it all off.

He put me in charge of making the shells and cheese after giving me the recipe and telling me how, while he made the red sauce that topped them. This was my dad's favorite dish so obviously Max was trying to butter him up for something. And I fully intended to figure out just what it was that he was working so hard for. Since Max is a part of the Hera family, he is as stubborn as a mule. But he has always kept things bottled up inside more than the rest of us, which ticks me off more than I can explain. I suppose he gets that from our father.

"So," I began when I was mixing the cheeses together. "Tell me exactly why you are making this delicious food tonight."

He glanced at me out of the corner of his eye and I briefly saw his cheeks go red with embarrassment. Or maybe it was anger, I can never tell. It's just sad that we're twins and I should know everything about him. Our twin telepathy had faded out years ago. He cleared his throat and tried to play it off as if he didn't hear me, but I know he did and I wasn't going to be ignored.

"Max, come on, just tell me." I pleaded.

He swirled the sauce covered spoon in the large pot of red, thick liquid bubbling on the stove, trying to avoid eye contact with his sister before he spoke.

"I need five hundred dollars for a ticket." He finally responded.

My mouth dropped so low, I thought it had hit the bowl that the cheese was in. I was hoping to God's sweet feet that he meant a ticket for a concert. Because I knew if he meant a speeding ticket, my dad would literally send him flying into next week. He already has two on his record already, he couldn't get anymore. So I stared him down to make sure he knew that I was irate with him for doing such a thing. Will he ever learn?

"You do realize that if you keep this up, you'll end up in juvey. Dad can't handle you alone anymore and I'm starting to think that having your head shaved and getting up at four in the morning to do nothing but work will be good for you. Maybe then you'd finally realize that racing is ridiculously stupid and not worth your time."

"Ok, first of all," Max turned to me with anger burning in his eyes. "Racing is more to me than just time to waste for me, Scarlett. You don't know a thing about it. Second, it wasn't for speeding. I was coming home from the party the other night and the cops pulled me over. They made me do a breathalyzer and I got a DWI. Nothing major, so just drop it."

"How on earth is that not—" I began to shout but stopped when he gave me the "just drop it" face. So I did. But I couldn't stop myself from thinking of yelling at him. How could someone be so stupid? My brother must have some screws loose because this just isn't normal behavior for a boy his age. Not the racing or the getting DWI's. Why couldn't he just be a nerd like me? That would make not only my life easier, but my father's as well as his.

Maybe that Caleb kid was having some influence on him while we were here? No, that couldn't be true. If anything, Max would have an influence on him, not the other way around. Not to say that Caleb is an angel or anything. But Max makes his own decisions and has since the day he could walk. And even on that day he destroyed my mother's antique lamp.

The silence cut through both of us as if we were butter. Neither he nor I wanted to be mad at each other. But he hated it when I pried into his life and I hated it when he made me. He's my brother after all. If I didn't worry about him; who would? My mother isn't here to . . .

That sentence is better left incomplete for now. Talking about my mother is such a sore subject with everyone lately that she is never brought up. They weren't there, however. Each night I've been having very vivid dreams about the accident. Piecing in the spots that I missed the first time. It's the most horrific sights I have ever seen in my life. They make me thankful that I blacked out during the whole ordeal.

I couldn't take the silence anymore. Someone had to say something otherwise I would start thinking about mom again. And I knew that Max wouldn't start a conversation even if it meant getting a new car, being the stubborn mule that he is and all. So it had to be me.

"What does it feel like?"

I believe I had given Max a heart attack at that very moment with what I had said. But it didn't register that it could have been taken as something perverted before I said it. And just my luck, Max has one of the dirtiest minds I know. I honestly didn't mean that, however.

"Racing a car, I mean." I clarified.

"Oh," he picked up a knife and started to play with it, passing it back and forth between both hands. "Well, you get that rush of a feeling that you get whenever adrenaline is pumping through your veins. Mostly I like to race because it makes me feel important. I can't do much else and it seems that people like me more when I race."

I looked at his face and knew that he was about to say something else, but changed his mind at the last minute. What could he have possibly been about to say? And why was he keeping whatever that was from me? I'm his sister for God's sakes; he should be able to tell me anything that's on his mind. I wish he could realize this.

"Do you remember that Portia girl?" He asked randomly.

"Yeah," I dragged it out to show him I was confused. "She's a nice girl, what about her?"

"Well, has she said anything about me whenever you two talk? Like, does she say that she thinks I'm cool?" He asked.

Why would Max ask me a question like that? Did he have a little crush on my friend Portia? But Max never had a crush on anyone before. He was always the one the girls were crushing on. There must be another underlying reason to his question. Max is too mysterious to just be blunt about something like this too. So what is it that he's asking me?

"No not really. The only time we've talked other than the party is at work and even then, we have more fun talking about the customers that come in there. Why do you ask?"

I watched as a faint frown crossed his lips and his eyes drooped down just a bit more than usual. But the pain only lasted him about a millisecond before he bounced right back to being his confident self and replied with, "Because someone had told me she had a crush on me and I wanted to set her straight right away."

"Set her straight how?" I asked.

"I was going to tell her that I would never be interested in some freak like her and to just keep away from me. I mean come on; she dances around like she's some mythical character and she's too happy *all the time.* Nobody's happy all the time . . . nobody." He responded.

"Excuse me, but Portia is one of the best friends I've ever had!" I started to yell again. "And to hear you insult her like you just did really gets on my last nerve. You don't know her; you don't have the right to judge her before you even try to get to know her. She's a very nice person and she deserves the best. You, Maxwell, are certainly not for her!"

"I'm your brother, Scarlett—" "He tried to interject but I wouldn't let him.

"And I do love you to death because of that. But your shallowness is something I just can't handle. You pass up perfectly good girls because you or one of your dumb jock friends thinks that she's weird and that's just not right, Max. You need to grow up and mature or else you will miss out on true love."

He stared at me with large, saucer-like eyes as if he had never seen me before in his life. And he hasn't seen this side of me ever before. This was the straw that had broken the camel's back and I had just told him exactly how his words made not only me feel, but the girls he talks about. How could someone be so cruel is beyond me. But I wouldn't allow one of my close family members to be the one to treat someone as such.

He finally found his voice again and had the gall to state, "But she was mean enough to call me an igoramon."

I through my arms up in the air in frustration and said, "No, she called you an ignoramus and that's because you are one!" Before stomping out of the kitchen and away from my idiot brother, I made a loud huff at his incompetency to grasp human emotion. Max likes to put himself in front of everyone and make everyone pity him instead. Well, this is one person that won't ever feel pity on him again. He had lost that gift when he stepped into that car the previous night to race that gorilla.

# Chapter 9

$\mathcal{I}$T WAS THE END OF June and I had finally received the privilege to work by myself at the book store. Life, at the moment, was going by rather slowly. Or so it seemed on days like this. The morning rush had passed and I had nothing to do but sit on the stool and file my nails. I had already stacked the shelves full of books, I had cleaned the floors and the dishes from the coffee we serve, and I had straightened up the storage closet. Angel was lying lazily in a sunspot near the window. I had the radio on country (which I now have Portia hooked on as well) and I was bored out of my mind.

Nothing has happened for the last week and I'm beginning to consider this town just as sleepy as the stereotype claims it to be. Small towns have always carried a bad reputation of simply being slow, and now I'm beginning to believe it. I haven't hung out with anyone but Portia in that time and I'm probably getting on her nerves by now. It's not my fault though!

I must have scared off all boys that had been interested in me when I first arrived. Gunnar hasn't said one word about me to Portia and it worries me. He was a guy that I could really see myself liking a lot. But apparently, he doesn't feel the same way about me. Not even Caleb was bothering me anymore . . . which I have to say, kind of ticked me off. Why and how did I scare away every boy I've met so far? Was I some sort of social leper or something?

"Dig your party shoes out of your closet; we are going out this Friday!"

Portia burst into the store often with news for me but it had always been about gossip in the town or just to say hi to me. Angel had been spooked by the door flying open and booked it as fast as he could in the back room, knocking things over in the process. I couldn't help but laugh at his reactions. But Portia's sentence sunk in slowly after. This, this was very good news to me! It meant I wasn't fully shunned from everyone around me.

"Who's party?" I asked.

She handed me a flier and spoke.

"It's an annual party thrown by Kenny and Fritz. They call it the 'Halloween doom in June' party. It's basically the whole class getting together in Kenny's barn and dressing up in costumes, getting wasted and sleeping in the haylofts."

"Sounds . . . interesting."

"It's a lot more fun that it sounds right now. Trust me; you're going to have a blast. Now, what should your costume be?"

"Nothing too outrageous Porsh', please. I'm not partial to being the center of attention and you know it. Subtlety goes a long way for me."

Did I forget to mention that Portia's niche is designing and sewing clothing? She told me about it one day and I thought it was the coolest thing I've ever heard. I mean, to be able to make your own clothes would be a major bonus in life. You would never have to fidget with designer labels or sizes or anything of that magnitude. And she's really good at what she does too.

"I can figure something out; just don't you worry your pretty little head over anything. I'll make your costume and all you have to do is wear it this Friday. Trust me; you'll be the hottest thing in that place."

She was collecting her things to leave when she turned to me and said, "Oh and by the way, Gunnar is going to be your date for this party. Is that OK with you?"

"Are—are you kidding me?"

"He approached me today at the diner and asked if you wouldn't mind going with him. I told him that you wouldn't have a problem with it but I can still say no if you don't want to."

"No, no I'll go with him. That's fine by me." I answered her.

Truth be told, I was jumping around screaming with glee at the top of my lungs. Inside my head, that is. It's not every day that a really, really hot boy asks you to accompany him to a party. Well, at least it's not normal for me to get a date like this. You know, being a nerd and everything, I didn't get many dates back in California.

She told me that I wasn't allowed to see the costume until Friday right before we left. That didn't sound like a good thing to me. Portia was definitely plotting something and I had a feeling that it wasn't good.

For me at least. She even went as far as locking it in another room when I stopped at her house to see the progress she'd been making. I swear that girl has one weird brain! But who am I to talk, right?

"No . . . No . . . Absolutely not!"

"Oh come on Scar', I've already made it and you look hot. You're wearing that if I have to strap you down in it and carry you to that party, even if it's the last thing I do."

It's not as if I really had a choice to say no to her. I mean, she made it just for me and she already told Gunnar I would go with him. He should be here in about an hour or so too. Basically, it was too late to run away this time. Darn!

I said, "Uh, alright but you have to help me put it on."

Do you know those old saloon girls back in like the late 1800's that served alcohol to cowboys, as well as certain other pleasures? Well, I was one of them tonight. She even made me wear that stupid corset looking thing and black fishnet stockings with leather boots. My dress was black with red lace and frills lining the bottom and I had a matching black rose comb to put in my hair after she was done curling it and such. I couldn't complain all too much. I mean, for once in my life, I had cleavage to show off. There is only one downside to having such privileges. Although it makes you look smoking hot . . . you can't breathe worth anything in corsets.

Portia had to upstage me on her costume once more, however. She told me I had nothing to worry about, that the boys would be too busy drooling over me to notice her, but I didn't buy it for a second. She was going as a vampire/saloon girl with me. Portia figured I shouldn't suffer completely alone tonight so she made a dress for herself. Hers was black with dark purple lace instead of red and her hair was up.

"Boy Portia, those teeth almost look real! And did you get colored contacts?" I asked her as we were in the bathroom finishing our preparations.

She must have bought those fangs at a custom shop because, honestly, they looked like they could do some serious damage to anyone's jugular. They were pearly white and appeared super sharp.

And her eyes . . . well her eyes were ice blue instead of her normal green. There's no way on Earth that contacts could hide some tint in her natural color. But these did. Oddly enough, she could pass as the real thing tonight.

I know I'm being stupid but I was just thinking out loud is all. I mean, who had actually heard of vampires being real? Come on, you have to get up pretty early in the morning to try and con me in that way. Not only is that scientifically impossible but also illogical. No being could live purely off of blood, human or otherwise. Well . . . leeches and ticks maybe but I'm talking about a life form that's at least bigger than a paperclip.

We were still held up in the bathroom when Gunnar and David arrived. Gunnar hadn't been too happy when Portia said David was coming with us and to tell you the truth, I'm not so sure I wanted him to go either. Max is going to be at this party too and I would rather stay away from any repeats of last week. I know my brother very well and he would try it again if the situation ever presented itself. And this time, I don't think I could stop him from making an idiot of himself.

I knew that Portia did a very good job on my costume when Gunnar's mouth dropped about a foot down. David's did the same but I wouldn't know if it was for me or Portia . . . and I'd like to keep it a mystery. We rode in Portia's SUV but David insisted on driving (so sexist in my opinion). Honestly, what does Portia see in him?

"You look really pretty tonight," said Gunnar when we began to pull out of the driveway. I turned to look him in the eyes but he certainly wasn't staring into mine. No, his line of vision was further south of my neck. Which I couldn't really complain, I knew it was going to happen. With this dress, you couldn't really expect much more from a male. They are only human after all.

Gunnar blushed when I noticed this and I started to laugh quietly to myself. It's not as if I'm going to chastise him for just seeing what's in front of him. Although it was a bit much when I caught him a few more times doing the same thing before we even arrived at the party. I don't know what he's thinking about and I'd particularly not like to know. Again, male minds don't have the same intentions (or same locations in the anatomy, metaphorically that is) as the female brain. Look it up; men are focused on only one thing while females are prone to think about several things at the same time.

Anyways, Gunnar wasn't being that bad I have to admit. It could be worse; I could have had to go with David. I shudder to think about the consequences of that evening. But when we arrived, he was a perfect gentleman . . . Gunnar, I mean. Ironically enough, he was dressed as Zorro for the night. Complete with mask and black cape and a dashing sword to finish it off. He looked really good, and I mean *really* good! The only thing I didn't like about his costume is that his black bandana and cowboy hat covered up that luscious curly hair. Oh well, you can't have everything after all.

The minute David stepped in my house, I laughed quietly to myself. His body builder outfit was a plain white wife beater tank-top with rips and tears in it as if he did it himself. He wore jean shorts that pleated at the bottom as if he were some surfer guy or something. I've seen surfer guys plenty of times back in California and trust me; they'd just laugh at his attire. He had that nasty orange, self-tanning lotion on and I'm pretty sure he thought himself to be the best looking thing at the party.

You know, the party wouldn't have been half bad if the first thing I saw wasn't the last thing I could ever imagine stomaching.

I've already told you Max would be there with a few of his friends, right? Well they brought dates with them too. My brother, dressed in a Jack Sparrow costume had some skanky looking, raven haired girl dressed in a bunny costume (lingerie was more like it) hanging all over him while I witnessed them in a battle of whose tongue could make it all the way down to the other person's spleen first. Honestly, get a room or something! I would never like to see Max slobbering down anyone but he's not what sent me to the keg early in the evening.

I was slurping down a delicious drink the maker had called a Screwdriver when Portia caught up with me again. I was about this close to getting up on a table they had placed in the middle of the barn for the beverages when she found me and stopped me from giving everyone a good little show. Hey, I was upset and nothing could make me feel better but the sweet release alcohol provided.

"P—Por . . . hic . . . Portia!" I screeched drunkenly.

I wrapped my arms around her and hugged her tightly, mostly to keep myself from toppling over, but don't tell her that!

"Oh no, Scarlett I'm so sorry!"

"For . . . hic . . . for what?"

I was stumbling a little with the plastic cup in my hand and it had sloshed and spilled a bit on the bottom of the barn. I might have been wasted, but I was still conscious of everything I was doing at the current moment.

"For getting you trashed at a party you didn't want to even be at. God, I feel like such a crappy friend right now. Please forgive me?"

"Portia," I placed my shaking hand on her shoulder and leaned in so I could whisper in her ear. "Don't tell anyone, but I'm having fun!"

I pulled away in a giggle and let out a rebel yell before downing the remaining contents of my glass. Liquid courage helped me out in this next stunt I pulled. But that doesn't mean I regret what I did.

"Gunnar!" I shouted.

He was sitting with a few of his other friends on those plastic white chairs and chatting it up when I approached him, stumbling the whole way over there. He never saw it coming and that, I was very proud of. I grabbed the back of his neck, titled his head up to face me and planted one right on the kisser. It lasted no more than five or six seconds but I doubt he will be forgetting it any time soon. Even if I was drunk at the current moment and the rest of my body was protesting, I'm aware that my lips worked perfectly fine.

Instead of sticking around and having that awkward conversation as to why I sexually assaulted him at the party, I walked in the opposite direction. Back to the drink table, if you must know. However, I don't think Gunnar would look at it being sexual harassment. If I knew boys, any feature of the female form is welcome to touch any part of them any time we wish. Some exceptions are only if the male thinks the female is ugly or "not sexually fit", but I'd bet they would welcome it if alcohol was thrown into the mix. They'd accept anyone just fine if that were the case.

The drink maker gave me something red in a tiny shot glass and told me to shoot it. It was a hot liquid and tasted as if it were being lit on fire when it traveled down my throat. I remember coughing and sputtering after the drink was swallowed but that's about it. Everything went a little hazy after that.

Voices all around me hummed in a tone that made the floor vibrate underneath my feet. Cold liquid kept being poured into my mouth (which at the time, I had no idea it was being poured by my hand) and my body was swaying to some kind of gyrating sounds from off in the distance. A body was pressed to mine as I moved to the sounds and I remember it feeling really good.

My arm was being pulled out of my socket before I could wrestle it away from whomever was trying to rip it out and my feet were moving at an alarming rate. I no longer saw any light and or anything in front of me. All I could make out was a body standing in my view of the moon, obviously male by size, and a rather large hat sitting on top of its head.

The first name that popped into my mind was Gunnar and his costume. But why was Gunnar pulling me into the darkness?

"I can't believe how you're behaving right now, Red. You're in public! At least *try* and pull yourself together."

"Mmmhmmm . . . "

That was about the only thing I could manage to get out at that moment. Because what I was concentrating on was not vomiting up all the alcohol I had consumed and not fainting from the lack of oxygen passing through my lungs. That corset was sucking the life right out of me, it was almost unbearable.

"Are you even paying attention to me?" The dark figure screamed.

Why was he mad at me?

"Mmmhmm . . . " I mumbled again.

As much as I tried to resist the pain happening in my ribs, I succumbed to it and fell to the ground . . . hard. I'm not going to say I passed out right then, because I didn't. I was fully aware of the dark figure that had been yelling at me a short while previously, shouting my name before scooping me up off the ground and carrying me into a vehicle. What vehicle you might ask? To tell you the God's honest truth, I didn't pay much attention.

I really should have, I know this now, what with the whole rape factor and everything. But when you're drunk you really don't worry about anything but staying upright. The dark figure with the hat was talking to someone outside of the vehicle and then he climbed in and started the engine.

And *that* was the last thing I remember before the lights went out.

# Chapter 10

$\mathcal{M}$Y DREAM THAT NIGHT WAS a bit . . . unconventional at best. Before I begin to explain it, you all have to promise me not to laugh. I know I will sound like I'm insane but please, just give me the benefit of the doubt.

It started off giving me a recap of what happened that same night.

*"Are you cold? Would you like my jacket?" Gunnar asked when we exited the car. It was cold but I would not want to wear that cape if my life depended on it. Not to say that Gunnar was disgusting, but it was a cape! I was already making a fool of myself with the dress; I didn't need any more humiliation.*

*"No thank you," I replied sweetly.*

*We were wandering around and attempting to find someone we knew and wanted to talk to but no such luck came along. Portia kept pointing out to me the people to stay away from when school started. Let me tell you, the list was quite a long one. She obviously didn't get along with very many people. Well, at least I can say that I won't be on that list anytime soon. In my opinion, it's a very good thing to have Portia as your friend. If you had any idea how sarcastically vicious she could be to other people, you would be too.*

*"And that's Daisy Menendez. Don't talk to her unless you want a good laugh. She's the second stupidest person in high school, and that's not an exaggeration."*

*A young girl with shiny, fake blonde hair and brunette highlights was sitting in a portion of the hay on the floor of the barn. Her costume was that of the cat persuasion but rather slutty in appearance. I think she was trying to look like cat woman but didn't pull it off very well. She'd look like cat woman if cat woman was in porn! Her six inch heels zipped up past her knees that were currently wrapped around a boy's waist.*

*"God, why do people have to suck face in front of everyone else? At least take it outside so we don't have to keep our vomit back."*

She shouted her last sentence in order to get the attention of the two make-out artists. Surprisingly, they listened to her and started to stand up and move. That's when I noticed who this Daisy girl was actually sucking face with. Caleb had his hand intertwined with hers and he was pulling her out the barn door. He gave me a quick smile before disappearing into the darkness.

Maybe it was the way his chaps hugged his hips in all the right ways. Or the mesmerizing sounds that his spurs made on the back of his boots when he walked. I was even considering the way that black cowboy hat sat on top of his head and how it went beautifully with that black vest and flowing white shirt. Or perhaps it was just his entire style, personality and everything that made up him that made me follow the two of them outside and peer just beyond the barn door to try and figure out just exactly what they were doing. But, as I suspected, they were already going at it once more on the grass.

Something inside of me snapped and that's when I went to go get drunk. It started off with one simple beer and tumbled downhill from there. I was only planning on getting a little buzz but apparently, fate had other plans for me.

The only thing that set the dream apart from reality was when I turned to go and find Portia with a drink in my hand, I saw something, or rather someone, standing in the middle of the barn doors as clear as day. The only problem was no one else seemed to notice her. Her figure floated (actually floated) over to me and stared me in the eyes. Her facial expression took on that of mystery yet caring at the same time. She looked as if she had a secret to tell me . . . but she said nothing.

The figure was middle aged with flowing red hair and freckles lining her nose. She was wearing a light pink t-shirt and jeans with white tennis shoes gracing her feet. I just couldn't believe my eyes. It was my mother, dropping in on my party to haunt me. Her hand outstretched to my face and brushed my hair out of my eyes. It occurred to me that this was impossible and that it was just a dream, but it felt so real. Someone had turned sprinklers on or something because my face was growing wet.

Her hands moved from my face to my shoulders and she gave me a hard shove, sending me backward and into nothingness. I caught one last glimpse of her eyes before she sent me spiraling out of the dream world and back into reality.

My eyelids snapped open as if on reflex and I jumped about a foot off of my mattress. Max sat on the corner of my bed, right by my head, and his hair was wet and slightly bent to the side. He had certainly been the one who made my face wet, making me wake up from the dream. I should have known. He usually does this when he tries to wake me up after he's had a shower. It probably sounds mean or sadistic to some of you. Any brother waking their sister up gently doesn't sound typical, you forget that I have two of them and I know how they act! But today, Max knew that I had a hangover; he probably had one himself. So I was grateful that he did so somewhat gently. Well, as gently as he thought was fitting in such a case.

"What did you do to Caleb?" He asked me with a smile.

I answered in a wee bit of a panic with, "What do you mean?"

"He's passed out cold on the couch downstairs. I can't even wake him up he's so out of it. Say . . . why is he on *our* couch anyway?"

His smile grew into a wicked grin and I don't even want to know what he was thinking about. Actually, I did know what he was thinking about but I certainly don't want to discuss that with him. Besides, I don't even know why he was on the couch. Even if I did *anything* with him, he would have gone home. So don't ask me why he is down there.

"When did you get home?" I asked him trying to avoid his question.

"A couple of minutes ago. Dad and Holden went to work early so no one's here but us. What do you want for breakfast?"

This is another bonus of having a brother that's sensitive and can cook. Especially when your headache is raging and your stomach is so nauseated you don't want to move. Max figured I didn't want to talk about the events that occurred last night and he knows when to keep his mouth shut when he needs to. I swear Max is a life-saver sometimes. And at the moment, there is only one thing that will make me feel better.

"French toast and bacon, please," I answered with a weak smile.

He left the room and I fell back onto my mattress in exhaustion. I contemplated going back to sleep for a while longer but knew that it was a bad idea. The 1800's dress was still plastered onto my body like glue but my corset was semi-unlaced at the bottom. Someone was clearly trying to help me breathe properly.

I had the day off today but Portia didn't and I needed to talk to her about my actions last night. Maybe apologize for something I might have done to her or someone she liked. So I dragged myself out of bed and grabbed my black Ramones t-shirt and a pair of faded jeans out of my closet. I wanted a hot shower right now and nothing will get in my way of getting what I want.

There was one particular image that kept repeating over and over again in my mind when I was showering. And it happened to involve Caleb. No, not that, so get your minds out of the gutters!

Was he the one who carried my drunken body to his truck last night and took me home? If so, does this mean he forgave me for that little scene I pulled in the parking lot of the diner? I had a hunch that it was the reason he has been avoiding me for the past week. And if he has forgiven me, what does all of what I felt for him last night mean? I blew dry my hair thinking of every emotion that had coursed through my heart as I envisioned Caleb and Daisy's lip lock.

The first one, I knew very well to be anger. I've been feeling that emotion a lot over the past couple of months and half of it had been directed at Caleb. The next one I couldn't pin at first. It could have been hurt or it could have been jealousy, I honestly didn't know. Maybe it was both? And the third emotion . . . pure, grotesque disgust pointed toward Daisy. Anyone with eyes could see that Caleb was a player and yet she lowered herself to accompany him on the grass. Granted, if you saw her you wouldn't consider it lowering. She had some smutty qualities to account for herself and there's no doubt in my mind that she wasn't the hardest girl to acquire in the school.

But why him? Why did she have to go after Caleb? There were plenty of other guys at the party she could persuade to do the same thing. So why did she have to chose Caleb out of everyone else? It's just not fair!

What's happening to me? Montana is having weird affects on my judgment calls. Or maybe it was just the people in Willow Creek? I would have never fallen for the players at my other school. Even if someone were to pay me to date one, I would turn the money down. They aren't a particular species I would have the pleasure to tango with. So why does thinking about Caleb and Daisy together make my blood burn hotter than a soldering iron?

I finished getting ready for the day and made my way down the stairs and into the living room. The delicious smell of vanilla and cinnamon followed by the meaty, greasy scent of bacon permeated from the kitchen like a snake coiling around its prey. I inhaled a big whiff of it, not noticing the sound of someone snoring until I exhaled.

He was still in his cowboy attire sound asleep. His hat was tilted over his eyes and his arms were crossed over his chest. How could he sleep through that food smell? Caleb was certainly a hard sleeper if he could withstand all of that. He needed to wake up though if we were going to eat. I am leaving for the bookstore after I'm finished with breakfast and Max has to go to work. Although I don't think anyone would mind leaving him here to sleep while we are gone, it's the principle of the matter. I really didn't want him to have the opportunity to rummage through my stuff when he did wake up. And something inside me said that he would.

An idea of how to wake him up hit me like a ton of bricks. Don't ask how it happened, but for some odd reason, I knew it would work. So I removed his cowboy hat and knelt down to his eye level.

Looking at his sleeping form made me think. How in the world could I have been so malignant toward him? His eyelids were loosely closed and his mouth was slightly parted with a small drop of drool running down his chin. His hair was severely disheveled but still looked perfectly in place. He looked so innocent and sweet; I couldn't help but sigh a bit. I used the pad of my thumb to first wipe off the driblet of drool. I know it might sound disgusting but it was just drool after all. And I wiped it off on my pants right afterward, so no harm done really!

I moved my mouth just an inch away from his ear and used the tip of my index finger to stroke his right eyebrow while whispering, "Caleb, bacon's on the table."

He responded to that all right! I have never seen someone's body move that fast in my life. It was as if he moved at lightning speed or something. Whatever it was, he made a mad dash out to the kitchen before I could even pull myself up. He's such a guy! But I suppose that's not a bad quality to have for him. It definitely suits him well.

Guys might be fun to look at sometimes, but I'd pass on watching one of them eat any day. I had to hurry up and snatch two pieces of French toast before they could be wolfed down. The bacon was almost gone the second I walked into the kitchen. Half of it, the bacon I mean, was in Caleb's mouth or on his plate while Max talked to him with mushy cooked bread in his. How could someone be able to stand this for an extended period of time was beyond me?

"Well, I'm off to the bookstore," I said while getting up and rinsing my dirty plate in the sink. Not that there was much on it, but still.

"Bye Scar'," was followed by "See you later Red!" Not that I condone any nicknames for myself, but if I did, Red or Scar' would definitely not be any of them. I know a lot of people use Scar' but truth be told, I hate it. And Red . . . come on, how thick can you get? It did, however, bring me back into perspective. You can imagine that having Caleb say that to me brought me down to reality. He just had to have been the one to use that ignorant little nickname for me.

I thought about, ironically, my scars in my truck while I was driving to the bookstore. I know they won't go away ever and it makes me angry in a way. A little anger is directed at my mother in this case. Only because she was in the car that caused these ugly scars. But that's childish and wrong to blame someone that's dead for an accident they didn't cause. I wonder if that scar-be-gone I saw in the store the other day would do anything with the one on my leg? With my luck, most likely not!

"Portia?" I called into the empty room when I arrived at the store.

No one answered.

So I called a bit louder, "Porsh' it's me, Scarlett!"

I heard something hit the floor and break from the back room and the first thought that came to my mind was "please don't let her be cutting herself again! I don't want to see the blood!" That's honestly what I thought. Truth be told, I am a squeamish person when it comes to blood. Guts and missing body limbs are fine, as long as they are visibly clean from anything red and thick.

I ran to the back room and threw open the door to a very interesting sight. Portia wasn't cutting herself, oh no, but crouched on the floor cleaning something up. Her back was facing me and I caught quite a glimpse of a tattoo that she had mentioned to me before. It was a silver, shaded sword with a cobra snake wrapped around the blade and handle that took over her entire back. Blood was dripping out of the snake's mouth and at the bottom of the sword as well. The blood was the only part that was colored.

"Portia, what are you do—"

Her head whipped around to look at me in an impressive speed. Her eyes were large and icy blue once more. The fangs she had worn the night before were still intact and dripping with some sort of deep crimson liquid which was also coating her entire mouth. She couldn't be this crazy, could she? I mean she doesn't have some vampire complex or anything, does she?

A low, menacing growl tore through her throat that made my knees quiver and almost give in. The way she stood up from the floor screamed sex appeal and danger at the same time. Just beyond her lay a large pool of the same substance smeared all over her face. It was definitely blood! I could smell the tin-y scent of it while I was standing feet away from it. My head became dizzy at the simple thought of it.

"Porsh', Portia what's going on?"

A vindictive smile spread across her lips as she sauntered over to me, swaying her hips as she went. That voice in my head kept screaming for me to run but my heart told me to stay put. And, stupid me, I listened to my heart.

I suddenly realized just how ironic that tattoo is and it made me give out a semi-loud, half between a giggle and a nervous laugh. I don't think this made Portia happy because she was running toward me at an alarming rate . . . sharp incisors bared and ready.

I was a goner!

# Chapter 11

"PORTIA! PORTIA DON'T, IT'S ME, Scarlett!"

I had attempted to run away from the maniacal being coming toward me but it didn't work very well. She had me pinned to the ground and placing all of her body weight onto me. She told me once that she weighed one hundred and twenty-five pounds, but this wasn't one hundred and twenty-five pounds! This was more like a bus full of overweight tourists trapping me under its wheels as it squealed them over and over again.

The blood kept dripping off of her teeth and chin which, in turn, landed on me. She moved her smiling mouth toward the base of my neck and inhaled a large amount of air into her lungs. Did she just smell me?!

A strange feeling consumed my entire being all of a sudden. It was like I was at ease with the fact that Portia was about to make me her dinner. Seriously, it was like I welcomed the fact that it was her doing the killing. I tried to push the feeling away, but it wouldn't go anywhere. I've seen movies like this and I know just where this mind controlling power is coming from. Portia's influencing me so I don't try and stop her. But I wouldn't give into her just yet!

Her body shuddered on top of me and she let more weight drop down. I couldn't breathe! I was sure I was going to pass out and die of suffocation at any minute. At least I wouldn't have to see her rip me to shreds with those teeth of hers. She opened wide and was about to rip open my jugular when I used my only oxygen to utter, "Portia, please don't."

She titled her head and snarled one last time before I placed my thumb on the pressure point on her neck. I suppose that snapped her out of whatever state she was in. I had no idea what was going on or what exactly she was, but it certainly scared the heck out of me. In a way, it also fascinated me to watch her eyes fade back to her normal tea green color.

Oh and did I mention, HER FANGS RETRACTED BACK INTO HER GUMS! This was absolutely no trick because normal people can't change their appearance in the blink of an eye.

Not only did she return to normal, she also reeled back as if struck by lightning. Her expression also changed into fear . . . as if she were the one needing to be afraid of me! I was frozen to the ground, just attacked by something that tried to rip my throat out, and she was the one worried about her life!

"Oh my God Scarlett, I am *so* sorry!"

She was crying! Why was she crying? Well, I know why she'd have a right to be angry with me. I had burst in on her feeding and made the choice to stick around and let her emotions, as well as instincts, run amuck. But there was no reason for her to cry about it.

"It's OK," I reassured while picking myself up off the ground. "Just . . . tell me, what in the world that was all about!"

"Well, OK but you have to promise not to be mad at me. I can't help it, really!"

We moved out into the empty main shop before talking. It wasn't spoken of but I could tell being near that blood made her nervous still. And we didn't want a repeat of *that* any more than we have to. The stool I had taken to sitting on while she paced seemed to be unnaturally soft all of a sudden. Maybe it was because I had just had about three tons of inhuman girl pinning me to a hard, cement surface?

"Scarlett, I really don't know how to start this so I'm just going to state the obvious right now. I'm a vampire."

I knew this was going to come out of her mouth but Portia actually saying it still sent shivers through me. It's like when someone tells you Santa Claus isn't real and, somewhere deep down you knew it, but you didn't want to accept it. That was what I was going through then. But if vampires existed, does that mean other mythical creatures exist as well? Maybe Santa Claus is real?

So when she said this, I couldn't make words form in my mouth so I just silently nodded my head yes. She got the hint and continued to explain the rest of her supernatural heritage to me.

"My parents and I moved out to Montana about a year ago," She has parents?! Whoever they were didn't seem as important right now so I let her continue on talking. "And we have been getting along with the locals all right but we certainly don't fit in like everyone else assumes we do."

"Is—is it hard for you? I mean, standing the blood smell and all."

"I'm . . . " She dragged the word out to make it sound as if it were more than one syllable. "Older so I can control it much better than some of the others. It's a complicated concept but if you're able to imagine standing in a room with food around you and not eat it, then it's basically the same thing."

"Can you eat real food? Or is it strictly blood for you?" I asked in curiosity. See, I told you I'm a curious person. Here I am talking to a vampire and I'm asking a bunch of questions like it will be on a test or something.

"Come on Scar, you've seen me eat real food before. You know the answer to that question. The taste of it is a bit different but it's still the same as when we were alive. We just need to drink blood to survive."

"And does it have to be from a living person?"

SHUT UP ALREADY, SCARLETT!

"Well, when you interrupted me in there, I had just grabbed a donated bag and poured it in a glass. So, technically the blood needs to be from a once or still living being but we don't need to attack them anymore to get it."

A moment of silence passed while I was thinking of my next question. I had so many zooming around in my head it was hard to single one out long enough to tell if it's a good idea or a bad idea to ask her. There was one that stood out from the rest. Actually, it just seemed like the bigger one in my head. And it was definitely not harmful to ask, so why not?

"Portia, how old are you?"

She giggled quietly before answering with, "Well, I'll put it this way . . . that dress you wore last night used to be mine back when it was in style. I didn't make it on a whim."

"Do you actually make your own clothes then?"

"Yes, I still do. Most clothes made today won't work with the temper I have when I get angry, so I only stick to the designer brand when I'm calm. And you know by now that my rage happens often, so I learned how to sew a while back and kept the knowledge."

So, my best friend was a vampire. I think I could accept that enough without losing my mind. I mean, I also have an aunt that thinks she's psychic in case you've forgotten so I'm used to weird things. But if Portia is a vampire, then there are others out there like her. Do all vampires have similar features or was it just her family? And if she had parents, where were they? She said that she was a lot older than she led on, so maybe they're dead. But she said that she moved here with them last year! Does that mean vampires can have children? I thought they stayed the same age forever.

See, so many questions and I wasn't sure if I should ask them or not. I wanted to . . . more than anything, I wanted to. But would it be too inappropriate in a time like this to play 20 questions with a vampire? I mean, she did just finish eating and I would *never* like to see her that angry again. Declining the chance to grill her some more about her life was easy. Because someone had walked in and interrupted our conversation.

"Hey guys! Whatcha doing?" The little 9 year old voice asked.

Kate's blonde hair was held out of her eyes with a twisty that made her tiny, angular face appear thinner. She had to be the most beautiful child I had ever seen. Was she a vampire too? It's only logical that I assume since she's a part of their family, she too must carry the vampire trait. Did they bite her when she was walking home from school one day? It was the only scenario that seemed to make sense as to why, if Kate is, she is a vampire.

"Katie, can you come back a bit later. Scarlett and I are discussing something important and you don't need to hear."

Maybe Kate still doesn't know she lives with ravenous blood suckers? How would that make you feel? You're nine years old and you have been lied to all, or most, of your life. The people that you live with aren't the people that you thought they were. If it were I and I found out, I'd never speak to any of my family members again.

After some persistent bickering between the two of them, Kate finally left, leaving me alone with Portia again. But no matter how hard I tried, I couldn't bring myself to ask the questions I wanted so badly to know the truth to. It was Portia who changed the subject almost immediately after Kate left the store. I had to be alright with this. It's not like I had the guts to spark up the conversation we were having before once again. I might be a strong person but I'm certainly not that strong.

"So, how are you and Caleb doing?" She asked me.

Sadly, I think I knew this question was coming up sooner or later.

"Contrary to what everyone believes and wishes to be true, nothing is going on between Caleb and me. That's probably something you don't want to hear but I can't—"

"No, that's exactly what I wanted to hear!" She shouted with glee.

"Really?"

"Really! Gunnar has been asking . . . well, more like grilling me for answers on you and how you thought the date went last night. He called me ten times from the time I got home until I came into work today and left me messages on each one . . . pertaining to you. So, what should I tell him?"

I took a moment to think about this. Because something so monumental like this needs to be re-evaluated before any serious decisions are made. There is the whole Caleb factor to work into this situation. He and I aren't dating and probably never will, but I couldn't deny the fact that I am attracted to him anymore. I wouldn't say that it's full blown lust that I'm feeling but something has to be there. You can't just be jealous of some random girl at a party that sucks face with a guy you know and not have it mean something. Even if it's miniscule, there is a part of me that holds a special place for Caleb.

Then there was the fact that I've only had one boyfriend my entire life. Now that I'm older and the guys my age are much more interested in becoming physical, I really don't know how to handle that. I mean how to say no and alleviate myself from such situations. There is no doubt that I could take care of myself if a guy wouldn't stop if I told him to but there is still that worry. Gunnar doesn't seem like that kind of guy though. Maybe I should give him a chance to prove himself a good boyfriend?

"Well, I had a really good time with him when I was sober. And what I remember from the kiss, he doesn't slobber all over a girl. I'd give him another chance if he asked me."

Portia flipped out. She was happier than I was that I was dating Gunnar again. Confusing? Yes, yes it is but hey, if she's happy that a guy wants me in a more than platonic way then I'm happy to oblige. If we were back in California, this sort of thing would never happen to me. And I am talking about this entire day. Honestly, who can say that they found out that their best friend is really a mythical undead creature that sucks blood *and* got asked out by a very hot boy? Not even a handful that I am 100% positive about. Well, 90% at least. But that's taking in account of how much vampire knowledge I am in the dark about still.

# Chapter 12

THE FIFTEEN MINUTE DRIVE HOME was very interesting, if you must know. First off, I found Angel walking down the road in town as plain as day with no motive in being there at all. After I picked her up and put her in my truck, I started to drive once more.

Maybe about three or four minutes away from my driveway, in the middle of the forest that extends to our house and located to the left of our back porch, I spotted a wolf running, well playing really, through the trees. It was a deep grey with black all around its face and a streak of white going along the top of its back. Now I wasn't close enough to see perfect details but it was semi-large for even being a full grown wolf. I've never seen one that close before . . . it was kind of cool. Especially considering I've never even seen one on TV with that sort of coloring! It was beautiful.

I wasn't going to worry about some miscellaneous animal right now. I had bigger fish to fry and it didn't involve another species. Well, if you want to call a boy a different species then so be it. I do.

As soon as I turned the ignition in THE BEAST off, I heard the phone from inside ringing. I had a strong feeling I knew who it was but I wasn't going to jump to any conclusions yet. Running down a rocky driveway sounded like a good idea at the time but I wouldn't recommend anyone else doing it. Yeah, I fell flat on my face as soon as my foot hit a rock sticking out of the dirt. It hurt so much. I stumbled up and kept running for the door, however, praying that whoever it was calling wouldn't hang up yet.

"Hello?" I asked, out of breath and sweating a bit, through the receiver.

"Hello, is Scarlett there?" A male voice asked politely on the other end of the line.

It was exactly who I expected it to be. Although I had just met him only a few weeks ago, I knew that voice all too well. It had a very smooth, soothing tone to it. Sort of like my mother had when she was alive. God, I missed her!

"This is she," I answered.

"Oh, hi Scarlett, this is Gunnar. Do you remember me?"

His insecurities were so adorable. Of course I'd remember him, how could I not? Unlike a certain member of the male species who thinks he is the best thing to ever walk this Earth. And guess who decides to walk into the sliding glass doors (scaring me witless) leading to the backyard at the exact same moment I thought about him? If you said Caleb, you'd be right. It was hilarious to see his face print on the glass but I contained my chuckles so Gunnar wouldn't think I was laughing at him.

You know the saying, "Speak of the Devil and then he shall appear"? Well, something like that, but in this case I was thinking of instead of speaking of him.

He was naked from the waist up with a towel wrapped loosely around his neck and a pair of Max's jeans resting low on his hips. You know that little V-shape that appears on the sides of a body that is perfectly sculpted? Well, Caleb would be a marble statue placed in the Louvre if it were up to me. His stomach was flat and had abdominals that any girl would kill just to touch. Caleb had pecks with a dip right in the middle where his sternum ended and biceps that were the right size for his body structure. Beads of water were sliding down every inch of him. His hair was sticking up everywhere and held there by the water soaking through it. He was obviously just coming in from a dip in our pool.

There was one feature I couldn't take my eyes off of, however. And it just happened to be his mouth. It was curved into his crooked smile and was directed straight at me. How could something so beautiful be so . . . so . . . immature, egotistical, shallow, easy and annoying? That's just the way heartbreakers are, I suppose.

"Scarlett? Are you still there?"

Gunnar's voice interrupted my daydreams of Caleb and his fantastic body. Mainly I was thinking about how good he would taste if I licked off the drops of water that were so tempting, it was almost unbearable. Stop it! I need to concentrate on Gunnar. Yes, Gunnar is going to ask me out and I need to pay full attention to the boy that would actually be good for me rather than the one who would end up tearing my heart into a million pieces.

"Yeah, sorry. How are you?" I asked.

"I'm fine. How are you feeling after . . . you know?"

He was talking about all the alcohol I had consumed.

"I'm feeling better now that I've slept and had some food. Thank you for asking, I really appreciate your concern for my well-being."

"Y-Yeah, no problem. So listen—"

I became distracted again. Caleb was sauntering over to me while taking the towel off of his shoulders—his broad, muscular shoulders—and putting it on our counter. In my defense, I doubt any girl would be able to concentrate on a conversation with another person with this beautiful specimen right in front of them. His mouth moved to form the words "who is that," but I didn't answer him. Something inside of me told me not to tell Caleb anything about Gunnar, and just in case, I was heeding the advice for once.

"Pardon me; can you repeat that one more time?" I asked courteously.

"Yeah sure, I was wondering if you were free tomorrow at around 7 o'clock to go and see a movie or something. You don't have to if you don't want to but—"

"No, no I'll go."

Caleb moved to the bar stool he was sitting on and stood smack dab in front of me. I know he was trying to listen in on part of the conversation in order to find out just who I'm talking to. His brows were furrowed and his lips were pulled into a hard line. Why was he becoming angry? I'm not doing anything to hurt him or even make him remotely mad in any way. He can be so childish sometimes it's unreal!

"Really?!" He shrieked over the receiver.

You know, with the way he is reacting, you'd think that *he* was the nerd.

"Yeah, that sounds great."

"OK then I'll see you around 6:45 or so."

"OK cool. Can't wait!" I finished.

We hung up at the same time. Gunnar and I haven't even started dating each other and we are already so in sync it's a bit strange. The person in front of me, however, I still had to deal with. And I have a feeling that this conversation won't turn out as pleasant as the one I just left. Darn!

"Who was on the phone, Red?" He gritted through his teeth.

"None of your business, Darwin."

To prove that it wasn't that big of a deal, I walked over to the fridge like I was on a Sunday stroll and grabbed a soda out. I was never expecting him to grab the can out of my hand and slam it on the table like he did. It even imploded on itself! What he did after that though had me floored. His arms shot out and cornered me so that my back was pressed against the island in the middle of the kitchen. Caleb's eyes were burning a hole through my own, hitting my soul and setting it on fire.

"Tell me *now*," He growled . . . actually growled!

The feeling returned and screamed louder inside my head not to tell him about Gunnar and me. But this time, I didn't listen to it.

"It—It was Gunnar Belwin."

"What did he want?"

His body was moving closer to mine until his torso was just barely grazing mine through my shirt. His face was just inches away from my own and I could feel the heat radiate off of him and onto me in waves. I'm not going to lie, I had a very strong urge to wrap my fingers through his hair and pull until our lips met. But I fought that urge and won. I didn't win the battle to keep my mouth shut, however. The little voice screamed louder but my voice seemed to have a mind of its own.

"We're going to the movies tomorrow night."

"Like a date?"

He nonchalantly smelled my neck! I was instantly reminded of Portia and the incident that had just occurred in the Bookstore. Was I being pinned up against a counter top by another vampire? Oh, say it isn't so! Not him . . . not Caleb, because I know if he had the same power and influence on human emotions like I knew Portia to have, I was done for. I don't think I could ever be able to fight off his advances if it ever came down to it. Honestly, I don't think I'd *want* to even fight him off!

"More or less," I almost whispered my reply.

His palms, located beside me, took on their own fury and slammed down on the counter top with such force that it made me shake where I stood. It might have been my imagination but I caught a glimpse of his eyes and I swear that they momentarily turned an eerie yellow. But Portia's eyes didn't do that when she was about to make me her meal. I'd prefer not to question his eye color when I so clearly needed to concentrate on getting away from him.

I took my chances and placed both of my palms on the front of his chest and shoved. I figured if he was going to eat me, he'd have tried it already. He wasn't as heavy as Portia was, but was obviously heavier than any human. Even for a teenage boy. I did end up moving him though.

Only a few feet from me but it did give me enough space to move away from the island and several away from him.

"What was that all about, Caleb?" My voice came out in a fury of hurt and rage. What can I say, the boy made me so angry I could punch him. But I think it would hurt me more than it would hurt him. Whether he is a vampire or not, it probably wouldn't affect him in the least bit. Which, in turn, made me even madder at him.

"I—he . . . he's just not . . . he's just not the guy for you, OK Red?" His hand raked through his wet hair while he said this.

"Who are you to tell me whom I can and cannot date? The last time I checked, I was perfectly capable of making my own decisions and judgments, in case you haven't noticed."

"What's that supposed to mean?" He asked becoming mad himself.

"I didn't date you!" I hissed at him.

"You know, you're no picnic to be around either princess. You're rude, stuck up, and not as pretty as you seem to think you are."

That was a massive blow to my ego, right there. You never tell a girl she's ugly, even if she is. For one, you can do some major damage to the girl's psyche and make her either 1.) Need massive amounts of therapy to recover or 2.) Do so much mental damage that she feels she isn't worthy of being in this world and do something drastic. Now, I will do neither considering I have a date with a very nice boy tomorrow that thinks the total opposite of Caleb, but I'm not saying that it couldn't happen.

"Get out!"

"What?" He asked in shock.

"I said get out of my house right now!" I yelled at him.

"Come on Red, I wasn't being ser—"

To make my point perfectly clear to him, I found the nearest heavy object and chucked it at his head. Granted, it ended up being a soup ladle but it very effectively did its job. He was hit square in the eye before he had the opportunity to duck. After he came back to his senses from the blow the ladle gave him, he grabbed a shirt that was lying on the arm of the couch and booked it out the door and into his truck. I heard the engine roar and he was gone.

There was a small part of me that felt guilty about the whole 'hitting him ruthlessly in the head with a soup ladle' thing . . . but I didn't. I might agree that I'm not very pretty, but he didn't have to point it out so bluntly like that. Just because we were in the throes of a fight doesn't give him the right to call me names and make fun of my physical appearance. That's just low!

I need to calm down and just let everything he said roll off of my shoulders because I have at least one guy that wants me. And we are going to the movies tomorrow as an actual date. I couldn't be happier even if you bought me a new puppy. Can any of you tell that I'm lying? In the back recesses of my mind still lay a thought about Caleb's words that cut me like a knife.

To clear my head of all thoughts, I walked up to my room and shut my door. Angel was there lying on my pillow, dozing soundly like he normally does. I turned on my stereo and cranked up country and the tears started to flow like a waterfall. I told you, Caleb's words really hurt my feelings and I couldn't help that my emotions got the best of me in the end.

It was going to be a long night of cleaning and nobody had better interrupt me or else they might be injured in the line of fire just like Caleb had.

# Chapter 13

ACKIE MADE ME WORK THE morning shift the next day. I told her about my date and she switched spots with me so I had enough time to get ready for it. It's one of the bonuses of having a boss that's only a few years older than you I suppose. She can be a great advantage to my social life, like her sister in a way. Too bad it unnerved me to no extent to be around her or any of her family members without Portia around. Remember, they are vampires after all.

The morning rush slowly dissipated into nothing, leaving me sitting all alone with nothing to do. No matter how much I complain about how sleepy this town is, I can't hate it entirely. I've been through a lot and certain residents helped me cope with my losses and, in a way, saved me from becoming a mopey, wreck of a person. So in a way, I should really thank them instead of making hurtful remarks about how slow the town is. Even if the evidence proves it to be true.

Jackie showed up around 2 o'clock and wished me luck on my date before I left. I wasn't nervous or anything but maybe I should be. What if he doesn't like me and he is just going out with me because Portia told him to? Maybe Caleb was right about me not being pretty enough. That would certainly explain my luck with boys most of my life. I guess I'll just have to wait until Gunnar picks me up to make any permanent assumptions about how he feels for me. It's mostly up to him anyway.

But as much as I tried to push back the disturbing mental images of Gunnar going in for a kiss and suddenly coming into his senses—calling me ugly as well—fought its way to the surface and won. I couldn't concentrate on what to wear so I chose a simple pair of distress jeans and a brown, off the shoulder American Eagle t-shirt. I looked OK once I curled my thick hair to a more manageable appearance but I could still see all of the flaws in the mirror.

Do you know when you stare at your reflection in the mirror for so long, the image starts to distort? Well, I began to mentally write down everything I found that I considered wrong.

I was skinny but my stomach had enough soft curves visible through my shirt, making me seem fat. My dark red hair was plain and dry and much too thick for my own liking. Max had it easy . . . his hair was short and smooth with natural copper highlights that shine in the sun. I have no such luck with that. As I said before, my face wasn't full of freckles but the ones on my cheekbones and nose are very visible. My legs are too long but I'm still short for my family's standards. And, last but certainly not least, my mouth. Shape, form and fullness, I hated everything about it. My lips were full but the bottom one always seemed to be a bit thicker than the top.

And don't get me started on those nasty scar lines on my face, sides and my thigh. Albeit you cannot see the one on my leg it still doesn't make it any less ugly. The tiny line running across the crease of my lip wasn't that noticeable anymore, which made me happy, but ever since I became tanner, the one in my eyebrow stood out like a shockingly white line. And I hated it.

And those thoughts didn't exit my mind when Gunnar came to pick me up, when we took our seats in the theater or even when the movie started. Honestly, my flaws were eating away at me while Caleb's voice kept repeating, "You're not as pretty as u seem to think you are." I didn't even know I was that conceded but apparently I've been going around flaunting myself like someone his lips were distinctly attached to at the party. I'm going to have to work and get better at not being so narcissistic I suppose.

For Gunnar being as good looking as he is, he sure isn't full of himself. When I thought about how this date would go, I pictured him to be more like David or Max or even Caleb. He wasn't very affectionate in the least. Not that I was expecting a full make-out session in a dark corner of the theater, but he didn't even hold my hand or anything. I'm not going to lie, that hurt more than I was expecting it to. What's wrong with me? Maybe I have cooties like every boy thought I had back when I was seven. Why do guys have to be so complicated?!

I heard Gunnar snicker at something beside me just then. He wasn't laughing at the screen because we were in a horror movie and there were no funny parts coming up anytime soon. My hand felt something brush up against the top of my fingers and intertwine with them shortly after two or three strokes against my palm. Maybe Gunnar had gotten the hint and decided to act on his feelings.

Or maybe he was just trying to spare mine and be a gentleman on our date. If so, that is about the lowest thing anyone could do. I mean, think about it! You ask a girl out only to find out that you aren't as attracted to her as you previously had thought, but you still try and be courteous by holding her hand. That's leading someone on, that is! And why would you go to all that trouble if you don't like that person? It's not as if holding my hand will benefit him in his life. So why must it be me that gets deceived into thinking this?

"Scarlett?" Gunnar asked me.

"Yes?"

"I don't want you to take this the wrong way Scarlett, but I have to get it off of my chest or my head just might burst from retaining it for so long. I'd like you to know that you're the most beautiful girl I've ever seen."

Well . . . that stunned me to the point where I couldn't get my vocal cords to work properly. I stuttered and stammered and ended up just smiling in his direction because I didn't want to make a bigger fool of myself. As if I didn't do that already! I don't think Gunnar was going to hold a few babbling words against me though. It means that I actually liked what he said to me, if that was any help.

The movie ended but our hands never unlocked from one another. All the way out to the parking lot, they stayed together. His touch was a bit cold but nothing to unmanageable. It was like sticking your hand in front of the air conditioner vent in a car. You know you can do it for hours on end but it gets numb after a while. Oh crap, I just remembered that I was supposed to pick up my paycheck before my date.

"Gunnar, would you mind if we made a quick stop at the bookstore before you drop me off at my house. I forgot to pick up my check."

"Sure thing."

The fifteen minute car ride was slower than usual. I think he was purposefully taking his time in order to spend more time with me. That's sweet but I'm not that interesting and I really need to get this check before the shop closes and Jackie goes home.

The car spontaneously accelerated.

"Alright, here we are gorgeous." He said while putting the car in park.

I jumped out and ran into the bookstore as fast as I could. If the evening was going in the direction I had hoped, I will most likely get a kiss goodnight after he walks me to my door. So I was determined to spend as little time as necessary in the store to get that one simple kiss. What can I say; Gunnar is a major fox!

I couldn't find Jackie around anywhere. This, you know, worried me a little because the sign was still reading open and the front of the shop was empty. Maybe she was in the back of the store sucking up blood like Portia loves to do? OK, I know that was a little insensitive but she's not around at the moment and I'm still freaking out about what she really is. You would be too if your best friend just sprung the most frightful news on you. Even if you were the one that caught her in the act.

"Jackie?" I yelled before traveling through the door that led to the back room. I don't want a repeat of what happened last time.

Oh, but what I saw when I peeked through the crack of the door was much, much worse than Jackie sucking on a bag of blood. I'd take that over what I was witnessing any day. Heck, I'd even take the blood being from my body if it were capable of erasing this brutal mental image. OK, that was a bit extreme but if you knew what I saw you'd be siding with me one hundred percent. I'm not sure whether to explain to you what this audacious sight was or to leave you in the dark. Because once I share it with you, you will never be able to rid your mind of it ever again.

Oh well, I'll tell you anyway. No point in being the only person to know it. So the room was pitch black save for the stream of light coming from where I was peeking in through. There was a desk currently being occupied by two dark figures doing unspeakable things. If you looked close enough to see their faces, you could make out every feature. Sounds of pleasure that I wish to never hear ever again filled the entire room. Brace yourselves because knowing who it was that was rocking the desk in a grotesque manner is the one that might make you vomit.

At first I thought it was Portia because the only thing I could make out was long brown hair. That was before I saw the short black hair along with the brown. I knew David didn't have black hair and that's when it tipped me off. I looked closer at their faces and realized that it wasn't Portia and David in the least. But instead, the bodies on the desk were Jackie and Andrew! And they weren't doing anything siblings do. Or at least supposed to do.

A sheen of wet, red liquid dripped down onto the floor and into my line of vision. That was the moment were I realized I shouldn't be here for this . . . in any sense of the word. I quickly shut the door and booked it out to the parking spaces where Gunnar was waiting quietly for me.

"Did you get your check?" Gunnar asked me when I hopped into the passenger's seat.

I completely forgot to look for that when I was busy ruining my eyes for the rest of my existence. I think I'm going to rub hydrogen peroxide in them when I get home in attempt to rid them of the obscenities I had just witnessed. But I couldn't tell him this so I need to make up a lie. What to tell him?

"Umm, Jackie said that she would have them ready for us to take tomorrow." I replied in almost a whisper.

He didn't question me like someone else I knew would have. And if you don't know who I'm talking about now, I'd suggest you all go back and start reading this book again. I know for a fact that he would grill me until I told him exactly what happened in the bookstore. He's only concerned about my well being but when he pushes too much, it's hard not to become angry with him.

The ride home was sufficiently quieter than I'd liked. Right now, I just needed someone to talk to so I wouldn't keep thinking about Jackie's and Andrew's incestual problems. But I didn't know what to say and it looked like Gunnar didn't know either. Luckily, we were at my house before I even realized it. Gunnar was a gentleman and walked me to my door. Or maybe it was just because he was looking to get that goodnight kiss I had mentioned earlier. Yeah, I believe the latter to be right.

"So, I had a good time tonight," I started off with when we were in front of my door.

"Me too," he responded.

"I-I really appreciate you being so nice to me. Not many people have been so welcoming like you and Portia have been."

"I don't see why not. But you're very welcome. Besides, it's not that hard to be nice to you Scarlett."

I gave him a wide smile and that's when his head started to lean down. This was it! This was the moment I would finally be kissed by a boy without any braces and animal crackers stuck in the wiring! Don't get me wrong, Carter's kisses were nice and all, but they were usually just a quick peck and a small, very girly giggle. And the girly giggle was not by me, just to throw that out there.

Our lips were a few inches apart now and just about to touch when . . .

"Good evening kiddies! What's going on out here?"

You'd think it would be my father or Holden, thinking they were being chivalrous or something, but it wasn't. A sweat pants clad Caleb stood in the doorframe with a smile/scowl on his face. And he was only wearing sweatpants too. God, I hate it when that boy decides to show off those muscles he works so hard for. They make you utterly incapable of forming a coherent sentence let alone look at anything other than him.

"Caleb, go away!" I gritted through my teeth.

"I think it's time for you to come in now. Portia's here and she's upset about something." Caleb stated.

Now whether or not that was true, I had to talk to her anyway.

"OK, I'll be inside in a minute."

He didn't move. He just kept standing in the doorway and looking back and forth from Gunnar to me as if he was waiting for something. I know him well enough to know that he wasn't going to move until I accompanied him back into the house. I, however, wasn't going to go without kissing Gunnar in some way tonight. And it had an added bonus of making Caleb mad and jealous so it was a win-win situation.

So I let out a huff before saying, "Goodnight Gunnar, I'll see you later."

It was a quick peck on the lips but it got my point across very well. I know it wasn't our first kiss, the drunken stupor I was in that night took perfectly good care of that, but I wanted to at least kiss him better than I had. But with Caleb in my line of vision looking severely scrumptious, I couldn't accomplish anything. So after I kissed Gunnar, I turned on him and grabbed Caleb by the scruff of the neck and pulled him inside.

# Chapter 14

"Ow, ow, ow, Red, let go!" Caleb whimpered.

"That will teach you to never interrupt my dates ever again!"

I was yelling at him very loudly. And just to make my point count even more, still grasping the hairs on the base of his neck, I threw him down on the nearest chair in the kitchen as hard as I could. It didn't have the desired effect that I wanted. But then again, I don't think spontaneous combustion via mind powers is possible yet. Darn scientific evolution!

"I wasn't interrupting, I was . . . observing . . . from a very close distance."

I folded my arms across my chest and look him straight in the eye with one eyebrow cocked and my mouth pulled into a thin line.

"Did you imagine that would somehow magically work on me? Make me forgive you for all that you've done to me? 'Oh, I understand Caleb. That makes perfect sense to me. And now, with your smooth talking words, I think I'll dump Gunnar and only go out with you . . . take me, you big stud muffin you.'"

When I finished mocking him in my squeaky, girly voice, I went back to staring him down in order to get my point across. But I can almost guarantee that my point was completely moot with this big buffoon anyhow. So I guess I was just doing the typical 'angry female' routine to make myself feel better. And it was semi working.

"You know, that was just cruel. You could really mess a guy up, leading him on like that."

"Somehow, I think you'll survive."

My throat was as dry as the Sahara desert by now. Not that I didn't drink anything at the movie theater, but when you're eating popcorn, the sensation to quench your thirst is almost as important as oxygen. So I walked myself over to my fridge with muscle man still sitting in the seat not knowing what to say and grabbed myself a soda. But, like the first time I told Caleb about my date with Gunnar, he made his way off of his seat and over to me before I could even realize he moved. This little thing he's doing, the 'being as silent as a mouse' thing. Yeah, that's got to stop.

"He's not respecting my personal property, Red."

His voice was no more than a whisper but, for some odd reason, my ears had bat-like capabilities all of a sudden. I could have heard that sentence from a mile away if it were put to the test.

"What do you mean by your personal property? Do you mean *our* house or something? Just because you befriended my brother before Gunnar did . . . or ever does . . . doesn't mean that its—"

"I'm not talking about your house, Scarlett . . . " followed by the longest pause of my life before, "I'm talking about you."

He was being serious about this. Would you like to know how I knew this? Because he used my name and not his little nickname. Ever since I arrived in Willow Creek, he has called me nothing but Red unless he's drunk or having a serious conversation with me. I'd think it's sweet if he and I weren't in a massive fight at the moment. I am no one's property and never will be. And for him to think that somehow telling me that he owns me would make me change my mind all of a sudden is just ridiculous. Male chauvinism is too much sometimes.

"What do you mean by 'your personal property'? Did you mark your territory on me or something?"

I meant it as a joke but by the facial expression he was giving me, I don't think I was too far off on my assumptions. His eyes were wide and his lips formed a guilty smile while the redness of a blush began to appear on his cheeks. My stomach turned at the thought of him urinating on me at any point just to stake his territory over another male.

"You-you did, didn't you? That's disgusting!" I yelled while shoving him away from me.

Even though he had marked me permanently in the most sickening way anyone could ever imagine, and I would be forever irate about, the feeling of his skin was just too powerful to ignore. It was like velvet or something. Way too much for me to handle, that's for certain. He more or less stumbled back and rested on the counter. In my opinion, I think he pretended that he lost his balance in order to give me some space but I could be wrong. Don't think I am though.

"You don't understand, Scarlett. I had to claim you somehow and I did the only thing I could think of. It seemed fitting at the time—"

"You think secreting bodily fluids on me without my permission is fitting? You are seriously disturbed." I needed to get away from him now. If I didn't, I swear I would end up chucking another kitchen utensil at his head.

"I didn't pee on you, alright?! I just . . . rubbed up against you as much as I could to make sure that my smell was fully imbedded in your skin. See, no urination involved."

"When?" I asked bluntly.

"Excuse me?"

"When did you do this?" I asked louder.

He sheepishly turned away from me and started to pick at a piece of the counter top that was peeling away. Why was he nervous? Even though I'm mad at him, I couldn't physically hurt him to the point where he should be cowering away from me. I know I'm intimidating but come on, this is just absurd. The silence was so deep that it made me jump when he started talking again.

"It was the night of the Halloween party when I took you home. After I untied that stupid vice you called a dress to let you breathe, I-I got an idea. It seemed like a good idea at the time because I didn't think you'd find out."

I began to think about Caleb rubbing up against me while I was fast asleep. If he did what he said he did, can I smell him on me too? Or is it just a male thing? Where did he get this idea and why did he think it would work? Most guys would stake their territory by just asking the girl out first. Or fighting; which I wouldn't put past Caleb to do. I don't know who would win if Gunnar and Caleb were to solve this dilemma through violence but I know it would be interesting to watch. Wait a minute, did he rape me? Sex is in every male's psyche and to have a female passed out in a bed with semi-open dress certainly factors in on the easiness of the situation. I wouldn't even be able to struggle or anything.

"Did-did you . . . I mean, did we—"

I made a gesture with my hands instead of actually putting it into words. Asking something like that out loud would be just too awful to bear, especially to Caleb. I ran through every possible way Caleb could have reacted to my question but I was *never* expecting him to laugh at me like he did. I couldn't help but glare at him over his insensitivity to this situation. How would you like it if you just asked a guy a serious question and they laughed in your face?

"Do you—ha, ha—do you actually believe I'm that kind of guy? When I do take your virginity, I would like you to be conscious at the time to at least enjoy it."

I don't find it hard to believe that he used the term "when" and not "if" while talking about he and I getting to know each other in the biblical sense. But what I did find odd was the fact that he knew I was still a virgin. I don't recall even talking about it to Portia let alone him. So how on Earth did he know something so personal about me without exploring it further? I shuttered to think about what he did.

"How-how did you—"

"Hey Caleb," my brother came from upstairs and interrupted before I could finish that sentence. "Robin just called me and wants you and me to go and meet Daisy and her at the diner."

Max was followed quickly by Portia. She had a large smile on her face and a skip in her step. I'd prefer not to know what had made her so happy when just a few minutes ago Caleb told me she was in pieces about something. And if it had to do with my brother, I'd rather be stabbed with hot pokers than hear any of the gory details. This brought that sickening mental image of Portia's brother and sister back to the front of my brain. The boys were leaving and my dad and Holden didn't seem to be anywhere around . . . now's the perfect time to get more answers from her.

# Chapter 15

$\mathscr{I}$F ANY OF YOU COULD actually have seen what I saw at the bookstore, I don't think that you would be so calm about it. I was doing my best because Portia obviously had something else on her mind before she came here and needed to vent before I started to pry in on her family problems. I just didn't expect them to be as typical as every other teenage girl in the country.

"And-and when he said that she was a better kisser than I was I sort of . . . snapped."

Let me give everyone at home a quick recap of what Portia had told me before this was said. Basically David is in the hospital right now with a broken nose, three cracked ribs and two broken legs because he was stupid enough to bring the girl he was cheating on Portia with to the diner at the same time Portia decided to go and get a bite to eat. And no pun was intended in that sentence. When she confronted him about it in the parking lot of the diner, she ended up beating him to a bloody pulp after certain things were said. And with her super vampire strength, I am still shocked that she didn't kill him.

I felt her pain in a way. I do not condone the fact that she almost massacred a boy outside of a local hang out. But the honest truth behind the reason she did so made perfect sense to me. I know if Caleb ever did such a thing to me, I wouldn't be as lenient as Portia had been to David. Oops, I meant Gunnar. If Gunnar ever did that to me I would beat him so bad that the FBI couldn't identify the remains. So I was doing my best to sympathize with her situation the best I could without being too hypocritical.

"I'm sorry about you and David breaking up Portia, and I don't mean to be rude, but I think that you finding this out is the greatest thing that could ever happen to you." I said as I handed her a tissue from the bathroom down the hall from my bedroom.

"I know this," I certainly wasn't expecting that response. "But I can't wrap my head around the fact of whom he was cheating on me with. I mean Rachael Yates! He could have at least picked someone with surviving brain cells. That girl lights up almost every free chance she gets!"

"Forgive me, I'm in a bit of a shock, but did you really just say that you knew this was the best thing for you? I thought you loved the guy?"

"Oh, heck no! He was sort of . . . an in-between guy if you will. I know who I'm meant to be with whether he knows it or not. That's why I'm not too broken up about it."

"If that was you going easy on him, remind me never to never get you angry with me." I said with a smile. I was only kidding after all. She would never do such a thing to me and I know this for a fact. Beside the fact that we had only known each other for a few weeks, I know she's not a violent person . . . or couldn't be on purpose, I should say . . . toward me.

The long silence between the two of us gave me a chance to think about some things that she had said. With what she said about knowing who she was meant to be with, I was curious. Did she really mean she knows or was she just guessing? Maybe it was some special vampire quality to know who the one you were meant to be with is even before they do. I really do want to ask her, but should I? Yes, yes I should!

"I know I'll probably regret ever asking you this, but how do you know?" I asked.

"How do I know what?"

"How do you know who you're meant to be with?"

She was quiet; I imagine thinking about how to word this explanation, before actually responding with, "There's this thing that vampires go through when they first grow their adult fangs. It's weird at first because you hear a voice inside of your head other than your own and you really don't know how to handle it. But once an older vampire, such as my parents, explains to you what's happening everything comes into perspective."

"And just what is this thing called?"

"Vilis Futurus means 'meant to be' in Latin. The voice in your head, the one I was talking about, is owned by the one person you will meet and fall in love with. That person was, in a way, made for you and only you. You're able to hear all of their thoughts and if they are a vampire too, they can hear yours as well. It makes it easier to have private conversations with one another and not have someone interrupt but it also makes it hard to keep any secrets as well." She finished.

"And David isn't your Vilis Futurus?" I asked.

"No, he isn't."

"Do you know who is?"

The voice in *my* head was doing a crappy job at shutting me up. Albeit it was mine and only mine, it definitely doesn't know me well enough to be able to get me to stop talking. I am a curious person and I wanted to know but I also know that this is considered prying into someone else's personal life. But if she was willing to give it out, then I'm willing to listen.

"Yes I do," she answered.

I waited for the name but it never came.

"And . . . who is it?"

"I don't know if you'd want to know Scarlett. I mean, on one hand you might be curious. But I've gotten to know you over the past couple of weeks and if I tell you who it is, you might never speak to me again. And I really don't want that to happen. I'd prefer to keep you as another friend in my arsenal before I have to leave again."

The first name that popped into my mind was Caleb. By reflex only, I swear it! Then I began to wonder how I would actually feel if Portia and Caleb were soul mates. I know I'd be mad and I know I'd be jealous, but would I actually stop talking to Portia just because she's dating a guy that I have the tiniest feelings for? To be honest, I couldn't answer that question for myself let alone give a straight answer to another person. So I just have to suck it up and take the blow to see what the consequences will be.

"I can take it."

"Alright, but don't say that I didn't warn you. It's . . . " Why does everyone insist on pausing whenever they're telling me something important? Do they like torturing me or something? Because it's working if that's the case.

"Max." She finally finished.

I actually turned around as if she was saying his name because he was entering the room. It was probably a stupid move but to think that my twin brother would be anyone's soul mate is just ludicrous. He can't even hold down a girlfriend let alone be with someone for the rest of his life. The conversation from the kitchen had popped up into my head once more. And that's when I began to laugh, loud and long.

"You're joking, right?" I managed to choke out through giggles.

A blush crept up on her cheeks and she became bright red. She was serious! Her embarrassment made me think about how much blood was actually circulated through her body. Vampires are supposed to be the living dead but they are portrayed in entertainment not to have any blood. It's only probable that I bring this into question whenever Portia is around me. A frame of reference is good to have with anything and it seems as though Hollywood is my only one when it comes to vampires. I suppose that it's not such a good thing.

"Oh, oh, I'm sorry for laughing."

"It's alright, I knew you would react somehow and laughing was the easier one for me." She responded.

"Has anything even happened between you and my brother yet? Are you two at least getting along now?"

"No, he's still a clueless, bullying ignoramus. But he'll eventually see it my way and fall for me just the same."

"So, you really love him, don't you?" She nodded and bent her head to avoid eye contact with me. She looked sad that Max didn't know this about her. Heck, I would be too if the boy I was in love with still saw me as just another friend . . . if that. I hope whatever is between Portia and Max works itself out soon, because both of them deserve happiness and love. Plus, I'm sick of their avoiding each other at all costs.

With that little detail out of the way, I felt it the perfect opportune moment to bring up what happened earlier tonight. You know, in the bookstore and all. It was going to be weird but it has to be cleared up if I'm going to be friends with her.

"Portia . . . I-I saw something today that I need to bring up with you. Now, I don't want you to overreact but what I'm about to tell you probably won't sit well. So I'd just like to warn you before I go into this conversation."

"Alright, my stomach muscles will be clenched tightly to hold in my lunch until you're done. Now, go!"

"OK, I forgot to pick up my paycheck earlier today so I told Gunnar to stop by the bookstore to help me out. When I walked in the store, I tried to find Jackie but she wasn't in the front room. I figured she was in the back so I walked back there and opened the door and saw Andrew and she doing . . . well, something that shouldn't be done by brothers and sisters. I don't want you to freak out but I thought you should know." I finished with a sigh.

She burst out into raucous laughter. Of course, it was only fair that I laugh at her expense so she has to return the favor. I couldn't be completely mad at her but a small twinge of anger did pass through me. It's only fitting. Portia eventually stopped laughing and wiped her eyes of all the running make-up before speaking again.

"That's a typical thing for my parents to do, Scar'"

"P-parents?"

"Yes, my parents. I thought you would catch on that Jaclyn and Andrew are my mom and dad. I suppose I shouldn't have assumed that right away. They go at it like rabbits all the time I guess I should have warned you before something like this happened. I'm sorry."

Well, that was a lot to take in. Also . . . still kind of disturbing now that I know I witnessed Portia's mom and dad doing that. Not as bad as the whole incest thing, but still gross. You would never want to see your own parents doing such a thing; it's just as bad seeing someone else's.

"Want to go swimming?" Portia asked me.

I thought it was a random question but I thought she was just trying to lighten the mood after what we had just talked about. And I had to agree with her in some way. Learning so much in so little time was overwhelming and you need a little break from reality. Good thing we had a pool in our backyard, otherwise we wouldn't know what to do.

So I said yes with enthusiasm but slowly declined on participating in any actual swimming. What made me do this, you may be asking yourself. Remember the scars on me that I so frequently remind you of? You have to be quicker than that if you're going to read what I write. But I still went outside with her while she planned on jumping in the water. And what I saw when she did so was nothing I was going to be able to forget any time soon.

Her skin was *metallic black*! Her whole body was covered in what looked like black paint while her eyes were the same, icy blue that they were the night of the costume party. Her teeth were sharp and pointy and protruding once more. In a way, it still unnerved me but strangely, it comforted me as well. I don't know why but it did. Does this happen every time she goes into water?

Portia explained to me that it's a genetic anomaly with which the hydrogen reacts with their blood (they do have it) and creates this black sheath around their skin. It's an amazing sight to witness, however I wouldn't recommend it to anyone that doesn't know about vampires beforehand. It would scare the living daylights out of you.

Portia was still floating in the water while I sat on the edge with my feet dangling in the now warm water. I started to think about the vampire process as I stared at her shimmering skin underneath the water. Since the Hollywood genre of vampires weren't true, what exactly was it like to be one?

"Hey Porsh', does it hurt?" I asked.

"Does what hurt?"

"Being a vampire," I clarified.

She looked down toward the ground and started playing with a puddle of water near her. Well, this seemed familiar. Max and she were more alike than anyone knew. And I suppose that it's what draws them together more or less. Well, that and that vampire soul mate business, whatever that may be.

"Well, I've heard that the pain is unbearable when you are bitten. Of course, I don't know that first hand, but I can imagine. The emotional pain, on the other hand, his just as bad if not worse. Going through centuries and centuries, making new friends just to watch them die. I don't ever wish it upon anyone ever. There's also the thirst for blood. It's more or less a dull, numbing sensation at first, but when you go longer without, it turns into a sharp, stabbing feeling. Other than that, no being a vampire doesn't hurt."

"Other than that?! Jease, that's enough to turn me off even the thought of becoming a vampire!" I replied.

"And you won't ever be. Scarlett, no vampire will ever bite you as long as I'm around. I'm going to make sure of it. You don't deserve the same things we have to go through. You deserve much more."

I started to think about all the things that Portia was talking about. To think that you can't even fall in love with anyone but the one voice that's in your head. What if you don't love them back? What if you found love in another person and they didn't want to be a vampire with you. To suffer through that would be indescribable. And not to mention losing the ones you care about to the hands of time. I couldn't imagine what it would be like to watch my brothers and my parents growing old, knowing that I would live on forever while they died. Portia was lucky to have the family she does.

And what about the blood? Is there any remorse after how many years of sucking fresh human blood? Does the killing become just like a routine to a vampire? I doubt that I could ever not feel guilty about taking another person's life no matter how old I would be. No, being a vampire is definitely not on top of my list of things to do right now.

We both went inside after several hours of sitting around and talking about everything but the supernatural. The car accident was something

Portia was very interested in hearing. I couldn't blame her, everyone that knows anything about it would love to get the inside scoop from me. I would be the only person they could ask and get a straight answer from. So I told her the entire story from my perspective and she listened intently. Then, after I was finished, she hugged me as tightly as her strength allowed without strangling me. It was very comforting.

Portia fell asleep first. I bet with everything she's been through tonight, sleep was welcomed strongly. Really, I couldn't blame her. I dosed off almost directly after her and the moment my head it the pillow, the lights went out.

I was having a very good dream about Caleb saving me from a pirate ship back in the late 1800's, when I felt myself being shaken awake. As soon as my eyes opened I saw a figure standing above me in the darkness. Screaming wasn't an option for me after a hand was slammed against my mouth and muffled my cries. In layman's terms . . . I was screwed!

# Chapter 16

$\mathcal{N}$o MATTER HOW MUCH I struggled against the stranger's hand, I couldn't make my screams loud enough to be heard by anyone. An idea popped into my head so I just went with it. It was the only thing I was capable of doing at the time, so why not give it a try? My knee bent at the crease, flying up and hitting my assailant rather forcefully in spot that gives a male the most pain when hit. The silhouette of the stranger doubled over and started to let out gasps of air.

"What'd you do that for, Red?" was asked followed by more coughing and sputtering.

"Oh, Caleb, I'm so sorry—wait, why are you in my room?!" I asked, my tone growing with anger.

He was still rolling around on the floor at the base of my bed, clutching his male part as if somehow that would make it magically better. I'm not going to lie, seeing him in this much pain was somewhat enjoyable. You would feel the same way too if you just had pulled off massive, unknown payback on a guy who called you ugly. The simple pleasures in life shouldn't be overlooked in the slightest. And, trust me; this was a *majorly important* pleasure in my book!

"I came in to see if you wanted to go for a ride so that I could show you something. God Red, I think you really did a number on me. Even my puppies will feel this one! SWEET JESUS!"

Did he just say puppies? Was he calling himself a dog or was he just trying to make light of the situation and joke around? Whatever it was, it was way too creepy for my taste in humor.

I had enough of his whining anyway so I through the covers off of me and climbed out of bed. He stopped rolling from side to side but didn't release his hand from its current position. Not that I was going to touch anything below his belt, but he was being a baby about this. I know I didn't hit him *that* hard. And even if I did, he should be a man about it and act like I didn't do any damage. But what if I really did to severe damage? I might not like him but I don't, in any way, want to harm the poor boy so much that he won't be able to reproduce with anyone else.

"Do you think you can stand?" I asked him.

"Maybe with some help, yeah."

I stuck out my hand in attempts to help him out like he asked. As soon as his fingertips grazed the base of my palm, I felt a strong jolt of electricity pump through my veins and make my heart leap about a mile into my throat. That has never happened with *anyone* before!

I believe he felt it too by the way his mouth fell into an "o" shape and a small tuft of air was sucked into the open hole. It shocked the both of us and I wanted to pull my hand away to make the sensation stop, but he wouldn't let me. His hand was securely holding onto my own like it was his lifeline and he was on his death bed. Our eyes met for a brief moment.

"What's going on?"

Portia propped herself up on her elbows and with sleepy eyes and a raspy voice, interrupted the moment. Boy was I grateful for this! I have no idea what would have happened next if she hadn't. Part of me would kill to find out but on the other hand, fate had other plans (obviously) and Caleb and I weren't meant to kiss in that particular moment.

"Nothing Porsh', just go back to sleep."

And that's exactly what she did. Caleb let his eyes roam away from me and onto Portia quickly but I took that time to remove my hand from his. The feelings that we both felt were too strong for me to sift through for any logical reasoning present and I'd prefer not to think that hard right now. Caleb wasn't very happy when I disappeared from his grip but he'd just have to live with it.

I was surprised after he walked to the door and turned to whisper, "You coming?" to me before exiting down the stairs. I was sure he wouldn't want to go through with whatever he had plans for after what just happened. But, I have to say, I was curious as to what exactly he had to show me. And the curious part of me won the battle of wills. All I can say is that if it's anything weird, gross, perverted or any combination of the three, I'm leaving immediately. There's no possible way I will stick around and witness him try and kiss me after showing me a fungus growing on his foot or anything. That was a bit of a stretch but I think I got my point across.

He took me about five miles out of town to a river bank called Jefferson. I remember hearing about this place once. My grandma told me that the founder of the town, Robert Pauling, proposed to his love, Katherine, under the full moon one evening. It would be a great romance story if she didn't run off with the stable boy just hours before the wedding, leaving Robert to die of Cholera no more than two months later. I find it a bit ironic that Caleb wants to show me this place out of everywhere else in town. I still haven't done much exploring but I know there are much better spots to go to than this one.

"Close your eyes," he commanded once we were parked and I was sitting on the door of his truck bed.

Without even a fleeting second thought, I did as he told me to do and slowly shut my eyes. It somehow makes this seem more exciting . . . a mystery perhaps.

"Now, I brought you out here for a reason, Red. I don't want you to freak out about what I am about to show you so I'll give you a quick recap while you're just sitting here. I lied about not knowing who you were the very first time I met you. My dad told me all about you when I was younger and when I found out that it was your mom that died, in a way, I was happy because it meant I was able to meet you.

"I know that makes me sound selfish and awful but it's the truth. I was there at the funeral and it took all of my strength not to be the one to run after you and consol you."

I took a chance and peeked through my fingers to see what he was doing. His shirt was being pulled over his head and his jeans were already off, leaving him to only wear his boxers. What was he doing?! But before I go and ruin another moment, I'm going to take a short while to admire those sculpted abs of his once more. It wasn't only his upper body that was muscular though. Oh no, his thighs were strong and his calves were lean and beautiful with just the right amount of hair covering them. It made me want to jump his bones . . . however, I stayed put.

"What are you doing?" I randomly spoke before I even had the chance to register it in my brain. Oh well, too late now.

"No peeking! You're not allowed to look until I say you can!" He said forcefully.

I put my hands over my eyes once more and waited in anticipation. The truck bed sunk down a bit which gave me the idea that Caleb was leaning on it slightly, or sitting on it. What was he planning to do exactly? Seriously, the wait is *killing* me!

"My dad used to tell me about the love that he let go back in high school. 'She was a real beauty' he used to say to me. I was very young at the time and didn't pay much attention to this part. I was too busy listening to the part where the woman that left him became pregnant and had a daughter. But the story had always been the same and the lady turned out to be your mom.

"Now, a few days before I was told this story, I also found out about what I truly am. It's rather shocking so I have to warn you beforehand. I feel that I can trust you well enough to show you the secret I have kept all of my life from everyone else in this sleepy little town. Prepare yourself and open your eyes now."

The weight lifted from the truck just before I removed my hands in front of my face to look at Caleb once more. He smiled at me as I noticed his body twisting and molding into something else. It was as if he was disappearing before my eyes and I was too slow on the upkeep to actually do anything about it. So I watched; it was all I could do. And when I could no longer see him in front of the truck, I bent my own body forward to see over the opened bed door.

There was a jolt that shocked the door, making me fly back and hit the windshield that separated the taxi and me. Do you remember that large wolf I had talked about earlier on? The one with black and grey fur with a white streak on its back? Well it was larger up close, let me tell you! The massive, animal body hopped up onto Caleb's truck and sauntered over to me on all fours. I was being stalked by a wolf!

I cringed away as its hot breath grazed the side of my cheek. I didn't want to see its mouth open up and swallow me whole so I clenched my eyelids shut as tight as they could go and prayed that nothing would happen.

# Chapter 17

UT SOMETHING DID HAPPEN. THE cold, wet muzzle of the animal pressed on the side of my cheek and let out a small whimper through its throat. Something about those penetrating yellow eyes made it impossible for me to look away. Almost as if a steel tether was connecting his soul with my own, it was that strong. Then it occurred to me then that this oversized dog could actually be Caleb. Is this what he wanted me to see? If so, I am very satisfied with the results and am happy that I came with him when my brain protested strongly. Why would anyone ever want to miss out on something this mind-blowingly awesome?!

The large dog let out a bark and turned so it could jump out of the truck and back on the ground. It disappeared underneath and a different body came back up.

"You're-you're a—"

I couldn't finish that sentence I was still in so much shock.

"A werewolf . . . yes, I am." He blatantly answered.

"But-but . . . and you-you . . . huh?"

"I'm not allowed to tell anyone about my abilities in order to save the species. If people knew, they wouldn't be so accepting and that's why I have to beg you not to speak a word of this. Can you do that for me?"

I nodded my head instead of struggling to get a word out. No point in trying when I already knew that it wouldn't work. I'd just start to babble unintelligibly and no one wants to see that.

After the initial shock of being in a truck bed with a werewolf wore off, everything was alright. The both of us were lying down (about a 2x4's distance away from each other) and looking up at the stars. But I began to think; did Caleb think that just because he had shown me what he is, I would telling him something about myself? My scars that nobody outside of my immediate family has seen could be a great secret to reveal to him. But am I ready to reveal something so big that I haven't even told Portia about? Until I sort through this completely, I'll just start up another conversation. The overpowering silence was getting old anyway.

"So . . . when you said that you knew about me before the funeral, how much are we talking about?"

"Not much. Your mom kept in touch with my dad several years into your childhood and he'd read the letters she sent out loud to me like a bedtime story each night. Back then, you were always Princess Scarlett trapped in some dragon guarded castle and needed saving by a strong knight. I kept dreaming that I was the knight and ever since then, I've wanted to meet you so badly."

"That's all well and good but you still didn't answer my question."

I turned my head to face him briefly with a tiny smile to see how he reacted to my sarcasm. His chest heaved and I watched every motion as it rose up and fell back down. It was almost mesmerizing to watch.

"How much do I know about you . . . hmm, let's see. Well, I knew back then that you were obsessed with the color pink. I know about when you took pink magic marker and used it to 'decorate' your entire room. What else? Oh, I know about the time when you were seven and you ate a whole handful of dirt because you wanted to know what it tasted like."

"Hey, in my defense, I was expecting it to be like chocolate. Who knew that it would taste about as awful as it sounded?"

"Everyone on the planet," He responded while laughing.

I was only seven and I couldn't help myself. Max dared me to do it and, I'll admit, the part about me curious as to what exactly it tasted like is true. But when I was telling my parents why I was covered in it and sobbing uncontrollably, I left out the part about Max. Back then, Max and I were joined at the hip and that meant covering each other when necessary. If it happened today . . . I'd call him out on it the second my dad asks me what happened. Albeit, it probably wouldn't have anything to do with dirt nowadays, but that's beside the point.

"So you know a few facts about my past, big deal. I've changed since I was seven years old."

"I still know a lot about you," he stated smugly.

"Oh yeah," I laughed off. "Like what?"

"Your favorite color is still pink."

I was utterly shocked. I mean it. Not because he knew this but because he took the time to actually pay attention to me. Then again, he *is* a player and most likely studies his next victims before he strikes. Maybe those weren't the correct words at this very moment, but you get what I'm trying to say. Right? Because if not; I don't feel like explaining it again. I honestly don't know if I can explain it again and have it make sense to myself let alone all of you. So good luck trying to figure out what I just said!

"That's-that's not that hard to guess." I tried to reassure myself a little in that sentence.

"Oh so you want it more personal? OK, how about how you hate to be touched but when you're alone someplace you become so nervous your foot shakes uncontrollably. Or how when you want to be polite, your smile twitches at the corner, right at the spot where the scar crosses through. And if you didn't like those, how about when you look at someone you really love, everyone else around you disappears and your focus is only on them. And your eyes may be blue but in certain lights, or when you're smiling, they have a green tint to them. And when you get close enough to see, they have almost a smear of black as if the cornea exploded. I've got plenty more . . . if you'd like to hear it."

BREATHE! BREATHE SCARLETT, YOU HAVE TO BREATHE! I opened my mouth and my lungs were flooded with what felt like something foreign to me. How did he know so much? What he said was sweet but had a bit of a stalker's edge to it. I know Caleb would never stalk me, but it's the principle of the matter. No one knows *that* much about me . . . not even my dad. I bet you there is something that he knew nothing about. And I think this is the perfect time to show him what exactly he is missing.

"C-Caleb?" I almost whispered.

His dog hearing picked it up, however.

"Yeah?"

His head turned to face me and I could feel his gaze so hard that I thought I had been set on fire. Honestly, it was as if my insides were a burning inferno and I couldn't put it out. I wonder what it would be like to kiss him. No, I can't think about him like that! He's just a friend . . . if that.

"There's something you don't know about me. Actually, nobody outside of my family knows this. But I think in light of the current situation, I should show you."

I sat up and he followed suit. This was going to take a lot of courage to pull off for me. They were ugly and I don't like showing them off in the least. I think I'm going to save the inner thigh one for another day, if he gets that lucky. But I suppose I could show him the ones on my ribs. They were just as ugly but not in an awkward place. I don't think I'd be able to look Caleb in the face if I were to take my pants off for that purpose only. I shudder to think what he would think I was doing.

"You're not going to like this . . . so prepare yourself," I stated.

And it was the truth. I've gotten to know Caleb over the last month and he's become very protective of me. Seeing the remnants of my injuries won't do his temper justice but it was worth a shot. I had this image in my head about him going berserk and running away at full speed in his werewolf form. It would be entertaining but hurtful at the same time. Just because it meant that he didn't accept them and I had made a mistake. It's now or never! I wrapped my fingers underneath the hem of my shirt and began to raise it until my bra was covered but my mid-section was completely exposed. His eyes shifted to yellow like his wolf form, I'm guessing, to see better in the dark.

"Oh my god, Scarlett! Are these from the accident?"

I nodded my response. His mouth hung open but his eyes slanted as he examined them. I didn't expect him to reach out and graze the two lines with his fingers. Shivers visibly traveled through my body and a sharp intake of breath passed through my teeth. These sensations whenever Caleb touches me have got to stop! They are becoming quite bothersome.

"Are you cold?" He asked me.

"No," I responded plainly.

His exploration continued along every inch of the scars and my feelings had gotten so bad that I was positive I would pass out from the headiness of his touch. His hands were large but his fingers were elegant and lean, making them appear able and strong. The hands that were innocently moving along my scars were venturing a little too far north and, surprisingly, I wasn't doing anything to stop him. I DIDN'T WANT TO STOP HIM!

Just before he reached the point of no return, something off in the distance rustled loudly. In a way, the sound saved us from making the biggest mistake of both of our lives. I took the opportunity to pull my shirt down as he looked behind him to identify whatever it was. Something in the air didn't smell right to Caleb, literally, and he became frantic.

"I'm going to check it out. Get in the truck and lock the doors!" He commanded.

Caleb disappeared and the werewolf jumped out of the truck and ran into the trees and down the road. Not saying that I will obey him whenever he tells me to do something, but I think this is a relevant situation to do as he says. It could be something trying to harm us. I'd prefer not to take my chances. Oh, the perks of having a werewolf as a friend! Which reminds me; does Caleb know about Portia being a vampire? And vice versa?

A large, dark object slammed against the window and I saw blood!

# Chapter 18

"**O**H MY GOD PORTIA, I'VE never been more frightened in my life!"

The next morning at breakfast, I decided to tell her everything that happened minus a few details. Details such as: Caleb being a werewolf and that I almost let him feel me up. Major gossip should never be shared with anyone. Even if it's someone you want to tell so badly and are your best friend. I'd advise that shutting your mouth about it is best for everybody that's involved.

"Did you guys ever figure out what you hit?"

I never answered her. Partly because Portia's rendition of what happened last night was that Caleb and I went out to get breakfast for the next morning at the 24 hour mini-mart and we hit something in the middle of the road coming back. The truth is that Caleb had flung himself against the driver's side window to freak me out and had gotten cut up when he was running through the trees. Don't think that his little stunt didn't go unpunished. As soon as he stepped foot in his truck, I formed my palm into a fist and connected it to the side of his face. Sadly, no permanent damage done but I did give him a bloody nose for about five seconds

Werewolves heal very quickly, or so Caleb told me. It was actually cool to see the blood just stop flowing that fast. Also . . . a little bit stomach churning. I've always had a bit of a weak stomach though.

Not only was I frightened last night, but this morning as well. And still am scared witless about not being able to do anything about it. I'll explain to you what happened and then you'll know what has me freaked out to the point of hyperventilation.

I woke up around eight o'clock and quickly learned that no one else was awake except me. Making my way down to the refrigerator for something to eat, I began to think about the ramifications that last night might have upon Caleb and me. What if he took the whole "feeling me up" thing to mean that I do have feelings for him that are more than platonic? What if I actually *do* have some feelings for him that is more than platonic? Now, those thoughts were too much for me to think about that early in the morning.

So I made my way down to the kitchen all frazzled over the guy who was asleep upstairs, when I noticed a note laying on the island in the middle of the kitchen. Right away, I knew who it was from because the handwriting was so familiar I would be able to recognize it in the dark. I picked the note up and scanned over it before actually reading what it said. It was from my dad and it read:

"Kids,

I'm so sorry about this but I have no other choice. I'll be gone before you wake up and I want you to know that I love you more than anything in this world and nothing can take that away, not even death. But I have to go and say goodbye; it's for the best. I hope that one day you guys will understand my side in all of this. Holden . . . take care of your brother and sister while I'm gone.

Love forever,
Dad"

By that point, my heart stopped beating. This note—the note that my dad had written just this morning—sounded like a suicide letter. Just where did he go? To work? No, he wouldn't have any purpose in going there if he were to do that. To Oliver and Grandma's? No, they aren't his parents and he dislikes them much more than he leads on. Where did he go?

And just like that, it dawned on me.

"Hey Scarlett, what's going on? Where's dad?" Holden asked from behind me.

I threw the note at him and commanded him to read it. Thoughts were zooming through my head at the speed of light and my heart was telling me to get out of there now and run to him. But my feet stayed glued to the floor as Holden read the note. His reaction was as if watching day turn into night. Scary, but not as horrifying as to why he was mirroring my reaction in the least. He had a right to be like this and no one would be able to stop him.

"I think I know where he went," I plainly said in a panic.

"Let's go then! We'll take my car," Holden said. Instead of relying solely on just telling me to get in his car, he grabbed my wrist and pulled me outside. And it hurt! We might be trying to save dad but there's no need to be brutal about it. But his emotions were all mixed up right now and his adrenaline was pumping fast through his blood stream so I suppose I can forgive him . . . just this once.

Holden's driving has always been a little on the manic side, but every swerve or bump felt like it was magnified by twenty percent. As if every speeding ticket he had ever gotten before was a ticket to Disneyland. They all paled in comparison. But when we arrived at our destination, I wanted to stay in the car forever. Facing the real thing was a lot different than facing the big bad in your head.

Considering it was summer, the sun was shining and the trees had bright green leaves on them. There was an older looking man mowing the grass off in the distance and you could faintly smell the finished product whenever the wind blew just right. A small, stone bench was located next to a very large oak tree and the limbs hung down so far down that if you were sitting down, they'd just barely graze the top of your head. The silence was so eerie that if you stood there long enough, you'd go crazy. Or start to talk to yourself (which I often did on my own).

A taller, younger gentleman was standing pin straight in front of an arched stone located in the ground. He hadn't shaved yet which made him look scraggly and his eyes were bloodshot and puffy, as if he'd been crying. The figure was simply staring at the lifeless stone saying nothing. I tell you, he looked like a zombie from where we were standing. If you were able to read the engraving on the stone, you would see:

"Jane Elizabeth Hera
1971-2009
Beloved mother, wife, daughter and sister

Even though the body lies in the ground, the soul lives free and soars"

My mother's grave had haunted my dreams ever since the funeral. I could tell you every detail about it but I would most likely break down and cry. Just like my father seemed to be doing at the current time. He looked rough and a surge of pity washed over me.

Luckily, we were quick to find out there was no gun nor sharp implement in his hand so no immediate danger was happening. Holden started to walk in his direction but my hand flew out and stopped him before he could get too far. Dad had started to talk and the voice inside my head told me that he needed time to get things off his chest. He needed to be alone with mom right now and we shouldn't intervene. And since it was so quiet in the cemetery, we heard every word that he was saying. Don't judge; it wasn't our fault that we overheard.

"I can't live without you Jane." He was saying. "I've been trying but every day has been torture. You need to come back; we all can't survive without you. Please come back to me Janey. You're my everything and I need you."

A moment passed by and nothing happened, as we all expected it to do. No matter how much any of us begged, she will never come back to us. I wish time and space could bend in such a way to make that possible, but that's impossible. My cheeks felt wet all of a sudden. I reached up and grazed them, only to feel the salty remnants of tears falling freely. It was only fitting that I'd be crying over my dad's pain. I looked over at Holden and noticed he was crying too.

Dad reached down and placed his hand on top of the gravestone before saying, "she meant nothing to me Janey. Honestly she didn't."

Who meant nothing to him? Did Dad cheat on Mom before the accident? Why, that lying, cheating lowlife! Mom was the best thing that happened to him and he was capable of throwing it all away for some cheap floozy. I bet it was his assistant back in California. She always did wear extra make-up when he was around.

"I've been stupid lately and I take full responsibilities for my actions. I think it all started when I found one of his letters in our closet. Why didn't you ever tell me you kept in touch with Jack over the years? Did you love him more than me? I could accept that, if it were the case.

"I wish I could have given you all you've ever wanted and deserved because you meant . . . mean, the world to me. I love you and I always will. Goodbye Janey."

My dad turned and spotted us. Looking him in the face after what I just heard was like a knife stabbing into in an already infected burn wound. You could never understand the true magnitude of his pain unless you saw it with your own eyes. But then again, who could really blame him for beating himself up over mom's death. Even though it was partly my fault we had gotten hit—and before you all tell me otherwise, just listen to this: If I had actually listened to her that night at the diner instead of storming out like a small child without candy, the truck would have never hit us and we would still be safe in California. But is that what I actually want?—my dad had cheated on my mom, leading to her wanting a divorce and needing to tell me before anything progressed.

While leaving the cemetery, the man mowing the lawn earlier was standing off in the distance, watching us leave. His face had wrinkles and his eyes were sunken in and tired. The sleeves of his sweater covered his hands and he was standing with his back slumped over. Not only did he look creepy, but the fact that he was staring directly at me (not Holden or my father) magnified that factor about ten times.

There was a decrepit, old dog sitting on the ground looking exactly where his owner was looking . . . at me. He was brown with black spots covering his body with an odd design in the front of his chest. He was so worn out that his body was shaking while just sitting there.

Do you remember the cat that my aunt has? Well this dog had piercing blue eyes and the black mark on his chest resembled an eye, just like Jinx. My thoughts quickly turned from the dog standing a few yards away from me to the cat I had acquired about a month ago. She had come out of nowhere with an almost human-like personality and an unforgettable mark on her side. Albeit, nothing like this dog or my aunt's cat, but just as strange.

The old man waved a finger at me to provoke me to walk to him. And, stupid me, I actually did as he asked and went over there. He wasn't as scary up close; he reminded me of my grandfather in a way. His face had hard planes and it looked as if he never smiled. And when he spoke, his voice was scratchy and not so friendly.

"You're her, aren't you?" He asked me.

I honestly didn't know how to respond to that, so I just gave him a confused look and answered with, "Umm, sure."

"I've heard the stories growing up but I've never thought them to be true. It just seemed too impossible for reality. Can I—Can I shake your hand?"

I had no idea what was going on and why the man was acting like this to me, but I shook his hand just the same. He didn't look too harmful and it was just a handshake after all. It was what he did when our hands were interlocked that had me so scared. His arms looked to be weak with age so I was never expecting him to use all of his strength to pull me over to him and whisper to me something I will never forget. Because I still have no idea what it means.

"Enjoy the rest of your glimpse, darling. It won't last long," is what he said to me. And in that creepy, raspy voice of his too.

I rode home with my dad to make sure everything was alright and he wouldn't try and drive off of a cliff or something. The old man and his dog took over my mind. Something about them, although still creepy, comforted me deep down. It was as if a part of me knew and respected this man almost to the point where we were friends. Whatever it was, it sure scared the pants off of me.

I didn't tell Portia about the old man and his canine friend and I'm certainly not saying anything to Caleb and or Max due to the fact that they'd probably think I was crazy. No, this was an episode that I am going to keep to myself for quite some time.

# Chapter 19

ULY 4$^{TH}$, 1990. NOT JUST a national holiday, but the date of Max's and my birth. I had mistakenly told Portia about this little fact two weeks before. Now she is planning a birthday party for us and I can't stop her. Honestly, I think it's her life goal to make mine miserable. And I have a completely legitimate reason for my moodiness lately. Caleb hasn't stopped by or even said one word to me since the truck incident. I would normally be ecstatic about this, but ever since then, I couldn't get him out of my mind.

Gunnar, however, hasn't left my side since our date. It gets annoying but I have to admit, he is good looking. At least it gives me something pretty to look at while I'm being annoyed. Even when it's just Gunnar and I, I somehow end up thinking about Caleb. When we're making out on my couch while watching a movie, I imagine its Caleb's tongue in my mouth instead of Gunnar's. When we're walking down the street holding hands, I wish I could feel the electric pulses that Caleb causes me whenever we touch. But, sadly, none of this is possible.

The preparations for the party were underway and Portia was in heaven. She wants it to take place at our house and before I had a chance to protest at this, she talked to my dad and he agreed it would be a great idea. How on earth could I dodge the party now? This is going to take skills and I might have to consult the master on getting out of things . . . Max. OK, so it was a wee bit of an exaggeration, but that's beside the point. He wouldn't help me anyhow.

Not only did Portia want me to help her with planning the whole thing, but I was the 'go to' girl as well. She must have sent me to the Wal-Mart in Harrison maybe twenty times before I refused. I should have thought about saying no after the second time she asked me, but it's hard to say no to a very persistent vampire. I had once been threatened by her sharp teeth and I don't ever want that to happen again. There was, however, this one run I went on that I enjoyed . . . somewhat.

She sent me to get pink streamers after someone (Max) had let it slip that it was my favorite color. After apologizing about a million times for not knowing this, and getting green and purple ones instead, she asked me if I wouldn't mind going to get some. Me being the pushover that I am (sometimes), I left for Wal-Mart once more. I was walking into the super store and he was walking out but I clearly saw him. I had been mumbling to myself about Portia's forgetfulness and hadn't been paying much attention, but I wouldn't be able to miss him even if I tried. And I couldn't help but call out his name to get him to look at me. It had been several days since I've seen him, remember?

"Caleb!"

He turned around to look and see who was calling his name. I'll bet all the money on the planet that he had either seen me first or heard my voice and knew who it was even before I saw him. Those dog ears of his can only be useful at certain times. Even though I waved to him, I wasn't expecting him to come over and start talking to me. Honestly, I thought he would pretend like he didn't know me or something.

"Hey Red, long time no see." He said nonchalantly.

Don't I know this?! I couldn't believe he had the gall to bring up something so painful. He knew what he was doing too. You couldn't say that without wanting some sort of rise to happen. But I swallowed my anger and pride and had a full conversation about the auto shop and—can you believe it?—his new girlfriend.

I've only met her once but ever since then, I didn't like her. Her name is Shaylee Morgan and she's on the cheerleading team with Daisy and Robin. And if a survey was taken at random, she would win the most beautiful girl in school. Shaylee has caramel hair cut shorter to show off her perfectly smooth, flawless, heart shaped face. For being so petite, she certainly was blessed at having the biggest boobs I have ever seen on someone weighing no more than one hundred and fifteen pounds. Oh, and did I mention, she's a real ditz too. If you ask her what 3+3 is, she would most likely answer with "four . . . duh!" As if you were the stupid one for even asking a question like that. But it's Caleb's choice and I really should be happy for him. God, I hope that little witch falls on an old, rusty screw or something!

Caleb was bragging about Shaylee like she was something to rub in my face. Such a sweet boy I've fallen for, huh? It was the first time I've ever admitted that little detail to myself and, I have to say, it feels good to get it off my chest. Well, sort of. But, boy does it smart to hear the boy of your dreams talk about another girl like he was doing. I needed to get out of this conversation before I start crying.

"Are you coming to my birthday party?" I asked him, hoping he would say yes and at the same time no.

"Depends . . . am I invited?"

"I just asked you, didn't I?" I replied smugly.

"Alright, I'll go. But I have to get this bedding to my mom so I'll see you then."

"Bye," I said somewhat sadly.

"Bye."

I couldn't believe that he felt nothing, *nothing* over our meeting. How could he be so cold and distant after he spent so long trying to win me over? Since I wasn't putting up much of a fight now, was he done with chasing me? That's low, even for his standards. See if I ever think about him again! OK now I was just lying to myself. This isn't good. Never how I pictured my summer before junior year to go. Then again, I don't think I could ever in my wildest dreams imagine that I would be best friends with a vampire and in love with a werewolf.

I purchased the pink streamers and hurried out of Wal-Mart as fast as I could to avoid anyone else I knew. It didn't happen but it was just a precaution I was willing to take. Portia was waiting at my house and overseeing Max's attempts to hang balloons on the banisters. I guarantee she was just "supervising" to get a good look at his backside. Eww, I believe bile just rose up in my throat at the thought of my brother and his girl issues. Never again do I want that sick mental image in my brain! Gunnar was on our porch with confetti and fake palm trees, setting up for the supposed luau theme the party had taken on. So, I made my way outside in order to avoid Portia and her many errands.

Doomsday finally arrived. With everything that happened these past months, I suppose those aren't the right words to use. But when you hear what happened, you will think otherwise. Because what was meant to be a fun, happy birthday party for two people turned into something worthy of America's Funniest Home Videos and UFC. Just wait and hear out the entire evening before I tell you anything further.

Portia spent the night at my house and changed with me. Actually, she found it best if she was the one to dress me for my own party. I could understand that she didn't like the first outfit I tried on, but to call it hideous and demand it be burned right away was a bit over the top. I mean, it was just a simple Journey t-shirt and shorts that I had had for three years now. But she said that I was better off taking a knife to my heart than wear that in front of Caleb.

"How—how did you know?" I asked her in shock when she said this.

"Come on Scarlett, I'm a mythical creature . . . not blind! A girl—no matter what species—knows when another is in love. I just didn't say anything because I thought you would tell me when you accepted this." She responded smiling.

A moment of silence passed between us before . . .

"I don't know how Gunnar is reacting to this, but that doesn't matter."

It might sound stupid but I really didn't think about how I should deal with Gunnar. Caleb is dating Shaylee right now but what if he wasn't? What if I realized my love for Caleb before he felt it right to give me Grand-Canyon-sized space? Would I go out with him knowing everything I know about his past and how many girls he has hurt? My confusion to this whole subject made me feel like some silly follower of Daisy. Like I was one of her mindless cheerleading zombies hanging on her every word.

"Oh, now this is more like it!" I heard her voice in my closet.

I was frightened to know what she found in there. Portia was partial to short, show-off outfits and I . . . well, I'm not. So when she brought the thing out of my closet, I had prepared myself. But I don't think anyone could have been really ready for what she had chosen as my party outfit.

"No! No, absolutely not!" I said shaking my head.

"Aw, come on Scar' you're hurting my style pride here. This will look A-M-A-Z-I-N-G on you and you're wearing it if I have to force you into it."

To prove her point, she let her sharp; canine teeth slide down and bare themselves. She sure knows how to fight dirty!

"Uh, fine! Give me the dress you scheming, little tick."

If anyone else said that to her, I'm pretty sure their jugular would be lying on the floor by now. But since I inquired that I would wear the scrap of material, I suppose she overlooked the small insult I gave her. Remind me to never call her that in a real argument though.

Walking down the stairs was meant to be my own little "Grace Kelly" moment but it didn't work out. Not in the death trap Portia called heals that she put me in. She will be the death of me one of these days! Everyone else that had arrived already thought that I looked fantastic. How do I know this, you may be asking yourself? I heard about fifty gasps escape from people's mouths at the exact same time. And I know it was for me because Portia had already been downstairs and was the one to announce me. I thought it was downright hilarious when she asked me to wait upstairs but I appreciate the outcome.

Portia stayed glued to me for about an hour, making it impossible for me to escape like I wanted to. Everyone was making me feel uncomfortable with all the attention I was getting and I wanted to get away. It would make my break a lot easier if Max were here. He called my phone when we were still getting ready and told me he would be there later. My guess would be that he was with Caleb and their little play things. And by play things, I hope you all know I mean Shaylee and Robin. If not, keep up!

Gunnar was the second person to give me a present. Portia had been a little anxious before and accidently blurted out what she had given me. So after the surprise had been ruined, she handed me the box and let me unwrap the silver plated picture frame with tiny red roses lining the edges. It had already contained a picture of Portia and me at the bookstore. Tears welled in my eyes but didn't spill over when I hugged and thanked her for her present. But Gunnar's was different . . . if not a bit odd.

He had sat me down on one of our beach chairs by the pool and handed me the box. With the way it was shaped, I knew it was a book. It was either that, or a very heavy movie. But I was right the first time, just not any book I had ever imagined my boyfriend to buy for me. The title of it was *Love the One You're With* by Emily Griffin. I read the description on the back and it was about a woman trying to fight off the temptations to cheat on her husband of one year with her old flame. Why on Earth would Gunnar give me a book like this?

"Umm . . . thank you," I chose my words carefully. Because if I didn't, I know I would end up blurting out something I probably shouldn't say. Something like, "What are you getting at Gunnar?" or "Are you trying to send me a message about obedience?" But I refrained myself well.

"You're welcome. I thought you'd like something like this." He replied with a smile that looked like I had just lifted a weight off of his shoulders.

"It's . . . um . . . it's something."

"Wow Gunnar, next time your girlfriend has a birthday, why not get her something better than a book on how to stay faithful to your boyfriend."

Oh no, that voice wasn't from anyone I wanted to be there at that moment. He would just make fun of my boyfriend's sense of kindness, just like he is now. This *really* isn't good!

"How about you mind your own business, grease monkey." Gunnar snapped at Caleb.

"I will as soon as your business isn't with her," Caleb remarked.

Oh crap!

Gunnar laughed quietly to himself before coming back with, "Well, that's not going to happen any time soon. So I suggest you back off and leave *my* girlfriend alone."

"If you knew your girlfriend at all, you'd know that she doesn't want me to leave her alone. She cares for me too much."

Digging himself into a deeper hole!

"Oh is that so?" Gunnar said with a smirk. Which could only mean he had something happening in his mind. Something good that he could use against Caleb.

"Yeah, that's so." Caleb pushed.

"Hmm, then tell me Caleb . . . how many times have *you* tasted her tongue in your mouth? Because I have it perfectly memorized . . . texture and flavor."

Caleb gave no answer but you could visibly see the hurt in his eyes. It was an emotional blow right to his ego and he wasn't happy about it. You could tell by the way his hands were tightening into fists.

"Hey guys, that's enough," I tried to interject.

Gunnar had stood up from the chair we had been sitting on and was now only inches away from Caleb's face. No doubt, getting ready to fight him at all costs. But nothing happened . . . yet.

"And just how many times have you heard her sigh as she melts into your arms? I can tell you . . . zero."

It was true, physically at least. Because those times that I have done that with Gunnar, I was thinking about Caleb and not him. So I guess it works both ways, but I'm not saying this out loud. At least not now.

"She wants me, not you so accept the facts and move on! Just like you're pretending to do with that little slut Shaylee. Scarlett would rather have a real man than a little mutt like you, so crawl back to your date with your tail between your legs!"

Oh . . . My . . . GOD!

"Gunnar!" I shrieked. Caleb's eyes drifted to me and stared for the longest time. He looked like a puppy that had just gotten his chew toy ripped away from him for being bad. I couldn't handle looking him in the eye directly so I turned away, only to catch glimpses from my peripheral vision. The eyes that were so innocently hurt just a moment ago were now turning black with rage and fury. And I do mean literally black, in case you were wondering. That was a color I have never seen on him before.

But it was too late to stop him. The first punch had been thrown and landed square on Gunnar's eye. I distinctly remember hearing bone crunch underneath Caleb's fist, but it could have been either boy. And Gunnar couldn't leave well enough alone so he began to retaliate and tackled Caleb to the ground and hit him again and again until Caleb twisted his body and had Gunnar pinned underneath him.

This continued for about three minutes and I did nothing to stop it. I couldn't do anything to stop it. Imagine a small, newborn kitten trying to stop a fight between two grown tigers. This was my predicament at the moment and I couldn't do anything but yell at them to "stop it now!" They didn't listen, I expected them not to. But with the way Gunnar was throwing punch after punch, I think it will at least do some damage to Caleb's bone structure.

I thought of the only person at the party capable of helping me stop them.

"Portia!" I shouted off to the house.

In seconds, a small brunette came running out with an indifferent expression on her face. That is, until she saw the two boys on the ground pummeling each other to a pulp. Then she became worried and frightened. She ran up to me and asked what was going on. Caleb and Gunnar were inches away from the pool's edge when she and I saw Caleb land a blow straight into Gunnar's stomach, sending him as close to the water's edge as he could get with touching the pool.

"We have to get them away from the water!" Portia yelled in hushed tones at me.

"Why?" I asked.

It didn't occur to me until something actually happened. Gunnar pulled at Caleb's shirt and Caleb lost his footing, sending them both into the water. Neither of them gave up even when fully submerged and lacking oxygen. Caleb's head popped out of the water and held Gunnar's under. It was then that I actually looked down to see Gunnar's skin changing into something normal people would find off-putting. Some would say frightening even. Because all of a sudden, Gunnar was a shiny, black, flailing thing in the pool underneath Caleb's hands.

"Caleb, let go!" I shouted to him.

And this time, he listened. He let the struggle end and Gunnar float to the surface, still soaking wet and black. But that's not all; everyone could see the icy blue eyes staring at them and the sharp canine teeth protrude from his mouth as he stood in the shallow end, panting to catch his breath. No one moved an inch in fear Gunnar would attack.

"That's why," Portia responded next to me.

# Chapter 20

$\mathscr{E}$VERYONE HAD CLEARED OUT AFTER Portia had lied to them all and said that Gunnar had a skin condition that had made his skin turn color. Oh, there was plenty of screaming and running when they saw Gunnar like that, but nothing Portia couldn't handle. She influenced the minds of everyone at the party until they all forgot about the scene they had just witnessed. But in no means was I finished with the two of them. And since Caleb was the closest one I could reach, I grasped him by the wrist and pulled him in the house. I know he could have easily shaken me off, but he didn't. Probably to hear what I had to say.

We entered my room but neither of us said a thing yet. I was searching in my drawer for my Ramones t-shirt and pink plaid sweat pants to put on instead of the skin tight, black dress Portia had made me wear earlier. When I found them, I walked to the door before saying, "Stay here! I'll be back in one minute." And he did. I had removed the dress that I was wearing against my will but my hair stayed up in a messy, curly ponytail as Portia had done for me before the party.

"How could you be so stupid to start a fight in the middle of my party?" I began to chide. He was pacing in the middle of my room like some sort of caged animal, drenched from head to toe. I threw the towel I had taken from the bathroom at his head with force.

"Did you hear the things he said about you? I couldn't let him demean your reputation like that."

Is it just me, or do any of you remember Gunnar saying anything to "demean my reputation"? Is Caleb seriously going to try and make up excuses that aren't even probable to make me think he didn't beat Gunnar up because he was jealous? How dumb do I look? Honestly, boy brains need to be removed and put in jars for observation.

"Caleb, Gunnar didn't say anything that wasn't true. I mean it's not like he was calling me names or anything. You shouldn't have punched him like that and, you know, you sort of deserve that cut below your eye."

And that's when I realized it wasn't going away. Normally, Caleb's injuries just disappear within seconds. But these weren't going anywhere. His left eye was puffy and red with a gash underneath, gushing blood. His shirt was ripped and torn and had dirt all over it. His fingers brushed up against the cut and I heard him suck a sharp intake of breath between his teeth.

"That's the first time I've felt pain in years." And the dummy kept touching it.

"Come on, I'll clean it up for you in the bathroom."

I grabbed the wrist of the hand he was using to cause himself further pain and pulled so that he would follow me into the hallway. So, when we reached the bathroom and Caleb was sitting down on the bathtub's rim waiting for me to put antibacterial cream on his cut, I couldn't help but revel at a certain fact. Caleb looked HOT all beaten up like this. And it only furthered the hotness to know that it was all for me.

We sat there in silence while I cleaned and bandaged his wounds. But don't think I didn't notice him staring at me with those large, brown, puppy dog eyes of his the entire time. I couldn't for the life of me describe what his gaze meant. It was too deep and brooding for me to decipher it, but it felt nice to be looked at in such a manner. Even if he did look like he wanted to eat me whole.

"You really need to stop doing this to me, Red." He finally spoke.

"In case you haven't noticed, I'm pretty sure you did this to yourself when you punched Gunnar in the nose. So don't try and turn this around on me, this is all you."

I put liquid Band-Aid on his eye and stood up to avoid eye contact any longer. There is only a certain time limit that I can stand to look into them without going crazy. And I just surpassed it by like . . . ten minutes or so. So instead of confronting him about anything too deep, I walked over to the counter and began to put the first-aid kit away.

"I wasn't talking about the fight, Scarlett." He was right behind me. I didn't look in the mirror to find out, but I could feel his warmth behind me as his breath grazed my hair. "I was talking about the way you make me feel whenever you're around."

I was about to stutter unintelligibly but he stopped me and continued talking instead. "There isn't a moment in the day that doesn't go by that

I don't think about you. You've consumed my whole heart and . . . and I love you."

Those last three words hit me like a battering ram right to my chest. Not because he was finally admitting the truth, because that was the furthest thing from my mind. No, what I was thinking about was how many girls he has said this to before me. It was too rehearsed to come from the heart and that thought was the hardest to cope with. Caleb didn't love me and he never would. I was just another pawn in his game and that's all I ever would be to him.

"Don't lie to me, Caleb. The only person you're capable of loving is yourself and don't try to say otherwise. I've gotten to know you over the past months and the amount of girls you 'happen to know' seem to keep piling up. Have they gotten the same speech as I am right now?"

I was getting angry.

"What? No, Scarlett this isn't coming out right." He tried to defend himself.

"Oh really? Then tell me the God's honest truth, right now. No lines, no tender words used on many before me. I want what's actually in your heart."

"Do you want to know what's really going on inside of me?" Now he was shouting. He couldn't stand in one spot so he began to pace the length of the bathroom. "Alright, here it goes. I can't think when I'm around you because all I am capable of is thinking about how breathtakingly beautiful you are! Every time we're close, my hands shake uncontrollably because I want to reach out and touch you. Whenever I see you with Gunnar, I want to rip him to shreds with my bare teeth because he has you and I don't. I want you Scarlett! No, I *need* you and if you don't feel the same way about me, it will kill me. I can't live without you."

He finally stopped moving back and forth and I just stood there and started at him while his breaths were coming short and shallow. That was certainly never used on any girl before me. I could tell because of the way his face was becoming red with embarrassment. He wasn't planning on revealing so much at one time and it scared him.

Caleb reached in his back pocket and pulled out a small box wrapped in shiny, silver paper with a red bow tied to the top. He handed it to me and said Happy Birthday. I hadn't realized that the entire time I was unwrapping his present, I was holding my breath. Inside the tiny, white box lay a beautiful platinum chain with a heart in the center. The heart had a keyhole in the middle of it with a diamond on top. Next to the heart was a silver key with a matching diamond in the handle.

"Now your heart will stay locked up until you're ready to give someone the key." He said with a smile.

He helped me put it on my neck where I was planning on it permanently staying for the rest of my life. It was a gorgeous gift and must have cost him a pretty penny to buy. I tried to say thank you when he was putting it on me but I couldn't make my mouth form the words. So, I got an idea when he was finished.

"Caleb?" I almost whispered.

"Yeah?"

Instead of fumbling with words, I thought of a better way to get my message across to him. So I grabbed the collar of his shirt and pulled him to me until he was pressed against my chest. Then, I kissed him.

His mouth tasted like honey and cinnamon toothpaste which surprised me considering all of the raw meat he eats. The kiss was so powerful that I began to see stars through the black lids of my eyes. Man, this boy can kiss. His tongue wasn't at all probing like Carter or Gunnar's is. I felt his arms wrap around my waist and hoist me up closer so that he didn't have to bend down so much. I was now on my tip toes and felt like I was flying. Kissing Caleb was like Heaven. I had died and gone to Heaven and that was that. It was almost as if he made me melt into him or something. Whatever the sensation was, it should be bottled up and sold on shelves at every store in the country. God, I could kiss him for days and never get bored!

As intense as the kiss was, it had to be stopped eventually. And Caleb was the one to separate us. He looked severely disheveled and it was then that I noticed my hands had worked their way up to his head on their own accord and my fingers were tangled in his hair. I moved them to his neck and rested my forehead against his. Our breathing intermingled and it was perfect. Well, up until the ignoramus made this comment.

"I suppose this could be considered the silver lining of your mother's death, huh?"

If my mother hadn't died in that horrible car accident, I would have never met Caleb. With all that wishing of her return, if such things were possible, would that mean my family would still be in California? And if so, would my parents still be getting divorced? Would my mother still move out? Is that what I really want? To think about making a decision after that incredible kiss whether if I would chose Caleb over my mom. This is all too much to think about at once.

"Caleb, I think you should go home now." I said as I pushed him out of my bathroom door.

For once, he steeled himself to the floor and wouldn't budge when I tried with all my might. He didn't want to leave me right now but I needed to be alone and think about everything. So I mustered up the best pleading face I could and directed it straight at Caleb. He let out a huff and kissed me on the cheek.

"Call me tomorrow so we can talk about this more," he said.

I quickly locked the door and slid down to the ground, balling my eyes out until it hurt. Everything hurt. Because that's what my mother deserves; all of my pain and suffering for hers. After all, the last words I had said to her were words of hate, literally. So why should I deserve such happiness after what I had done to her? I've been acting selfish ever since I survived, thinking that I was the only person to lose someone so important to me. What about my brothers? What about my Grandparents? Jease, what about my father?! How had I been treating him after such a tragedy?

A scratch on the window startled me from out of my cloudy, crying stupor. I crawled to it and unlatched the handle, not expecting it to push itself open and have Angel hop from the tree branch outside into the bathroom with me. But he accomplished the feat somehow and I wasn't complaining. At least now I have a companion in here that won't judge me.

I cried myself to sleep on the bathroom tiles, snuggling with Angel in my arms that night, pouring my heart and soul into the tears my mom should have received from me the moment I found out she didn't make it.

# Chapter 21

*I* DECIDED TO TAKE A DRIVE the next morning to clear my head. A destination wasn't planned but somehow, out of the blue, I was parked in my grandparent's driveway. You all were expecting somewhere else, weren't you? Don't worry, because I was too. I just wanted to make one stop before I made my way over to the cemetery. I had been avoiding the visit long enough and now, it was time to pay my respects. On both parts.

"Grandma?" I called when I went inside the house.

"In the kitchen, dear," was my response.

I trailed rather slowly through the little house in attempts to avoid the inevitable. Maybe I'm a chicken, but what I planned on doing would take a lot of courage. So don't criticize me for taking my time!

As rough and tumble as my grandfather is, my grandma did an excellent job of decorating their home. It was a beautiful two story farm house with log paneling (my grandfather built it) and a wraparound porch. My grandma let it slip that I would inherit it one day, but that's beside the point right now. The inside was lined with every piece of wood furniture you could imagine. I will get to the reason why in a minute.

Flowers littered every open table and countertop in the house. My grandmother loves to garden and her favorite thing to grow are lilies, so they are more prominent everywhere. The flowers made the house smell amazing but it was the cooking that will overtake you first. Grandma could seriously be a gourmet chef if she wished but she's taking her family recipes to the grave. She's Polish/Irish, so I suppose it's how she was raised. Max learned everything he knows from her. She makes a mean Kielbasa and Sauerkraut that the neighbors would kill to know how to create.

So it was no shock to me that she was in the kitchen when I came over that day. She was in the process of making my grandfather's favorite . . . baked ziti. And, truth be told, my favorite as well. She puts extra ingredients in it that makes it explode on your taste buds. Every time I come over, she always asks me if I would like to help. So it was no surprise that this time wasn't any different.

"Hello sweetheart, would you like to get me the mushrooms out of the ice box please. You can start cutting them up if you'd like."

For those of you living in the 21st century, the ice box is the refrigerator. Just a little tidbit so you all don't assume I'm making something up. But I did as she asked and placed the package next to the bowl she was working at and gave her a hug to say hi.

"Actually grandma, I need to talk to Oli—grandpa." She hates it when I call him by his first name around her. So I changed it at the last minute after I was shot a death glare that would scare the pants off of Portia even.

"He's in the barn," She replied while getting back to work.

I gave her a kiss on the cheek and ran out the screen door in the back of the house. Their house was lying on about 50 acres of land that a company called Green Acres Homes has always been trying to purchase off of them for a new condominium spot. Oliver, being as stubborn as he is, won't sell it for all the money in the world. I can't say that I object to him not selling. After all, this will all be mine one day. I'd kind of like to raise a family here and settle down, maybe buy cows and horses and such. It's a beautiful place.

The barn is located off to the side and in the middle of the land, the only downside of having so much space. So, I slowly made my way down to the old, rickety, red barn and pushed open the doors. They always make a creaking sound as if a warning to anyone that's in there that someone else is entering. I was sort of expecting Oliver to yell out a few choice swear words in Italian when I did so.

"Who is there?"

Oliver still has a bit of an accent from living in Italy until he was twenty, so he doesn't really use contractions like the rest of us. I think it's funny sometimes when he's trying to talk to someone new in town and they have no idea what he's saying. I try not to laugh but it just spills out sometimes and I can't really control it.

"It's me Oliver" I yelled out.

Although grandma doesn't like it when I call him by his first name, he's used to it by now and I think he prefers that I do. My brother's rarely call him this but; again, they aren't told they inherited all of his Italian emotions like I do. I suppose that's why we clash so much.

I walked inside the hay-smelling barn and was met by a tall, muscular looking man with a scowl on his face. Since my mom was conceived at a young age, my grandparents are still in good looking shape. Albeit, the test of time has rounded my grandma a bit more than she used to be, her hair was still rich auburn and there were sparsely any wrinkles anywhere on her. The same goes for Oliver as well.

Oliver had a darker complexion from working out in the sun his whole life and thick, dark hair. It has just recent developed a few grays but it makes him look more distinguished rather than old. His jaw line is still wide and strong and he was a very intimidating man. I would be frightened of him if it weren't for the fact that we are related and he would never even think about laying a hand on me. He didn't hug me like my grandma does . . . he never seems to.

"What do you want?"

Such kind words from kin, right?

"I was hoping to talk to you about mom," I responded.

"Oh, well, hurry up. I have things to do and I do not need you bugging me all day."

"OK, I'll try and make this quick."

He escorted me to two wooden chairs in the back of the barn that he made a while back. Oliver is very handy and is a pro at making stuff out of the blue. That is exactly why the house is filled with all sorts of hand-crafted furniture and what not. The things he makes are really beautiful though. He should really think about selling them sometime.

"How old was Aunt Cassie when she got Jinx?" I asked.

"I thought you said this was about your mother. I do not wish to speak about Cassie." His voice thundered.

This was a typical response whenever someone brings my aunt up. In some way, I believe Oliver thinks Cassie betrayed him by spouting off her "abilities" at the Thanksgiving table. It was over twelve years ago . . . he needs to let it go once and for all. I mean, she's his daughter for Pete's sake!

"Please Oliver, I just need to know."

"Oi! Fine, she was around seventeen years old I believe. The kitten just found her one day and would not leave her alone. Why do you want to know this?" He answered.

"Just curious. Did mom ever have a pet when she was younger?"

I don't know why I wanted to know this, but it was like my mouth was on auto pilot and I couldn't control what it was asking. What I had asked him though was something interesting.

"No, your mother was more social than Cassie was. She did not have time for animals of her own. Damn cat drove Cassie nuts. Did your mother ever tell you about the first time Cassie came running inside screaming about how she had just saw the future? The cat had showed up right after and she never stopped the insanity since. I blame my mother for all of this." He finished.

"Why? What does Grandma Liliana have to do with this?"

My great grandmother died when I was three years old. I met her once before her death and she seemed like a sweet old woman. Her mind did seem to wander off randomly when someone was talking to her, but that's to be expected of someone her age. She was one hundred years old when she died.

"She filled Cassie's head with outrageous ideas whenever she visited and put her head in the clouds. It was her fault that Cassie is crazy."

"Cassie isn't crazy Oliver. She's just . . . a bit stranger than the rest of us."

"That is what your grandmother says as well. I will not be made a fool of in such a manner by my own flesh and blood!" He had begun to shout and stood up from the wooden chair with such force, it knocked the chair over.

"That's just it Oliver, Aunt Cassie *is* your flesh and blood. She's family! You learn to take their faults no matter what they are and love them anyway. Not seclude them from the ones they love like they're some kind of freak. Imagine what she's feeling right now. How she's coping with her life by herself with only a nurse to keep her company. It shouldn't be like this." I yelled back at him.

Silence as thick as brick too over us both and I didn't expect for him to say anything more. So instead of furthering the shouting match, I stood up from the wooden chair and began to walk to the barn doors. This was how every meeting between us ended . . . with a battle of words. And it always ends with me leaving, both of us still furious with each other. I can accept this, but I just hope that one day it can end with something better.

"You remind me so much of her," I heard in the distance.

I slowly turned around to see Oliver staring back at me with an actual smile on his face. This was one for the history books as well. Hurry, someone call the presses! Oliver Costarelli just broke a smile!

"Who? Aunt Cassie?" I asked.

"No," He responded while walking toward me. "Of your mother."

I wasn't expecting that to come out of his mouth in the least bit. Because saying something like that takes heart. Something most people were sure Oliver did not possess. But here it was; something so meaningful that you would think I made it up in my head.

"Umm, thanks," I was only capable of saying.

As we stood there, facing each other without a word left to say, all of the awkwardness that should have been there, wasn't. It was as if we talked like this my whole life. And there was only one thing standing in the way of the dawning of our new relationship. Well, a better relationship at least. Because I wouldn't say everything could be fixed between us. Only mended. So I walked over to him and wrapped my arms around his waist and squeezed as tight as I could.

"Goodbye . . . grandpa," I whispered.

"Goodbye miele," He responded, hugging me back.

I could swear I saw a tear after I pulled away and began to walk to the door again. But I wasn't going to call him out on it. After all, I think I might have shed a few myself back there. That was the easier thing I had to do, however. Because as I climbed into THE BEAST, I had one destination in mind. I had to go there and say goodbye. I owed it to her.

# Chapter 22

*I* SAT IN MY TRUCK FOR about ten minutes trying to build up the courage to stand in front of my mom's grave and say the things I came here to say. She might not be able to hear me, but it's still hard to bring yourself to talk to a spirit . . . if there was one. I just hope I don't make a fool of myself.

"Hi mom," I began. After placing the yellow daisies (her favorite) on the bottom rim of the stone, I sat down in front of it with my hand lying on the top of it. For some reason, I felt it made us closer. "I don't know where to begin so I'll just start off with a quick recap of what happened since . . . since the accident.

"Max and I made some new friends. I'm working at the bookstore with a girl named Portia. You'd really like her. She's a vampire but she's been the nicest person to me yet. Max works at the auto shop with a boy named Caleb."

The memory of the night before came flooding back into my mind and brought me to clutch at the necklace hanging from my neck. This was going to be harder than I thought it would be.

"I fell in love with him mom. I didn't mean to, it just sort of happened and now I don't know what to do." Tears gathered in my eyes but did not yet spill over. "He's dating a girl named Shaylee and I'm seeing a boy named Gunnar and it's too late. I should have told him my feelings as soon as I figured them out myself, but I waited and waited like you told me never to do."

I found a blade of grass on the ground and started to pick at it and break it into pieces. It was the only thing I could do to keep myself from crying. Yeah, didn't work out too well if you ask me.

"I kissed him last night. I know that's something you might not care to hear, but I thought it's important to share. Do you know when the main characters kiss in fairytales and they try to explain it with birds chirping and bells going off? You aren't going to believe me, but that's how it felt. It was like . . . I don't know, my feet were on the ground but my body was flying. It was amazing."

I bent my head down for this next part.

"He said something after that made me think though. He said that he was the silver lining after you're . . . after the accident. Umm, and it made me think. What if—what if the accident had never happened?" The tears started to fall slowly. "On one hand, I would still have you and we'd still be living in California. But then I began to think about everything and everyone I'd be leaving behind here if by some miracle you could come back and this whole incident was erased."

I wiped my cheeks and continued.

"That's selfish, right? That's what I had been thinking after I realized I thought about it. I mean, who would pick a boy they fell in love with after knowing him for a few months over their own mother. I-I didn't mean to do it, I swear."

Now my tears were gushing out at full force and I couldn't stop them even if I tried. But I don't think that I should stop them after what I did to her. Then, it was time for my apology.

"About-about what I said to you. You know, before the truck slammed into the car. I didn't mean it. I don't hate you, not at all. If I could go back and change everything, that would be my first regret. I love you mom, and I don't ever expect you to forgive me. I just wanted to let you know that I should have listened to everything that you had to say before assuming the worst. It was yours and dad's business, not mine."

I paused and inhaled a great deal of air before clearly stating, "I'm sorry mom."

Just that simple phrase was like a weight lifted off of my shoulders and I already felt better. It's amazing how saying something out loud can make the worst pain in the world go away instantly. It was time for me to leave. Nothing could get any better after this.

I kissed the tips of my fingers and placed them on the top of the stone before saying, "I love you," and standing up. It was the least of my worries that I had an audience listening off in the distance. But when I did see the old man and his dog standing by a grave a few feet away from me, I didn't freak out. He was smiling, making his face look misshapen and mean. More like a grimace than anything. He was obviously trying too hard.

My hand rose on its own and waved back and forth toward the man. He waved hello back but not in the enthusiastic way I had done. But as I was walking to my truck, concentrating on everything else in the world except what was in front of me, I heard a very loud, muffled meow. I didn't expect anything of it, just some random neighborhood cat that had stopped by to say hello. When I didn't see anything at my feet, I continued my trek to my truck.

I reached for my handle and heard the meowing again. Ignoring it once more, I opened my door and was hit by something flying at me from inside. I saw streaks of white and black before I fell into something strange. It was swirls of multi-colored lights surrounding my entire body and wrapping me in warmth like I've never felt before. Smells assaulted my nostrils that triggered memories from my past, present and future.

Jasmine and Fuchsia were first and most prominent of the aromas. It was the way my mom's perfume that she wore every day smelled. Next was the smell of lumber and pine needles. I couldn't quite tell if it reminded me more of my grandfather or Holden, ever since he started working at the lumber yard. Either way, it was powerful. Then, lilies and chocolate chip cookies passed through the swirling lights that made me remember my grandmother. The smell of fresh air and grass reminded me of Angel, when he just comes home from wandering the town. And the final smell that came was vanilla. For some odd reason, a picture of a face was created in the lights as if the smell came to life. I recognized the face to be Caleb.

My body shocked itself out of reverie and I rocked back on my heels but did not fall over. Something square was weighing my hands down and from my weakened state; I let it fall to the ground. The loud thud cleared my head and I finally opened my eyes. What I saw, however, made me convinced that I was still dreaming. Either that or I knocked my head on something harder than I thought.

"Scarlett, can you come down here for a minute?" I heard a voice from somewhere below me.

This was not possible!

# Chapter 23

THE THING THAT HAD FALLEN out of my hand was lying at my feet, taunting me with what was reality. The title read *Twilight* which was the last book I had been putting away before my mom had called me downstairs that night. I remember every single detail of that night by heart and I also remember storing that book away in a box that I haven't yet unpacked.

I was standing in the exact same spot in the exact same room wearing the exact same clothes at the exact same time I heard my mother's voice calling me down. Which I had heard again moments ago. How was this even possible? This has got to be off of the "X Files" or something!

"Scarlett, I need to talk to you!" The voice came again.

That was my mom's voice coming from below me. I would recognize that sweet sound anywhere. Was this Hell? Did I die back in Willow Creek and this was God's way of punishing me? There was only one way to find out for sure or not. So I ran downstairs at full speed, trying my best not to trip and fall.

I passed the living room and heard the same hollering coming from the sofa as the TV played the baseball game it had been before. My brothers' and dad's voice echoed through the walls and it was strangely comforting. I literally ran into my mom while walking into the kitchen. This was something that didn't happen before.

Her eyes were still puffy and bloodshot due to her silent crying over my dad. I should have been more sympathetic, but I couldn't concentrate on anything but her being alive, standing right in front of me. Breathing . . . blinking . . . smiling at me like it was any other day. Normally, my weak stomach doesn't travel to my head, but I couldn't help it when the room started to spin. I lost my footing and fell to the floor in a crumpled mess.

Go figure . . . I see my mom, the moment I had been waiting for since the accident, and I pass out. Heart of a lion I have, right?

When I finally gained consciousness again, my mom was standing over me, fanning her hands to give me more air. A question popped into my head that I must ask immediately.

"What's the date today?"

It came out groggy and slurred so I was a bit surprised that my mom understood what I said. But she replied with, "It's June 2nd," and my heart leapt with fear, confusion, and happiness all at the same time.

I couldn't stop myself from lunging at her and hugging her as tight as I could. And I certainly couldn't stop the tears from releasing and streaming down my face as hard as they could. Even though she had no idea why I was acting like this, she hugged me back.

"I love you mom!" I cried into her shoulder.

"Well, I love you too Scarlett." She responded back to me.

I didn't let go of her until well after I knew this was real . . . she was real. And even then, I never took my eyes off of her. Afraid that she would disappear and this would all be a dream. She didn't though. We both stood up from the ground and my mom made me sit on the chair to make sure I was stable.

"What was that about? Do you need a doctor or something? Oh my God, should I call an ambulance?" She asked in a panic, reaching for the phone to dial the number.

Who could really blame her for being worried? I mean, if I had a daughter and she fainted right in front of me for no apparent reason (to my knowledge), I would be asking the same questions. But it's not as if I could tell her the truth as to why I had hit the floor like that. I'd be locked up in a house like Aunt Cassie . . . or worse, locked up in a mental hospital. So, I lied.

"I didn't have very much to eat today and my blood sugar is on the low side right now. I'm alright, I promise."

"Oh, well then can we go and get a burger or something? I need to talk to you about some things and I think that it would be better if we left the house for this." She asked.

I know what happens next and I am certain that I was meant to stop it. That's why I was sent back here . . . to prevent all of this horrible mess from happening in the first place. Why else would I be reliving this awful day for any other reason? So I racked my brain to come up with excuses to make us stay inside the house. There was only one that had a good possibility of working out.

"*Small Town Dreams* is on in like five minutes though and I want to watch it. Can we just go up in my room and talk about it there?"

"*Small Town Dreams*? I thought you hated that show?" She asked me with a confused expression. Which, I don't blame her for having after what I had just owned up to.

It's a soap opera in case you all were wondering. I don't think anyone actually watches it, but it's still on the air so I suppose I'm wrong about that. One of the main characters I guess I could sort of relate to. Her name is Haley Miller and she's in love with a man who's married happily with two children. She battles to contain her feelings but it doesn't help that she works at the police station with this man. Lisa Robertson, Haley's best female friend helps out a lot with her inner turmoil by giving her advice.

The man that Haley fell head over heels for is Luke Arthur and his wife is Cheyenne. Cheyenne cheats on Luke frequently with a man named Dylan Derrickson. They both work at a local bar with the owner, Chris Laughlin, who wants to make the bar into a strip club instead, Cheyenne being his main attraction. Steven Cartwright is in love with Haley but they are just best friends. The town drunk, Zach Dewitt, is frequently wandering in and out of scenes with all sorts of alcoholic beverages, trying to loosen up the episodes a little. Sometimes it makes it funny, but most of the time, it's just lame.

Eric Hart entered the town, making the show tolerable to watch with his movie star good looks. Not that any of the other male characters are in any way ugly . . . far from it. He's considered the bad boy that cares for everyone deep down. His main goal is to get what he can't have . . . Haley. Because she is the goody two shoes of the place which only makes her feelings for a married man worse. Oh and don't get me started on Haley's dad, Scott, who secretly sleeps with Haley's friend Victoria Madison. Her mom, Natalie, still has no idea of her husband's infidelity. All in all, the show has plenty of drama and it's rather funny to watch if you enjoy watching people complain about their lives.

But convincing my mom that I'm addicted to it is a different story. She knows me and I've told her time and time again that Soap Operas were created to make people feel better about their own lives. I was trying to save her life . . . it was the only thing I could think of, give me a break!

She agreed to stay with me though which made me feel like a huge weight was lifted off of my shoulders.

She sat with me on my bed upstairs and I flipped the channel to The BNC and waited for the show to start. I couldn't believe I was about to watch this horrific, train wreck of a show and pretend that I like it. But then again, I couldn't believe that I'm watching it with my mom as well. So I suppose it can be considered a win-lose situation. Winning with the fact that she's here and losing for forcing my eyes and ears to witness this torture. So I apologize to those particular body parts for what they are about to go through.

And it started.

# Chapter 24

*D*O YOU KNOW HOW MANY commercial breaks *Small Town Dreams* contain? I do. Three . . . THREE in a one hour time span! How on Earth could this network put people through this kind of torture? Boy was I ecstatic whenever one came on though! Normally, people hate commercials, but in this case I welcomed them with open arms. Eventually, it was over and time to talk about the dreaded subject . . . divorce.

"Sweetie, what would you say if I told you that your dad and I aren't getting along as well as we should be right now?" She began.

"Well, I would say that I saw this coming . . . literally." Maybe it was too soon for inside jokes with only me? OK, think about being a little more sympathetic and maybe she will change her mind. Doubtful, but it's worth a shot. "But just because you two aren't getting along perfectly right now, doesn't mean you should do anything drastic."

"Your father passed drastic about three months ago," she mumbled under her breath so I wouldn't hear her. But I did.

"Are you talking about daddy's affair with that woman?" I asked.

"How did you—?"

"It doesn't matter how I found out right now mom, but I know he regrets it."

"It's been going on ever since March sweetie, he doesn't regret a thing about it. I should have been smarter and seen the signs before anything happened. I told Ben not to hire someone fifteen years younger than him, but he just wouldn't listen."

I knew it was his assistant! I've heard temptation is a hard thing to overcome, but cheating shouldn't be an option when it's your devoted wife that you're hurting. God, my dad isn't the person I thought he was! How could he stand to cheat on my mom over and over again like that without a second thought? I've heard what he said at the funeral and at the cemetery, how could this be so? Well, I'm still not so sure if that was all just a dream or what. But that's not my point at the moment.

"So go to couples counseling or something. Divorce can't be your only option yet."

"I want him to fight for me Scarlett, I honestly do, but he obviously wants to be with his assistant more than me. I'm not going to stand in the way of his happiness . . . I love him too much for that. Even if what makes him happy is something that will never last."

I couldn't help but to laugh with her at her last comment. Because it's true. Dad could never be as happy as he wanted to be with a twenty-something over my mom. But none of us could stop him once he had his mind set on something. Especially when it's something blonde with really long legs and a brain the size of a peanut. It means that she doesn't know any better when hooking up with a married man.

"Scarlett?" I heard her asked me.

I looked at her only to see a glum smile on her face. Why was she smiling about something so serious? Then, something hit me. I went back to the cemetery scene from before and realized that it had been ever since I was born that my mom had been keeping in touch with someone. Someone that my dad had no clue about. And that someone was Caleb's dad, Jack. Could her smile mean something awful? Because I have a thought in mind about what she could be so happy about in all of this and it's nothing good. Well, depending on how you look at it, it would seem to be good or bad in my case.

Because if my mom did move back to Willow Creek, it would mean I get to see Caleb again. But on the other hand, it would mean my mom would divorce my dad forever and I certainly didn't want that. And then there was the whole travel situation. If my mom were to get into any form of transportation, what would happen? Would she get into another accident or stay safe and sound the whole trip?

"You can't leave mom! You just—you can't!"

"I have to, honey. I've already contacted one of my friends back in my hometown and he's expecting me in a matter of days. He's been nice enough to let me stay at his house and I won't insult his hospitality by changing my mind. Besides, I need some time away from your father right now and seeing his face every day sure won't help my decision to divorce him."

The thought of my mom living in Caleb's house sickened me. What if my mom started to date his dad and they got married? That would make Caleb and I step siblings! I have to prevent this at all costs!

"What—what if you stayed at least until Max's and my birthday? Then, after that, if you still want to leave I'll let you go without any more questions."

Mom sat there thinking about this proposition while I chewed on my bottom lip in worry. What if she didn't take the bait? What would I do then if she didn't think waiting a whole month would suit her? Maybe I should be coming up with better options than just thinking about her answer. Yeah, that might be a better idea!

"Alright, if I stay until your birthday, you have to promise me one thing."

"Name it!" I replied with enthusiasm.

"You have to consider the idea of coming with me to Willow Creek. I'd like to have you and Max come with me to stay for a month or so to see how you like it and maybe move there with me."

"What about Holden?" I asked her.

"Holden would never leave your dad. Even if he was in the wrong, Holden is very attached to him and I could never see him leaving Beverly Hills for a place like Willow Creek anyway. So, what's your answer?"

I wasn't going to Willow Creek without my whole family with me. I refuse to leave any one of them behind in fear that something might happen to them. But I couldn't tell her this. Because if I did, she would just leave in a few days by herself. Which could possibly mean she would die in another crash. So I had to stall somehow. I lied . . . again.

"Yeah mom, I'll think about it." I answered her.

"Good! I'll go and tell Max then!"

And she left. My room, that is. I don't understand why she was so excited about leaving Beverly Hills *and* my dad. Does Jack have some sugar coated lips or something? I shuttered to think of the image my mom and Jack making out portray in my head. EWWW!

To do a little background check on this guy, I pulled out my laptop and typed in Jack Darwin. Not that I don't trust the love of my life's father, but it's better safe than sorry.

Do you know how many hits there are for Jack Darwin out there? Two million five hundred and fifty two . . . on the same guy! Jack Darwin is the sole proprietor of Green Acres Homes. It's that condominium company who is trying to buy out my grandparents' farm! With offices all around the country, they are very important. Their most prominent location is actually in California . . . Beverly Hills to be exact. With seven-hundred thousand homes being built every year, Jack's roughly worth nine-hundred million dollars. Wow, my mom sure knows how to pick 'em!

A link appeared at the side of one of the websites I went to that said "about Jack". Curiosity got the best of me and I ended up clicking on it. Here's what it read:

"Jack was born in the small town of Willow Creek, Montana to a family of bakers. He worked at his family's bakery from the time he was ten and, there, he received all of his entrepreneurial skills. At the ripe age of eighteen, Jack broke out of the family business and started a small project of his own while going to college. He met the love of his life in business school and married quickly, producing the first heir to the family fortune shortly thereafter.

The ending of Jack's marriage was difficult on everyone. Especially Jack. His ex-wife left him with their two children, Caleb and Emma, while his business was just getting off the ground. But the challenge of fatherhood didn't hinder Jack's marketing skills. His business flourished and is now a multi-million dollar company. With so much money, Jack expanded his family homes. He now owns a condominium in Maui, a castle in Scotland, a cabin in the Alps and, of course, a mansion back in his home town which his family chooses to occupy year round. A link will appear at the bottom of this page with pictures of every one of their homes.

Still single, Jack takes on the title of number three on America's most eligible, richest bachelors. Although he does not date just anyone, he is still looking for the right person to become a motherly figure in his kid's lives. What a wonderful father he is!

To purchase one of Green Acres Homes many properties, contact the number on the home page. Or, email us at www.greenacreshomes.com. And remember, Green Acres wants to put you in a home without all of the mule!"

You have *got* to be kidding me with this! What is up with their slogan? "Green Acres wants to put you in a home without all of the mule"? I'm guessing that was a play on words . . . just a little. Mule being a substitute for Bull. But whatever, it's their option to commit that kind of shameful humiliation on themselves.

I decided to click on the link for pictures of the houses. I never did have the opportunity to see Caleb's house. He was always over at mine for some odd reason. But boy would I just have a heart attack if I saw this place in person! Especially thinking of Caleb working at the auto shop when he has a place like this!

It lies on an isolated, sixty acres of freshly cut, green grass decorated with exotic and local flowers alike lining the property and the house itself.

You were met by a gate in the front which was about ten feet high with beautiful, black bars and spikes on the top. The yard was surrounded by a wall of perfectly trimmed bushes that wrapped around the entire property. In front of the house was a paved driveway in a loop-like fashion that seemed to go on for miles. The Darwin house was made of stone and had an asymmetrical appearance to it. A caption under the picture read: "forty five windows total . . . I counted." The person who posted this picture must have been proud of themselves.

The backyard was shown from an aerial view that showed a twenty foot swimming pool with a waterfall streaming into the hot tub. A basketball court was to the left of it several yards away and a cabana area was to the right, conjoining with the pool. Oh, and before I forget to mention, there was a dirt bike track in the very back of the yard. It was the biggest thing back there too.

Now I could see why Caleb didn't take it so well when I said no to him so many times. He was probably used to getting whatever he wanted and I was the only thing he couldn't have. Boy, my life resembles that character from the soap opera more and more! But seeing Caleb's house made me think of my birthday present for some odd reason. I know his truck must have cost him a fortune, but just how much had Caleb spent on me?

I typed in several jewelry stores that came to mind like Zales and Jarred and even Kay, but none of them held the same one he had bought me. There was only one more shop that I could think of. And if he bought it from this store I would be speechless. If I was capable of beating him up from miles and miles away, let alone a time paradox, I would, if this is true. So I typed in the store's site and waited for the home page to pop up.

I must have spent an hour looking through each category but still did not find the necklace. Oh, thank God! He wasn't as stupid as I thought he was. I was in the diamonds section of the website and thought I was done, when I noticed I still had another page I hadn't seen. Holding my breath, I clicked next and the page loaded. There it was.

I couldn't stop staring at the page with my mouth open because I still couldn't believe he bought me a birthday present from Tiffany & Co. He must have swapped out the boxes before bringing it to me so I wouldn't know he was rich. I feel it more shocking for all of you to know the price if I actually wrote the numbers instead of lettering, so here it goes. $2, 825! Almost three thousand dollars on a stupid necklace! Well, I would never have called it stupid, but that's not the point. The point is I lost that necklace when I traveled through space and time and now I will never be able to treasure the luxurious gift ever again.

My fingers reached up to graze my collarbone, where the necklace would be if I still had it. But there was something there. I scrunched up my face in confusion and looked downward. There, hanging from my neck, was very same locket whose picture was on my computer screen. I hadn't lost it! But what does this mean? If I went back in time, I wouldn't have the same things from before . . . would I? Ugh, my brain hurts!

A cold breeze blew through my window that made the trees rustle loudly and ferociously. Scratching followed by a loud thud made me pull my eyes from the necklace and look up. There, in the middle of my room, sat a full grown, white cat with streaks of black on each side shaped like angel wings. He kept staring at me with such intensity; I could have sworn he was trying to set me on fire with his gaze.

Angel was back.

# Chapter 25

GETTING A JOB IN CALIFORNIA just didn't feel right to me. I mean, my dad had asked me if I was going to apply anywhere but I couldn't see myself working anywhere but the bookstore back in Willow Creek. Sad, I know, because it will never turn out like it was before. Even if I do go with my mom when she leaves, no one there knows me like I know them. They don't even know my name yet! I think it'd be kind of strange to just walk up to one of them and have a full conversation with Portia or Caleb when they have no idea what I'm talking about.

It certainly hurts to hold my necklace each night and know that Caleb doesn't even know he gave it to me. I can't say that he knows nothing about me, because he does. Well, he knows the toddler form of me at least. My mom's letters to his dad was the only benefit from their relationship in my eyes. There's no doubt in my mind that my mom has intentions to date Jack as soon as she reaches Montana. If she isn't dating him now!

Having Angel back with me makes things a little better. Beside the necklace, he's a part of my experiences there too. And it helps to have him cuddle up to me when I start to cry. Mostly about losing all of my friends, but even more about Caleb. I must sound obsessive, but give me a break. I loved him after all, remember?

It was a week before our birthday and my mom was behaving in a manner that I have never seen on her. She's been distant and secretive and won't tell me what's wrong. Some of the blame can be placed on that stupid couch downstairs that she chose to sleep on every night. But I understand perfectly why she had chosen to take up that current sleeping spot. Who would want to sleep with a man whom their divorcing? The point is the couch is so horribly built that it makes her cranky from lack of sleep.

I tried to be the one to cheer her up by having a romance movie marathon with plenty of Strawberry Cheesecake ice cream, courtesy of

Ben and Jerry of course. But as soon as *Gone with the Wind* ended, she started to ball into my pillow. And these were full out sobs too, not some wimpy tear rolling down her cheek. It made me feel partly responsible for making her stay when she doesn't want to. But I needed her with me now too! I know it's selfish, but after the ordeal I just went through, I don't really care what people decide to think of me.

Seriously, I couldn't get her to stop crying for the life of me. Max helped me put her to sleep after she ended up exhausting herself.

I went to sleep that night worried for her. What if this crying thing never stopped? With the both of us! Because, I'll admit, I cried myself to sleep that night as well. Just one of many, I'm afraid. But at least I had a legitimate reason for not telling her why I continue to do this to myself. She had no excuse not to share her problems with me. It's not as if I'd be judgmental or anything. So, I expected to confront her the very next day and demand answers. Too bad she wasn't there!

I did find a note in her sloppy handwriting (she's a doctor, remember?) laying on my nightstand, however. It still pains me to think about it, but this is what it read:

"Dear Scarlett,

I know I made a promise to you that I would wait until after your birthday to go to Montana and I'm sorry. But I couldn't spend one more second looking at your father knowing he's in love with another woman and not me. I'm sorry for leaving nothing but a note and I know you probably won't forgive me for this but I had to do it. And as for Max and you coming with me to Montana, I feel it best that you two should stay in Beverly Hills with your father right now and help him out. As soon as I'm on my feet with my own house, I will agree to let you two come and live with me. Only if it's what you really want, that is. I want you to know that I love you no matter what anyone says and it tears me apart to leave you like this. I'll call you as soon as I land.

Love,
Mom"

135

Why does everyone find it fitting to leave me with a note? First dad does it and I think that he's gone to commit suicide. Now my mom does it and all I'm worried about is if the plane doesn't smash into some mountains or something. Why couldn't she at least leave me with a hug and a decent goodbye? It slowly began to sink in that my mom had already left. I needed to do something about this! And I know just the person to go to.

"Max, can you give me a ride to dad's work?" I asked him after bursting into the kitchen.

His mouth was filled with Trix cereal and his hand was clutching a silver spoon. I didn't even notice what time it was until I looked at our clock, but Max must have been about to leave for work. His *Ray's Put Put Golf and Food Court* logo on his t-shirt sort of gave it away along with the fact that it was seven fifty in the morning. Normally, he doesn't wake up until noon. When he looked up at me with large eyes, I laughed. Max had milk dribbling down his chin and multicolored mush showing when he asked, "huh?" How on Earth could he be made to love anyone, let alone Portia, was beyond me!

"Can you drop me off at dad's office before heading to work?" I asked him again.

He let out a huff but chugged the rest of his milk in the bowl and set it in the sink. I grabbed the car keys from him and headed out the door while he was taking his lazy time slumping out the door. What's wrong with him? Did he lose a race last night or something? Oh well, I have bigger fish to fry this morning and my brother wasn't on the list. And when I said fry, I meant it!

"Thanks Max!" I yelled through the open window when I exited the car at Cohen, Redmond and Hera.

"Hey, wait!" I did so. "Whatever you're planning on doing to dad; make sure you don't drag me into any of this. I have a feeling that he's getting me a new 2009 Mustang Bullitt and I'd prefer not to get it taken away before I even drive it."

I smirked at him before walking away. What's the big obsession between boys and cars? I mean there only a motorized box with wheels on it. Nothing special! But I guess it's like girls and scars on boys. You'll never figure out why they're so tantalizing but you can't help but stare when a boy shows them to you. It probably had something to do with being capable of defending us. Who knows, I'm not a psychologist!

Speaking of scars . . . mine were gone! It was one thing I was happy to lose when coming back in time. And believe me; I checked everywhere just to make sure. It made summer in California so much easier being able to wear shorts and not be worried about ugly scars poking out. I couldn't wait to go to the beach and wear a bikini again! Well, if what I'm about to do works, it won't be in California when I'm lying out on the beach. But we'll see what happens.

"Well, Miss Hera! Don't you look lovely this morning! Big plans today?"

The doorman outside my dad's office building is probably the nicest man you will ever meet. Henry is friendly and actually *tries* to get to know you instead of just pretending because you're one of the boss's offspring. As far as my memory goes back, I've always known him. That's probably because my dad has been at the office most of my life instead of around any of his children. My mom used to frequently bring us here to say hi to him, but he was always busy. I ended up seeing Henry more than my own father.

"Nope Henry, just going to do some screaming at my dad. What about you?" I asked courteously.

"Just standing out here as usual. Go easy on your dad today; he has a lot on his mind lately."

"Don't I know it?!" I grumbled before entering the door Henry was holding open for me. In no way did I plan on going easy on my father after what he has caused.

The large lobby was quiet and empty due to it being very early in the morning. Most lawyers don't see their clients until ten or later so I have plenty of time. I burst through there so fast I didn't notice the person who was sitting at the front desk said anything to me, let alone was telling me to stop. It finally registered in my brain when I was on the elevator and pressed the number fifteen. Not that I care if I hurt that person's feelings. He works for a lawyer's office. It's not as if he had a soul anyway!

I stormed through the hallway after getting off the elevator and tried to avoid as much eye contact as I could. Especially with one person. And that person's desk was placed just outside of my dad's office. Her name is Tina Grey and she's a twenty two year old intern. She is very petite and wears stiletto heels all the time to make her look taller. Brunette hair fell over her shoulder and her eyes were almost black. I'm not making it up for dramatic effect, they really were! Also, she happens to be my father's assistant. So you can all imagine why I was avoiding her altogether. I shoved my dad's door open as hard as I could and then slammed it. I was lucky not to knock any of his awards off the wall behind him. Albeit, that would be somewhat of a bonus.

"Oh, hey sweets. What's wrong?" He asked, looking up from whatever papers he was working on.

Instead of unnecessary shouting (right now anyway), I threw my mom's letter down on the table right in front of him and barked out, "read!" While taking a seat in the chair right across from him, I waited while my dad followed my orders. I wonder what was going through his mind in that moment. What would reading my mom's words of goodbye to me do to him? I was pretty much preparing myself for anything.

"Has—has she called you yet?" He asked first.

I could tell he was somewhat shocked by this. His hand was covering his mouth and his eyes kept searching the letter in front of him for something. In a way, I could say I sort of regretted springing this on him without warning. But then again, everything lately had been sprung on me, so why stop the trend now?

"No, she hasn't." I responded.

"Alright, thank you for showing me this."

And he went right back to writing on the papers lying on his desk.

"'Thank you for showing me this'! 'Thank you for showing me this' is all you have to say? I—I can't believe you right now!" I shouted as I stood up from my chair.

"Scarlett, lower your voice."

"I'll lower my voice when you stop thinking that hussy out there can ever compare to mom! How can you just let her go like this?!" I shouted.

The hallway outside went quiet and I could feel Tina watching me from through the glass. Like I care what she does? I was irate right now and no amount of staring or telling me to calm down will help. Actually, it might end up with someone getting maimed!

"She doesn't want to be with me, Scarlett, I can't do anything about that," he gritted through his teeth to keep from yelling back. "I don't think your mom ever knew what she wanted. So don't come storming in here and think that you know everything about what's happening."

"I know a lot more than you think, dad. Starting with the letters from Jack that you found."

His mouth almost hit the floor.

"The ones she sent him weren't about how much she loved him dad, they were about me! Me and Max and Holden and how good her life was now that she was with you. Mom loved you with all of her heart and you're just going to throw that away for the first pair of legs that looks in your direction." I finished while panting for air.

Neither of us said a word in fear something was going to explode. That's how thick the tension between the two of us was. This is why I don't confront him unless I have to. His stubbornness collides with the hard-headedness I inherited from Oliver and it all goes downhill. But I suppose it's a good thing that we can finally get this all out. He needed to know that I knew a lot more than he thought.

"She's gone now, Scarlett. There's nothing I can do about it." He mumbled.

He was so frustrating; I had to clap my hands together with each word when I said, "Fight for her, dad." The clapping stopped. "She wants you to fight for her. Make an outstanding gesture or something. *Do anything!*"

"But her letter said—"

"Ugh, stop being such a guy and *read between the lines*, dad! She wants you to follow her and tell her how much you still love her. God, why do men have to be so stupid?!"

I started to stomp my way out of the door to give him time to think about everything I had just said when I stopped in the door frame. I pointed toward Tina and said, "Oh, and stop dating this little twit behind mom's back. She's not even remotely as beautiful as mom and so not worth your time."

And then I left.

# Chapter 26

$\mathcal{H}$E DIDN'T COME HOME THAT night. Max made dinner for only Holden, him and me and even then we were worried. With dad's job as a lawyer, he used to miss dinners all the time. But after mom made it a rule that we would eat together as a family every night, he did as she told him to do. Now, three children with parents nowhere in sight were digging into their chicken cacciatore at the kitchen table alone. Mom called after dinner and told us that she was OK and that Jack had been nothing but gentlemanly ever since she arrived. I'll bet he has, what with him wanting mom back for himself and all.

Even when I walked up the stairs to sleep that night, thoughts were whisking around in my head as to just where dad could be. I could think of no answers this time like I had the last. But that was a simple reasoning problem while this . . . well, it's much more complicated than just reading between the lines of a letter and throwing out every unethical possibility. This was my dad's mind, almost too impenetrable than anything anyone has ever come across. Other than his heart, that is. But my mom had seemed to conquer that for at least a little while. Sleep sounded so inviting after such a stressful day that I almost didn't make it past getting changed without falling over and shutting my eyes.

*"Scarlett! Max! Holden! Wake up now!"*

The sound of someone's voice reverberated off of my eardrums but did not get through to my brain until I rolled over and read the clock. It was two thirty in the morning and my dad was shouting about something. The first thought that occurred to me was that he could be hurt, so I removed my nice, warm covers and sluggishly made my way down the stair well and into the living room where he stood with a large smile overpowering his entire facial features.

"What's going on dad?" Holden asked from the couch. He was sprawled out so much that there was no chance in me squeezing my body into a seat. And Max was sitting on the Laz-E boy, so I just used the armrest to sit down on.

"All of you need to pack a bag now and get in the car as fast as you can." He responded with the same, wide smile on his lips.

Since it was so late at night (or early in the morning, depending on how you look at it), my brain was still on REM mode. Not comprehending a word my dad was saying, I just stared into his eyes in a dream-like state. My head was cocked to the side and my eye lids were guaranteed to be slanted down to barely look like I was awake. I probably looked cross eyed or something.

"What are you talking about? It's too early in the morning to go anywhere. Did you hit your head or something, dad? Because you're making no sense right now." Max said as his input to the whole ordeal.

"Scarlett made me think of a few things today and I've been walking around all of Beverly Hills for hours just trying to clear my head. I'm taking your advice, Scarlett."

"What advice dad?" I asked groggily while wiping the sleep from my eyes.

"We're going to Montana to win your mom back!" He simply stated.

Nobody spoke for several seconds after he said this. We thought he had gone insane or something. I knew my brothers felt this way because they had the same look on their faces as I did. But my dad was serious about this. We were going to Montana in the wee hours of the morning just so he can make a fool of himself. I know my mother and she won't get back with him until she knows dad is absolutely positive that it's what he wants. So it was good news for me because it meant that if dad was serious about winning mom back at all costs, we would have to move to Montana. My mouth pulled into a smile on its own accord at the thought of seeing Caleb again.

It took us seventeen hours to get to Willow Creek from Beverly Hills. We took two cars up there because Max couldn't stand to be parted from his mustang for five minutes. In his defense, it's nice . . . but it's still just a car! Dad and Holden were in the Bentley in front and I rode with Max in his car. It was such a long drive that when we finally stopped at the hotel we were staying at, I burst out of the car and ran around the parking lot three times to get my legs working again. And I wasn't the only one doing so too. My brothers looked like morons doing the same thing as well.

But I'd like to share a conversation that Max and I had in the car before I get too carried away with the arrival. It was a monumental occasion and shouldn't be skipped over. Because it actually showed me that my brother has feelings. Who would have thought? We had just passed the California exit sign when he let out a sigh that couldn't be good. His head was facing the road but looked slightly bent down and sullen. Max wasn't smiling or even expressionless like he was most of the time . . . he had a frown on.

"What's wrong?" I asked him.

"Nothing," He bit out.

I knew he wouldn't tell me right away, but there was no need for the defensive tone. I'm his twin sister after all and who can you trust if not her? So I was determined to get it out of him if it's the last thing I do. He's not keeping any big secrets from me in this day and age!

"Something's obviously wrong with you, Max. Now tell me right now or I'm going to give you a Charlie horse so bad that you'll have to pull over because the pain will be too blinding!"

My hand balled up into a fist and I positioned it right over his leg to be ready when he said he wasn't going to tell me again. That little bugger won't get away with it this time. But what he said was nothing I was expecting.

"Go ahead, I've already been in enough pain to last me quite a while."

My hand dropped in sync with my mouth at those words. What could be bothering Max so much that he's in pain? I'm beginning to worry he might do something stupid about it too. Like drive off a cliff or something. Let's hope it doesn't come to that today! I had to dig through my mind to come up with some way for him to tell me. I finally came up with a solution.

"How about if I tell you something secretive about me. Would you tell me what's going on with you then?"

"Maybe . . . depends on what you tell me." He shrugged.

"O-OK, well it's going to make me sound crazy but I think you need to hear this. We've been to Montana before Maxi," I said, trying to use his nickname so that he'd be less freaked out. It had the added bonus of getting on his nerves as well. He told me he hates it when I call him that because it makes him sound like a feminine product or something. Albeit, he didn't use that discreet of language while explaining this to me.

"Call me Maxi again, and you will be walking to Montana by yourself! But yeah, I know. We've been to grandma and grandpa's for Christmas. Is that what you're telling me, because it's a sucky secret if so?!"

"No, that's not what I meant. We've lived in Montana before! Mom and I were in a car accident and she died so we moved to Montana to be closer to her grave. And I had a job at the bookstore and you had a job at the auto shop with . . . " I couldn't finish that statement. "And we had friends here and I found Angel here and it all happened in Willow Creek!"

I then proceeded to give him details about the alternate reality. Including the part about our birthday (which was still three days away) and the necklace Caleb gave to me. Although I didn't tell him it was from a boy whom I loved. He was staring at me like I was insane. It's a lot to take in, I'll admit, but there's no need to look at me like that. I know what I'm talking about even if nobody else does. And I kind of figured he wouldn't believe a word I was saying. Not many people would believe me and what I went through.

"That was a dream Scarlett, not worth me telling you what I'm going through. Sorry, but it's just how it goes."

"It wasn't a dream and I can prove it!"

I pulled the platinum chain around my neck to make it visible on the outside of my shirt. Max was the first person to see it. I didn't know how to tell people where I had gotten a Tiffany's necklace without telling them the whole crazy story. And I didn't want to end up in a psychiatric hospital, so I kept my mouth shut. Until now, that is. I had to get my point across somehow.

"How does that prove anything? You probably bought that yourself!"

"Fine, if you don't want to believe me then I don't care! Keep your problems to yourself!"

I crossed my arms and faced my window in anger. He was being a stubborn mule and I wouldn't deal with it. Even with twin telepathy, he couldn't possibly figure out the fire bolt comments I was shooting in his direction in my head. Well, I hate being out of the loop!

"If you're going to be a baby about it, fine! You can pout all you want!"

And then it was quiet. We didn't talk to each other, partly because Max started to blast his radio and partly because we didn't know what to say to each other. Even if we were brother and sister, it doesn't change the fact that he is keeping something from me. And I wanted to know what.

While merging into Idaho, I finally heard this, "I feel empty."

"Get some gas in the next town then." I answered, thinking he was talking about his car.

"No, I mean I feel like there's a giant, gaping hole in my insides and it won't go away. And the weird thing is I don't know where and why it's there."

I looked at him and I could tell he was being serious. His eyes were straight on the road but I could still make out something inside of them that made this statement true. It was as if his soul had been ripped out of him by some unknown force and he was in pain . . . physical and emotional pain.

I hadn't really noticed this much back in Beverly Hills, but Max had lost some weight. He was much, much skinnier than he was months ago and it was scary. His cheekbones were sunken in and I could clearly see his ribs through his shirt. Max's arms were smaller than mine and his clothing seemed ten times too big for him. His hands gripped the steering wheel so tight that I could see every vein in his hand poking through his skin. Have I been selfishly blind this whole time not to notice that my brother was dying before my eyes?

"Have you been to the doctor?" I asked.

"I'm not going to get some quack prescription for something that I know isn't really there. I've been dealing with it in my own way and it will go away eventually."

His statement worried me to no extent.

"What do you mean by 'dealing with it', Max?"

"You don't want to hear it, so don't ask." He replied.

"I asked, didn't I?"

Max wouldn't say anything. He kept clenching his jaw and I could see every muscle tense up and release, it was disgusting. He needs help one way or the other and self infliction won't do anything like he wants it to. I needed to get through to him somehow. But he needs to tell me what he's been doing first. I needed to get his attention in a critically frightened voice.

"Max?" I asked quietly

"I've been sleeping around, Scarlett! I'm not proud of it and I never want to admit it ever again, but I am. It takes the pain away for a few minutes anyway and I'm working on getting better. So don't even think about judging me!" He shouted.

Even though his confession sickened me to my core, I couldn't say anything. Because like he said, I couldn't judge him. With the way he was talking about it made me think that it was actually true. That it did take his pain away for a few minutes and I never want my brother to be in pain. But he couldn't keep doing this to himself. He will make himself very sick with the way he's going and nobody wants that. Not even him.

"What does it feel like? The gaping hole inside of you I mean." I asked curiously.

"It feels like it sounds; a giant hole in my center. Like something's missing in my life and without having it, life's not worth living."

Something in his voice and the words that he said triggered a reaction from my brain. I knew right away what was making him act like this and it wasn't anything that he could help. I know why he's been sleeping with other girls, I know why he hasn't been eating, I know why he hurts so much and I know why he doesn't want to seek a doctor for something they can't even cure. Because the doctors don't have any drug to cure what Max was going through right now. The gaping hole that he's talking about isn't from anything he's even aware exists.

Max missed Portia.

It's a confusing concept to get, because Portia had been ripped from Max's memory before anything could happen between the two of them. Obviously Max had feelings for her that hadn't been sifted through before I was forced back in time to stop everything from happening, though. He was suffering from lovesickness and doesn't even know the woman he's in love with yet. Sad, it really is, but soon everything will turn out better. I hope.

# Chapter 27

$\mathcal{M}$Y DAD AND BROTHERS BROUGHT in our luggage while I made a phone call to someone I needed to talk too immediately. I won't burden you with the whole conversation because you will soon find out exactly who I was talking to. And it was of the utmost importance at the moment. As soon as they were done unloading the car, I told them I was leaving.

"I'm going to explore the town for a little while. I'll be back soon." I said.

"Wait, I'm coming with you."

Max leapt over the bed that he was behind and ran to meet me at the door. I was shocked that his twig-like legs didn't just snap in half with that amount of physical activity. Seriously, seeing him stand up was worse than seeing him sitting down in the car. How could I have not noticed this at all until now? Maybe I should keep a closer eye on him from now on. Just to make sure he doesn't keep doing this to himself.

"So where are we going?" He asked me once we exited the hotel.

"I have no idea. We are going to wander around until we find . . . something."

I couldn't tell him where I was actually going. He wouldn't approve of my choice and try and talk me out of it. But I'm not giving in until I talk to her. Answers are what I need and she is the only person who can give me a straight answer about what's really happening.

It didn't take us long to reach the downtown area from our hotel. It was only about a mile walk and it gave Max and me a chance to catch up with everything we've missed with each other. More than he told me in the car, that is. Despite the fact that Max has been sleeping with other girls, he's learned ten new recipes for barbeque (which I am claiming to be the official taste tester for!), won three races and had snuck out of the house for each one. And they were all followed by, or in association with, massive amounts of alcoholic consumption. I asked him straight up if he drove drunk but he said no.

While in the long process of drilling my brother for information about his life, I happened to noticed we had stumbled upon the diner. Max thought we should go in and try the food, but I already knew that it would be delicious. Psychic, remember? Well actually, I don't know if that's true or not yet, so we'll just have to wait and see.

Kitty was my waitress again. I liked her, but there was something about her that just seemed strange to me. Maybe it was because she was one of the only beautiful girls that isn't a complete snob? No, I don't think that's it at all. But whatever it is that is so off putting about her, I *will* find out eventually! She won't be dating my eldest brother without some background information. If Holden ever does decide to work up the courage, that is.

You know, there was something about the way his insecurities come out whenever she's around. Holden had never had a problem talking to girls at Beverly Hills Prep, so why all of a sudden is he a fumbling idiot when it comes to Kitty? I know nothing has happened yet, but what separates her apart from the rest of the girls in the world?

So, pop quiz for all of you readers! What's the worst thing that could happen while Max and I were preparing to leave? Who does it involve and what would provoke me to do what I did? I don't care if you think you're one hundred percent positive about your answers, you're wrong! I will, however, tell you the correct response to all of them in a short recap.

Kitty picked up our empty plates from the table and asked us if we would like dessert when I heard her first mumble. She said something about "insufferable little toe rag" and "should be emasculated". My brain didn't register right away whom she could be talking about until I heard the most annoyingly high, almost screech-like laugh come from behind me. Shaylee's laugh.

My body moved on its own accord before my mind could have any say in the matter. So the next thing I knew, I was running up to Caleb and throwing my arms around his neck and holding on as if trying to choke him. My eyes became blurred with tears and all I cared about was the fact that I was able to touch Caleb for the first time since I was forced to leave. But it was a shock to me when I didn't feel the hug reciprocated. I did, however, feel that strong fire between us like before.

Honestly, I was expecting to feel his arms wrap around my waist or something . . . but no such thing happened. His arms stayed out to the side and Shaylee began to noisily pout. What a drama queen! I could see why she would be angry, though. A random girl hugging the stuffing out of my boyfriend wouldn't sound too peachy to me either. And I guess that having some stranger come up to you and latch on wouldn't be so pleasant too. But they weren't strangers to me, now were they?

"Umm, Scarlett?" I heard Max say in confusion.

I don't blame him for being confused as to what I was doing. But it finally became awkward after about twenty seconds of one-sided hugging and I let go of him. Slowly . . . but I let him go nonetheless.

"Do I know you?" He asked, tilting his head in the adorable, puppy dog manner.

"Not yet; no. My name is Scarlett Hera," my brother had approached us and I introduced him as well. "And this is my brother Max."

"Caleb Darwin," he replied while shaking both of our hands. I think he was more comfortable doing that than full on physical contact. I would prefer the hug—well; actually I would prefer a real kiss. But I know I can't have that just yet.—however I am going to respect his perimeter and stay a few feet away right now. Who knows how long it will be if that changes. If it changes.

"Nice to meet you and hope to see you around town," was the last thing I said to him.

We left the diner with Max hounding me with loads of questions about Caleb and how I knew him. Of course I didn't tell him the truth as to where I was going; he wouldn't believe me if I did. So I stuck to telling him that I had seen him here last Christmas and he looked like an interesting person to meet. Max wasn't stupid so I know he didn't buy one word that I had said. But at least he left it at that. Besides, I was too busy worrying about how to ditch him without making it too obvious. So I racked my brain for the best possible excuse but only could come up with one.

"I'm not feeling very well Max. Woman problems and all that so I think I'm just going to head back to the hotel and take a nap or something."

Every guy on the planet hates to talk about a woman's "time of the month" and it was the only excuse he wouldn't ask questions about.

"Do you want me to walk you back?" He asked brotherly.

"No, I'm fine. You should keep walking around. Maybe you'll end up finding something interesting."

I was talking about Portia, of course.

"Very unlikely. Hope you feel better, sis."

And I started to walk in the opposite direction. It roughly took me half an hour to reach the house I was looking so diligently for. I felt strange being in front of her house after all these years, but it felt good. She would be the only person to understand what I'm going through and I'm happy I have her to talk to. If she wasn't around, I'd probably be in a mental hospital or something.

I rang the doorbell of the small, one story house and waited for a rather large, older woman to open the door in a white overcoat. She led me into a very warm and appealing living room and a very frail looking woman sitting on a Laz-E boy recliner. Her face lit up with a very wide smile when she saw me. I walked to the woman and sat down on the couch next to the chair she was occupying.

"Hello Aunt Cassie," I said to the woman.

# Chapter 28

$\mathcal{I}$N A WAY, HER WEAK appearance reminded me of Max and his current stature. And with her bright red hair cut short, it only helped the mental image increase. What kind of treatment had my aunt been getting these past few years by her nurse? I'm definitely talking to my family about this when I get home. No one should be put up to this if they didn't have to.

"What can I do for you, little one?" She asked me.

It was as if my vocal cords were swollen shut for some strange reason. I couldn't even think about asking her what I came here for. Not that Cassie is in any way intimidating, but I could only think about how ridiculously stupid I would sound when I did ask her. Can you imagine that? I'm afraid of asking just what was going on with me to someone who claims to be psychic!

"I was hoping you could tell me some things about yourself," I answered after a long pause.

"Alright, I'm all ears."

I needed to figure out what order to put my questions in. I know I should have been more prepared for this moment considering I was planning it from the moment I saw my mom again. But I was a little preoccupied with enjoying the time with my mom to think about this. Besides, I thought I had more time! It's not my fault that my mom decided to up and leave us on a moment's notice without leaving anything but a note. So I suppose I'm just going to have to wing this and hope for the best. Who knows; that might be the better choice in all this!

"Umm, when you first got Jinx, did you have . . . certain . . . dreams before hand?" Was my first question.

"By dreams, do you mean one life changing situation that rocks you to your core before being dropped back to reality like a sack of potatoes?"

"Yeah, something like that."

"Well then, yes, yes I did." She stated with a smile.

I was awestruck. Not that I wasn't expecting her to say yes, because I was. It's just, I was never fully ready to hear her say it like it was the easiest and the most normal thing in the world. Why was she so at ease with this? Does she know how people look at her after she gives out this information? It's nothing good, let me tell you.

"Can you-can you explain it to me?" I asked her.

She nodded and told me everything. "Well, I was sitting out in our pasture one afternoon when I was sixteen and I was called in by your grandpa. When I walked inside, he immediately took me outside. It was walking through the field that he told me about Grandma Liliana's illness. She had fallen ill with the flu a few days earlier and they didn't expect her to make it through the week. Grandpa bought plane tickets and we left as soon as we were ready."

How is it possible that I know what happened to her before she even told it to me? I'm not going to spoil the surprise for all of you . . . you can wait until she says it herself. But every word she had already said was like someone hit replay on a tape recorder and it wasn't the first time I heard it. And a vivid mental image of Aunt Cassie and Oliver walking in the field was the first of many throughout the story.

"Grandma Liliana died about a day after we arrived, making your grandpa obligated to stay and tend to the funeral processions and what not. Jane went back to the States with your grandma but I stayed. It was about a month later when we were still in Italy, where I overheard a doctor telling grandpa that they found something that could have saved Grandma Liliana's life. I was transported back to that first day in the field before my dad talked to me and I knew what I had to do."

I knew what that depressing gleam in her eye meant. And the fact that her voice had fallen an octave lower when she said the last part out loud only made things clearer for me. Because I had to deal with the same quandary she had and each of us had made the choice that affected our heads and what was right instead of what our hearts really wanted.

"You met a boy in Italy, didn't you Aunt Cassie?" I asked her.

She slowly nodded and I saw a tiny tear roll down her cheek. Cassie was remembering her love that she left in Italy. I felt bad for her, truly I did, but I could only think of Caleb and the time *we* had together before I left. It's about as selfish as you can get, but it's not as if I could stop myself.

"His name was Santo Giovanni and he was the son of a Blacksmith. He swept me off of my feet the moment I met him. His favorite thing to do was bring me one of the most gorgeous red rose from his mother's garden and tell me 'the beauty of this rose cannot compare to the beauty of your soul'. He was my first and only love and I will never forget him." She finished.

"Well, why didn't you return to him after you saved Grandma Liliana? I mean, you could have just gone back to Italy and married him, couldn't you?"

"No darling, because he wouldn't have remembered anything about me. And I couldn't handle seeing him again with the fact that I was in love with a man who didn't even know my name. Besides, plane tickets were expensive back then and I was only sixteen. I certainly didn't have the money to buy one anyway."

I tried to imagine not being able to come back to Montana to see Caleb again . . . but I couldn't. Times were different back then and I had to wrap my head around the fact that Aunt Cassie had no chance at seeing Santo after that.

"But why don't you go to Italy now? Why not just buy a plane ticket and search him out? Get to know him all over again and live happily ever after!"

It was such an easy solution in my eyes, but she had obviously seen it otherwise.

"I did go to Italy, Scarlett, about five years ago. He has a wife and a family and he's happy. That's all I wish for him is to be happy; whether it's with me or not, that's all I want."

What she said made me think of Max's predicament. Without Portia in his life, he was a waif of a person and he wasn't happy in the least. So how is it that Santo could forget my Aunt Cassie without a second thought? How could he not be alone and depressed, wishing he was dead like Max is doing? Maybe he did? Maybe there was a yearly time period before Aunt Cassie saw him that he was so down on himself that he couldn't walk? Perhaps he had just found this woman and married her to try and fill that void.

Cassie wiped her tears away and drank from a glass of something I didn't know beside her. I don't think it was anything strong, but I couldn't tell for sure. It was several seconds until she finally asked me, "So . . . what was your glimpse like?" And I told her everything.

At times, during my story, I thought it would be best if I left out the facts about Portia and her family being vampires or that the love of my life is a werewolf but the boy I was dating is a vampire. So she still doesn't know about my supernatural adventures, but she knows everything else. I even told her about how Max misses Portia without even the slightest knowledge of her existence.

"That's common as far as these things go." Aunt Cassie told me. "Max will eventually get over the feeling and live his life as he normally would."

I don't know how true that is considering Max and Portia are meant for each other. Remember how Portia told me that her life mate was Max? And how Max was made for her and only her? Yeah, I don't think Max will be getting over this as fast as Aunt Cassie claims he will. But that's something that will just have to wade itself out in the long run. Right now, I had more important questions to ask of her.

"I wanted to talk to you about something else that happened in my glimpse, Aunt Cassie." I began.

"Alright, I probably have the answers," she said in a joking manner. Because she knows she'll have the answers. One hundred percent, she knows that whatever I ask her, she'll tell me exactly what I need to know. Lucky for me that I have an intellectual, psychic aunt!

"I met this man when I was visiting my mom's grave one afternoon and he said something to me that I had no idea what it meant."

"What did he say?" She asked in worried tones.

"He said to me, 'you're her, aren't you' and then asked to shake my hand. I didn't know who he was talking about but I think he mistook me for someone else."

Cassie's eyes widened a considerable amount. She stood up from her chair and walked off without saying a word.

# Chapter 29

$\mathcal{I}$ DID NOTHING BUT JUST SIT there in awe and say nothing. My eyes flittered around the room as if someone was going to pop out and say surprise at any moment. It was the only solution I could come up with as to why Cassie would just up and leave for no apparent reason. And without answering my question as well. Do I leave now, or what?

"I think you should see something before I explain this to you."

Cassie entered the room carrying several scrolls under her arms and a wild look in her eyes. It kind of scared me what she had to show me if it had anything to do with what the man said about me. She set the four decrepit, yellow papers on her coffee table and spread them out in front of me. They looked as if you'd touch them, they'd crumble to pieces. So I gently picked up the scroll closer to me and began to unfold it with such care that it took me half a minute to open it. And this is what it said:

"A child born on the fourth day in the seventh month to an unexpected family will change the lives of many. This child will have powers like no one has seen before and must be taught how to use them. If not, the world will be in peril of this child's strength. As the child grows, it will be not aware of what she possesses until her sixteenth year. Up until then will this child's soul be wild and free. As the soul dies, it will be replaced by an immortal counterpart and will only make the child stronger. Beware the suitors of the child, for they are not human and love her more than their own life. This one will have many alliances but more enemies than she can handle. Many will deceive and betray her for she only sees the good in people. Keep the child safe and reap the rewards of the ever powerful Immortal Savior."

My breath had caught in my throat a long time ago but it didn't occur to me that I had not been breathing until I had to cough and sputter after I had finished reading the scroll. The old man thought that I was this child some old piece of paper had told him. How on earth could this ever be me?

"How—and I'm—what?" I stammered.

"These scrolls have been passed down our female generation for hundreds of years. They have been the property of philosophers, queens, inventors, outlaws and modern day housewives . . . all of which have been psychic. Each one have been trained and prepared to teach the 'Immortal Savior'. I was taught by Grandma Liliana from the tender age of five and I am prepared to teach you . . . how to use all of your powers."

Oh, she doesn't think that I am this 'Immortal Savior', does she? I mean, yes, some of the statements in the scroll did sound exactly like me. But it doesn't mean that I am the one that so many people have waited on! I couldn't be that person! I'm just regular old Scarlett Hera . . . nothing important. Certainly not someone who's capable of saving many people. Can anyone else see how ridiculous this is?!

"Here, read this one! It's about the men in your life." She said excitedly.

I took the scroll from her outstretched hand and opened it.

"The Immortal Savior will have three suitors. The Warrior will be the only one the Savior will truly love. Like his name, he will be brave and courageous and willing to sacrifice his own life to save the Savior. His willingness will be put to the test many times over. Their love for one other will be the most powerful thing in the universe. The Snake will love her unconditionally but will not be loved back. Leaving him to betray the Savior and try to capture her power to make it his own. Protect the Savior from this man at all costs for he will manipulate the Savior to use her powers for evil instead of good. The Guardian will be an unexpected suitor for the Savior. He will be the most beautiful man in history and will be in the Savior's life well before she begins to love him. He will always grace her side for his love for her runs deep within his soul. These men will be useful in the Savior's life and will help with the growth of her powers."

OK, well I could try and pinpoint each one by name, but I'd rather not. I know the Warrior would be Caleb. That's an obvious one. But as for the Snake, there's only one person I could think of and he would never betray me. If I did have powers, I don't think he'd try and use them against me. Oh, and I forgot to tell you, the Snake, or who I thought it was, is Gunnar. Can any of you imagine Gunnar manipulating me into doing anything I don't want to do? I didn't think so.

But as for the Guardian, I'm stumped. There is no guy that comes to mind that has been around me that I haven't loved. I haven't really had many male friends to begin with. So that part was confusing.

Jinx jumped on my lap and I began to pet him. Aunt Cassie's mouth pulled into a smile and she stared at me like I was supposed to know what she was thinking. Well, even if I was, I had no idea what could be going through that maze she calls a brain. So forgive me if I'm not catching on to my powers right away. I returned an awkward smile and continued to pet Jinx behind his ear.

"What's your spirit animal?" She asked me.

"My what?" I asked in shock.

"Your spirit animal. Mine is Jinx and the man you saw in the cemetery had his dog. It's the animal the Higher Power sends to you for protection."

"Oh, well I guess you could be talking about Angel."

"Ooo, Angel, huh? What is it?"

"He's a cat. I named him Angel 'cause of him being pure white with black markings shaped like wings on his sides."

Her mouth dropped open and her eyes bugged out of her skull. Oh Lord, what now?! I mean how many new, strange factoids about myself can I handle in one day? Not as many as she's throwing out, let me tell you! How could anyone my age handle something like this and not wig out or become insane?

"What?" I asked her.

"I had expected you to have a different animal from the rest of us, but I never imagined it would be *that* different!"

I waited for her to explain more.

"Normal spirit animals are dark in color so that it's easier for them to be stealthy in protecting their charge. But you say that your cat is white—"

"As white as snow," I interrupted.

"And every single spirit animal I have heard of has had the marking of the Egyptian eye like Jinx has on his chest. But Angel has black markings of wings, you say?"

I nodded yes.

"Oh, oh, this is so much cooler than I expected."

"I'm sorry to burst your happy bubble, Aunt Cassie, but there's one little problem you seem to be overlooking. The scrolls say that the Savior is immortal and the last time I checked, I still have a human soul."

She bent her body toward me and glared at me with piercing blue eyes and whispered, "For now."

# Chapter 30

*I* RAN OUT OF THERE AS fast as I could. Well, I shouldn't say that I ran, because that would be rude to do in front of my creepy fortune teller aunt who just told me I was going to die soon. So I made up an excuse and exited out of the front door in a timely fashion. Too bad I think she saw right through my charade. Oh well, if she knew that I was freaked out by what she said, then why did she say it? Answer me that!

It was dark by the time I reached town. And I don't mean that "starting to get dark but still a small glow from the sun'. No, I'm talking 'pitch black, can't see unless you're by a street lamp' darkness. I didn't have my cell phone with me so I couldn't tell you the time, but I knew it was probably well past dinner time. My stomach growled with hunger and I hoped that there would be left-over's from whatever Chinese restaurant they decided to order from.

As I walked down Main Street, my thoughts were consumed with the image of Caleb's face. I know I'm a bit obsessive at the moment, but I'm in love. And women in love aren't accountable for the actions that take place during said time. So it's really not even my fault that I can't stop thinking about him. There was a tiny voice that told me to stop but I couldn't listen to it.

I heard footsteps behind me. There was no one on the sidewalk but me, however, so I tried to dismiss it as my imagination. I was probably still freaked out by my aunt's words. Yeah, that's it! I walked straight, trying to keep my eyes dead set to the ground. It was harder than anyone might think, not looking up. You have this odd sensation that you're going to run into something but you know if you look up you might see something you'd wish you hadn't. That's how I felt at that exact moment.

There it was again! Was someone following me? You'd think there would be better people to stalk than me. It sounded like they were trying to put as much distance in between us as possible while still keeping a decent pace so as to not lose sight of me. I chanced a glance behind my shoulder and saw nothing but an empty sidewalk where someone should have been. I quickened my steps subconsciously and purposely to get away from the horrible feeling of being followed.

I made it in front of *Betsy's Ice Cream Parlor* before slowing down and catching my breath. It felt like I had just run that last mile or so and I was severely out of shape. A low growl and a glimpse of something as quick as lightening out of the corner of my eye later and I was running as fast as I could down the street. I'm not kidding you: I was running faster than I ever had in my life. With no intention to stop, at that. Oh no, because stopping would mean getting caught by whatever was chasing me and I didn't want that.

It was, however, ten times faster than me and overshot my distance by about thirty feet. In the bright light of the street lamp, I could make out exactly what it was that was chasing me. Or, more fitting, *who* was chasing me. Portia's incisors were bared and her eyes were the purest and brightest blue I have ever seen. She was hungry and looking for a fresh meal. And I was the closest, easiest, and unknown thing to her at the moment. Lucky me, huh?

I turned on my heels and bolted in the opposite direction as Portia. I knew I couldn't outrun her, but I had to try. If only I could maybe confuse her and throw her off my scent then maybe I could get away. The closest alleyway to me was between the auto shop and the arcade. It was darker than the open sidewalk but I took a chance and ran inside, resting my back against one of the walls and breathing so hard I thought I'd pass out.

A few minutes passed with Portia nowhere in sight. I thought I was in the clear and it was safe enough to look around the corner to leave. So I stuck my head out and twisted it from side to side in order to look both ways. And that was when Portia's heavy, inhuman body hit me from the side and forced me back in the darkness of the alleyway.

I felt everything. The exact moment that her sharp vampire teeth pierced the skin at the base of my neck . . . I felt it. The blinding, white hot pain traveling from my neck all the way through my entire body . . . I felt it. Her hands crushing my shoulders to prevent me from struggling any . . . I felt it. The bones breaking under her grip . . . I felt it. Buckets and buckets of blood leaving me from those two, tiny holes where she was sucking from . . . I felt it. And last but not least, falling into unconsciousness while the warmth of dying enveloped me . . . I felt it . . . very, very vividly.

The last thing that entered my mind was the date. A week ago that day, Portia found out about David cheating on her. And she didn't have me to console her or to vent to. She never met Max as her reassurance.

# Chapter 31

*I* WAS CARRYING A SILVER TRAY *with a pitcher of lemonade and a basket of rolls on it to a distant stable. I felt the long fabric of a dress hit my ankles and the restraint of an apron tied to my waist. I looked down to notice I was wearing a pale blue dress with a flowery pattern. My hair was up off my neck and the sun was beating down on it strongly. Why was I walking to a barn? Was this some kind of 'Heaven' ploy? If I eventually reach it, will that get me into Heaven? Was there a Heaven to get into?*

*A man a few years older than me stepped out of the barn and smiled at me. I felt myself smile back at him. This man had an uncanny resemblance to Caleb. Every feature was identical to him right down to the fact that he wasn't wearing a shirt. Even his crooked smile flipped upward in all the right places. Although, I doubt you'd ever catch Caleb wearing those black, skin tight pants. His arms unfolded from his chest as I approached him.*

*"Good afternoon, Miss Katherine," he said to me.*

*"Good afternoon Henry; how are you this fine day?"*

*He took the glass from the tray and poured himself a glass of lemonade. I watched as his Adam's apple bobbed up and down while he drank, mesmerized by the motion. When he was finished, he wiped his mouth with his forearm and continued to look into my eyes. Henry's fingers had brushed against my own until they intertwined. I didn't pull away but I could feel that insecurity overtaking me as I knew we shouldn't.*

*"Robert will be home in a matter of minutes. You know I can't do this." I heard myself say.*

*"Then why did you come here?" He asked.*

*Before I could get a word out, he had taken the tray from my hands and laid it on the ground. Then, he gripped my legs behind the knees*

160

*and scooped me up off the ground . . . taking me into the barn with him. I knew what was going to happen, but I'm not going to say it here. I will continue on with whatever this was, however.*

*"Henry, this isn't proper. Robert and I are getting married in one week."*

*I was trying to protest his advances, but it was much too difficult with the way he kept kissing my neck like he did. He stopped abruptly and looked me in the face.*

*"Then don't marry him. Marry me instead."*

*"You—you don't know what you're saying Henry. I think the heat has finally gotten to you out here."*

*"No it hasn't, Katherine. You know I don't do anything drastic unless I am absolutely sure it's what I want . . . and what I want is you. I love you Katherine James and I wish to marry you today if it is possible."*

*"Oh I wish it were possible Henry," I touched his cheek lightly, "But it is not. My family as well as Robert's is expecting a wedding in one week and I cannot call it off now."*

*He seized my shoulders and searched my eyes passionately.*

*"Then run away with me, love. Run away and never look back at this awful town holding such sorrow for you."*

Someone was shaking me wildly and desperately calling out my name. For a moment, I was reminded of my time in the hospital after the accident and how it had been the exact same way I had been awakened then. Was it all a dream induced from a coma? It would be just my luck if so. But the voice that was calling my name did not sound like my dad's. Actually, it was a female's voice trying to wake me up. I did, however, recognize the voice almost immediately.

"Come on, Scarlett wake up! You need to feed and the Doctors are starting to get suspicious."

Portia's voice echoed in my ears and it sounded like music. Not because she was happy, oh no, she sounded worried. But because it was the first time hearing her voice in a long time. A scent entered the air like nothing I have ever experienced before. It smelled like chocolate and I wanted . . . no, I *needed* to have it now.

My eyes snapped open and, with lightening fast reflexes, I grabbed the flask from Portia's hand and slammed the lid to my lips, sucking up every last bit of the delicious flavors inside. I even stuck my tongue down inside to lick up the excess liquid . . . yeah, it got stuck. Portia started to laugh at me while I yanked it away from my mouth. The flask went flying and hit the opposite wall. Only, it didn't bounce off like I was expecting it to do.

A giant, gaping hole took the place of where the flask had hit the wall. Plaster was raining down from inside and the support boards were clearly visible through the dust. What did I just do?! And how did I do it?! My eyes stayed glued to the same spot, the hole, and I just stared for the next several seconds. I could feel Portia trying to shake me out of it, but she was getting nowhere. And she wouldn't for several hours more.

I was left alone after my doctor came in to check my IV and shooed Portia out. He said that visiting hours were over until tomorrow at noon and she had to obey by leaving. The Doctor spotted the hole and forced her to explain what happened before she exited. Portia lied and told him it was from one of the chairs she tried to move earlier and lost her balance, sending it straight into the wall. Good thing he didn't look inside of it!

Portia whispered to me before she left, "I left another bottle in the bathroom cabinet behind the shampoo for later. Drink it!" Whatever *it* was, I didn't plan on moving . . . so her demands that I drink it were completely shot to smithereens.

I didn't sleep that night. Strangely enough, I didn't feel tired. Actually, I felt like I had just gotten the best night's sleep I'd ever had. It left me with one thing, however, and it was the last thing on Earth I ever wanted to do let alone admit to doing it. The TV in my room had been turned to The BNC and soap operas took over my entire night. Surprisingly, *Small Town Dreams* isn't the worst show on the planet. But it was either that, or watch infomercials until the uncontrollable urge to buy something overtook me. Trust me, it happens too!

Before I knew it, it was tomorrow and I had people to see. Not that it's a bad thing, but what am I going to tell them happened to me? I couldn't tell them that I was attacked by Portia in a dark alley and she almost killed me, could I? Luckily, Portia had burst through my door right when the minute hand on the clock hit twelve. Actually, it was rather funny to watch Portia speak in such a frantic tone that it looked like her head was going to explode.

"Did you drink it? If you didn't drink it, we're in trouble. You didn't attack one of your nurses, did you? Oh my God, how would I end up explaining that? Maybe I could ask dad to—"

"Portia, shut up! I drank it . . . OK?"

Her face relaxed and she sat at the foot of my bed. I wasn't lying either, I really did drink it. It was right after a show called *The Beautiful and the Young* when I smelled it. I was very shocked at first how my throat became as dry as the Sahara Desert and the scent was so powerful I couldn't think straight. I ended up sniffing everywhere else but the place where it actually was. Eventually I found it and cleaned the entire bottle in seconds. The sickest part of it all was the slurping and purring sounds I was producing through it all.

"How do you know my name?" Her eyes slanted in curiosity.

I couldn't tell her the truth, so I lied. "One of the nurses told me after you left last night."

She nodded her head in acceptance.

"How do you know mine?" I asked her, because this was so obviously not possible in this dimension. She's never met me before.

A blush crept up on her face before she answered with, "I looked at your license after I took you to the hospital. They needed identification and I couldn't give it to them without spying. I'm sorry, will you forgive me?"

"Yeah, I forgive you."

It was kind of funny . . . a vampire with a guilty conscience over something so little as to snooping inside of a purse to find ID. Oh well, she'll eventually know the truth about me if we are to become friends once more.

"Your mom and dad are waiting downstairs. I told them I needed to talk to you first alone and they bought it. Hope you don't mind but I sort of told them we are friends in order for them to let me check on you. You know, so they won't ask questions as to why I'm visiting. I brought you a mirror," she said to me.

I didn't think about looking at my reflection, honestly. I just figured that since I've recently become a vampire—I grasped that concept shortly after I dripped some of the liquid from the flask onto my hand and noticed it was blood. Trust me; the reaction that I gave was quite a sight! The bathroom was pretty much destroyed after that. Luckily, I am the world's fastest cleaner!—I wouldn't have a reflection. So when I was in the bathroom all those times, I just avoided looking into the mirror. But Portia's telling me I can?

She gave me a small, rectangular hand mirror that was surrounded by black plastic and smiled at me. I inhaled a long, deep breath before turning the mirror over and looking at myself. The image brought a gasp to my lips.

I was beautiful! Not to sound so conceited, but if you saw what I saw, you'd think so too. Compared to what I used to look like, of course. My hair was still dark auburn, but it was shining bright and smooth instead of the rat's nest it was before. My skin was perfectly pale white without a single blemish and so velvety smooth, I couldn't stop touching it. My eyes weren't the same shade of blue like they used to but instead, a very clear, very brilliant shade of tea green. Which, I have to say, went much better with my hair than the blue ever did.

"I-I'm . . . but I'm-I'm—"

"You're a vampire." She finished for me. Not the word I was looking for, but it would do.

She spent the next fifteen minutes going over everything that I could and could not do, which was a bit of a recap if you ask me. Not that she knew it was a recap, but nothing she told me shocked me like it had before. She did, however, tell me that we heal remarkably fast. It made me wonder what I was still doing here in the hospital if that were the case. I thought it wouldn't hurt to ask her that one, tiny question.

"I'm keeping an eye out for you just for now, until I know you can handle yourself. You're being released tomorrow anyway."

"How long have I been here for?" I asked her.

She winced before saying, "three days."

"THREE DAYS?! THREE DAYS, UNCONSCIOUS IN THE HOSPITAL FOR A BITE WOUND?!" I shouted.

"It wasn't just a bite wound Scarlett, you were changing and I needed to make sure you were still alive. I thought I had killed out for the longest time."

"Wasn't that what you were aiming for in the alley? To kill a poor, innocent stranger so you could get your next meal?" I bit out sadistically.

"You know, I don't appreciate your sarcasm and for your information, I wasn't *trying* to kill you! I just wanted a taste of a real flesh and blood human and you were the closest one. I pulled away before your heart stopped."

"Barely! And now I'm a vampire like you . . . oh, this is just great," I huffed and crossed my arms over my chest in anger.

"Fine," She crossed her arms as well, "If you don't want my help then I won't give it to you!"

A few seconds of pouting like three year olds and we were laughing at each other. It broke the ice and we couldn't be mad at each other after that.

I suppose it's not such a bad thing that I am a vampire. But it does prove my aunt's theory of me being the one the prophecy had been talking about to be one hundred percent true now. I don't think I'm going to admit that to her just yet. I'd rather keep my pride intact for a few days at least.

"Knock, knock."

Someone entered the door at that moment carrying a bouquet of store bought flowers. My parents and Holden followed directly behind Max and his flower replaced face. Portia look in their direction and stood, beginning to make her exit, before my brother set down the flowers on my bedside desk, revealing himself. I heard her let out a small gasp, incapable of hearing to the untrained ear. That's another one on of the perks of being a vampire: Portia told me, is that my senses are heightened and I'd be able to feel, see, smell, taste and hear things at a much clearer frequency now.

He turned in her direction and paused in his steps. Max couldn't help but stare at her. He could, however, stop the driblet of drool from escaping his mouth and running down his chin. Yeah, he didn't catch that in time. And I suppose that's what triggered a reaction from Portia. Too bad it wasn't the proper reaction you all would be expecting.

"Ew, why don't you take a picture? It will last longer."

Max couldn't let her insult him without a comeback.

"You'd probably break my camera with that hideous face if I did."

"Oh please, you wish you could have this." She retaliated.

"You'd be lucky if I gave you a first glance let alone a double take. So I believe it would be the other way around."

"I don't date guys who could quite possibly blow away in the wind."

"Oh honey, you might want to take a look in the mirror before you make that accusation. All it would take for you is just one puff of air and off you'd go."

"Alright, that's enough!" My dad interrupted in his "fatherly voice". "Max, apologize this instant to Scarlett's friend!"

"But she started it!" he whined.

"It's alright Mr. Hera, I know he's sorry." She sneered at him and then said, "Scarlett, I'll talk with you tomorrow when you get home. See you everyone!" And she left.

Why couldn't I go home today? I felt perfectly fine and I didn't need to stay in a hospital at all. So why do I have to wait until tomorrow to go ho—wait a second, did she just say I was going home? What "home" did she mean?

"Um, excuse me, but did Portia just say I was going 'home' tomorrow?" I asked everyone in the room.

Holden was the one to actually answer me, however. "Oh yeah, dad bought a house when you were unconscious!" He was quite happy about his answer as well. He has obviously met Kitty once more then. Lucky me I was to get bitten and transformed before I had any say in which house we bought. Hopefully it was a nice one . . . and close to where mom is staying and Caleb lived.

# Chapter 32

$\mathcal{M}$Y MOM KEPT FUSSING OVER me the entire time while my dad sat in the chair and avoided any conversation with anyone. Max was making fun of my bandage and Holden was checking out the nurses in the hallway. This was how their visiting hours went. Don't get me wrong; I love my family and all, but the way they acted most of the time was downright ridiculous. You can only be forced to put up with their shenanigans for so long.

They left after my nurse told them I needed my rest. People need to start listening to me when I say I am not in the least bit tired. Little did I know how tired I actually was! I ended up falling asleep almost immediately after they left my room. But it really wasn't my fault after the ordeal I had just been through. And it was so nice not to dream a thing for once in my life. I needed at least one night of dream free, REM sleep. And that's what I received.

When I opened my eyes, however, I did not expect anyone to be sitting at my bedside waiting for me. Especially not who actually took over the chair closest to me. It was around seven o'clock at night and the sun was going down but here was Caleb sitting in my hospital room, doodling something in a Sketchbook. He was really concentrating too. You could tell by the way he bit his lip and furrowed his brow, every now and then sticking his tongue out slightly. It was the cutest thing I've ever seen. The smell of vanilla overpowered my nose as I watched him draw. It was quickly over when some of his charcoal dust floated over and up into my nostrils, making me sneeze loudly.

"Oh, you're awake!" He said surprised.

I couldn't do anything but nod to him. His appearance here made me confused and I couldn't figure out what dimension I was in. Was I back in a time where Caleb knew me and has already fallen in love with me? No, that couldn't be possible with how I had just seen my mother only a few hours ago. So Caleb still didn't know me and I was in love with someone who barely knew me.

'Say something you dummy!' I heard inside of my head. Only, it wasn't my voice saying it.

"So, Sarah—"

"Scarlett." I interrupted him.

"Pardon me?"

"My name is Scarlett, not Sarah," I told him with a smile.

I'd have to make a correction on the whole 'cutest thing I've ever seen' I threw out before. His blush is the cutest thing I've ever seen. And the way he cussed himself under his breath just made me laugh. No, the creepy, weird part came after the blush. Another sentence formed inside of my head without my voice being its owner.

'Oh nice one, this is a great first impression! Get her name wrong before you even know her. Bravo champ, bravo!'

It didn't register in my brain as to why this was happening. Whatever was happening, that is, was too strange for words. I had to start talking otherwise this might just keep occurring. And the only potential spark that popped into my head was the thing he had been drawing previously.

"What was it that you were drawing?" I asked him.

"Oh, umm well, you see I like to sketch random things here and there. You sort of gave me inspiration while you were sleeping . . . so I hope you don't mind that I . . . "

He flipped his sketch book over to let me see his work instead of just telling me. But I wasn't complaining after what I had seen. He has sketched me, in charcoal pencil, with my eyes loosely shut and a smile on my face lying in my hospital bed. It was honestly the most beautiful drawing I had thus seen. Not because it was of me, so keep all of your narcissistic comments to yourself! No, but because his sketch had perfect detail and wasn't in the least flawed.

"Ho-How long have you been here?" I asked him in shock.

"Just a little over two hours now," he answered after looking at the clock on my wall.

"Why?!" I looked at him in puzzlement. His head bent down as if to be hurt by my words. "I mean, why would you stay in a hospital room for two hours waiting on a complete stranger to wake up? I know you have more important things to do than that."

'I've been here longer than two hours.' I heard in my head.

"I wanted to see if you were alright. I heard about your accident from your mother and thought I'd come here and see if there was anything I could do for your family. Sorry if I've been a nuisance to you!" He said angrily.

"Well, it's not as if I'm *that* interesting of a person to watch sleep or anything! Why didn't you just go home or go to your girlfriend's house or something?"

"How did you know she was my girlfriend?" He asked abruptly.

"Umm, that's-that's not important right now. What's important is that I know why you're stalking me in my hospital room. Do you have a reason, or is it your normal routine to watch some stranger sleep?" I steered the attention away from me.

'It's fun watching you sleep,' the voice said.

"I don't have to take this from you. I'm out of here!" And he was. He stomped out of the door after grabbing his sketchbook and pencil. What a baby!

'Don't worry, we don't need him.'

That was a different voice entirely. Oh, it wasn't mine, but it wasn't like the first one either. Does being a vampire make me Schizophrenic? All of a sudden, a flashback of Portia's discussion occurred in my head. Replaying it fully so I grasped how serious this situation really is.

"Vilis Futurus means 'meant to be' in Latin. The voice in your head, the one I was talking about, is owned by the one person you will meet and fall in love with. That person was, in a way, made for you and only you. You're able to hear all of their thoughts and if they are a vampire too, they can hear yours as well. It makes it easier to have private conversations with one another and not have someone interrupt but it also makes it hard to keep any secrets as well."

It figures that the Immortal Savior has to have two voices inside of her head at all times! Why me?! The first one was obvious to me after I remembered this conversation with Portia. I was hearing Caleb's one-sided thoughts while he was here but he couldn't hear mine still. The second voice had been a bit harder to figure out at first . . . but now, I know exactly who it is.

'That's right, Scarlett, welcome to the vampire world! I'll be your host 24/7 live from inside your head. Give it up for . . . The Snake!'

Gunnar's voice rang through my ears in the most maniacal snicker I've ever heard. Maybe I was wrong about him? Maybe he would try and make me use my powers for evil instead of good. Only time can tell with something like that. This is going to be one heck of a journey, let me tell you!

'And with me along for the ride, it's guaranteed not to be boring!' Gunnar added.

I clutched at my throat as if from reflex and found my necklace still there. Oh thank God nothing happened to it! Well, I wouldn't go as far as to say that *nothing* happened to it. The diamond in the key handle was missing and the heart had a tiny dent in the side of it, but save for all of that, it was still good as new. And in no way was I willing to give up Caleb's necklace that he had bought for me and had endured time travel with me!

'What if I bought you a new one?' Gunnar asked me.

'I would never wear it,' I responded inside of my head . . . and something told me he got my message.

Boy, I am *way* more messed up than I ever thought. I couldn't even be normal and have only one Vilis Futurus, no Scarlett Evangeline Hera *had* to have two! What am I going to do with two voices inside of my head not letting me keep any of my secrets? Could I handle two people with me every second of every day?

'Don't forget me, love!'

Oh, you have *got* to be kidding me!

# Chapter 33

*I* WAS GOING HOME TODAY. My mom packed up all of my things while I changed in the bathroom and I was so ecstatic to leave this horrid place I almost forgot to put on my pants. Almost being the key word here! And let me tell all of you how hard it is to change with a person inside of your head that can see everything you see and hear all of your thoughts. It's the hardest thing in the world. So I have to make sure never to change in front of a mirror nor look down ever again until I am fully clothed. There's no doubt in my mind that Gunnar would try and sneak a peek if he ever could.

I still haven't figured out who the third person is yet. Identifying the other two was no problem for me, but the other one I do not recognize to save my life. I think it's because I haven't met him yet. But you can never be too sure as far as these things go. Portia still doesn't know about this genetic problem I am having yet and I plan to tell her when I get home. Maybe she will have some insight as to what exactly is going on with me.

The house was nowhere near the one we had before. Actually, it was on the exact opposite end of town. Near the bookstore to be completely honest. Our backyard was still in front of a forest, but it wasn't the same. It still had a pool in the backyard, smaller in size but just as luxurious. It had four bedrooms and two bathrooms. The only thing setting it apart from the other one was the location, color and the fact that we had neighbors. A large moving van was parked in the driveway, taking up half of the spaces.

I rode there with my mom in her car while my brothers rode with my dad in the Bentley.

"We have a surprise for you, Scarlett." My mom had told me as she helped me exit the car. I was still a little wobbly from being off my feet for four days but at least I wasn't being forced to ride in a wheelchair like they insisted upon before we left.

"Oh yeah, what is it?" I asked.

I was hoping that she was going to tell me that her and my dad had worked out their differences and were back together again. But that's not what she had for me at all. I heard the roar of an engine and gravel crunched underneath tires from the driveway. Oh crap! THE BEAST had been still available and my dad bought it from the guy all over again. NOOOO!

I saw pink instead of rusty blue. And it was new paint and not chipped or anything. This wasn't THE BEAST they were giving me, was it? Nope! The car that they were giving me was a 1967 Chevrolet Camaro Convertible customized to my liking. Like I said before, it was pink in color with black, exotic flower designs and swirls on the side and hood. The interior was cream colored suede and a pair of pink dice hung from the rearview mirror. It was beautiful!

"Thank you so much!"

My mom was the closest person to me so she was the one I latched onto and started to hug tightly, trying to remember I am much, much stronger than I used to be in the process. After my dad exited the car, I hugged him just as much as my mom. And then I did something that would probably draw attention to me in a bad way. I ran to the car and hugged the hood of it. I even kissed it! But hey, this *is* the best car in the world after all!

"We figured since you've been in the hospital, we'd give you your birthday present a bit early." My mom said happily.

My stomach clenched and my insides twisted at something she had said. Not quite knowing what it was yet, I dismissed it out of my mind and hopped in the driver's seat of the car. I wasn't planning on taking it anywhere (I probably wasn't in the best condition to drive yet) but just sitting in the thing made it all seem too real or something. Everyone else went inside but I stayed in my new car. I finally knew why Max has been so attached to his Mustang all these years. Just the fact that it's yours gives you the biggest high ever! I shut my eyes and listened to the sound of the engine purring.

"Sweet ride!"

It was the voice of the unknown speaker inside of my head. I tried to ignore it the best I could because I knew Gunnar would soon find out what he said and start an argument up. Its how things normally work inside of my head. He will say something Gunnar doesn't like and it will be a battle of words until one of them gives up. And let me tell you, they are both *really* stubborn!

"Are you deaf?"

'Shut up John!' It's the nickname I've given the unknown one. You know, as in John Doe.

'Sorry to say sweetheart, but this time, it's real,' Gunnar said to me.

My eyes shot open and saw a stranger kneeling against my door with his arms crossed and his head resting against them. He had a smile on which blinded me. I was so embarrassed I couldn't even begin to put it into words for all of you to read.

"Umm, sorry, I guess I must have . . . dozed off or something," I told the handsome stranger.

"It's alright. You just move in?" He asked me.

"Yeah, my dad just bought the house a few days ago and we're in the process of getting everything over here."

"Where are you from?"

"Beverly Hills," I answered him.

"Ooo, California girl, huh? Well, welcome to the neighborhood. My name is Griffon Hallowell."

He stuck his hand out and waited for me to shake it. I took it in my hand and replied back with, "Scarlett Hera."

"And she has a semi-famous name people! This girl has it all!"

He finally stood up, putting his arms up in the air as to be funny, giving me a perfect opportunity to fully look him over. He was several inches taller than Gunnar and Caleb but not freakishly tall. The first thing I noticed was his eyes. What can I say; I have a thing for eye color. Griffon's were teal . . . half way in between blue and green, and ever so clear. Next thing I noticed was his smile. His teeth were perfectly straight and shining white as if he brushes ten times a day. He had longer hair that curled at the back of his neck and was espresso brown. His features were sharp yet had a certain boyish charm to them. He was definitely good looking! And funny to boot, how often does that happen?

A black SUV pulled into the driveway, right next to my new car, and I had to hold my breath for it had gotten so close to mine, I swear it was going to hit. It didn't, thank God, and Portia hopped out shortly after putting it in park.

"Hey Scar', I thought I'd come over and help your family with moving and stuff."

It was the first time I've seen Portia wear something other than designer or designer looking clothes. She was dressed in a pair of men's blue basketball shorts with a t-shirt she had cut the sleeves off. You could see her sports bra through the holes in the sides of the shirt but nothing to worry about. Black sandals were her shoe apparel and her hair was tied up in a loose bun and out of her face. Honestly, even when she doesn't even *try* she looks beautiful! Now tell me, is that fair?

"Oh, hey Griffon, what's going on?" Portia asked, only looking at him from the corner of her eye.

Griffon did a mock bow toward Portia and said, "Madam," to her. She sneered at him and turned back to me. What was with the cold shoulder? You see, this is why I wish everyone new you meet would come with an instruction manual. It would certainly have come in handy if something simply said 'Keep Portia away from Griffon'.

"Well, I'll leave you two beautiful ladies to your work. I hope to see you around soon." Griffon said to me.

"OK, see you later," I replied.

"Bye Griffon," Portia bit out seething.

Griffon left, leaving me to glare at Portia for how rude she had been to him for no apparent reason. Wondering so strongly why Portia dislikes him so much, I decided to talk to her about it. And she will answer me whether she likes it or not . . . because now she can't threaten me with her sharp, vampire teeth for I have a pair myself to fight back with.

"What?" She sounded guilty.

"Why were you so mean to Griffon?"

"I barely said ten words to the guy." She quipped.

This was true. I don't think she even spoke ten words the entire time to him. That was somewhat of a tipoff in my eyes that something happened between them to put them in such horrible terms.

"You seemed so . . . cold, when you were around him. Why?"

"Well, I'm hungry! What do you say we go inside and have ourselves a quick snack before starting to unload?"

She started to walk away from me in order to further avoid the question, but I stopped her by saying, "Portia, get your skinny, immortal butt back here this instant and tell me what's going on!"

Portia turned her head to me and it was then that I saw the remnants of tears swimming in her eyes. Griffon had done something to her! And I had been so sure that she was the one to hurt him, with the way she was

174

behaving and all. But no girl cries after she had been the one to hurt some guy. It's usually the opposite. Did he break her heart or something? But Portia didn't seem to be too torn up when she lost David. Well, the first time she lost him anyway. Remember, her life mate is my brother after all. So why would she be this torn up about something he did?

"Please tell me why you acted the way you did just a minute ago." I begged.

Portia let out a deep, long breath before stating, "Griffon had an older sister. She was murdered about ten years ago after walking home from the park late one night. They never found her killer, or a body to bury in the town's cemetery. She was barely nine years old."

The tears had fallen from her eyes and were now streaming down her snow white cheeks. Something was really bothering her about this story and now I'm not quite so sure if I want to hear the rest of it or not.

Portia looked straight at me and said in the most eerie of tones, "Her name was Kate."

# Chapter 34

MY MOUTH HUNG WIDE OPEN as I stood there in shock of what Portia had just revealed. Well, actually I really didn't understand what she was trying to reveal to me fully. What did Griffon's older sister having the same name as Portia's niece have to do with anything? I mean, she didn't even know I knew about Kate! So why was she telling me about Griffon's older sister? Unless . . .

"You don't mean . . . "

"I was going through a bit of a phase," she didn't hear me, "where I wanted to be alone and away from my parents. It's normal for a vampire after several hundred years to stray from the path and try life on their own for a while. When I stumbled on this town, I didn't realize how thirsty I was.

"It had been almost three days since I fed and my throat felt like it was on fire because it was so dry. I didn't plan on doing anything but she looked so appetizing, I couldn't help myself. I cornered her between the slides and I just . . . attacked her. It was the worst feeling, seeing her lying there on the ground writhing in pain . . . so I took her back to my parents and they helped her out. She's been living with us ever since under the disguise of being my niece."

"Time out, I have a question. How do you hide Kate from her real parents then? I mean, wouldn't they see her at some point in time?" I asked.

"Kate's convinced that she is my sister and she's too dangerous and new to be out in the real world. My mom home school's her and she stays in the shop and reads books most of the time. It's sad but she's still waiting to turn seventeen like me."

Thinking about Kate's innocence and naivety made me finally get why my insides had twisted earlier when my mom mentioned my birthday. I wouldn't be turning seventeen this year or any year after that. Due to Portia biting me a few days before-hand, I would be forever sixteen. But it did stir up some interesting questions for me though. Like how come Kate, Jackie and I have different shades of eye color than Portia and her dad? Or how is it that Portia has managed to stay seventeen years old when she was born a vampire?

While walking into the house, I came up with a great idea to bond like we used to.

"Hey, how about we play twenty questions?"

"OK, sounds like fun!"

"OK, first question is, what was up with the insult match between my brother and you in the hospital?"

Her eyes narrowed as she sat down on one of the counters. She didn't want to answer the question I threw out to her . . . well too bad! Granted, I already knew the answer, but that's not the point. She needs to know that I know what's happening between the two of them and I'm perfectly fine with it.

"Promise not to tell anyone?"

I silently nodded.

"He's my Vilis Futurus. I'm in love with him but I don't think I should be."

"Why do you say that?" I asked her, taking a seat on the kitchen floor and leaning against one of the cabinets.

"Because I believe in free will and he obviously didn't have the slightest interest in me. So if he doesn't want me, I'm not going to challenge what he wants."

You see, I *could* tell her about the whole 'drooling when he saw her' thing. But I'm not going to, unless Max wants her to know that. Or he makes me furious, either excuse will do. I really do hope that he's the one who tells her about his feelings in the long run. I'd hate to ruin the perfect moment for them, if it ever comes.

"So, have you ever been in love?"

My hand reflexively roamed up to the partially embossed heart and key on my neck. And before all of you start in on me for thinking about Caleb again, SHUT UP! Obviously you've never been in love!

"Yes," I shyly answered.

"What was his name?"

"I-I don't want to bring him up again. The heartbreak was too strong and I'd rather not relive it." I lied . . . well, sort of. But for good reason! I couldn't tell her I was in love with Caleb when Caleb barely knows who

I am. And she probably would think that I barely knew him, seeing as I "just met him" a few days ago. So for the moment, I needed to bend the truth as far as I can.

"Has there been any other vampire ever with more than one Vilis Futurus?"

"Not that I know of. I suppose it's possible but it's never happened before. My family, at least, has all had only one."

Well that's just fantastic! I really am as much of a freak as my aunt led on after bringing out those stupid prophecies. Why me?

"When's your birthday?" She asked me.

"July 4th."

Her eyes brightened up and a smile appeared on her face. I already knew what was going on in her mind. Portia is like some sort of social butterfly that needs to help others achieve popularity if it's the last thing she does. Not that it's a bad thing, but it can get annoying.

"Yes, you are invited to my party."

Her smile became wider.

"Why do I have a different eye color than you?" I asked her.

"Because those who are turned have vampire blood given to them by a third party instead of being born with it. My mother is the same way as you and Kate. She was bitten when she was twenty two by my father. They were each other's Vilis Futurus and he thought it was time for her to become a vampire."

Well, now that I know more of the story behind her parents I feel a bit better about them. Not that I've met them yet . . . in this dimension . . . but it's only a matter of time.

"What brings you to Willow Creek?" She asked me.

"My dad was having an affair with his assistant so my mom left him and came back here, where she was born and raised. I talked some sense into my dad about winning her back but my mom isn't that into the fact that he's come here. She doesn't think that it's really what he wants, so it will take some time . . . but I'm not complaining."

"So *that's* why your mom said she had to be home soon. I was so confused."

Portia was the only person I told about this. I know how well she is with secrets and she won't be blabbing my parent's dilemma any time soon. So I was perfectly at ease with her knowing this about my life. Anything deeper than this, and I was in trouble.

"How is it that you're seventeen forever when you were born a vampire? What was your childhood like?" I asked her.

"My childhood was just like yours. I grew up from a baby to a toddler and so on at a normal rate, just stopped growing when I reached my current age. Every vampire that's born into this sort of family goes through a normal childhood. As for the staying seventeen part . . . my dad was seventeen when he was turned. It tends to settle upon the eldest of your parents and he so happens to be it. Actually, that's why his eyes are so blue because he's so much older than the rest of us." She replied.

"How old is he?"

She began to count on her fingers while silently counting in her head. It was taking her quite a while to answer the question, which made me think he was older than dirt . . . literally.

"Almost fifteen centuries old now."

My mouth hung open. I would probably never be able to stand in his presence again and not think about everything he's been through. Could you imagine living through that much change in your whole life? How far medicinal advances came and how many lives they've saved. How many wars to be a part of and survive like that. How many loved ones to watch die while you live on forever. Honestly, I will never look at Andrew the same way *ever* again!

"How old are you?"

"Oh, I'm just over a century and a half old. I was born in 1870 a few years after my mother was turned in her hometown of Pinos Altos, New Mexico."

So she probably has Mexican blood running in her veins. That's why her eyes look like they do. I bet if she wasn't a vampire, her tan would be wicked in the summer and all of the girls at school would be jealous of it. I'm saving her dad's nationality for my next question.

"What's your biggest secret?"

Well I wasn't expecting *that*! Should I tell her my actual biggest secret or make one up for her benefit. Because I'm pretty sure if I tell her what I am—other than a vampire—she won't want to be my friend anymore. She could possibly think I'm insane even. And I don't want Portia to think that about me. She *is* my best friend after all. Or . . . will be, at one point, right?

But then there might be some bonuses to having her know everything about me. I'd have someone to talk to about it that's not my brother or my creepy aunt. And she was the one asking me, not like I'm just blurting it out randomly and freaking her out. So I should tell her, right? Whatever, I'm going to tell her whether it's the right thing to do or not. She should know what she's getting herself into before we become any closer.

"My biggest secret . . . is that I'm psychic." I told her while fiddling with my fingers nails, trying to avoid eye contact as much as possible.

"Cool!"

Did I just hear her correctly?

"What? But-but Portia, I just told you I was psychic . . . you know, as in I can see the future."

"Yeah, I heard you. And I think that it's cool."

"You believe me?"

"Of course! Why wouldn't I believe my friend?" she asked with a smile and a small giggle. I couldn't imagine how at ease she was with what I am. You would think she'd be in denial or at least think I'm lying to sound better than I was. But she honestly believed everything I told her because she thought we were friends. How sweet is that?

So she and I now know almost everything about each other. Portia knows about my glimpse and that she and I were best friends before. I know that she's Mexican/Greek and sometimes regrets being a vampire. And we both hate peanut butter and popcorn. With the way this all started, who would have thought that our friendship was even possible?

# Chapter 35

𝒥 FOUND MY BROTHER SITTING POOLSIDE, sulking over his lack of new car. He was wrong about his birthday present and instead had gotten a new computer. Yeah, he wasn't too happy with them after that. So all throughout our birthday party they threw us (with the help of Portia, of course) he hadn't said one word to anyone. And that's when he went missing and I had to be the one to go and find him.

Since we've moved to Willow Creek, he's been slowly gaining his weight back. Now he doesn't look like a scary skeleton man! He has a long way to go before he reaches a healthy place, but I'm happy that he's at least trying to get better.

"Hey, cheer up Kurt Cobain," I nudged him in the arm as I sat down, "It's your seventeenth birthday. Don't worry, be happy!"

Don't ask me why I was in such a good mood; I don't know the answer to that. But I was. It was like nothing in the world could bother me that day and I was truly happy. And if I was going to be happy, so would everyone else! Otherwise they just might bring me down and I certainly don't want that.

"Leave me alone, Scarlett." He scowled.

"Aw come on, what's the matter?"

"I don't want to talk about it!"

Now he was mad.

His eyes were fixated on something off in the distance and weren't moving from that spot. I followed his gaze to the sliding glass door leading into the kitchen. There, a group of people stood in front of it talking animatedly to one another. One specific brunette vampire was touching a boy's shoulder and laughing at a joke he must have told. Now I understand what his problem is!

The boy Portia had been flirting with is Alex Johnson. He's not very popular but he's *very* good looking. I wouldn't expect anything less for Portia to flirt with. She doesn't deserve anything less.

Alex's café-au-lait skin color complemented her snow white tone perfectly. I know, surprising to accept, but it's true. His head is shaved and he's a bit taller than Portia. I've only met him once but he's really nice. He happens to be good friends with Griffon so I know that laugh Portia had just pulled off was completely genuine. The crowd that both of them hang out with are downright hilarious.

"Let it go, bro! Just . . . let it go." I told him as I patted his back.

I couldn't take his depressed mood anymore! So I stood up and made my way to where Portia and the group of people were. Max wouldn't be happy to know where I had gone, but he was being a sour puss and I don't associate with downers at my birthday party. Even though I will forever be sixteen and won't experience an actual birthday ever again. When I had reached the group, several people scattered leaving just the three of us.

"Well, seems like you two are enjoying the party . . . unlike some people." I broke the ice.

Portia and Alex looked over to the pool where Max was sitting and Portia scoffed at him. I couldn't blame her, really. She could hear his thoughts inside of her head and I'm sure they aren't too pleasant at the current moment. Actually, they were probably the last thing that Portia wanted to hear right now. Who wants to hear their life mate whine while you're trying to flirt with an incredibly cute guy?

Somebody had come up behind me and placed their hands over my eyes while asking, "Guess who?"

Speaking of life mates . . .

"Oh, hey Griffon! What's up?"

He removed his hands and stood at my side. I loved the fact that his tall frame towered over my own. It felt right that he was so much taller than me. In a way, it was like he could protect me better. Like . . . a better vantage point to see any evil coming toward me. But in reality, I have the "gift" to see what's going to happen before it does. So I guess that's my job, so to speak.

"So are we going to the fair this weekend or what?" He asked me.

"Depends . . . are you going to buy me cotton candy and win me one of those giant stuffed bears?"

"I only live to serve my Queen," he bowed. "Of course I will."

"Are you two coming along?" I asked Portia and Alex.

Ever since Portia confided her little secret about Griffon's older sister to me, their relationship has improved immensely. I can't say that I'm complaining, because Griffon and I have become close over the last month. He *is* my next door neighbor after all. We were bound to run into each other frequently so why not just form a friendship? Although, hearing his voice inside of my head made it a bit awkward on my part.

"Why would we miss it?"

"'Cause we be . . . Going to the fair, going to the fair . . . " Alex began in a country accent, slapping his knee and hopping up and down, and soon enough, Griffon caught on. Pretty soon their arms were linked and they were performing a hoedown right in the middle of the party. Portia and I were clutching our sides and trying to control our laughter.

They eventually stopped and we were back to talking. See, I told you, they are hilarious. Especially when you get them together.

"Does anyone want something to drink?" I asked them.

"Umm, I'll take a Coca Cola," Griffon replied.

"Me too," Portia followed.

"None for me thank you," Alex said politely.

"Ok, I'll be right back then."

I slowly walked over to the food and drink table on the other side of the lawn and reached inside of the cooler to grab three Coke's. Something didn't feel right when I had looked around my party. Where was Caleb? Did he realize he was invited to this thing for being my brother's friend? Did he want to be here? You see, Caleb and I really haven't talked since I had been released from the hospital a few weeks before. I know, I know, it's been too long for a fight to continue between us, but I am not going to be the first one to break down and apologize for something I didn't do. He didn't really do anything either, but that's not the point in all of this.

"Hey, need some help with those?"

Caleb's voice was right behind me as he started to grab two of the sodas from my full hands.

"No, I do not need any help!" I gritted through my teeth as I clutched the sodas closer to my chest so he couldn't take them. For one minute, I could have sworn that they were going to be crushed underneath my vice grip, but they weren't. Thankfully. I turned my back toward him and started to walk back when his hand lightly took hold of my elbow. He twirled me around and looked at me with those innocent brown eyes. Why me?

"How long are you going to stay mad at me?" He asked with a weak smile.

"As long as it takes for you to realize that I'm not worth sitting in a hospital for more than two hours each day."

He began to laugh at me. Yeah, that made me mad.

"Fine, I'll admit that you aren't worth sitting in a hospital for two hours each day if you stop hating me."

"I could never hate you Caleb," I whispered under my breath. No doubt in my mind that he heard every word, however.

"Fine," I said aloud.

Griffon had called my name from off in the distance. I turned around and saw him waving at me with a large smile on his face. He was sure a happy person, for the most part. I've never actually seen him angry or anything like that since I've known him. I waved back.

"Figures," I heard Caleb grumble behind me.

"What do you mean by that?"

"Huh?"

He was obviously shocked that I heard something that was so quiet to him. Oh well, no point in taking the time to explain right now.

"Why did you say 'figures' when I waved at Griffon?" I asked him angrily.

"Nothing at all."

"You obviously meant something when you said it; otherwise you wouldn't have said it! So if you don't tell me right now what you meant by it, I'm leaving and never talking to you ever—"

"Alright, alright, it's just . . . he's a clown."

"And what exactly are you?" I asked crossing my arms tighter over the sodas.

"Well, I'm better than him!" he said a little loud.

"You might think you're better than him, but you aren't. I don't want to *ever* hear you say that you're better than any of my friends ever again! Nobody is better than anyone else. No matter how much money their daddy has in his bank account."

"How did you . . . ?"

"Need some help over here, Scarlett?"

Griffon had come to my rescue no doubt after hearing Caleb's voice raise earlier. It's not that I will ever need protection from Caleb but I was glad that Griffon had come over. It stopped the argument and future explanations I might owe Caleb have been put on hold for a while.

Griffon, however, was in a very protective stance next to me. His shoulders were squared and his jaw was set. It was as if he was trying to make his presence known to Caleb. Like he was capable of saving me even though Caleb could rip Griffon to shreds without even trying. Not that Griffon knew this or anything. But I think it was purely a male thing. Caleb, however, just simply smirked at Griffon's demeanor.

"Nope, I was just about to head back," I answered.

"Good, let's go then."

Griffon wrapped an arm around my shoulder and started to guide me away from the food and drink table. Mostly away from Caleb, though. I will never be able to understand boys in the least. But I suppose it's on equal territory considering they will never understand us either.

"Thank you Griffon for getting me out of there."

"No problem! Just think of me as your guardian."

And just like that, hearing that phrase slip out of his mouth, it all became clear to me. I already knew that his voice had sounded similar to the unknown in my head. But this right here confirms that he is, in fact, the third voice. The scroll's words began to replay themselves in my head.

"The Guardian will be an unexpected suitor for the Savior. He will be the most beautiful man in history and will be in the Savior's life well before she begins to love him. He will always grace her side for his love for her runs deep within his soul."

I don't know if I'd consider Griffon to be the most beautiful man in history, but he is very good looking. As far as I'm concerned, Caleb is the most beautiful thing I have ever seen. Not that I would tell him any time soon, but I hope he knows this. After everything he just said, however, I need to do some re-evaluating on his character. Nothing will hinder my feelings for him, though.

I just wish we get whatever it is between us resolved soon. I miss having Caleb in my life, no matter if it's just as a friend or perhaps more, later down the line. Caleb has my whole heart in his hands and he could do either of two things with it; crush it . . . or love it back.

# Chapter 36

GRIFFON IS A REALLY GREAT guy, but he is terrible with heights. If you ever put him on a dinky little Farris Wheel, he will whimper the whole time. Don't think I'm making fun of him, because I'm not. OK, well maybe I'm making fun of him a little . . . but you should have seen his face! That was mean, I'm sorry, and I didn't mean to make it sound like he is a wimp.

The day went by fast and before any of us knew it, the night sky had taken over the fair grounds. Alex and Portia had gone off to ride another ride (because Alex isn't afraid of heights) while Griffon and I stayed on the ground. He said he wanted to prove to me that he isn't a complete and total wuss and win me that bear I had been talking about a few days previously. Lucky for him, it only took two tries to knock down the milk bottles.

"Five years of baseball will give you killer aim," he told me as we started to walk around again.

So, you know how I said before that Caleb is the only one with my heart? That's not exactly true anymore. Oh, he still and forever will hold the biggest piece of it, but there are two others with their own pieces too. Portia and Griffon being the two. Portia is like the sister I never had and it feels right to say that she will always be in my life as such. Griffon . . . well, Griffon's a different story.

I don't know what it is about him that I like most, but whenever I look at him, I feel as if I'm betraying Caleb. He doesn't give me those same shock waves when he touches me like Caleb does, but there is still a spark somewhere and it frightens me. What does it mean? I don't want to like Griffon more than I love Caleb and that's how it's turning out to be. Is it possible to fall in love with two guys at the same time?

"Do you want some cotton candy?" He asked me.

"Wasn't that part of the agreement to come here with you?"

"Ooo, touché! I'll be right back." And he was off.

I took the time to wander around for a short time. I won a goldfish by tossing a little yellow ball in his tank. I wonder how Angel will take the new addition to our family. Will he try and eat Freddy the fish or leave him alone? Griffon was still not back with my cotton candy and I spotted one of my favorite attractions . . . the fun house.

I bought my ticket and entered the house of creepy looking mirrors. This was a bit scarier than I had thought. They put clown faces on the top of the mirrors and in corners and such and add the creepy music they were playing; it would be a perfect setting for a horror flick. Being inside made me paranoid and skittish but I couldn't find my way out. It would have been alright in the daytime to go through this particular attraction . . . but at night, not at all. How pathetic is this, a vampire afraid of mirrors? I suppose some things don't change with genetic mutation.

Someone was laughing maniacally in the background. I don't know if it was a part of the show or what but it made me quicken my pace and made me frantically start searching for the exit. A hand shot out from out of nowhere and grabbed a hold of my wrist painfully. *And I was a vampire!* That hand pulled me forcefully up against another body and the smell of someone all-too-familiar wafted up my nose. Another arm wrapped around my waist and held me in place.

"Just look at how great we look together."

Gunnar's voice was dripping with venom and hate while he was trying to sound loving. His nose pressed into my neck and inhaled the scent of me. I cringed away from him but it did no good. While struggling to become free of his grip, he pulled me outside from the back door located behind a curtain. This was just too much!

He slammed me against the trailer holding the fun house inside and pinned me against it with his body. His midsection was keeping me firmly in place and I couldn't move an inch. But I was still trying!

"Stop fighting me, Scarlett. You know you want me, too."

"I will never want you, Gunnar . . . just like the prophecy says!"

He knew about it too from hearing it inside of my head so why not call him out on the truth.

"The prophecy is just a silly piece of paper that means nothing!" he growled while trying to kiss me on the mouth.

I twisted my head away from his reach and bit out, "you will never be anything to me but a lowly, slimy snake!"

"Why you little—you'll pay for that!"

His teeth slid out of his mouth and his eyes turned blue. To defend myself, I let my own canines slide down in case of an emergency. But I didn't have to use them. No, because before I could register what was happening, Gunnar was being ripped away from me by an unknown force. I couldn't be happier that someone had come to help me, even though I didn't know who it was. But once I did know, the feeling of worry rushed through me.

"Stop it! Both of you; stop it *right now!*" I yelled to the fighting boys rolling around on the ground.

I didn't get any further than that, however, because a vision had interrupted everything else in front of me. A head rush had swept my brain and everything went black.

> *I was in Willow Creek forest near dusk, looking over what appeared to be a battle scene. Everything was eerily quiet and the rain was falling against my face in large, hard drops. Bodies were lying on the forest floor and blood was everywhere. I could hear snaps and growls followed by a distinct, wolfish howl a few yards in front of me. When I looked up, my ears had not betrayed me. There, taking enormous chunks out of an already dead wolf beneath him was a very large, very ferocious looking white wolf. And next to him was yet another, grey wolf tearing at the flesh of the dead one as well.*
>
> *I began to look around me as everything began to sink in. The bodies lying at my feet were my family members and friends. My mom's body was lying against a tree near me. Blood was escaping her mouth but her body was still and unmoving. Next to her was my father, draped over her legs and clearly dead. On the other side of me was Max's battered body. The wolves had really done a number on him. Lying next to him, holding his limp hand, was Portia. Her cheeks still had black streaks on them from what were so obvious, tears she had cried for my brother's death. It was as if every bone in her body had been broken.*
>
> *To my surprise . . . and confusion . . . Angel's body was also lying motionless on the ground underneath a*

*tree. Why was he dead? What did he ever do to these wolves that deserved to die for? He is my Spirit animal; was he protecting me from them?*

*I began to approach the wolves and, shockingly enough, they didn't even see me. It was as if I was completely invisible to them and could do whatever I wanted. To be honest, the only thing I was curious about was who they were tearing apart. Although I had a pretty good feeling of who it was, I still needed confirmation. But, as I stepped closer to them, the feeling of denial washed over me. This isn't real and yet I am feeling as if it all happened just a few moments ago . . . right in front of me. And I did nothing to stop it. What could I have done, though?*

*I peered over the ravenous wolves and saw exactly what I had feared. A deep grey wolf with black all around its face and a streak of white going along the top of its back had been mutilated. This particular wolf I knew all too well. This particular wolf had his eyes permanently opened and as I stared into those cold, yellow walls of nothingness, I began to cry.*

"Scarlett? Scarlett, are you alright?"

Caleb's voice sounded worried and yet so calm and loving. My eyes fluttered open as I heard him call my name one more time. Boy, I could listen to him talk for days!

"Oh thank God, you're OK!"

I was lying down on hard ground with dirt and grass poking into my flesh at odd angles. It was very uncomfortable, let me tell you! Not that I had passed out and hit the ground below me, no, but the fact that a lot of people were looking down at me as if I was a sideshow freak . . . yeah, that would do it. God, I'm so humiliated!

"What happened?" I asked groggily while attempting to sit up by myself. Both Caleb and Griffon stepped in to help after they had seen I couldn't do it alone.

"You just passed out." Caleb stated. "I thought he had done something to you to make you do that. Did he?"

I knew who Caleb was talking about, but he didn't want to say it in front of everyone at the fair. So he kept it in code as I shook my head no. Thankfully, his tight expression loosened a fair amount after he knew the truth. Well, the only truth he wanted to hear that is. I doubt Caleb wants to hear about me being psychic or what part of my prophecy he takes place in. He'd be a little creeped if I just busted out and told him that he and I are meant to be forever and he's supposed to die for me after I had just fainted.

Everyone cleared away from me after they found out I was alright.

"So much for a fun evening at the fair, huh? I'm sorry Griffon."

He had pulled me into a hug and said, "Are you kidding?! I'm just happy you're alright. Thought you'd gone into another coma for a second there."

I heard Caleb cough behind me and knew what I had to do.

"Thanks but I'm fine. Can you take me home though?"

"Yeah, just let me find Portia and Alex and then we'll leave."

"Alright," and then he left.

I turned to Caleb with an innocent smile on my face in hopes of lightening his mood. But as I expected, his stance, facial expression and demeanor screamed anger, but his eyes whispered hurt. Why must he force me to sit back and watch him do this to himself when there is such a simple solution? All he has to do is dump Shaylee and ask me out. I'll say yes in an instant! But I have a feeling that's not going to happen any time soon. Oh well, I can wait forever for Caleb . . . I don't want to, but I can.

'Why did she hug that dweeb and not me? I'm the one who saved her from Gunnar. Why don't I get a—'

I interrupted his thoughts by wrapping my arms around his waist and squeezing just a tad. After a few seconds of surprise on his part, he warmed up to me and followed suit by putting his arms around me as well.

It wasn't the same burning fire like before. No, it sort of dissipated into a slow, buzzing hum between our bodies as we hugged each other. I loved how perfectly our bodies fit together. It was like magic! I could stay in his arms my whole life (however long that might be) and I'd be perfectly content. Why does he have to fight this force between us?

'Oh crap, Shaylee's coming!' he thought.

Instead of waiting for the hurt to seep in as he quickly pulled away from me, I was the one who ended the hug.

"Thank you very much for saving me tonight. I owe you one," I told him.

"You're welcome and you don't owe me anything. Consider it an apology for the way I've been treating you ever since you've arrived in Willow Creek."

"Apology accepted."

"Oh there you are Kay-Kay!"

Kay-Kay?

"I've been looking all over the fair for you! What were you doing without me?"

To stake her territory on Caleb, she put her arm through his and glared at me, pulling him as close to her as she could. You see, this is how females mark what's there's in society. They rub it in their competitions face what they have to prove that they are the best. This will not end until the competition either moves away or gets a boyfriend themselves and leaves the first prize alone. Lucky for me, Griffon walked up at the very same moment this was happening.

"You ready?" he asked me.

"Almost."

"Ahh, if it isn't the fair Miss Morgan. What bringeth you to these fine festivities on this, such a beautiful evening?"

"Huh?" She asked with a befuddled expression.

Griffon was mocking her intelligence. Remember when I was explaining to you all that Shaylee is the most idiotic person you will ever meet? Well, this proves it! And I couldn't help but giggle under my breath as Griffon insulted her without actually insulting her. It was just too perfect of an opportunity to pass up!

"He asked you why you two came to the fair tonight," I answered for Griffon.

"Oh, well Kay-Kay has to work the next three nights at the auto shop so he thought he'd be a good boyfriend and bring me tonight. Wasn't that sweet of him?"

"Almost too sweet I think he's given you a cavity," Griffon retorted.

"What?!" She was spazzing out. She opened her mouth and started to tap her teeth and even brought out a small make-up mirror from her pocket to look inside of her mouth. Seriously, this girl was ridiculous!

"He was just making a joke, Shaylee." Caleb reassured her.

"Oh, well it wasn't very funny!"

"To you," I mumbled.

"Daisy, Robin and her date are waiting for us by the Tilt-O-Whirl, Kay-Kay." Shaylee said to Caleb.

One hundred bucks says that Robin's date is Max! Earlier he told me he was going out, but he never mentioned any specifics. He's still trying to get over the empty feeling inside of him in any way possible. And so he's discovered Robin a few days before the fair. I believe Caleb introduced the two of them after Shaylee heard he was single. Oh well, it's Max's business to sort through his feelings. I'll try and hold off as long as I can without interfering any. But I can't make any promises!

Griffon and I began to walk to his car shortly after Caleb and Shaylee had left our sights. He asked a few questions about Caleb and me and our history together, but I just told him that we were friends and it was no big deal. This was true . . . at the time. I think he accepted it, I can never be sure.

Portia sat next to me in the back for a change as the two boys were in front. We were a little ways down the road when Portia asked me this:

"What happened tonight?"

She asked it in a whisper so that neither boy could hear it. I just dismissed answering her and told her that I would tell her all about it when we got back to my house. She was staying overnight so I had plenty of time to explain everything in wonderful detail . . . including the vision I had when I passed out. I think she will be very excited to know what I saw, but after she hears the entire thing, I don't know how excited she will be.

The situation between Caleb and I will probably be confusing for a long time. I have no idea what will go on between the two of us right now, but I hope everything is sorted out as fate intended. If it doesn't . . . the ending to my story will probably not include a happily ever after!

# Chapter 37

*I*T'S NEVER EASY . . . BEING A vampire in love with a werewolf. Especially if the werewolf doesn't know you're in love with him. Don't get me wrong; I'm happy to be in love, I really am. But sometimes I wish I was in love with someone of my own species.

I've been a vampire exactly three months now so I don't know everything there is to know about being one. Lucky for me, I have a best friend who's also a vampire. She's the only one who knows what I really am, because she's the one that made me this way. Not that I'm blaming her anymore, because I'm not, but I do sometimes wish she wouldn't have. But then again, who wouldn't wish that? Oh sure, you have eternal life and powers beyond your wildest dreams . . . but who would want all of that without love?

And now I have to endure the love of my life dating some ditzy cheerleader and not say one word about it. Talk about your extreme pain! Anyone that's been turned knows that it hurts more than anything to get bitten. As your soul dies, it feels as if (while it's leaving you) you've been submerged in freezing, arctic ice water and you can't move anything. You feel as if hypothermia should have set in hours ago . . . but it doesn't. You feel everything and anything imaginable when you become a vampire! I'd rather be forced to sit through being bitten again and again before I'd ever want to see Caleb and Shaylee together. I only want him to be happy, though, and that is exactly why I keep my mouth shut.

It just (excuse the pun) sucks that I can't tell him how I feel whenever I'm around him. And considering my mom lives at his house now, I happen to run into him more than I wish to.

I am, however, learning things about him that I never knew before. I still have that sketch he made of me up on my wall . . . at my dad's house of course. I don't know how he'd take it if he ever saw it hanging anywhere in the room I sleep in at his house.

Oh, and did I mention that Caleb's dad is filthy rich? Oh, I did? Oh well, I get to brag just a bit about this, because you'd never believe it any other way. House is not the appropriate term to use where Caleb lives. It's a huge mansion just a few miles away from town. I have my own room close to my mom's in the west wing even though I only stay there about once a week or so. It's a nice room complete with a beautiful dark mahogany bed post, but it always seemed so . . . cold to me. I can't explain it any other way than that. It's probably because his dad casts this creepy aura around the entire house.

He's always working in his den save for dinner time. My mom is the only one who can get him to come out of that place and to be honest, I don't like it one bit. They aren't dating (I don't think) and yet I know for a fact that Jack Darwin has the hots for my mom. It's disgusting, I know, but I can't really blame him. She's a very beautiful and smart woman with loads going on for her. But to think about anyone other than my dad loving my mom is just *weird*! I don't like it.

'Good thing you received most of your mom's looks, otherwise I might not like you as much!'

'Shut up Gunnar!'

Portia says that I should practice using my powers so that I don't end up hurting anyone by accident. Lately, she and I have been going running every morning just to release stress and what not. But you see, when vampires run, it's nothing like humans. We run the full length of Montana—which usually only takes us about thirty minutes to an hour—cut through to the middle and climb Granite Peak. It's the highest point in Montana but it's easy as pie for Portia and me to climb. We don't have to breathe, for future reference. She hasn't taken me to test my strength yet, but I'm pretty sure I'd have that down pat when she does.

She has, however, taken me into the forest to show me just how powerful my senses have become. It was the most amazing thing I've ever experienced. To feel the crisp morning air on my cold skin, see with perfect clarity every strand of light and color watching the sun rise, hear every forest animal, big and small. It was the most beautiful thing on Earth and I wish all of you could experience it just once.

There is one thing I hate about being a vampire and that is the smells. No, I don't mean anything disgusting by it! Things just smell different than before. Whenever I'm around my family members or any other human being, I smell an overpowering scent of chocolate. And it's true about how it's very hard for a woman to resist chocolate. But it's worse than that, because what's making them smell that way to me is their blood. They smell so warm and delicious; I have to take three doses of donated blood from Portia's parent's bookstore before I am around one. I've never tasted fresh human blood before, but Portia says that it's nothing like the ones we drink from bags.

And then there is our kind. We vampires smell more like cinnamon but it's not as strong as other scents. It's easy being around other vampires and not feel any hostile feelings toward them. I believe we only have this distinct aroma to warn any other vampire what we are. And this is why I'm very confused about Griffon. He still smells like chocolate, so why can he hear and respond to me in my head?

Werewolves smell different than humans or vampires. Whenever I'm around Caleb and his family, all I smell is vanilla. I've always loved vanilla so I can't help myself when I inhaled large amounts of oxygen around one of them. Caleb's little sister Emma loves to hang out with my in my room. Emma idolizes me for being three years older (even though I'm not) than her and already experienced high school. She makes it easy to catch sniffs here and there without being noticed. Mainly because she thinks I'm popular and has it drilled in her head that I would destroy her high school years if she said anything to make me angry. I wouldn't under any circumstances ever hate Emma that much. And besides, performing acts of shunning young adolescents for no particular reason what-so-ever is more of Daisy's forte.

Emma isn't as observant as her older brother which brings me to the beginning of this story. I was over at the Darwin mansion like I normally am every Sunday night. I had just changed into my boxers and t-shirt and snuggled into bed with my laptop about ready to start a new book when my door flew open and someone burst in without knocking.

"Hey Red, how's it hangin'?"

# Chapter 38

"Have you ever heard of knocking by any chance, Caleb? Or do you think just because you're the new football co-captain you can do anything?" I yelled at him.

"Hey, it's not easy being me!" He quipped.

"Oh yeah, why?"

"You try and go out in the streets being this good looking and talented and still act so calm and cool."

"I don't know if my brain could ever fathom being as conceited as you, Caleb." I retaliated.

He threw himself on my bed and disturbed my cat from his nap. Angel found me during the vision I had before and I've had him ever since. He's my spirit animal that the higher power sent me when I was receiving my own power. He follows me everywhere I go. The only other psychic I know has a cat as well, but she doesn't have one that looks like mine. I'm . . . special, even for a psychic. Angel hissed at Caleb, hopped off of my bed and ran out of the room.

'Stupid boy! Doesn't have manners!'

That was Griffon's voice giving his input on how Caleb just acted toward me. He's very chivalrous, but I can handle myself when it comes to this little show off. He's just a werewolf, after all.

"We start school tomorrow. Are you excited?" He asked me.

"Not really, no."

"Why not?"

"I've always been invisible at my other school. It's not the greatest feeling in the world when people walk past you without saying one word every day of your life."

'I don't think anyone would consider you invisible here!' Caleb's voice echoed in my head.

He was so sweet. I just wish I could tell him thank you for the things he thinks about me. But of course he doesn't know I can hear him, so I have to keep myself quiet. I've been taught ever since I was little to be polite and say thank you every time someone compliments me, but I can't. It makes me feel like a bad person or something. It's awful!

"I'm sorry you've been treated that way."

"It's alright; it's just what happens when you're the nerd." I responded.

'You deserve to be treated better'

'Oh please, this guy is such a sissy it's unreal!' Gunnar's voice followed Caleb's in my head.

'You're just jealous because he's getting further and further into my heart and you will never be able to,' I replied silently.

'Yeah, I'm really jealous of Mr. Football Star over here!'

"Well, it's getting late and I think I should go to bed." I said, ignoring the obvious fight brewing between Gunnar and me.

"OK, I just came in to tell you good luck tomorrow and that we leave at seven o'clock." Caleb beamed.

He stood from my bed and walked to my door. Abandonment flooded my emotions but I kept them locked inside. This usually happened when Caleb left me whether it is from my room or anywhere else. It's not my fault, it just happens and I can't stop it. As he exited, the feeling became stronger. I pushed it aside and climbed into my sheets to prepare for sleep. I was tired; there was no doubt about that. But, of course, the Higher Power couldn't leave me to slumber until I had a vision first.

I've only had one other since my first and it was something I didn't want to see. But this one was not as gruesome as the other. In fact, it was actually normal compared to the odd twists of the last one. Just like the last one, my eyes rolled in the back of my head and my body dropped down as if it weighed five hundred pounds. Luckily I had a soft mattress this time to protect me from the awful fall.

*I was walking down the hallway of a school I had not yet entered. People were passing me but did not see me. Not because I was "invisible" but because I was invisible. They seriously couldn't see me even if they tried. Teenagers kept bumping into me but only I could feel their touches. I was moving at an alarming rate through the building when I finally turned down another hallway. I have no idea where I was going or in which direction this thing was they so desperately wanted me to see, but it was weird.*

*Standing by light grey, regulation lockers, was a very familiar looking redhead surrounded by my friends. It was the first time I saw me in a vision ever. It was the weirdest thing imaginable to be looking at yourself acting like you normally do without a care in the world. That's what I was doing; just talking with my friends like nothing was wrong. Griffon, Alex, Caleb, Portia and Max were standing around me, which was odd, because Caleb and Max despise Griffon and Alex. There was no fighting going on, however, just talking.*

*"Did you hear we're getting a new student?" Griffon was the first I heard.*

*"Really? Boy or girl?" Max asked.*

*"Girl," he replied.*

*All of the boys smiled a sort of cheesy half smile which made my stomach churn. No doubt that the real me standing right there was feeling the same exact way. My eyes flew directly at Caleb the minute I noticed the other boys' expression. His was the same way as theirs. Now I felt like I was going to lose my dinner all over the fake hallway I was standing in.*

*"Pardon me," a very high pitched, feminine voice came from behind me.*

*The real me as well as the vision me looked to see who was asking us to move aside. A very petite yet big breasted girl stood there with books in her hand and a large, white smile on her face. Her long, bright blonde hair fell below her shoulders and down her back and took on a silky smooth appearance. Her eyes were pale blue and her features were perfectly symmetrical and there wasn't a single blemish on her skin. Her color reminded me of my own . . . pale and radiant. To make sure she wasn't a vampire, I smelled the air. Yup, she was human . . . with a hint of sea spray body wash. But if she still had her soul, why did she look like she does?*

*She gave a small cough to bring all of us back to attention and we moved three inches to the right. As if on purpose, her books fell to the ground and she let out a tiny, "oops" as she looked at them. The girl didn't even have to ask for help when the guys basically threw themselves on the floor in front of her, gathering up all of the spilt books for her. And what's more ridiculous is that Griffon and Caleb began to play tug-of-war with one of them. Not for fun, no, but to determine who would give it back to her. They were all like children over some girl they didn't even know. I mean, yes she's pretty. But that doesn't mean you should almost hurt yourself and others just to perform a simple task for her.*

*As I looked at the stranger, something inside of my blood boiled as if to warn me about her. There was certainly something wrong with this girl and the Higher Power obviously wants me to know about it. But what exactly could it be?*

I was thrown out of the vision in an instant and back into my bedroom once more. I have to admit, I was a bit disappointed that I couldn't see the rest of the vision to find out more. But there probably wasn't much I was missing. Otherwise the HP (Higher Power) would have let me stay longer to see it. What could possibly be dangerous about a pretty, new girl? Then again, Gunnar looks normal and he's going to try and use my powers for evil.

'Hey I resent that! I haven't figured out what I'm going to do yet.'

I knew he was going to say something like that. It made me smile most of the time to make fun of Gunnar just to see what he'll say.

'Well, aren't you just a wonderful person!'

'Yes, yes I am,' I responded sarcastically.

And he shut up. Finally! Peace and quiet so I could once and for all fall asleep. I bet you're all wondering why if I'm a vampire how I have to sleep. Everything you've heard about vampires—well, almost everything—isn't true, and I've learned that first hand. Yes, we have super strength and suck people's blood. But we can go out in sunlight, eat garlic whole (even though I prefer not to), touch crosses without burning and we can't turn into bats and fly away. I tried that once and nothing came of it.

The moment I closed my eyes, the dream I've been having for months entered my mind. It's weird to see, but nothing to concern myself about. Back in the early eighteen hundreds, the founder of the town, Robert Pauling, proposed to a woman named Katherine James. Katherine, however, didn't love Robert the way he loved her and ran off with a stable hand named Henry Ashford hours before the wedding. Every night, I've been having these strange dreams that I'm Katherine and Caleb is Henry. I don't know why they're happening, but at least they're pleasant!

"What if none of the popular kids like me, Caleb?" Emma whined from the backseat of his 2008 Dodge Durango. "What if they hate me and they shove me in a trash can?"

"There are worse things than the popular kids not liking you Emma, trust me." I told her.

"Besides, if they even try and shove my little sister in a trash can, they will have to answer to me." Caleb said proudly.

He was being a true big brother to his little sister. I'm happy to know that he would defend his little sister if the opportunity ever presented itself. My brothers would do the same for me. It's nice to know that Caleb isn't a true jock like the ones from my old school. They would never even think about demeaning their reputation just because a family member was being picked on.

We arrived at the school and the three of us walked in with each other. Emma and I are both new to this school and have no idea where we are supposed to go. When we entered the main hallway, Emma kept worrying about how she wouldn't make friends with anyone and she will be a social outcast her entire high school career. I could tell Caleb was becoming sick of her but I never expected him to do what he did.

His hand shot out in front of us, grabbed an innocent boy by the collar of his shirt and placed him in front of Emma.

"There! This is going to be your new friend for the day. Run along with him and leave me alone!" He said exasperatedly.

The boy was scrawny yet tall with no muscles what-so-ever. He did have a pleasant face though. He sort of reminded me of Max back in his freshman year. Save for the red hair, this boy could be his look alike. It was so interesting to watch him try and fumble with words while talking to Emma. I couldn't help but watch the introduction of the two.

"C-Connor A-A-Alan," he stated.

"Emma Darwin," she replied with a small smile.

They shook each other's hand and were off to find their lockers. Aww, little children trying to impress each other was so adorable!

"Scarlett? Are you coming?" Caleb yelled from a few feet down the hall.

"Yes!" I angrily yelled back.

I ran to catch up with him and he found my locker for me. All my mind was capable of thinking at the moment was of Connor and Emma and if they were getting along. She's like my own little sister and I want her to be having fun with whomever she's with. And I hope Caleb made the right choice in friends for her when he man handled that boy into talking to her. They seemed to like each other, but you can never be too sure. All I can say is, he better not be anything mythical that wants to hurt her!

# Chapter 39

*I* TOOK SPANISH ONE IN BEVERLY Hills, but I was never good at it. And now that I'm at Willow Creek Public, I thought that I wouldn't have to take a second year. But apparently, the counselor thought that it would be better for my college applications to have two years of a foreign language. And who am I to argue if it will benefit my education? So I signed up for the dreaded class and came to find out, it was filled with sophomores. I was the only junior taking it this year and it made me embarrassed.

Luckily, it was the first class I had in the morning and I was with Portia and everyone else second period. The bad news about having everyone in our year together at once for this class . . . its Sexual Education. Well, the technical term for it is Health, but who are we kidding? It's Sex Ed and we all know it! Do you know how hard it is to have both boys and girls in there together and not laugh about every little term used? The first thing the teacher told us is that if we laugh at anything in her class, we would be forced to give a presentation on the reproductive system . . . male and female!

To make matters worse, Griffon and Alex sat next to Portia and me during that class, making it harder not to laugh. They like to make us giggle at the stupidest things at the worst of times. Not only is it hard to suppress the giggles, but Caleb sits a few seats away from us. Try and go through that while keeping your thoughts pure! It's not easy, let me tell you.

My favorite class, as you all might have guessed before, is English. I'm absolutely infatuated with reading and I love English. Ironically enough, my favorite part of the class is Mythology. It was after lunch and the teacher had said that it was what we were starting off with. I've always been a pro at memorizing information and Mythology requires that you can do so.

Plus, I like to hear about all of the love stories between the creatures. My favorite is Cupid and Psyche!

Cupid (or Eros in some cases) was one of the Gods of Olympus. His mother was Venus (Aphrodite), a very jealous Goddess of beauty and love. One day, she found a young peasant girl living on Earth more beautiful than she was. Venus sent her son, Cupid, to shoot Psyche (the peasant girl's name) with one of his arrows to make her fall in love with the vilest creature on Earth. To everyone's surprise, Cupid fell in love with her himself.

Venus wasn't too happy with Psyche marrying Cupid so she devised a plan to put the young wife through three impossible tasks. Venus had assumed that she would have to perform these tasks alone and, in turn, would die from at least one of them. Psyche had help, however, from an ant, an eagle, and her husband, who was angry with her for discovering who he really was before he had the chance to tell her.

In the end, Zeus granted the pregnant Psyche the drink of immortality and everyone lived happily ever after. It's an excellent story, but if you are depressed from the lack of lovin' you seem to be getting in your life . . . I wouldn't recommend it. That's why I had to choke back a few tears as we read it to ourselves in class my first day. I'm not a baby! I'm just a sucker for romance.

Caleb had football practice after school and made Emma wait in the library. She would have been by herself if I hadn't offered to stay with her and help her with her studies. I had assumed she would want to get a head start on her homework, but that's not how it went.

"Chad Michael's is the *hottest* boy in ninth grade! He likes Krissie Sanders but she is only into older boys. She's dating Riley Smith, can you believe it? Riley Smith!"

Riley is in my grade. As far as I'm concerned, he has no business dating a ninth grader. A few of my sources told me that he has already received a good verbal chastising from his friends. OK, so my only source is Portia, but it's still a legitimate source! They wouldn't stop making fun of him about it until he threatened to beat them up. I have a feeling it will still go on for quite some time even with the assault at hand.

"Oh, and guess what? Krissie wants to be *my best friend*! I wouldn't believe it myself if I wasn't standing there when she said it."

I set my Spanish book down on the table we were sitting at and looked Emma directly in the eye.

"Emma, did you ever think that Krissie wants to be your best friend just because of who your father is? I mean, you do have quite a bit of money and people like Krissie Sanders like to prey on innocent, influential girls like you."

Her eyes lost their excitement and her smile drooped into a frown when she heard my words. Her shoulders slumped down and I genuinely felt bad for her for not thinking of this before. I know girls like Krissie and they always seem to want something from you when you're as rich as Emma is. Oddly enough, the smile returned to Emma's lips and she perked right back up.

"Krissie would never do that to me. No, she really wants to be my best friend!" She stated cheerfully.

I had a feeling that Emma would be trying out for the junior varsity cheerleading squad in a matter of days. Krissie would talk her into it and Emma, being so naïve, would listen and obey her gracious leader. This was a beautiful, intelligent, talented young girl about to get destroyed by the popular crowd and I could do nothing but sit back and watch it happen. She wouldn't listen to me without experiencing it for herself first. Hopefully, Emma will come to her senses before the year is over.

"What about Connor?" I asked her. "You and he were looking like you were clicking this morning."

"Connor's just . . . well; I don't know how to explain him. Everyone kept calling him a spaz and I sort of . . . got into the habit as well."

"Emma, you didn't!" I gave her a look of disappointment.

"If I didn't, Krissie would have thought that I liked him! I had to make the sacrifice and I think I picked the right choice." She replied.

She tried to make herself sound proud of what she had done to Connor, but I could hear hints of guilt behind her charade. I just wish she could have heard it herself.

"Krissie says that it's a good thing that my older brother is dating Shaylee. She said that it means she could teach me some moves whenever she's at my house that would help me become a great cheerleader."

"Emma, you know Shaylee would never help you. She's too preoccupied with Kay-Kay to help anyone else."

I mocked Caleb's little nickname that Shaylee had given him. It sounds much more annoying when she says it, however. It's almost as if a million killer bees are hitting a windshield at the same time. I only wish I could be the driver of the car killing them all! Wow, I think being a vampire has made me a little evil. That sounded a bit maniacal . . . but you all get my point, right?

"I can at least try, Scarlett. And you can be a little more supportive of what I want to do. I thought you were my sister!"

"I am not your sister, Emma. Our parents aren't dating and they never will. My dad will soon win my mom back and I will be out of your house as soon as possible." I bit out.

OK so I should have been more sensitive in explaining this. But she was making me angry and I couldn't help but become a little defensive. You would act the same way if you were in my position. Maybe not exactly how I handled it, but I will not take back what I said. I meant every word of it and it's just the way it is from now on. I'm holding nothing back from her. If she wanted to become popular so bad, I was going to treat her like I do Daisy, Robin and Shaylee. All I have to say is that Krissie had better not come anywhere near me or else she might be missing several key organs for brainwashing this poor girl I once considered a friend.

"You two ready to go?"

Caleb showed up at exactly the right time. He had just gotten out of football practice, dripping wet from the shower he had taken after, and had come to get us. He was dropping me off at my dad's house but I wasn't going to stay there for very long. You see, I go to my aunts every Monday, Wednesday and Thursday for lessons. Lessons not to control my vampire powers, but to learn the full extent of my psychic powers. I haven't seen much of a change yet, but I suppose I just have to be patient.

Emma glared at me briefly, grumbled, "Yeah" to her brother, and threw back the chair she was sitting in to stomp out of the room properly. In my opinion, she was overreacting. However, I think I would probably act the same way if I had heard someone I looked up to say the things I said.

"What's got her training bra in a twist?" Caleb asked me as we were entering the hall.

"Don't ask," I responded.

# Chapter 40

"YOU HAVE TO KEEP YOUR concentration better!" My aunt snapped at me.

I was keeping my concentration the best I could! But considering everything else floating around in my head, I just couldn't. Emma took up most of my brain at the current moment, however. Would she ever forgive me for yelling at her and berating her for simply trying to make friends with kids in her class? What about the whole 'I'm not your sister and never will be' thing? She didn't think that I actually meant that, did she?

"Scarlett, if you don't try harder, you're never going to get this!"

"I'm trying as hard as I can, Aunt Cassie!"

But I wasn't. She had been teaching me to channel the HP and produce a vision on my own free will instead of receiving them sporadically. I've only accomplished this once the whole two months I've been at it. I don't think she's the best person to be teaching me this. Cassie doesn't have the gift like I do. No one does, and yet I have to learn from someone who thinks they know everything about this kind of thing. It just doesn't seem right.

"Empty your mind of everything. You have to free yourself or else it won't work!" She scolded.

I tried to do as she was telling me to do, but it didn't seem to work. This was becoming frustrating and I was getting a headache. I began to think, the faster I do this the faster I can leave. So I shut my eyes and with all of my power, I pushed everything out of my mind. And I was rewarded.

It was the same vision I had received the night before about the new girl in our school. She hadn't come today, so she must still be enrolled in another school, possibly threatening them instead of us. Not that I wish that on anyone, whatever she is, but better them than us. The vision was quickly over when she had approached our group. It didn't even let me stay to see the whole thing again.

I shook my head and opened my eyes to see Aunt Cassie staring at me with a smile on her face. She was proud of me; that you could tell. I'm glad I can make her happy with something I do not care to do. I could live without knowing how to use all of my powers. It would probably be a better thing considering Gunnar would try and use them against the ones I love.

'I told you last night, I don't—'

'Know what you're going to do yet . . . blah, blah, blah!' I interrupted Gunnar in my head.

'Well, I'm glad to hear that you do listen to me sometimes. That means we're making progress with our relationship.'

'There is no relationship between you and me Gunnar. There never will be so deal with it.'

"What did you see?" Cassie asked me.

"Just some girl I had a vision about before. She doesn't look harmful, but I can't be sure." I replied while taking a seat in the arm chair right next to us.

"What does she look like?"

Cassie took a seat in the rocker directly next to my chair and kept talking about my vision. This happened the last time I accomplished this power I have as well. She likes to know every single detail I see. Sometimes I don't even remember something and she will command me to Channel again just to find out one teensy little insignificant thing.

"She's your typical skinny blonde with big boobs and a low IQ boys bend over backwards for. Nothing important in the least, Aunt Cassie."

"I wouldn't be so sure about that just yet, darling. Did you find out a name?"

"No," I replied rather bored. "No names were given out just yet. But when she arrives at the school in person, I'll be sure to ask first thing."

I don't normally act so snobby toward her, but today everyone seemed to be getting on my nerves. I even snapped at Caleb in the car when he was trying to pry in about what Emma and I were fighting about in the library. I didn't mean to yell, but I couldn't help it. My buttons are easily being pushed today for no apparent reason. Maybe it's because I'm tired?

"I'm sorry, Aunt Cassie. I suppose today just isn't my day. Can we pick things up Wednesday? I'm not feeling very well now and I don't think this lesson will go as we wish it to."

"Will you work harder at concentrating for Wednesday?" She asked quizzically.

I nodded my head yes.

"Well then sure, you can leave and we can pick this back up on Wednesday. But I'm not happy about our session being cut short today."

"I know and I'm sorry. Thank you, Aunt Cassie!"

I kissed her cheek and bolted out of the room, grabbing my book bag before booking it out the door. After school, Caleb had driven me back to the mansion where my car was parked in the long driveway. Now my 1967 Chevy Camaro was parked directly in front of my aunt's house. I loved my car so much it was unreal!

When I arrived home, my twin brother, Max, was cooking dinner while my dad sat at the kitchen table working on a case his Legal Aid office just took on. He was always working and never gave up unless his case was won. I suppose it's a good thing for his clients . . . but not for his children. You could hear the sounds of a stereo being blasted from upstairs. I walked over to my dad, placed a kiss on his cheek and walked over to Max.

"What time is dinner?" I asked him, sneaking a piece of carrot being chopped up for beef stew.

"Six thirty," he responded.

He grabbed my wrist abruptly and slapped the carrot back on the cutting board. It didn't hurt one bit, but I still had to say "ouch" to keep up with the charade that I'm still human. I looked at the clock above the kitchen table and noticed I still had half an hour until we ate. That gave me plenty of time to check on my mopy older brother, Holden.

I glanced up at the ceiling before asking both of them, "Does anyone hear that?"

"Yeah, he's mad about something that happened in school today." Max replied.

"And does anyone feel the need to go up there and see what's wrong with him? Or were you just going to let him destroy that punching bag of his?"

"It's his way of releasing stress, Scarlett. Leave him alone and he will be just fine in a couple of hours." My dad said in a fatherly, know-it-all manner. I hated that voice!

I wasn't going to let Holden keep this locked inside like this. It's not healthy what he's doing and he needs someone to talk to. So, I took it upon myself to be the one to be the shoulder to lean on.

My brothers are sour sports when it comes to two things . . . sports and girls. Max gets out his frustrations by taking his Mustang to the nearest diner and finding someone to race down an abandoned road with. It cheers him up somehow, but scares the living daylights out of me every time.

Holden, however, is a different story. He wallows in self-pity until someone shakes him out of it. His way of getting over his problems is hiding up in his room, blasting Heavy Metal music and taking it out on a red punching bag he has up there. So it was no shock to me when I heard screaming voices coming from behind his door and a faint slamming of fists on polyester material. I opened the door without knocking (he would never hear me anyway) and sifted my way through dirty clothes and pizza boxes to reach his bed.

He knew I was in there with him, but didn't say anything. I don't think he knew what to say. So he kept beating the stuffing out of the punching bag as I watched. He would stop eventually; I just needed to be patient. In the meantime, however, I thought of all the possibilities he could be mad about.

It could possibly have something to do with football. Holden wasn't too happy when he found out that he was going to be co-captains with a junior. Especially when he was the quarterback and Caleb was simply the running back. A stupid philosophy to have, but I suppose it would make sense if you were male and understood the game. Something could have gone wrong in practice today and could have been twisted to go against his favor.

Or, more than logically, it could have something to do with Kitty. Kitty is in Holden's grade he has gotten a little crush on her. I've talked to her a few times at the diner where she works, but never talked about my brother with her. She's very beautiful, but very different from everyone in this town. Unlike Portia, she has lived here all of her life. I don't know how to explain it . . . there's just something odd about her I can't place. Holden thinks she's the greatest thing since sliced bread, though.

He gave the punching bag a few more good swings and finally gave up, collapsing on the floor at the foot of the bed a few feet away from me. I watched as his chest heaved up and down from exertion. Sweat was rolling off of his shirtless upper half like a river . . . a very disgusting, salty river. I cringed at the smell of his body odor filling the room. It was magnified with my vampire smell as well. And that's the downside of it!

"Are you done?" I asked sarcastically.

He nodded his head yes and threw it back to rest on his bed.

I could tell by his heavy pants that he needed water. My eyes searched his entire room for anything remotely close to me and found his Gatorade sports bottle on top of his dresser. It felt warm to me but it was water, none-the-less. As I was grabbing the water for him, I also turned the stereo down so I could actually think. I handed it to him and as he poured it in his open mouth I began the conversation.

"Do you mind telling me why you just unloaded on your Everlast?" I asked.

"Do you mind telling me why you're in my room without knocking?" He reciprocated.

"Point taken."

We sat there in silence as he continued to drink his water. I chewed on my lip and tapped my foot in boredom. A plus for that is it annoys the heck out of him. So when he threw his arms up in the air and let out a loud huff, I knew it was because of me. He had broken down and was about to tell me everything that was bothering him.

"She's way out of my league!"

"Who, Kitty?"

"Yes Kitty." He shifted to face me now but still sat down on the floor. "It turns out she's the smartest girl in my grade. I suppose I should have seen it coming, what with her being so beautiful and all. It's just the icing on the cake."

"So . . . what's the problem then?" I asked confusedly.

"The problem is what would Kitty want with a dumb jock like me if she's so perfect?"

I couldn't help but smile at his insecurities. What my brother didn't know about himself was that he had a lot going for him. And he wasn't just some dumb jock like everyone thinks he is.

"Oh don't be silly, you have brains. Somewhere deep down, but they're there."

He knew I was kidding so it was a relief when he laughed with me instead of putting me in a head lock like he used to do. Granted, it would hurt me any, but that's not the point. It would bring me closer to his armpits. The location of the putrid stench filling this room and nobody wants that.

"Seriously though, you don't give yourself enough credit," I stated. "You can't judge how a person thinks about you just because it's how everyone else sees you as. Who knows, Kitty might like you just as much as you like her? Give it time and see what happens."

"Thanks for the sisterly advice, Scar'. I appreciate it." He smiled at me.

"No problem. It's what I'm here for. Now, dinner's on the table and if we don't get down there soon, Max will have devoured it all."

I held out my hand and helped him off of the ground. He accompanied me downstairs and into the kitchen where we ate together as one, big, happy family. Too bad there was just one key ingredient missing in everything. My mom.

# Chapter 41

*A* WEEK HAD FLOWN BY AND I'm still not getting Channeling like I'm supposed to. Aunt Cassie isn't too happy with my progression in this whole thing and she's about to give up on me. Like she has a choice! But if you knew how hard it is to try and pull out a random vision from nowhere, you would be on my side. Aunt Cassie's just worried that I let the stress of my every day life rule over me, making it impossible for me to accomplish the tasks she wants me to perform. Well, she has a point . . . but I'll eventually Channel like a pro.

As for my social life, Portia had brought it up that the new movie *Blood Flesh and Tears* comes out this weekend. She thought it would be a fun bonding experience for the both of us to scream our heads off together at a horror flick instead of alone. So, I had plans to see a movie with my best friend . . . until somehow, they were all crumbling away like feta cheese.

I was sitting at a table next to Griffon and Alex, picking apart my bologna and salami sandwich (I've never been partial to salami) when Portia approached me with some news. She was half smiling, half appearing guilty and embarrassed. She obviously had done something she knew I wouldn't be to happy about.

"Hey guys!" She said cheerfully while sitting down next to me.

We all said hi to her in unison and the boys went back to eating. I, however, was going to get to the bottom of why she was acting like she was. Nervous, no doubt, about something.

"What's going on Portia?" I asked her.

"I'll tell you later," she responded.

What was with her today? Did it have something to do with Alex? Is that why she couldn't talk about it right now? Do I want to know what she's talking about if it has something to do with him? Well, whatever she's keeping from me, I am certainly going to talk with her about it later.

Later meant during Biology for me. We were dissecting sheep eyes today and she was my partner for the gruesome, gory job. I felt it the perfect time for us to discuss what she had done . . . over an open eyeball. I looked to my immediate left to see Griffon and Alex messing around with their eyeball, pretending like they were eating it, not paying any attention to us. It gave us the perfect opportune moment to talk alone. Too bad that once she told me the news, I wish I would have never asked.

"I was sitting in Computers class when your parasite of a brother asked me what I was doing this weekend." She paused and let out a deep breath. "I thought he was going to ask me out and I became nervous and babbled; letting it slip that we were going to the movies Saturday."

"Oh no," I grumbled.

"It's not my fault! He just sort of invited himself and I couldn't say no. I'm sorry, Scarlett, I really am." I glared at her.

"But that's not the worst part . . . " she whispered.

What could be worse than my brother coming along with us on a girl's night out? But realization hit me soon enough. My mouth dropped open and my eyes became slanted, shooting daggers in her direction. I was silent long enough for her to actually tell me what was worse. Even though I already knew before she said anything.

"He sort of asked me if Caleb could come along and I said yes."

"OK, so let me get this straight. You, me, my brother and the boy I despise," yet secretly love, "are going to see *Blood Flesh and Tears* this Saturday night? Oh, this is just dandy." I said angrily.

"What's this about movies?"

Griffon and Alex made their way to our table and joined in on our conversation. Both had sheep's blood running down their chin, giving the impression that they actually ate the eyeball . . . even though they didn't. Alex rested his chin on his hand and leaned in near Portia. He really liked her. Too bad the feelings weren't reciprocated. He really is a great guy.

"Portia and I had plans to go to the movies Saturday but . . . wait a minute . . . "

I had a perfect idea to make things less awkward between the four of us during the movies. Everyone might not like my plan, but in my eyes, it was the perfect solution. I hated the pressure of group dates and this way, everyone won't feel like it's a date. Oh, this is excellent!

"Would you guys like to go with us?" I asked them.

Their eyes lit up as they heard my offer. They certainly didn't hear anything about Caleb and Max going too. Oh well, that will be kept until the day we are going. I don't think they will be too happy with us, but they wouldn't want to go if I told them now. This way they will still go and I will be able to tolerate sitting next to Caleb the entire time . . . if I do, that is.

"Well, I don't know now. We weren't invited when this whole thing was brought up." Griffon whined.

"Maybe you didn't want us to even go. Maybe you just feel sorry for us right now." Alex added.

"We're asking you now, aren't we?"

Portia sounded annoyed. Was she mad that I invited them along with us? Well, I was mad that she invited my brother *and* Caleb without consulting me first, so we're even. Besides, she can at least tolerate the chuckle twins here without wanting to beat them into a bloody pulp. Then drink their blood afterwards . . . but that's not the point.

"Yeah, we'll go, I suppose." Griffon waved it off.

I know they were excited to come with us; they just didn't want to show it. I don't know how well Saturday will go with so much tension between the six of us. Not only will the sexual tension between Portia and Max and Caleb and I be a problem, but also the rivalry between Caleb and Griffon. Yup, I have a feeling something will be going down Saturday night, I just hope it's nothing like the fight between Caleb and Gunnar at my birthday party *and* the fair.

When I got home the same night and told Max about the extras tagging along with us, he didn't seem too happy.

"I thought it was supposed to be just the four of us?" He asked infuriated.

"Well, there has been some last minute add-ins. Do you mind that much?"

"Yeah, Scarlett, I kind of do. You know Alex and I don't get along well. And haven't you thought of what Caleb and I would think of this before you decided to ask them?"

"OK, time-out! First off, you invited yourself along to what was supposed to be a girl's night out with just Portia and I." I berated. "So don't even get me started on the whole 'consulting before asking' thing! Second of all, it's our decision if we want other people to come along or not. And thirdly, why do you care so much that those to will be coming with us or not? It's not as if you actually have to talk to them."

"Alright, well if you and Portia are bringing along dates, Caleb and I get to bring along Shaylee and Robin." He stated smugly.

Max pulled out his cell phone from his pocket and started to dial a number. "Dates? Who said anything about da—?"

"Hello, Robin? Hey, it's Max . . . Yeah, well I've been busy . . . no, I was wondering if you and Shaylee were up to going to the movies this weekend?" A short pause. "*Blood Flesh and Tears.*" He stated. "OK, well Caleb and I will be waiting to pick you up outside of your house are five thirty or so . . . see you later."

And he hung up. Dates? What did he mean when he said the word 'dates' to me? Did Max all of a sudden think that because Griffon and Alex were coming along, it was now some sort of octo-date? When was this decided? And how come I was never called to the meeting to discuss this? I don't think I have a say in the matter anymore. Somehow, it all became twisted and contorted and now we were all going to the movies with someone we each hated and didn't want to be there. Oh joy!

"Why?"

"I don't know why, Portia. Guys are just scum and can't ever think with their correct anatomy. But no worries! Tonight will be wonderfully blissful and nothing will go wrong."

Part of that sentence was me trying to convince myself of everything I was telling her. I was having no such luck, however. It was hard to tell yourself things will be alright when you know you'll be looking at the love of you life holding hands and sitting next to another girl. Every time I see them together I want to scream at him, "She's the wrong girl! It should be me you're with, not her!" But I hold it back because I know Shaylee makes him happy.

"Well, let's just hope that this movie will be good. Hey . . . I have an idea! What if we—"

"No Portia, we aren't going to stand outside Shaylee and Robin's window dressed in capes tonight and scare them into dumping the guys!" I finished for her.

"What about in tank tops and jeans? And-and we'll have our teeth out and . . . oh, oh, oh what if we went swimming before so that way our skin was that lovely shiny black color. Oh this will be excellent!"

"Sorry to douse your revenge plans there Portia, but you know we aren't capable of that. No, I suppose we're just going to have to endure this torture like the women before us have . . . stick it out and hope that one day they come to their senses."

Better said than done, however. I just hope that I follow my own advice and keep my hands—and teeth—to myself tonight. I can't promise anything though.

"How do I look?" Portia turned and asked me.

She had on a black mini-skirt that hugged her thighs and a red, over the shoulder short sleeve shirt from Baby Phat. The sleeves traveled down to her elbows and, while the upper half was loose, the lower half of the shirt has held tight to her tiny tummy and waist to make her look like utter perfection. And to top it all off, she was wearing red, four inch stiletto heels from Dolce and Gabbana. Her hair was down and she looked like she was going to a club instead of the movies.

"You look hot, but what's with the outfit? Do you know we're going to the movies, not to walk to catwalk or something?" I asked her.

"No, we're going out to eat before the movies," She replied.

"Where?"

"The Garden Café in Manhattan." She gave me an innocent smile.

"But that's the most expensive restaurant within miles of here! How are we supposed to pay for it all?" I asked her.

"Don't worry about it. My dad's friends with the owner of the restaurant and he got us a deal for the night. You worry too much. Besides, the guys already know about this and have agreed to go. Face it, you're stuck!"

I looked down at my outfit and noticed that jean shorts and a Hollister t-shirt might not be the best choice for this place. It's ranked four and a half stars and you don't wear something you'd wear to the beach to this place. Unless you wanted to commit social suicide, that is. Luckily, Portia had caught on to my fashion faux paw before I had to say anything.

"Don't worry, I have something for you."

She reached inside of her overnight bag and pulled out a very beautiful, very short, olive green dress from Donna Karan. The neck line of the dress went just a *little* too far down, if you know what I mean. And in her left hand—the one not holding the torture device she calls a dress—were heels like hers only a different color . . . black. It would look gorgeous on her . . . but would it have the same effect on me? How could she expect me to pull *that* off?!

# Chapter 42

*W*HAT IS IT WITH GUYS and boobs? They're just simple human flesh with mammary tissue packed inside. I mean, they're designed for feeding babies breast milk for heaven's sake! What's the big deal? But no matter how you spin it, guys just simply like to stare at them any chance they get . . . making things a little uncomfortable for the rest of us. Especially for the one whose body they are attached to.

I have a reason for starting off the chapter with such a taboo topic. It's because every guy that had gone with us to dinner (save for my brother, of course) kept looking down the dress Portia let me borrow and straight at my female anatomy. I even caught Alex staring once! I tried to ignore it, but it was hard to do when you know that they aren't looking because they're complimenting the dress. It didn't make it any easier that my hair was tied up, giving them easier access to glance at my fun bags.

'I wish I could be there to see it, honey.' Gunnar said.

'Don't start with me tonight, wise guy!' I bit back silently.

To make matters worse, we had been placed in a large booth in the corner of the restaurant and I was the one directly in the middle of everyone else. And just who was I sitting by, you may be asking? Well I bet you could all figure it out for yourselves, but I'll tell you anyway. To the right of me sat Caleb, his thigh being groped by the temptress sitting on the other side of him. It made me very uncomfortable to be able to witness such a grotesque scene when nobody else could. To the left of me was Griffon, trying his hardest to be a perfect gentleman and contain his jokes for the night.

"You going to our first game next week?" Caleb asked me when Shaylee was preoccupied with Robin.

"I have to be there to cheer on my big brother so yeah, I'll be there." I replied with a smile.

"That's great. I was hoping you—"

"Don't call me that!" I heard someone shout from across the table. It was Portia who had yelled it. She was standing from the table with her hands gripping the sides and leaning across it. Her mouth was pulled into a thin line and her eyes were emitting heat like I've never seen before. They were directed toward Max, who was also standing and leaning in, their faces were inches apart, and yet he had a mocking smile on his lips. He was making her mad any way he knew how . . . and apparently, he achieved his goal.

People were staring at the two of them from all over the restaurant and I knew it was a matter of time before . . .

"Excuse me."

Portia ran from our table and in the direction of the exit.

I tried to scoot my way out but no one got the hint until I shouted, "Will someone let me get through?!" The left side of me listened to my words and moved as fast as they could to get out of my way. It was the smarter choice on their part.

I darted outside and searched for Portia out in the parking lot. When I found her, she was slumped over my brother's Mustang and balling her eyes out. A very large dent by her knee had been newly formed in his car and I knew she had been kicking it. What did he say to her to make her this upset? I walked up to her slowly and placed my arm around her shoulder. She turned her body toward me and hugged me tightly. I was probably the only one she could be herself with this moment, so I knew that she was using most of her strength to hold onto me.

"What happened?"

She pulled away from me and sat back on his car. Wiping her tears away from her eyes before she spoke, I noticed her cheeks had black streaks not from her mascara running, but from the water in her tears.

"He-he told me I looked more like a Buick and called me Porshy. I-I *hate* that nickname and I told him to stop but he didn't!"

"Don't listen to him, Portia. He's just upset because you look so good and you're not fawning all over him like Robin does. I know Max didn't mean it and you shouldn't take what he said to heart."

"Yeah, I know. It's just . . . why did he have to say it?" She asked.

"Because he's a guy and they don't think before they let their large mouths speak."

She laughed at what I said and I knew she felt better already. Although nothing could make her happy like if Max would apologize for what he had said to her. But who are we kidding; he would never do such a thing. I led her back inside of the restaurant and we walked back to the table. Nobody said anything about what had just happened, but I know they were all thinking something awful about Portia.

I let Portia sit by me instead of making her sit across from my brother again. It meant she had to take the place of Caleb, but in a way, it helps me a lot. I couldn't stand sitting by him and watching Shaylee feel him up undetected by everyone else. We finished our meals in almost silence and left the restaurant soon after. Caleb, Max, Shaylee and Robin took the Mustang—which I was sad not to stick around to see my brother's reaction when he saw the dent in the side of his car—and Griffon, Alex, Portia and me took Griffon's Chevy Silverado. We all met up at the cinema, however.

We took up an entire aisle of seats in the theater. Just like the restaurant, Caleb and Griffon sat on either side of me. I'll give you how the seating chart went so you could get a clearer view of the conflict. Here it is: empty seat, Shaylee, Caleb, me, Griffon, Alex, Portia, empty seat. Can anyone see the problem with this seating chart? I hope so!

"Why don't we just sit somewhere else, Maxi?" Oh, bad choice of nickname to throw in there Robin. "I want to sit by you."

"Well I want to sit by my friends! So I'm sitting here," he pointed his finger at the seat next to Portia, "and you can go sit by your friend Shaylee. Capish?"

She let out a tiny huff, crossed her arms and stomped off in the direction of the seat he told her to take. He didn't seem too torn up about not sitting by his date. Portia, however, was furious that he was sitting by her. I could hear her mumbling bad things under her breath about Max that he could not hear. She didn't have time to voice her objections for the movie had started.

The movie had started out with a very pretty blonde chick getting her head chopped off in the shower. Great intro to the rest of the death scenes in the movie. Like this one where a boy and a girl were on a date up on a mountain, getting frisky, when the serial killer pops out of the bushes, chops off the guys head and stabs the girl right in the gut. Pulling the knife out and letting the blood drain out of her body. And you know what I was thinking the entire time?

'Mmm, I bet that blood would taste fantastic all young and fresh like that!'

No, that wasn't Gunnar, nor Caleb or Griffon. That was completely me. I couldn't believe how my sick mind works some times! But it didn't stop me from thinking about it as the killing on screen continued. I bet Portia was thinking the same thing. That made me feel a little better.

A scene where the two co-stars were sharing an intimate moment (code for having sex), I felt a hand touching mine. Its fingers intertwined with my own and rested there. His touch was warm and welcoming with a hint of power when the serial killer finally busted down the door and started to chase after our heroine. I wasn't prepared to hear what I did when I realized it was Griffon who was holding my hand.

'He had better keep his hands to himself otherwise he'll be dog food.'

It was Caleb's voice inside of my head being all manly and trying to threaten Griffon with his wolf-like powers. The only problem with that is . . . Griffon couldn't hear Caleb's thoughts. So his words were a waste of time.

Griffon's thumb began to move back and forth on top of my skin, caressing it in a loving manner.

'Hey, hey now! Get your hands off of my girl!' Gunnar's voice rang through my ears.

And when Caleb saw this action, he went off the handle. I actually heard him growl—actually growl—out loud. Luckily no one heard it but me. If they had, they would be severely confused.

'This is ridiculous! She shouldn't be with him, she should be with . . . well, someone else! How could she like him over . . . what am I saying?' He berated to himself.

His jealousy touched me, really it did, but he had no right to be jealous. He was here with his *girlfriend* and I'm just holding hands with one of my best friends. There's a huge difference there, in case you haven't noticed. Of course, this guy I claim to be best friends with, has a crush on me. And I liked holding his hand, but that didn't mean I stopped loving Caleb. I don't think I ever will.

"Stop it," I heard Portia hiss out quietly.

"Well then give me the popcorn bucket and we won't have this problem," Max retorted back to her.

I had a pretty good guess why Portia had told him to stop what he was doing. Is it appropriate for this? Probably not, but I'll tell you anyway. I've been to the movies with Portia before—she's my best friend, we've seen many—and I've noticed that she likes to hold the popcorn. I think what happened was that Max kept reaching into her lap to get a few kernels for himself more than one time, no doubt touching her hand in the process and making her nervous as to where he was reaching. It word unnerve me too if it were Caleb doing the same thing to me.

'Oh you are such a goner! I'm going to get you and you don't even know it.' Griffon's voice oddly continued in my head. 'Slowly . . . slowly . . . slowly stalking you until . . . . ha got you!'

"What?!" I asked in shock.

Oh no, and I said that out loud too! Everyone from our row snapped their heads to my direction and stared at me like I was a lunatic. But I was too busy staring at Griffon, thinking he is a complete nut job for thinking what he had just thought. It had sounded as though he was a hungry cat and I was the mouse!

"I-I didn't say anything," was his reply.

I accepted that it probably isn't the best place to have this discussion with him right now. A movie theater filled with other teens might not take it in kind if I screamed at Griffon for staking me as some prize to be won in his head. So I forced myself to turn around and watch the screen. Even if I wasn't paying *any* attention to the movie now!

'Oops, sorry about that Scarlett. Ignore what I just said.' The voice told me.

I don't know how I could when he sounded like that. What was he thinking? In a way, I would expect that from Gunnar . . . but never Griffon! If so, Griffon would be called the Snake in my prophecy and not Gunnar.

'I resent that,' Gunnar added in his two cents.

This night was just all too weird for me. I can't wait to get home and be rid of all these nut jobs around me. I can't wait to fall asleep and finally have my brain all to myself!

# Chapter 43

$\mathcal{T}$HE THUNDER CRACKED OUTSIDE AS rain poured over the window sill of Aunt Cassie's house. She was staring at me with an expression that said she had given up on me. I was sitting on her couch and she on her reclining chair. Her nurse had gone shopping for the day like usual—we can't have her seeing us doing what we were doing, it would bring up questions. Anyway, Cassie wasn't too happy with me.

"Considering you *haven't* been practicing your Channeling like you promised you would do, I guess we'll have to move on to something else." She leaned in closer to me. "We can start on Memory Transfer now."

"OK and how does this work?" I asked her.

"You are going to have to concentrate Scarlett, you always have to concentrate."

"Yeah, yeah, yeah, just tell me how to do it."

"Don't get pushy with me little missy! Now, you need to be in contact with the person you are trying to read. Because this is your first time, you will have to touch my hand in order to complete the transfer. I'll be thinking of a memory I want you to see and you will try and pull it into your own mind. Eventually, you will be able to do this to anyone you want without touching them at all. You will even be able to choose the memory you want to see. So let's get down to it."

Both of us moved forward so we were close enough together but far enough apart so we were still on our chairs. She reached out and opened her hand so her palm was facing upright. I took her hand in mine and closed my eyes to concentrate. Everything was black except a tiny box-like shape off in the distance. It was growing larger with every passing second until it was smack dab in front of me. I couldn't reach it. I tried to reach out and touch it, but it was like it was still too far away.

I could see what she meant by concentration. Because as soon as I pushed everything out of my mind and put all of my focus on trying to reach the shiny, golden box, it snapped to life, came straight at me and I was pulled into a different place involuntarily.

*This place was sunny and warm, unlike home was at the current moment. I was standing on cobblestones, surrounded by tall, beautiful, ancient buildings. Scooters were flying around every which way and I was lucky not to get run over by one of them. I suppose this was like my visions. They couldn't see me but I could see them. That's a good thing. It gives me an advantage to poke around and what not.*

*It was as if a tether was tied to my waist and was pulling me along the streets. It made me turn a corner and led me to where two people, a couple, were standing. They were holding each other and kissing while others walked past them.*

*When they pulled away from each other, I had a chance to look at who the kissers were. A skinny, bean pole of a woman stood there with red hair and a large smile on her lips. Well, who wouldn't be smiling after kissing this guy? He was down right gorgeous! His hair was longer than most men but it looked really good on him. His teeth were perfectly straight and pearly white and his golden tan brought the whiteness out further. The only flaw I could find on this guy was that his nose had a bump on the top of it. It just made him appear more distinguished and older than he probably was.*

*"I love you, Santo," the woman whispered to him.*

*"I love you too, Cassie. Forever and eternity." he replied.*

This was all the vision was capable of making me see. Aunt Cassie didn't want me to see any more of the memory and pushed me out of her mind. Maybe it was too emotional for her to see Santo again. In her mind, that is. When I looked up to see her face, I noticed that she had started to cry. I felt bad for her so I took the initiative to comfort her. She needed a hug from someone and I was the closest, available person.

Too bad hugging her because of the pain in her heart brought out the pain in my own. Seriously, it hurt *really* badly! Why do boys have to be so thick at times and then claim to be the simplest of creatures? Even though they might have simple intentions, you can't figure out how their brain works to save your life. And that is what I still hate about Caleb. There, I said it! A little part of me still hates him into oblivion and I'm not afraid to admit it. Only . . . now I have to work on saying it out loud. Preferably in front of him.

After I had finished up with my lessons and left my Aunt Cassie's house, I needed to clear my head. I thought back to how Holden clears his head and got an idea. I was going to work out the stress in my head by punching things to smithereens. And the only way I knew fitting was going to involve driving to Jefferson River. Things were going to become smashed and I couldn't wait to do some damage.

From my Camaro, I ran all the way through Willow Creek forest first at top speed to start the long workout. The wind whistling past me, trying to keep up with me as I ran at top speed was exhilarating. The stopping, however, was the tricky part. I was never very good at it when Portia and I do this every morning. All she has to do is gracefully put one foot in front of her at a different pace that the rest of her body is going and she stops. I, on the other hand, tend to stumble horribly and fall on my face. But I've gotten better at catching myself before I fall now. It's just more of a tripping motion now.

So when I stumbled to a complete stop, I opened up my senses and breathed it all in. The river water had always seemed to calm me down before when we come running out here. So I gave it a try. I was hoping that it would make me feel better . . . but it didn't. I was still stressed out of my mind and needed another way to release my tension. Several trees were standing in front of me and nobody would miss just one. But should I take out all of my problems on some innocent trees?

I slammed my fist out in front of me and punched a gigantic hole in the center of a trunk, sending bark flying everywhere.

Yes, yes I should!

That made me feel very good afterward, so I did it again only this time aiming a little higher. Another giant hole appeared where my fist had previously occupied. My arms did not hurt like I expected them to. Just the opposite, actually. It almost felt like they were somewhat freeing the rest of me by mutilating this tree in front of me. I wonder if this is how

Holden feels after using his punching bag. As the braches grew closer to me, I started to rip at them instead of continuing to punch. And actually ripping something apart with my bare hands felt better than I would have expected.

The tree was resulted into a woody mess of chips lying on the ground all broken. I was breathing hard and felt the familiar sting of tears. My fingertips brushed my cheeks and I had noticed wetness had been eminent on them as I pulled them away. When did I start crying? I fell to the ground and curled myself into a little ball, hugging my knees to my chest and leaning against another, fully intact tree nearby.

"Scarlett?"

At first I thought it was just in my head. But as the voice said it again, I knew that this was being said out loud. Oh, no! I lifted my head to see Caleb standing several feet away from me. His chest was heaving up and down and his large, brown eyes were even larger. He kept staring at me. Normally, I would absolutely love the attention from him. But seeing as the attention was drawn out of shock, I didn't feel all that loved. Hey, he shaved his head too. He looks good with very little hair! It shows off his eyes better.

My breath caught in my throat and I stumbled over my words. "H-How long have you been here?" I stutter.

"Long enough to know that you're either a being from another planet . . . " he paused to inhale a large amount of oxygen. "Or a vampire."

My head sunk back in between my knees to hide my shame from him. Sobs rocked through my body, making my shoulders shake and my cheeks no doubt black as coal. All of a sudden, I felt warmth radiating from in front of me and a large hand was being placed on my shoulder in comfort. He was kneeling in front of me, trying to show me his compassionate side . . . which, in turn, made me cry even more. Go figure.

I lifted my head briefly to see him smile a weak, yet reassuring smile in my direction. I couldn't take any more. My arms flung themselves around his neck and I cried into the crook of it. Surprised at first, he eventually warmed up to the idea and wrapped his own arms around my waist and hoisted me into his lap so he didn't have to lean in so much.

"You can hug me tighter if you want. I won't break, I promise," he whispered into my hair.

I tightened my grip around him slightly and found out that he was right. So I squeezed as much as I could and found out that werewolves are just as durable as vampires. This is a very good thing! We both sat there on the forest floor, me basically choking the life out of his neck and he rubbing my back and whispering to me "everything is going to be alright". It wasn't what I wanted from him at the moment . . . but it would certainly do.

# Chapter 44

"OH, NO! WHAT AM I going to do?!"

I was pacing back and forth in my room over at Caleb's house, fretting over the first Spanish test of the semester. There was no doubt in my mind that I was going to fail it horribly if I couldn't get this straight. Everyone else says that it's so easy, house vocabulary, but it isn't for me! You try and memorize a list of more than thirty words and then say it's easy. That's what I thought!

I picked up my Spanish book off of my bed and searched over the words for any hints to make them easier to remember, any anagrams or similes and what not. Too bad there weren't very many. I was so frustrated I was this close to throwing the book through the floor and hoping it rotted in the center of the Earth for all eternity when my door swung open. And in swaggered my heart and soul.

"Guess who's a shoe-in for junior homecoming prince?" He asked confidently.

"Umm, the Easter Bunny?" I replied sarcastically, not really paying much attention to his news anyway. Nope, I was too busy thinking of ways to get rid of my Spanish book without anyone finding any evidence.

"Ha-ha, very funny! I think you just might have a real career in stand-up comedy. You already have the whole school laughing at you for basically failing the easiest class on the planet!"

"You know what, Caleb; I don't need this from you too! Spanish might seem easy to everyone else, but I have a little bit of a hard time with it. So just *back off* or you'll be walking to class tomorrow with a limp!" I gritted through my teeth.

His hands flew up in that whole 'I surrender' stance. "Whoa, easy there, killer. I just thought I'd come up hear to ask if you want me to help you out."

"*You* want to tutor *me* in Spanish? Are you insane or have the car fumes finally gotten to you?"

"I'm serious. I was Senora Ramirez's star pupil when I took her class two years ago. I'm an ace at Spanish and I think I can really help you out if you just let me. What do you say, Red? ¿Le puedo ayudar yo?"

My mouth dropped open as I tried to picture him being the star of any class. You really can't see Caleb sitting up in the front of the room, listening to the teacher intently, ready to raise his and at any moment and answer the question right. But hearing him say a full sentence in Spanish without even blinking surely impressed me. So why not give it a shot? Besides, what could it hurt? If he's horrible at it, then I'll just be on my own again.

I sighed before answering with, "I suppose I can let you attempt to help me." Hey, I wasn't going to give him full satisfaction . . . that would be stupid!

"Great, then it's settled!"

He hopped off of my bed and did this funny skipping motion over to my dresser without saying a word. When I saw him pull open my top drawer I really didn't think anything of it. I was too busy looking at the way he was chewing on his lower lip to even care what he was doing. But when I saw him throw out a small piece of cotton, followed by more shortly after, I snapped back into reality.

"What do you think you're doing?!" I shouted at him.

"Huh? Oh, don't mind me," was his genius response.

Carelessly dangling from his fingers was a pair of my red lace thongs. My mom bought them for me when I turned sixteen thinking that I would wear them. I, however, thought that they looked too painful to even try so they've been buried in dressers for months now. Seeing him nonchalantly holding them in his hands set me off. I used my supersonic speed to run over to him and snatch them out of his hands, along with the rest of my underwear on the floor.

"I was looking for your swimsuit."

I opened up the drawer below and pulled out two pieces of lime green cloth and waved it in front of his face. To be smug about it, he gave me a large smile, showing his perfectly white teeth in the process. Oh, I really hated him sometimes!

"Next time just ask, please!"

"You got it, Boss," he continued to be smug.

'I just touched her underwear!'

Yeah, that was him inside of my head too. That I just had to keep myself from breaking out into a fit of raucous laughter. I mean come on, who would need to laugh after hearing that? He was like a thirteen year old seeing his first rated R movie all over again. I swear, if he ever pulls a stunt like that again, I will break each and every bone in his body!

"So just where are we going that I need my bikini for?" I asked him.

"You'll see."

Ah, I hated it when people put me in the dark about things. Seriously, why can't they just tell you what they mean and be done with it?

'Where's the fun in that?' Griffon's voice gave his input.

'I'd have plenty of fun without the mystery,' I shot back

But we both knew that wasn't true. If there was no mystery in life, it would be pretty boring. Imagine if you knew everything that was about to happen, before it actually happened. You'd never be able to think or dream in private because everyone would already know what you were thinking and dreaming of. I, for one, am thankful the smaller mysteries in life. Plus, it would mean that if you had a crush on a boy, he'd already know and you'd basically be rejected in silence. See, it's a better world now.

'Told you'

'Don't rub it in!'

I looked myself over in the bathroom mirror when I had the bikini on. If we were going swimming, he would see my body react to the water. It will turn metallic black and I don't quite know how he will respond to this. He knows quite a bit about vampires . . . but has he ever seen one wet before? God, I hope so for his sake! I threw a pair of cut-off jean shorts on and a simple pink t-shirt before leaving the over-sized bathroom.

When I stepped out of the bathroom, I noticed that Caleb was wearing a shirt underneath a sweatshirt (no doubt with a tank top underneath that) with a parka like jacket over everything else and jeans over his swim trunks. Wasn't he going to be hot in that? I mean it's not exactly summer here anymore, but it's not cold enough yet to wear that. Oh well, he's going to have to take it off to go swimming anyway. My senses went blank when I tried to picture Caleb in his swimming suit. I hope I don't drool!

That's all I could think about as we pulled up to Jefferson River in Caleb's truck; I hope I don't drool. Who could blame me, really? I've seen Caleb with his shirt off more than once, but each time there had been a reaction. Now I was going to be swimming with him in a lake and I'd have to control myself . . . because he has a girlfriend and I can't intervene. Seriously, why can't I be one of those seductresses who will do anything she can to get what she wants? Oh yeah, because I'm too much of a goody-two-shoes to even try something like that! I suppose I'll just have to wait my turn . . . if my turn ever comes.

"OK, here's what we're going to do." Caleb and I were standing a few feet away from the water and facing each other. I could feel the tide moving over my bare feet as I stared at him. "I'm going to give you a word in Spanish and I want you to translate it in English for me. If you get it right, I'll take off an article of clothing and we'll be much closer to the end and we'll go swimming after. If you get it wrong, however, you will have to take off a piece. I should have told you to wear something heavy. I have a feeling this will become quite a bit more interesting than I had planned."

My eyebrows slanted and my lips pursed into a thin line. If he thinks he's going to win so easily, I can't lose. I don't lose to cocky people whose ego is the size of Texas!

"Let's play, pretty boy!" I said with a smile.

He was in for it now.

"OK, wise guy . . . la sala?"

Without even thinking about it, I quickly blurted out, "living room." And I was right.

Off went that parka he had on. This was going to be much more fun than I had expected it to be. Honestly, it hadn't yet registered in my brain that Caleb was going to be removing his clothes one piece at a time every time I had gotten a question right. The power was in my hands all of a sudden and I didn't even know it. How thick can you get? But this was a fun game, though!

"La Puerta?"

I studied his lips as he said the words. How on God's good Earth can Spanish be *this* sexy? And why did it have to be him that is the Spanish pro and not someone like Griffon or Alex? They don't have girlfriends (yet) and I probably wouldn't feel that guilty basically playing strip study with them. Although I am not going to allow anything important to be revealed, it's still unnerving to watch Caleb inches away from me, taking off his clothes. Boy, did this book just take an interesting twist or what?!

"Door," I answered him.

Off went his sweatshirt. He was wearing a black t-shirt now that read "Bite me" in red, dripping lettering. I couldn't help but laugh at his small joke. Was he that immature? OK, so yes it's a little funny that I'm a vampire and he likes to rub it in my face, but still.

"Is that shirt for me?" I asked.

"I thought you'd get a kick out of it. La Terraza?"

This was one of the many I have trouble with. Oh crap!

"Umm, it's . . . I know this. Uh, don't tell me . . . kitchen?" was my answer. And I knew it wasn't right.

"Oo, I'm sorry that would be deck for those of you playing at home. Now, as for our contestant, that's one wrong."

"Don't be so cocky!"

He grinned at me as I removed my pink t-shirt and revealed how well that lime green bathing suit went with the color of my hair. That's why I bought it. Well, Portia was the one to actually push it on me, but I have to say I'm glad she did. It's my favorite thus far. I did realize, however, that I couldn't get more than one more wrong. Otherwise, Caleb will see more than he ever should at our age. Although, I'm almost certain he's had sex before, I'd rather not think about that at the current moment. Nope, he's just going to be a virgin in my eyes right now whether he knows it or not.

"I'll give you an easy one now. La escalera?" He asked me.

"In what world is that an easy one?!" I barked out. After he shot me a 'you know this' glare, I thought about it and realized that it was easy. "Stairs," I answered.

"Correct," he said as he removed his mocking t-shirt. And just as I suspected, he was wearing one of those white tank tops of his. Go figure, huh?

"El techo?"

"Ceiling," I replied.

I watched as his fingers traveled underneath the hem of his shirt and pulled upward. The boy has muscles that would make a nun drool! His chest was sculpted and hard with abs of steel that traveled down to his belly button and snuck down into his jeans. I shivered a bit but not because it was chilly out. We were finally even matched and I was nervous.

"El cuarto?" He asked.

My mind went blank as he raked his hand across his head where his hair used to be. It was a nervous habit of his that still hasn't changed, even though there isn't hair there to ruffle. He licked his lips and I chewed on my bottom one to keep from making a sound. Oh yeah, I forgot to answer his question. Why couldn't I think of the word now? I knew this one too, but it wasn't coming to mind any time soon.

"Umm . . . couch?" I weakly replied as I gave an innocent 'take pity on me' smile.

"Nope! Now off goes those shorts, little missy!"

I huffed in annoyance and quickly removed my shorts without saying a word. Until I had them off and caught him staring at me. Boys! I swear; they can't make up their mind even if you put the answer right in front of them and tell them to play "strip study" with it.

"Like what you see?" I cooed.

I saw him getting flustered and heard every single thought inside of his head. And they all were too dirty to put in this book. Let me tell you, though, I liked to hear him compliment me like this. It was rather flattering to hear. But it was all over in an instant. Everything went quiet; inside and out of my head and I became nervous.

His eyes became deviously slanted and his mouth pulled into a devilish crooked smile. It was clearly evident that he was up to something. It happened so fast that I didn't have any time to react. He didn't even think about what he was going to do before he did it. Probably because wanted it to be spontaneous and without plans. I felt his arms wrap around my waist and he hoisted me up and threw me over his shoulder. I let out a small yelp and smacked his back with my fists.

I was completely under the water when he finally let me go. I tried to stay under as long as I could to avoid coming up for air but there was only a certain amount of time my lungs could stand. Even though I was a vampire, we needed some oxygen every now and then. I guess you could compare us to dolphins. Yes we can hold our breaths for long periods of time, but eventually we need to come up for air. And I was just about to break my limit.

He was freaked out enough when he first found out I was a vampire, so the more I prolong the inevitable this time maybe he would prepare himself. My head popped up and I gasped in a heap of water. He was standing beside me with the same crooked smile on his face. His jeans were soaked and plastered to his dripping body. I reflexively shuttered at the sight of him.

"What?" I bit out toward him.

"I can't get over the fact that you look this hot every time you're in water. I guess I'm just not used to you being a vampire quite yet." He replied.

Did he just say that I looked hot?! I shook my head to process that information and stood up, showing the extent of the power. His eyes widened to take it all in. I couldn't believe what he did next. This boy really does surprise me at the most awkward of times.

He reached out his hand and let it glide over my face and eyes until it moved down to my mouth. I opened it slightly to give him better access. His fingers grazed the tips of my elongated fangs extremely light. Caleb's expression became softer but there seemed to be a hunger burning in his eyes. Our heads had slightly tilted to the side and were moving toward each other. This was it! This was going to be our first kiss and it couldn't come at a better time!

But before our lips could touch, a name had popped into both of our heads and ruined the moment. Shaylee. He pulled away and cleared his throat as if he had choked on something. Well, that was just a let down! Flustered, I began to gather my shirt and shorts and dry myself off. The black faded and I placed my clothes back on me. He took a little bit more time to come back to his senses and get dressed.

I couldn't believe that this was the moment I had been waiting months for and it had to be ruined because of his girlfriend. This is so typical!

# Chapter 45

THE NEXT DAY AT SCHOOL, I aced my Spanish test with ease. Caleb kept ignoring me, however. And to tell you the truth, that hurt more than anything I've ever been through . . . I was in a car crash *and* was turned into a vampire too! Portia had finally asked me why I was so mopey at lunch when we finally had some time alone.

"What's with the long face?" She asked me.

I paused and thought before I actually told her what was the matter with me. Should I tell her what happened last night with Caleb and I at the beach? I probably shouldn't tell anyone really that Caleb had almost cheated on his girlfriend with me. But this was Portia. I've told her everything since she bit me and she hasn't betrayed me once. So this little secret should be no different from the rest. I'm going to tell her.

"Caleb and I almost kissed last night," I revealed.

"Ohmigod Scarlett, that's so fantastic!" She shrieked out.

Well, she's taking this a bit better than I had ever dreamed of. A little better than I reacted as a matter of fact. That probably should have been what I did when we returned to the mansion and I was alone in my room. But I didn't. Instead I cried my eyes out on my bed and eventually exhausted myself enough to fall asleep. It was sad, really.

"It would be if it actually happened. We stopped when he thought about Shaylee. I swear Porsh', I wanted to walk up to her and rip her eyes out of her skull! I still do."

"Well here's your chance," Griffon entered in on the conversation along with Alex and sat down at the table with their lunches. "Daisy and she are bad mouthing you to all of the other sheep in their flock over there." He said.

Oh no, he heard me talking about Caleb! This isn't good . . . this isn't good in the least. How am I going to explain this to him without revealing that I'm a vampire? I do owe him an explanation . . . but how? Well, I'm certainly not doing it in the middle of a cafeteria with everyone around to hear me.

"Griffon, can we talk alone for a sec'?" I asked him.

Before he could respond, I was standing from the table, grabbing his forearm and pulling him in the direction of the hallway. That place is always empty during lunch. Yeah, this would be as could of a place as any to tell him I just don't have the same feelings for him as he has for me. The question is . . . how am I going to break it to him without hurting his feelings? Boys are always sensitive when it comes to rejection. So I have to go into this as easy and gentle as possible.

"Griffon, I'd just like to start off with the sentence that you really are a great guy and a terrific friend. But the thing is; I think our relationship can go no further than just being platonic. I know you're probably hurting right now but—"

"What makes you think I liked you like that?" He interrupted me.

Well, that was a shock! "I-I thought that since the movie and . . . and at my party you . . . the fair . . . am I completely wrong?"

He nodded his head yes.

"Oh, I feel so mortified!" I placed my hands over my eyes so I wouldn't have to look at him. "I shouldn't have jumped to conclusions. Wait a minute, if this was all just a friendship; why did you hold my hand and take me to the fair and buy me cotton candy. That's stuff that would be considered a date."

"Because I know you're in love with Caleb." He answered with a sort of skip in his voice.

Well, that just added on to my embarrassment! I removed my hands from my face and saw that he was smiling at me. Not only smiling at me, but laughing as well. Wow, was he sensitive or what?! Why does everyone else know about that except Caleb though? This really isn't fair.

"So? How would that help the situation?" I asked curiously.

"Men always like things they can't have. The more unattainable they are, the more they need to have it. I was just there to lend jealousy a helping hand. Don't tell me you didn't see his face when I held your hand? He was about to rip my head clear off."

Oh, if he only knew the truth to that statement right there, he probably wouldn't have said it. Heck, he probably would have run for the hills the moment he knew Caleb was actually capable of doing such a thing.

"How do you know all of this?" I asked flabbergasted.

"Because . . . I am having the same problem with someone right now too." He revealed.

His expression saddened as did my own. I felt bad for him, really I did. Because I knew how it felt to be in love with someone you can't have. So I sympathized immensely with his situation. The only problem is; he knows who I'm in love with but I know nothing of his crush. This just doesn't seem fair to me! I want to know the girl who stole away Griffon's heart out from under me.

"Who's the lucky girl?" I asked him.

He let out a pent up sigh and looked me square in the eyes. A few moments passed before he really said anything. "*His* name is Greg. He goes to Harrison High School and I met him a couple of months ago."

My eyes and mouth opened wide and I could say nothing . . . do nothing but just stare at him for several seconds. How did I not know that Griffon was gay?! Am I that clueless? This was just something I was never expecting. What did this mean about the voice inside of my head that sounds exactly like his? Well, obviously it isn't him. My potential life mate can't be gay. So begins the search for a body to place with the voice once more. But right now, I couldn't think about anything other than Griffon liking men.

Before I could reassure him that I was perfectly fine with his sexual preference, an uproarious wave of laughter came from inside of the lunch room and caught both of our attention. There's no doubt in my mind that it had to do with Daisy and what she was saying about me.

I turned back to Griffon and said, "Griffon, I hope you don't mind but right now I have to go and kick some major blonde booty in front of the entire school."

I threw open the door and stomped into the cafeteria with rage clearly imminent on my face. Everyone went silent and they knew that there was going to be a fight. Even the teachers acted as if nothing were going on. They were no doubt on my side in this whole thing.

"And here's the boyfriend stealer herself!" Daisy shouted from the table she was standing on. "Tell me Scarlett, how does it feel to be so desperate for a guy that you have to snake one away from an innocent girl like Shaylee?"

I walked over to the table and stood a few feet from it so I could look her directly in the face.

"I don't know, why doesn't Robin tell me? She's the one who has been making out with Freddy behind your back." I quipped.

The whole crowd snapped back to life and shouted "Oh!" as if to drag it out in ridicule. Freddy DeMarco is Daisy's new boyfriend. They have been dating for about a month now and she thinks everything is going fine . . . well, thought. About two weeks ago, Portia caught Robin and Freddy getting busy behind the bleachers after school and told me about it. I just never thought I would have to throw it Daisy's face like this. Oh well! That little scumbag beside of her (Freddy) started to creep away. I saw him . . . but Daisy was too preoccupied with me to notice her future ex running.

I saw Daisy shoot a glare in the direction of Robin who was blushing like a tomato. I kind of felt bad for saying it, but I don't take anything back about it. Even though Daisy is a horrible person, she deserves to know that one of her best friends is stabbing her in the back.

"You're just jealous because I'm in a healthy relationship with a man that likes me back!" She yelled at me. Obviously she's misplacing her anger right now.

"That's right Daisy, keep telling yourself that," I deadpanned.

"At least I'm not some freak with only one friend!"

"Was that supposed to hurt me? 'Oh ouch, I don't think I'll be able to survive a blow like that! You really got me, Daisy.' Besides, I think you underestimate your 'friends'." I performed air quotations to make it more effective in my liking. "Most of them don't even care one bit about you or your well being. I guarantee that they have wanted to push you off of a cliff at least once before. At least I have true friends that love me the way I am and don't want to cause bodily harm to me."

She said nothing but kept staring at me with a hurt expression.

"What, now you have nothing to say? Next time you want to insult someone behind their back, why don't you get your facts straight before you run that big, fat mouth of yours!"

And I walked easily in pride out of the cafeteria door.

# Chapter 46

$\mathcal{I}$ SPENT THE NEXT FEW DAYS running by myself instead of with Portia. There was just too much stress building up inside of me and the only thing that would cure it was listening to music while I ran my heart out. Lately I've been listening to things like *You Belong with Me* by Taylor Swift, *Cowboy Casanova* by Carrie Underwood, *You're So Gay* by Katy Perry, *Run* by Leona Lewis, and my all time favorite, *Let Down* by This Providence. You don't know how wonderful that song is. It's like therapy for me or something.

School was a bit odd, however. Everyone kept congratulating me since that day. They kept telling me that I was their hero for telling off Daisy like I did that day in the cafeteria. Honestly, I never expected this kind of hype all for saying what was on my mind at the time. It was kind of cool.

Oh, and the reason why this whole thing had been started was because Caleb had broken up with Shaylee the same night as the beach incident. She told Daisy who was insanely mad about the whole thing. If I could only tell her that she was the one sticking her tongue down Caleb's throat in my first vision. But I can't. I don't think everyone would take it in kind to know that I was an even bigger freak that I let on.

But if you all thought that just because Caleb dumped Shaylee that he would run to me and kiss the stuffing out of me, you'd be wrong. Nope, he's still ignoring me to no end. Which, I don't really have a problem with anymore now that I've been running. It would probably kill me inch by inch if I didn't have that simple, sweet release. But I've been getting through it.

The worst part of us both being single is that Homecoming is this weekend and we both have no dates. Griffon had asked me but I told them that he should take this chance to ask Greg. There's no sense in us both being depressed and with someone we didn't really want to be with that night. He wouldn't tell me if Greg said yes, but I have a feeling that he jumped at the opportunity. Griffon is, after all, *very* good looking. I still haven't figured out who the third voice is, but I'm not worrying about it now. He'll find me eventually and may or may not end up with me in the end.

'Oh he won't, because you will be married to me by then.' Gunnar's voice rang out.

Hmm, haven't heard from him in a while. I wonder who he's taking to the dance. Maybe he'd be willing to put up with me for one night.

'Sorry hon', but Lizzy Jackson already snatched me up. I would have said yes if you would have come to your senses sooner instead of filling your head with all sorts of garbage involving that Caleb guy.'

Hold on a minute, did I just consider going to one of the most crucial dances in high school with Gunnar?! What had gotten into me all of a sudden? Maybe it's all of this craziness finally going to my head. Yeah, that's it. Because under no normal circumstances would I ever even think about giving Gunnar the time of day. But at least he would have been a person to go with. It's Thursday; no one's going to ask me. Now I'm going to be basically the only one there, dateless and alone.

"Way to go, Scarlett!"

Some guy I don't even know came up and told me that. I was innocently sitting in Spanish, staring off into the distance as the teacher spoke about Subjunctive Conjugations. What was he talking about? He wasn't the only kid to congratulate me on something I knew nothing about as well. For the rest of the day, people kept coming up to me and telling me they voted for me or that I was the man. Yeah, I had no idea what they were talking about. I figured that they were still talking about the whole Daisy thing, but it had been days ago. Why would they still be talking about that? And what was the deal about something to do with voting?

I finally found out during my last class of the day. We were all sitting in the computer room when the principle came on the PA system and made an announcement.

"The ballots have been counted and recounted for the underclassmen Princes and Princesses and we have the results. For the freshmen class: Chad Michaels and Kristina Sanders." There were claps around the room as the principle fumble with some notes. "For the sophomore class: David Shaw and Marie Justice." More claps. "For the junior class:"

I think that the principle had dropped the papers at that point and was trying to search through them now. Because you'd have to be doing something to drag out a pause this long. Everyone already knew that Daisy would win by a landslide, however. And if it wasn't her, it would be one of her other two lemmings. She wouldn't be happy about that!

"Oh, I found them. OK and for the junior class: Caleb Darwin," what a shock. "And Scarlett Hera."

Cheers thrown in an uproar from everywhere. Not only from the room, but from the entire school. I looked at Daisy and could tell she was about to cry. I guess there would be one more person winning the spot she has always received that would make her angry. She was disgraced with the fact that I had won the vote over popularity. To be honest, I was in just as much shock as she was. Me being the junior class Princess?! Me?!

"The Senior King and Queen of homecoming will be announced during half time of the game tomorrow. This concludes this announcement."

The speakers clicked off and everyone came up and congratulated me, patted me on the back, and told me that they were rooting for me from the beginning. It was odd to wrap my head around the fact that people had actually chosen me to represent them. Just a few days ago, I was a boyfriend stealing freak with only one friend and now I'm the junior Princess. This was just too strange.

And things grew stranger as I walked to my Camaro after classes had gotten out. I had my ears plugged with my Ipod and had *Everything I Asked for* by a band called The Maine blasting. Even if someone shouted at the top of their lungs, I wouldn't be able to hear them. That's why I jumped about three feet off of the ground when someone grabbed my shoulder and shook it to get my attention. I know, I know, I must be the wimpiest vampire in history, but I still haven't gotten used to knowing that I am one of the most dangerous creatures in the universe. I removed my earphones and turned to see the person who had just scared the wits out of me.

"Freddy?!" I said in disbelief.

"Hey Scarlett, how are you doing? Congratulations on winning the Princess position. Daisy's really messed up about it." Only he didn't say messed up.

"Thanks," was my reply.

I started to walk to my car again, thinking the conversation was over when he said, "Do you have a date for the dance yet?"

I whirled around to face him and accidently ran into his chest. He was just a bit closer than I had liked him to be. Not that he wasn't attractive. He was; but not really my type. He's on the football team with Caleb (he's their second string quarterback) and he's the cockiest second string you've ever seen. There has been only one boy with as much confidence to be called cocky that I have ever liked. And he was standing a few feet away no doubt listening to the conversation with his super dog hearing.

"Umm, no I don't have a date yet. Why?" I asked.

"I was wondering if you wanted to go with me." He replied.

"Why?"

To tell you the truth, I was just shocked that he was asking me. Freddy and I don't exactly run in the same circles if you know what I mean.

"Well, I saw the whole scene with Daisy yesterday," he began. "And I couldn't stop thinking 'wow, this girl is really amazing'. No one has ever taken on Daisy Menendez and lived to tell the tale. And to think that you weren't worried at all to be cast out in social Siberia was what had caught my attention the most. So I knew I had to try and ask you to go to the dance with me. What do you say?"

I looked over to where Caleb stood and saw his eyebrows furrowed. I couldn't exactly pinpoint his expression. It was a multitude of them and you couldn't tell what he was thinking by just reading his face. Heck, he really didn't think anything! I would know if he did. Which kind of unnerved me. I would feel much better if he acted on his feelings and ran full speed at Freddy, taking him out in an instant. But with my luck these days, Caleb stayed put and just kept staring with that unknown expression.

"Well?" Freddy's voice brought me back to reality.

"Oh, uh yeah sure I'd love to go with you." I answered.

"OK great! I'll need to know where I can pick you before the dance. Would you like to go for dinner beforehand or what?"

"I think my mom will want to help me out with my dress and everything so I'll probably just eat before I have to get ready. And you can pick me up at 125 West Shallot Street."

"Caleb's house?" He asked as he screwed up his face like sucking on a sour lemon.

"Yeah, my mom has been living there for a while now and I have a room in the west wing. You don't mind picking me up there, do you?"

I had a feeling that he wasn't too happy about going to Caleb's house to pick up a girl he was going to a dance with. But hey, I can't help it that my mom has always wanted to see me off to my first social event in school. I was never very popular in Beverly Hills so I didn't go to many school functions when we lived there. She didn't push me to go, but I could see she wished I would.

So I'm now going to homecoming with a guy that I don't even know let alone like. How on Earth could life get better than this? That was in a sarcastic tone, by the way. Just so you know.

# Chapter 47

*P*ORTIA HAD MADE MY DRESS in advance, convincing herself that she knew I was going before I had even said yes. She brought it to the mansion after the big game (which we won) and stayed the night. I have to say, Portia sure knows how to dress me. She doesn't even need me around to know that what she is making for me will look fantastic.

This dress was a clover green strapless that had puffed out at the bottom but had no visible hem. The length was just above my knees and from the waist up synched to my body. My mom spent about an hour and a half curling my red hair into something manageable but would hold until at least midnight. They both worked on my make-up. I was completely finished with before Portia had even started with her own look. I felt a little bad for hogging all of her attention, but it didn't take her long to get ready.

She wore a cherry red halter that swooped to one side with a slit up the side of her thigh and two wide open slits on either side of her waist, connecting the back with the front. Jewels aligned the straps of the dress and her hair was pinned up to show it all off. A few strands had strategically fallen from the tie to frame her face. She always looks better than me . . . even if she didn't try.

Alex had arrived to pick up Portia first. She was so bummed when she found out that Max had already asked Robin to go with him to homecoming. So when Alex asked her, she more or less said yes to him out of spite. Max was going to pay tonight by being forced to see Portia with another guy. And there's no doubt in my mind that he would be torn up about it too. Even though he doesn't know it yet, Max views Portia as a possession of his. And he doesn't like other people touching his possessions. Never has and never will.

I waited for Freddy to pick me up, but he never showed. I'm not going to say it was a shock, because it wasn't. I was expecting something like this to happen tonight. And if he did end up taking me, he would have just ended up with Daisy on the dance floor anyway. Leaving me all alone to blend in with all of the other wallflowers. Just as the tears appeared in my eyes, Caleb appeared at the foot of the stairs.

"What's wrong?" He asked me.

I turned my head in the opposite direction so he didn't see my crying when I responded, "Freddy stood me up."

Angel rubbed up against my leg to make sure I knew he was still there. I reached down and scratched him behind the ear before standing up and heading toward the stairwell myself. My cat bounded after me and ran up the stairs before me. Caleb had a look of pity on his face that was directed at me and only me.

"Oh, don't feel bad for me," I sniffed. "I saw this coming from a mile away. I just should have spared myself the agony of putting this whole look together when I knew better. Have fun at the dance Caleb."

My foot was not yet on the third step when he stopped me by grabbing my elbow. I turned to question him but all I saw was that mocking smile on his face. He was happy that I wasn't going to the dance! How dare he be so smug about my pain like this? I guarantee there was a bet between him and my brother about if I would go or not. And it looks like he just won.

"Where are you going?" He finally asked me.

I ripped my arm out of his grip and bit out, "I'm going upstairs to take a nice, hot bath and escape this horrid reality for a few hours." And I started walking again.

"Hmm, because you're dressed for the dance and all, I was going to offer that I take you. But if you really want to soak in your own sorrow tonight then so be it. I'm off to have some fun."

I whirled around, causing my dress to twirl and reveal a bit more of my thigh than necessary. I don't think he noticed and if he did, he did say or think anything of it. My eyes grew wide at his offer as if it were the last thing on Earth I was expecting. Because it was. He had just asked me to the dance; give me some time to process the freaking information before you start to laugh at me. This was a big step for the two of us. For me!

"Are you serious?"

"As serious as a heart attack," he replied charmingly.

I looked into his eyes and saw no hint of jokes or trickery so I was in the clear. Caleb was really going to take me to homecoming. Granted, it's only because my first date stood me up like a coward. But it's still the way it should be. Me with Caleb and Freddy with some other girl I know nothing about. Too bad Portia didn't get to go with the person she belongs with. That would have made everything perfect.

"Let me get my coat."

I was having an excellent time at the dance. Dancing with everyone from Portia to Griffon (who by the way had a date that evening); I even danced with Alex once. The food was great and Freddy was even avoiding me, which is what I wanted. But what I truly wanted was to dance with Caleb. And not a fast song like I had already done. No, I'm talking a slow dance. The kind that I would need to wrap my arms around his neck for. The kind where he would be forced to confront some of his feelings for me . . . whatever they may be. But every time one came up, he somehow managed to dodge it and run away from me. It wasn't going to be the night I wanted until I was out on the dance floor, swaying back and forth with Caleb.

The two of us had to perform our royal duties by following up the other princes and princesses to the stage while they announced the winners of homecoming King and Queen. Our job was to stand there and look pretty while they had crowned the two seniors. It wasn't a tough job, but standing this close to Caleb and having his hand brush up against mine every now and then kind of distracted me.

"OK everyone, quiet down now!" The principle called out from the middle of the stage. "In this envelope holds the fate of two unsuspecting seniors. They've been waiting years for this moment and six dreams are about to be shattered. Because only two can be Willow Creek High's King and Queen of homecoming."

Our principle used to be a reality show host. Could you tell?

"And the winners of the crowns are . . . " he opened the envelope and my eyes began to wander. Give me a break, I was bored! "Rose Melbourne and Matthew Stevens!" He revealed finally.

Hmm, good for them.

"And now it's tradition for the King and Queen to dance with their royal court out on the dance floor. If you all would pair up with the appropriate classmate, we can get this started."

My jaw dropped clear to the floor. Fate does love me! I was getting to dance a slow dance with Caleb and there was nothing he could do about it now. He was trapped. Boy did I just sound sadistic or what?! Did he know about this tradition? Was he saving our only slow dance for this moment? Did I want to question it?

He led me out to the dance floor and placed my hands around his neck while the music started. And irony struck once more. The song played was a remake of the song *Who's Loving You* sung by HoneyHoney. It's a good song, don't get me wrong. But boy did it have undertones that stab into my heart like a serrated knife. Just listen to the song and you will know why almost instantly.

We swayed around the other couples in silence. I rested my head on his shoulder after he began to stroke my back ever so lightly. It felt nice to be this close to him and not have it mean anything. It was just two people dancing to music at a high school dance. It's been done for years and yet it felt so different. Right, almost.

'God, she's so beautiful!' Caleb said in his head . . . as well as mine.

I smiled into his neck as I buried my face in the crook of his throat. Vanilla. The overpowering scent of vanilla had made itself prominent on his skin. I loved the smell of him! He pressed his nose in my hair and inhaled a deep breath. He pulled away and looked me in the eyes.

"Don't take this the wrong way, but you sort of smell like me." He told me.

I let out a small giggle at the thought of what he just said. My memory brought me back to my first vision when he had revealed to me that he mark his territory by imbedding his scent on my skin. I really wished I was awake and sober to see that. But I was a bit . . . under the weather. Yeah, we'll go with that. Just the thought of him rubbing up against me sent shivers up and down my spine. I saw his eyes travel south.

"I've always been curious about that necklace of yours. Do you know it's broken?" He asked.

"Yes I do. I've been told this many times." I answered.

"Well, why don't you just replace it?"

"Because it has sentimental value to me. Someone special gave me this necklace and I'm never parting with it. No matter what the condition of it is."

I couldn't tell him it was actually he that gave me the necklace in an alternate reality. Speaking of which, I wonder how AR me is doing in her relationship with AR Caleb.

The song ended and Caleb released me like I was on fire or something. Well, that hurt. So we're back to just being friends. If that's what you could call our sick and twisted dance around each other. God, I tell you. Why can't boys just admit their feelings and be done with it? It would make our jobs as females much easier, let me tell you!

As soon as the shock wore off a little and I took one step forward, Freddy had blocked my exit and bombarded me with excuses as to how he had forgotten where the house was and how he felt so bad about leaving me there. Did I believe any of them? No, but it was the thought that he felt bad for standing me up that made it so delicious. And to make it up to me, he thought that dancing with me would be the only way to make him feel better about it. Of course, being the nice girl that I am, I *had* to say yes to him too.

So I danced a few fast ones with him, nothing too dangerous, and finally a slow one approached. I was planning on making a quick break as soon as the soft sounds hit the speakers. But Freddy wouldn't have that. He took me by the waist and pressed my body against his in a sort of sleazy yet demanding way.

"This is nice," he whispered into my ear.

I tried to pull away and put as much distance between us as possible and I had gotten quite far. Freddy, however, had a bigger advantage of being in public than I and much hornier at the time. It was one thing to grip my waist in a way that should be saved for one person and one person only (you all know who I am speaking of). But when his hands started to wander and reach my backside is when the final straw had broken the camel's back. I wasn't going to allow him to grope me at homecoming let alone any other day. I just wish he could have known that he had just pissed off a vampire!

My nails dug into his arms as much as they could without seriously injuring the boy as I pushed myself out of his hold. His eyes had a look of confusion in them that made me giggle on the inside. Who does he think he is; Fabio? The whole "Nobody turns me down," popped into my head at that very moment which only made me laugh out loud. Only when it came out, it was more or less a croak you'd hear from a toad or something.

"Listen, Freddy, I know you just broke up with Daisy and you're feeling a little bit vulnerable, but I—"

"Daisy and I didn't break up." He interrupted me.

"What?" I asked with outrage in the tone of my voice.

"We're still together. She's off drinking some spiked punch and getting sloshed and I didn't feel like dealing with her. So I came over to you."

His hands shot back out and tried to grab me once more but I stepped back so he couldn't reach.

"But-But you asked me to the dance! You told me you wanted to go with me after you and Daisy broke up!" I started shouting.

"Technically I never said Daisy and I had broken up. You insinuated that all on your own." He replied smugly.

"Ugh! How could you do that to her? She may not be my favorite person in the world, but she certainly doesn't deserve *that*. At least have the decency to tell her face to face that you want to see other girls. At least then she would have the opportunity to dump your sorry behind."

"Do you really believe that Daisy Menendez would break up with me? Me? I'm Freddy DeMarco, for crying out loud! No one in their right mind can pass up an opportunity to be my girl. Not even a little nerd like you." He bit out that last part in order to hurt me. And to tell you all the truth, it did just a bit.

It's moments like these that I wish I wasn't a vampire. If I had done what I wanted to do and slapped him upside the head at that crazy accusation, his head might have flown clear off his body. I tell you, having these powers can be a huge bummer sometimes. Instead, I had just shrugged it off and walked away. It was just as fulfilling for him to know that his words hadn't had the desired effect on me that he wanted.

I found Portia almost right away dancing with some random guy I did not know the name of, but knew he was in our biology class. She was grinding all over him like normal teenagers tend to do at dances while fast dancing. Nothing too raunchy, but I'd still pass every time I'm asked.

Portia knew how to make me feel better just by talking sense into my head about the whole nerd thing. "Freddy's just being a sore loser because you're too smart to fall for his little schemes he pulls," she reassured me. And I believed her. I had to believe her because if she was wrong, that would be the same thing as admitting that Freddy had been right.

"I need to get some air," I told Portia. "Would you like to come?"

"No, I think I'm going to find Brian again and dance with him. It was really getting to your brother. I heard him think about his killing Brian and hiding the body just for touching me." She replied.

"Sweet!" I shrieked in happiness.

She smiled her brilliant smile and I turned and left. I had felt a little better about my entire situation, but I couldn't help the doubt creep up right behind the confidence. Who could really blame me though? I have never had a boyfriend and most guys (pre-vamp) had always thought of me as average looking. Who would want average looking when they could have breath-taking? That's what Portia and Daisy are; I'd never be that beautiful.

And I am a nerd. There's no reason to deny what's obviously in front of your face. I like to read and be alone and I have my very own cat whom I have full conversations with sometimes; one sided, of course. If that doesn't scream nerd, I don't know what does.

As I stepped out into the hallway of the school, I heard someone laughing uproariously from several feet away from me. I couldn't see them but I knew that this person's laughter hadn't pleased another. I hid in one of the doorways just before the sounds and craned my neck as far as it could go without being seen. Although, I could clearly see the scene in front of me.

"Do you think I'm funny? Did you think I was kidding about what I said? She's a nice girl and nice girls should never run through such bad minds as yours. Trust me, if I ever see you around her again, I *will* rip you limb from limb with my bare hands."

Caleb had someone I couldn't quite see pinned up against one of the lockers with his hands balled up in fists around the shirt collar of the unknown person. Whoever it was obviously made Caleb so mad he has to resort to threats. Caleb never threatens anyone unless completely necessary. So, who exactly is the other guy?

"You know that's an empty threat Darwin as well as I do. Besides, you know you think about her tight little body and those big, full lips of hers too. Your mind isn't exactly on her smarts either, Champ." The curiously familiar voice replied confidently.

One swift, hard slam against the lockers and it shut him up.

"I promise you, DeMarco." Freddy?! "If you ever even think about Scarlett Hera in any way that's not strictly platonic, I will have to take action." Caleb had gotten inches away from Freddy's face and gritted through his teeth, "And you don't want to see me take action."

Caleb wanted to seem more ferocious so he thought it funny to scare the wits out of Freddy by letting his eyes go from that warm brown to the wolf's eerie yellow. And it had worked too. Freddy almost peed himself while struggling against Caleb's grip to get away. Eventually Caleb let go and Freddy scampered away like the little baby he was.

Did Caleb really just threaten some boy in order to protect me? Did it really happen or did I just dream up the entire thing? Nope, it really happened. Leaving a cocky Caleb, a frightened Freddy, and a surprised Scarlett. Not to mention the fact that now I have seen him defend my honor, I was more than a little irate. He could stand up for me and yet he couldn't tell me how he really felt about me? Ooo, if I ever get my hands on that boy, I swear I'll . . . .

# Chapter 48

AFTER THE DANCE THAT NIGHT, Emma had come to my room to talk with me about our fight. It was a brief conversation but meaningful nonetheless. She basically said that she was wrong about Krissie and finally came to her senses after she had told Emma that she thought Daisy was right to interfere in our little argument during lunch that day. There was one thing that she said that stuck with me to the next day. After I had apologized for telling her that I was never going to be her sister. She had hugged me and whispered something in my ear.

"I didn't mean that our parents were getting together in order for us to be sisters, Scarlett. I didn't mean that in the least. We're still going to be sisters one day."

What did she mean by that?

Caleb and I were standing by my locker with Griffon, Portia, Max and Alex around us. We were talking about absolutely nothing but how much fun we had at the dance. Useless gibberish, but we needed something to talk about. I was too wrapped up in the conversation with Emma I had the night before to even realize the scene right in front of me. Does anyone else know what I'm talking about?

"Did you hear that we're getting a new student?" Griffon said.

That got my attention.

"Boy or girl?" Max asked. Of course he would.

"Girl," Griffon replied.

All of the boys started smiling that cheesy smile I had seen them with in my vision. Oh no! Even though I was worried about what was about to happen next, I still wanted to slap Caleb silly. He was, after all, one of them who were smirking about a girl he didn't even know. None of us knew. Heck, they didn't even know if she was pretty or not yet. Griffon was the only one not to smile like a complete moron over the news. But you can all guess why.

"Pardon me," the high-pitched chirp said from behind me.

And there she was. In all of her blonde, curvy glory . . . my future project. There was a beam of light hanging over her light hair like a halo. It made me want to punch her square in that perfect jaw of hers. Not that I even know who she is . . . but a girl that can make four guys pick up all of her books without even saying a word has some sort of powers. Especially when one of those guys just happens to be gay.

"My name is Desiree Benoit," she chirped in a French accent.

I was polite and stuck out my hand for her to shake, but she just simply stared at it like it had some sort of incurable disease all over it and she was viable to catch it. Portia tried to be hospitable as well but that Desiree girl ignored her all together. Portia and I looked at each other out of the corner of our eyes and we both knew that this girl meant bad news.

Max was the lucky one to carry Desiree's books to her first class. That didn't stop the rest of our male group, not to mention the entire male population of our school to swoon behind her; looking like her eager lap dogs begging at her feet, waiting for a treat. The next few weeks were bafflement to all women in Willow Creek High. For once, Daisy, Robin, and Shaylee were without their usual posse of testosterone circling around their every move. The three of them were even caught in therapy, discussing their "problems" with new form self-esteem issues. I guess it pays to be semi-tight with the school psychiatrist.

It's the weirdest thing to see her in action. Every time you pass her in the hall she is with a boy. Except, if you look close enough, you'll see a very glazed over look in the guy's eyes and a spookily calm smile on his face. It doesn't matter who the boy is, they all look the same. She has some sort of power within her and I didn't like seeing Max, Alex, nor Caleb around her ever. But, they always were. It was as if Portia and I had been socially isolated by them all of a sudden and we weren't important anymore. She even had Griffon as her best friend!

Every girl despised that little pixie named Desiree but no one questioned her motives with the men in our lives. She was beautiful after all, so everyone just thought it was all about her looks. I, on the other hand, knew something else was behind her. When I had begun to research my case study (Desiree), Portia had started to become suspicious. She demanded for me to tell her what exactly I was doing in my spare time and why it involved the new girl.

I didn't find anything after a month and Aunt Cassie was starting to get edgy about the subject. "You need to figure her out, Scarlett. She could be the potential apocalypse for all we know and you aren't taking this as seriously as you should be." She said to me one afternoon at one of my lessons. OK, first of all, someone that looks like *that* could not bring the apocalypse. She's too dumb to even correctly remember her locker combination without writing it on a sheet of pink, scented paper let alone planning on destroying the world as we know it.

What Aunt Cassie didn't know is that I recruited Portia to find out anything from her father. She could explain to him perfectly the situation going on and hopefully his age will play some sort of benefit for us.

It was an early Wednesday morning in the middle of November and things were getting colder. Not anything out of the ordinary for fall in Willow Creek, Montana. But it certainly shouldn't be almost fifteen degrees already. Everyone was speaking of the massive weather shift and blaming it on the whole "Global Warming" crisis. Me? Well, I had a certain different ascertain on how things were changing. And it had nothing to do with the Earth itself.

"Hey Scar," Portia approached me at my locker sorrowfully.

"So, I'm guessing your dad didn't crack yet, huh?" I asked her.

The first time Portia had approached her father about the subject of Desiree, he told her to leave it alone. That she was just a simple young teen too beautiful for her own good. Portia kept pushing him and pushing him but he kept saying the same thing.

"I'm grounded for a week now. I've avoiding being grounded my whole one-hundred and fifty years of life and now I'm grounded for prying into something that doesn't even involve me. I'm sorry Scarlett, but I don't think there's anything going on here anymore."

"What?" I gritted my teeth in order to keep from losing my temper.

"We've been at this since October and we still haven't figured this out. You might as well accept the fact that Desiree is just a normal girl who can win any guy over just by shaking her ass. There's nothing wrong with that in the least and you know what, maybe I should start using my influencing powers on your brother. It seems to be working with her!" Portia began to tear up and I saw one slip out and cause a single black streak.

"Oh, Portia," I consoled her but pushed her into the nearest restroom to hide from all of the on-lookers who might accidentally see her black tears. She was a bit hesitant at first, but complied to do as I commanded once she realized we were in public and she was making a scene.

She flew into the restroom with some force behind her hands and let the door swing closed on my face. I brushed the gesture off as anger and quickly followed in behind her; only to hit her solid form just a few inches away from the door. Portia was standing there, staring at something and, whatever it was shocked her. It was when I looked to the front of us where I witnessed the most oddly horrifying sight

There, in the center of the restroom, a petite blonde with short, shoulder length straight hair stood. She was staring menacingly into the mirror, muttering some form of Latin to herself. A strange deep green glow was radiating off of her as if some sort of heat wave. She had hung her head and we thought that whatever she was doing was over. The green, string-like smoke had dissipated and the mood seemed to have lightened immensely. Just then, the girl shouted "Attero Sua" and a very powerful explosion spanned through the room.

No matter how massive the explosion seemed to be, it was nothing compared to the vision it had brought upon.

*I was in a hospital bed of some sort, screaming at the top of my lungs for a reason foreign to me. Somebody was telling me to breathe and push and I wasn't listening.*

*"Get them out of me!" I yelled. "They're going to die!"*

*Someone at the foot of my bed was placing my legs up in stirrups and probed my . . . private areas. Oh my sweet Jesus, I was having a baby! Whose baby was this? The room was still blurry and the scene was all in tunnel vision. I could feel someone's hand intertwining with mine and I was squeezing the life out of it. Whoever it was that was brave enough to put their hand in mine at a time like this, couldn't be human.*

*I had then realized that this was my first vision where I hadn't been the observer. Aunt Cassie had told me that once this happened, that my full powers would finally be in my control. I have a strong feeling that just because*

*this accidentally occurred one time, I still don't have full control over my powers. But who knows? This could be the turning point in my life. Back to the actual vision, however.*

*The doctor was placing my baby on my chest and I had a chance to look into the eyes of my future. Not to be taken as a pun. He was a beautiful baby boy with patches of dark chestnut hair atop of his little baby head. His eyes were a very bright, innocent green. No doubt he took after his mother, the vampire. I kissed the top of his forehead and smiled down at him. A pair of warm lips had been placed on my own head and gently nestled into my hair. This was obviously the father of my child. I was about to look up to take in the image of the stranger when the worst thing possible happened.*

*The little boy was being ripped from my grasp and I had felt a sharp, prodding pain down at the bottom of my abdomen. I let out an ear piercing yell and disappeared from the vision.*

Someone was shaking me with full force to wake me up. One voice was worried and frantic while the other had just said my name over and over again in a calm yet demanding manner. No doubt the serene voice was Portia.

"Scarlett, come on wake up," She said one last time before I opened my eyes.

"Oh thank God!"

Kitty was kneeling by my side while I was in my vision state and started to hug me tightly when I snapped out of it. She must have been worried about me the entire time. Portia, on the other hand, knew what was happening so she wasn't as worried. When Kitty had finally let go of me, I had realized what I had been witnessing previously.

"K-Kitty?" I stammered. "Umm, I think you should explain just what happened before I . . . passed out."

Hey, if she was some sort of evil being, I'm not going to let her know what I am until I'm fully aware of what she can do. I might be a vampire; but that can only take you so far. Now, was I planning on telling her even after she told me what she was, if she wasn't of any danger to Portia and me? Well, we'll save that for when it actually happens.

Kitty stood from the ground and walked back over to the sink. She couldn't face us for some odd reason.

"I'm a witch," she boldly stated.

"No you're not, Kit. You're a very nice girl—" Portia began before she was interrupted.

"No Portia, I'm an actual witch. You know, like magical powers and broomsticks and spells. I'm an honest to God witch and there's nothing I can do about it."

I was in shock. I've never seen one in real life before. Of course, I've watched *Sabrina the Teenage Witch* when I was younger. But to see one up close and personal like this was . . . well, I'm not going to lie. It was cool! Oh this is priceless, my brother's in love with a witch and he's utterly clueless about the whole thing. Too bad I couldn't tell him about this. I would have *loved* holding this over his head.

She was expecting us to hate her for this. To stone her or something. Well, I hate to break it to her, but there will be no stoning by the two of us any time soon. That would make us hypocrites and neither of us wants to be anything of such sorts.

"Cool," Portia said shrugging her shoulders.

"Did you hear me correctly? I'M A WITCH!" She said louder.

Portia and I looked at her before I said, "And we're vampires."

Kitty's jaw dropped almost to the floor.

"Are-are you serious?"

"Yeah. Actually, I'm psychic too so I have that going for me. You're not alone, Kitty. Trust me, there are others."

"Yeah, I know about Caleb; if that's what you're referring to." She told me.

Portia had glanced at me and it was as if I could see into her mind and knew what she was thinking. We wanted to know what she was doing in here before we were came inside. She was obviously up to something bad; otherwise there wouldn't have been that explosion. Well, actually I don't know much about witchcraft in real life, but explosions don't sound like anything good.

"Umm, Kitty, I don't mean to be nosy. But what where you doing in here anyway?"

She looked at us and blushed, "It's a long story."

"We've got time," Portia butted in.

"Well, I was walking in the hallway, going to my second period English class, when I spotted something off putting in the corner where the cafeteria meets the lockers. He-he was making out with her! She must not get away with that. Not when I'm still living!" She hollered.

"Who are you talking about? Who did you see?"

"Desiree . . . Desiree was . . . Desiree was making out with your brother!"

"What?!" I shouted in shock.

"Max?" Portia had asked angrily. I glanced over to her and saw she was elongating her fangs. Now, I don't know if she was about to attack Kitty for saying this or bust down the door and search for Desiree; either way, it wasn't good.

"No, Holden," Kitty corrected.

Oh, thank God! Kitty has no idea how close she had just come to her death. Good thing she has those powers to defend herself against Portia. I don't think I would be able to stop the massacre if it were actually Max. This was all just too sickening!

Don't get me wrong, my heart went out to the poor girls. But there's only so much unrequited love I could take. And it doesn't help that the two girls near me right now, my friends, were in love with my brothers. Who wants to hear about girls crushing on their kin? I'd prefer not to listen to the things Portia wants to do to Max. Or witnessing Kitty being the one to be making out with Holden instead of Desiree. But I guess you can't help who you love. I'm the walking example of that sentence right there.

Kitty was torn up about Holden, yes, but she could also help with the ongoing investigation of a Miss Desiree Benoit. She was another supernatural being, the only one we knew that wasn't being influenced by that succubus out there. Although that's one option, I highly doubt Desiree is *that* evil. But I am going to get to the bottom of this. I'm going to figure this out and I'm going to figure it out soon.

# Chapter 49

$\mathcal{K}$ITTY AND I WERE SITTING at the diner the night before the first of December, enjoying each other's company and sharing some pumpkin cheesecake (the diner's specialty). The diner was empty of all customers save for the two of us and Kitty was about the close up. It was nice being friends with an older person for a change. And I didn't mean by several centuries or anything, because that would mean I was crossing Portia out of the running. I meant physically older.

Every girl tried to ignore Desiree and her affect on the male population except the three of us. We were determined to figure her out even if it took years. There was also a part of me that wanted to figure Desiree out before Caleb actually fell for her. I didn't want him establishing any strong feelings for her unless they were created by her. That would just devastate me!

"So, how's your brother doing?" Kitty interrupted the silence while looking at me with sad eyes. It had been months since Holden had spoken two words to Kitty, inside or out of school. And to make matters worse, instead of talking about Kitty all the time, I have to suffer with hearing about Desiree from Holden. Even Max and Caleb where parading around the house with metaphorical t-shirts that read "Desiree's #1 Fan" on them. I couldn't escape it no matter what house I was staying at.

"Still as dumb as ever," I joked to lighten the mood.

And it worked, she was laughing. It was nice to hear her laugh for once. Kitty used to be such a cheerful person once upon a time, so it was very rare to see her lips crack at the seams to reveal a smile. It was almost as if she had become possessed by the personality I once took on when my mother had died. Right before I met Caleb.

Oh Caleb, the thick, clueless, idiot love of my life.

"I found it! I found it! I found it! I found it! I found it! I found it!" Portia came running up to the table screaming. She shoved a piece of paper down on the table and plopped down in the free seat next to me. "Read." She stated and slid the printed sheet over in my direction.

"Hey Porsh', did you want something to drink?" Kitty asked Portia.

"Umm," she thought for a moment. "How about a *Pepsi?*"

Instead of getting up from the table we were sitting at, she motioned her hand over to the cups on the counter, palm up, and waved it around. The cup had moved from the countertop as if by an invisible string pulling it along over to the soda nozzles near the back. She then lifted her other hand and made the nozzle that had the Pepsi logo on the front of it spray into the cup. She did this all without saying a word. When Portia had grasped the drink from out of mid-air, she glared at Kitty.

"OK Harry Potter. Let's stop showing off and get down to business, eh?"

Since we learned about Kitty's powers, Portia has been a bit jealous of Kitty. I think it's because Portia's no longer the cool, unique one of the group. But in everyone else's view Portia will always be unique no matter who joins in. I just think it's funny to watch.

I turned my eyes to the paper in front of me and read the title of what exactly this was about.

"Sirens?" I confusedly questioned Portia.

"Go on, read it," she pushed.

"Sirens were first introduced in Mythological history as devilish creatures known to lure sailors to their death by singing songs. They were known to resemble beautiful, youthful blonde women with no known physical flaws." My eyes were growing larger by the second.

"Some say that these wretched monsters were born from Venus herself, sent to Earth to destroy the pure and fittest to love. Sailors had seemed to be the only able victim of that time due to the Siren women needing water to survive. But in current studies, it has been shown that Siren's have now branched out, attacking any male victim that crosses their path.

It is said that Siren's, like werewolves, react to the lunar's beams during the full moon. The creature will need to feed on the soul of a pure at heart, otherwise she will die a horrible, and boisterous death. This is the only time the Siren uses "the sacred call" to lure the poor soul in. It resembles a lovely song on the outside, but the one she is targeting will be the only one to hear the message lying underneath. She will pull him to the closest body of water where she will devour him inside and out until he is just a shell of a person. This needs to occur every full moon before sunrise or else the Siren will die.

The Siren has no particular enemies at hand. Although she has specific powers targeting the male species, women should watch out for this devil as well. There has never been an attack on a female recorded in history, but it does not mean it couldn't happen.

*The Song of Sin* written by Doctor Andrew Gregory in 1742 is the most known artifact that produces all of his theories about Sirens as well as studies performed. To learn more about this topic click the link below or visit your local Barnes and Noble bookstore to check out Doctor Gregory's work."

"So, Desiree's a siren?" Kitty chimed in.

"Looks like it." I replied. "When's the next full moon?"

"Tomorrow," Portia answered.

"Well, that means we have less than twenty four hours to find out who Desiree is going to make her next meal and stop her. This should be easy as pie, huh? We just have to think; who do we know who is pure of heart and will most likely be stupid enough to fall under her spell?"

Just then my phone rang. Caleb's name lit up my caller id and the idea had hit me like a ton of bricks right to my heart.

She was spending much more time with Caleb lately than anyone else. It seemed as if she was . . . targeting him. Oh no, I've *got* to stop her! I slid open my sidekick and answered the phone with a swift, "hello?" Caleb's voice just seemed so innocent and naïve that I couldn't help but choke back a sob.

"Hey Scarlett it's me. I had a question I needed to ask you before tomorrow. Hope I didn't catch you at a bad time."

"No, not at all. What is it, Caleb." I replied with fake cheer in my voice.

"Did you plan on going to my birthday party tomorrow night?" He asked.

Oh God, not only was tomorrow night Caleb's birthday, but it was going to be his death too if we couldn't get to Desiree in time. To tell you the truth, I had forgotten that December first was Caleb's birthday.

"Umm, I'm not really sure yet. Why do you ask?"

"Because you kind of can't."

My jaw dropped open and tears had made their brief appearance in my eyes before rage took over. Why was he so mad at me to forbid me from going to his eighteenth birthday? I didn't do anything to him recently to make him do this to me. At least, not consciously anyway. Was it because Shaylee was going? Because if this was true; I'm about the reach through this phone and choke his little canine neck myself!

"Why not?" I softly asked him, trying to keep my control.

"Because you just can't!" He shouted. "Just accept it and stay home tomorrow night or else something bad will happen!" And then he hung up.

What was his problem?

# Chapter 50

*D*ESIREE WILL BE STOPPED BEFORE she has a chance get to Caleb. If it's the last thing I do, he *will* be protected. He's my world, my heart, and no matter what could happen—whatever powers Desiree may have—I won't let her touch a single hair on his head. Portia understood and respected this. Kitty was still trying to grasp the concept of the siren ways, but since she was in love with Holden, she can also grasp why I'm so protective of Caleb. I didn't care what Desiree could do to me. It didn't faze me one bit even if she does know how to kill me; I don't care.

Operation "destroy Desiree" was in full swing the second the three of us stepped out of Kitty's car. Of course, Caleb couldn't know I was there because he would probably go crazy and force me to go home. No this needed to be a covert case in which case I would be going in full undetected by the guest of honor.

I can't take credit for the name of our apparent mission. Portia had thought it would be more professional if we named it so she took the liberty and there it was. The plan was to just scare her a little. To make her cry her little eyes out and run back home to wherever it is that she came from. So simple, but it will most likely be effective enough to work. At least I hope it does. So I wandered around the party for about an hour searching for my prey. There must have been hundreds of people at this place but I never once say Caleb. I suppose it was a good thing, but it would still be nice to know where he was hiding. To know if he was hiding from me.

The pool made an eerie, luminescent glow to my already pale white skin. In a way, it actually *made* me look like a vampire for once since I became one. I hope that I find Desiree near the pool because there's no doubt in my mind that I would scare her witless in this state. But unbeknownst to me at the time, Desiree has already found Caleb and was trying her best to seduce him. However, there's one minor little detail that she had overlooked when choosing her meal for the month.

I had circled the drink table about three times before giving in and taking a cup with red liquid inside and gulping it down in one swallow. This wasn't normal punch. It was spiked with something other than alcohol too. I looked down into the glass and swirled it around to distinguish just what the strange substance was. It had the tang of the fruit punch with the bitterness of vodka and just a little hint of something extra. And as I dabbed my tongue on the roof of my mouth to identify it, I tasted chocolate. Just as I was thinking about someone adding chocolate sauce to the punch as a joke, I felt my fangs start to slide down my gums and poke down onto my lower lip.

Human blood.

"Scarlett!" Someone had yelled from behind me.

Portia ran up to me and took me by the wrist and started pulling me toward the mansion. She had claimed to have caught Desiree in the act and now was the perfect time to strike. But first, I needed to warn Portia that someone was trying to play a trick on us by spiking the punch with blood. Someone had a plan and it certainly didn't involve any friendly play to any vampires.

"Stop, stop! Wait a second, Portia I need to tell you something." I tried to get her attention by dragging my feet against the hardwood floor of the living area. I couldn't really call it a living *room* because honestly it could have its own zip code it's so big and unnecessary.

"What?" She grumbled facing me with my wrist still firmly in her hand.

"I think someone wants us to kill tonight," I told her.

She gave me a funny look and giggled at what I had just said. Did she think I was kidding? Maybe I was wrong and the blood in the punch really isn't a threat to us. To the humans, it would just make them sick to their stomach and their bodies would make them vomit it all back up. But if it didn't have any serious effects on us, then why did I want to run right through the sliding glass door and sink my teeth into Bobby Mason?

"I'm serious Portia. The punch is spiked with blood."

Her laughter stopped and she stared at me with such fear I've never seen before. She frantically darted to the sliding door and stared outside where the drink table sat. I watched as her eyes darted from person to person, each with a glass of the juice inside. They must just taste the alcohol as of right now. But there was too much blood in there to keep it down for them. There's no way any of them who took a drink will go home tonight and not get sick.

All of a sudden, Logan Pierce started to look very enticing to me. I stalked up to the window myself and watched him. He took a very large gulp of punch, bending his head backward and exposing the column of his neck to me. My mouth watered with the simple thought of plunging my fangs deep into his throat and sucking him dry. I felt my fingers grasp the handle of the door and began to slowly move it over so I could sneak my way out.

Logan turned toward me and saw me staring. He probably thought I was trying to seduce him or something. No doubt it's what I looked like. My body felt like it was on fire . . . but it felt good. It felt like I had power like I've never had before and I knew just what I needed to make the power grow stronger. And that, my friends, is Logan Pierce's blood!

"No!" I heard Portia shout as she slammed the door in my face. A second more of waiting and she would have crushed my face in between. Nonetheless, it snapped me back to consciousness and I began to see reason. But the blood lust was still lingering and begging to be brought to the surface.

"Scarlett we need to get out of here now," she calmly but firmly told me. But I wasn't listening. Something else had caught my attention at that point and held on stronger than the thirst had just moments ago.

I now had a clear vision of the kitchen in the mansion. The two of them were sitting in the same chair, him in the normal position and she straddling his lap. She was whispering in his ear and he was smiling like a stupid idiot clearly under her spell. The two giggled and he wrapped his arms around her waist and (if it were possible) brought her closer to him. I felt my fangs slide down even more and grow razor sharp. They were preparing themselves obviously. So, I did what my brain was screaming for me to do and started to walk over to them.

"What are you doing, Scarlett? I told you we have to leave. NOW!" I heard Portia yelling at me still from the living room.

I ignored her and kept on walking.

He didn't see me. I was in plain sight of him and he didn't even once pull his eyes from that seductress to see that I was coming after him. She had obviously already started her ritual because he was only concentrating on her. No guy, no matter who the girl is, would pass up looking at another hot girl sauntering over to you for the world. I still had to ask the question why Caleb though. Because I honestly didn't know out of all the guys in our class, how she picked him.

When I finally reached them, I cleared my throat to catch their attention and saw that Desiree had in fact already started. Not only were there sucking marks on his neck, but when he looked at me for the first time that night, I saw his eyes go from bright silver to his natural brown and briefly to yellow before returning. He hopped off the chair faster than I could imagine, dropping Desiree on the floor as well. I held back a chuckle as I saw her rubbing her back as she stood up.

"I told you not to come here tonight Red," He growled in my direction. He was mad at me? *At me?* Oh, you have got to be kidding me with this!

"Well, I had my own arrangements to attend to here. Sorry," I replied to him, but didn't take my eyes off of Desiree.

We were trapped in a battle of unspoken understanding and we both knew what needed to happen. Caleb, on the other hand, was completely clueless about the entire thing and probably thought it was all about him. Well, sorry to say to him, but it wasn't. Yes, I came here tonight to stop her from eating him. But it doesn't mean that I wouldn't stop her from doing it to anyone else I knew as well.

"Well, arrangements or not, you can't be here. I need to take you home right away or else—"

"Just let me talk to Desiree alone for a minute and I'll go." I interrupted him.

Caleb's eyes darted from me to Desiree about three times before agreeing to my commands and telling me he'd be waiting in his truck to take me home. This was such a great night! First off, I catch Miss Succubus making out with him in the kitchen and now I have to threaten her enough to scare her away. And I have to deal with him basically pushing me away too! How is this fair? Please tell me if anyone knows!

Once Caleb was gone, Desiree and I began to circle each other. In a way, I suppose it was our way of challenging one another to make the first move. More or less calling each other's bluff until something happened. And I made sure that I was the one to start it.

I grabbed her by the cheap cotton sweater she had on and shoved her against the refrigerator. The air went out of her lungs for a few brief seconds, but she caught it up and just simply laughed it off. Oh, that just got under my skin that did! So I slammed her up against it again with more force this time to make her see my point. She coughed and sputtered for a bit longer but she managed to speak.

"You can do that as many times as you want, I still won't be bothered by it," she gasped out.

"That's not what you're short breath is saying at the moment you little skank!" I bit out at her. I barred my fangs and hoped that it would start the scaring process.

"Speak for yourself, leech!" She spit her retort.

"Keep away from Caleb Darwin or else you will find yourself missing your jugular. Go home to wherever you came from and stay there. Because if I ever find out that you have come back to Willow Creek, I will personally make a surprise visit for you. And you won't be breathing when I leave."

I thought I was menacing. I think she thought I was menacing too because I could feel her slightly shake underneath my clutches even though her face was hard as stone. She was breaking and I was getting to her.

"And just what makes you so sure I won't go after your little boyfriend after he leaves you at home tonight? He was enjoying himself very much before you showed up and ruined our fun." She pouted.

"I'll warn him that you're trying to eat him and he'll stay away from you the rest of the night." I counteracted.

"Oh please Honey; you have no idea the powers I hold!" She cackled like a witch from those old time movies. She was scaring me more than I was scaring her. But I couldn't let her know that. So I got inches away from her face, tilted my head at the base of her throat, and grazed my canine teeth against her delicate flesh. And I received the response I wanted. She shuttered in fear against me and fought to be released from my grip.

"Fine! Fine!" She screamed. "I'll leave him alone!"

I put a bit more pressure onto her skin in order to make her feel my fangs just a bit more before saying, "And you'll leave Willow Creek?"

"Yes, yes I'll leave Willow Creek! Just please, don't puncture my perfect skin! I can't deal with a scar, I just . . . I can't be ugly!" She was finally crying.

Oh darling, if you only knew.

I let go of her sweater and her feet returned to the linoleum floor below the both of us. She clutched at her throat as if I actually had bitten her. What a drama queen! I started to walk away from her when I heard her mutter, "But before I go—"

Desiree started to spout off something in a language I had no idea. I didn't know what she was saying but nothing was happening. It was nothing that Kitty had ever said so she obviously wasn't part witch or anything like that. What was she saying? I watched her lips curl up into a mischievous smile when she was finished. A small buzzing sensation had filled my gut almost as if I had been drinking alcohol the whole night. It was a wonderful feeling, so it clearly wasn't from Desiree. She was looking to hurt me; not to make me feel good.

"Enjoy the rest of your night," she cooed before disappearing out the sliding glass door and back into the roaring party.

Well, that was easy. Almost . . . too easy. I guess I'll figure out that foreign language tomorrow and see what it means then. Right now, I had Caleb waiting to scold me inside his truck. Why oh why did he want me gone from his birthday party so bad was beyond me. But whatever the reason, it certainly wasn't necessary to bring me home himself.

# Chapter 51

'Breathe Scarlett, just breathe,' I kept telling myself as I approached his truck.

He opened the passenger's side door for me from the inside with a face that clearly represented anger. His lips were pulled into a thin line and his brows were drawn together. Not to mention his limbs were tenser than steel. I was in trouble, but I wasn't going to apologize for saving his life. And if he was expecting that, well he isn't going to get it!

"Why did you come here?" he asked me while I was buckling my seatbelt.

"I already told you, I came here because I had other—"

"Don't give me that crap Scarlett! I know better now tell me the truth!" He shouted.

I chewed my bottom lip for a few seconds in order to think about what to tell him. I had told Desiree I would warn him so that if she *did* go back to the party that night and try and eat Caleb, then he'd at least know. But what if she didn't go back? There's no need for him to worry about her and why I had protected him like I did. Plus, he would probably take my rescue the wrong way and explain to me how we're just friends and always will be. Then again . . . he could want more than friendship if I told him. What if?

"Promise not to be upset with me?" I asked.

"I can't make that promise," he replied through clenched teeth.

I blew out a breath and started to tell him the truth, "Portia, Kitty and I found out that Desiree is a siren and she wanted to eat you." I looked over at him briefly to see if he was taking it as well as I had hoped. He seemed to be concentrating on the road a bit too much. His hands were white-knuckling the steering wheel and his face looked like he was in pain. Was this hurting his feelings in some way?

"We read that sirens like her feed only during the full moon by a body of water. So I knew that when I saw you to on the chair that I had time before she sunk her teeth in you. I had to stop her Caleb, and I did. But I hope you're not mad at me for taking matters into my own hands." I finished.

I heard him breathing heavily with his eyelids droopy and his muscles were twitching as if he were trying so hard to keep it together. His tongue darted out and licked his lips while he rubbed his hands up and down the steering wheel in circular motions.

"Caleb, are you OK?" I asked him.

His head snapped to look at me and I saw those eerie yellow eyes glowing bright in the dark. Caleb's teeth were barred and his eyes were slanted as if to warn me to stay away from him. "Do I look OK?" He snarled.

I scooted toward the window to keep my distance from the maniac werewolf next to me in the truck.

'Jump out of the truck, Scarlett. Jump out now!' the unknown voice screamed inside my head.

Just then, Caleb screamed and grasped his head in his hands and squeezed. I couldn't just leave him like this. Not when he needed my help. So I pushed all of the warning calls in my mind aside and flew over to Caleb to grab the wheel and steer it for him. We were closest to Jefferson River so I turned the wheel toward the bank and moved my foot so I could press on the brake at the right time.

'Ahh, this is like torture! Oh god, just let me die!' Caleb's voice boomed inside my head.

He was snarling and howling behind me and kept bumping into me so much that I wasn't sure that I could park the truck without crashing it.

Which I did.

The grill of the truck smashed into a nearby tree just before the bank started to go downhill into the river. The airbags deployed but no one was hurt . . . not yet at least. I pulled a flailing Caleb out of the truck and sat by his side as he wiggled and screamed and gripped his head, riding out the pain. I didn't know what to do to help him. I felt like I was the one hurting him because I couldn't make his pain go away.

"Caleb? Caleb, what's wrong?" I begged.

Nothing came out of his mouth but more screams and moans. Do you realize how agonizing it is to stand there and watch the love of your life writhing around and you can't do anything to help them. Tears were pouring out of my eyes in an instant as I placed my own head in my hands and prayed that he would be alright.

Silence.

Oh no, did he die? I can't bear the thought if he had just given up and died on me. I searched my brain for any thoughts of his. I concentrated my hardest to try and delve into his mind but I came out empty handed. This was it. No more Caleb in my life. My head rose from behind my hands slowly and looked down where Caleb's body lay. I was hoping he would look peacefully asleep instead of dead as a doornail. But he looked neither. His yellow eyes were open and fixed on me and a *very* creepy smile took up most of his features. He was breathing steadily but as my hand rested on his arm, I could feel his pulse going absolutely crazy in his blood stream.

"Hello my love. What are you doing out on this beautiful, full moon night?" He asked me in the eeriest voice you could imagine.

"U-umm, C-Caleb you took me here." I stuttered, backing up slightly.

He got up on all fours and kept his eyes in my direction and whispered, "Well then, I mustn't disappoint." His butt planted itself on the dirt bellow him, his head rolled back and his right foot came up and scratched his ear like a dog with an itch would do. Then, he bayed at the moon like that of a wolf—which I knew he was, but it was still quite scary to see.

I tried once more to pry inside of his mind in order to hear his thoughts but it was no use. It was as if his mind had a lock on it and it was Scarlett proof. I would have to go figure out what's going on the old fashion way. And although it was very dangerous, I had to do it. I just hope I don't infuriate him in the process because I sure didn't need an angry werewolf in front of me right now!

"Caleb, what's going on?"

Instead of answering me, he rolled over on his back again and had his arms and legs bent in the air. That creepy smile he was wearing before had turned into one that a child would have on when they were about to get a piece of candy. His lower half was sort of wiggling back and forth as if . . . well, as if he had a tail and he was happy. What did he expect me to do?

"Caleb . . . ?"

"Rub my belly! Rub my belly! Please, please *phu-lease* rub my belly!" He begged in such an adorable voice. His tongue lolled out of his mouth and he began panting in anticipation. Honestly . . . I couldn't refuse.

"Aww, how could I say no to such cute little puppy?"

I placed one of my palms on his abdomen and began to slide it back and forth. The strange this is, it didn't feel weird at all. A small giggle escaped my mouth as I heard him whine in appreciation. He actually let out a little bark once I hit the right spot on his left side just below his rib cage. That's when one of his legs started to go. I brought both of my hands to that special spot and began to vigorously scratch until his whole leg was going insane shaking. It was the funniest sight you could ever imagine seeing.

Caleb shot up on his own accord, and sprang onto the banks right in front of the flowing river. I watched him remove all of his clothes—turning my head as he showed the important parts. No matter who he is, I'd rather not see a fully naked man quite yet in my life—transform into that grey, black and white wolf, and leap into the chilly waters. He splashed around, playing with the foamy current that swirled around him. I've never seen him happier in the short time that I've known him.

So I decided to join him.

The shore was only a short walk, but somewhere along the way between the crashed truck and the river, things got a little blurry. Literally. My sight grew foggy and I could barely make out objects not three feet from me. I reached out to clutch anything in front of me I could, but it happened to be a human shoulder. A naked human shoulder at that. I looked up to see a very fuzzy looking pink blob of male hotness. My head shook from side to side a couple of times in order to clear my vision but it was a failed attempt.

It didn't matter for much longer however. Because in the next second, I felt the familiar touch of Caleb's lips against my own. Caleb was kissing me again! Oh this is such a great moment I can't believe it's actually happening! I instantly forgot about my lack of vision, closed my eyes and enjoyed Caleb's mouth and tongue exploring my own. God, I love him.

'Scarlett.'

I tried to ignore the frightening voice that just whispered out my name inside of my head and concentrated on wrapping my arms around Caleb's neck and giving myself into the moment. But the voice came back with much more force and sounded like it was up to something evil. It was then that I heard Desiree's foreign language in her own tongue once more. The words played clear as day inside my head and I couldn't ignore them. But it was too late. Everything went black and my mind went blank.

A very strong heat streamed down from above me and seeped into my marble cold skin. It didn't rightly warm me, considering I'm a vampire and I can't ever be warm. But it did make me uncomfortable long enough for me to open my eyes and realize it was morning. I tried to twist my body in order to stretch myself fully awake but I couldn't. Something vise-like held me in place and even when I tried with my full strength I couldn't escape.

Nonetheless, I twisted enough to see what was behind me. I just never expected it to be Caleb. We must have fallen asleep here . . . in the bed of his truck. The ribbed bars on the bottom dug into my back even if there was a blanket underneath us. As I wiggled around to try and escape, a sharp pain shot up my legs and made me flinch. I ignored it the best I could and kept on trying to free myself. My fingers ended up doing their job and prying his hands from around my waist. I sat up only to realize something *very* important that I was missing.

My clothes.

I looked over at Caleb's sleeping form and noticed that he was still shirtless with only a very rough, wool blanket covering his important parts that were clearly naked as well. I quickly grabbed my clothes from the side of his truck, threw them on and ran as fast as my vampire speed could take me all the way back to my house before he had a chance to even open his eyes.

Now, I'm definitely not one to condone teenage sexual activities. I'm the type of person to believe that teens should wait a considerable amount of time to engage in such things. I myself didn't plan on losing my virginity until at least college. Even then, I would have needed to be in a committed relationship with a man I know I have at least some type of future with. But obviously that dream has been completely shot to Hell now. The strange thing is; I can't remember anything about it. It's not as if I was drinking last night either so I couldn't blame it on alcohol.

Wait a minute, could it have had something to do with the blood in the cup that someone had put there? But how would blood affect vampires like that? It would make them thirsty, granted, but it shouldn't make their sight blurry and cause blackouts. This was definitely not one big, long vision. I was clearly awake now and last night I didn't see anything after I blacked out. The only thing I could think of is that foreign language Desiree was spouting off at me right before I left the party.

I gathered up my laptop, sat on my bed and typed in what I could remember into the *Yahoo!* Search engine. What had come up was just some useless nonsense about the French language and sessions to sign up for to learn it. Not something I needed in the least. But I knew something that *could* possibly help me. Instead of typing in the words of the voodoo she was trying to perform, I typed in *Songs of Sin* by Andrew Gregory. And what do you know, there was tons of information useful to me.

Turns out Desiree had cursed me. She had used an ancient spell only sirens know that causes the person put under it to lose consciousness but still be capable to function for seven hours straight. Not a very useful spell on anyone else, but I suppose she had other plans in mind when casting it. Did she want something to happen to me and Caleb? That doesn't make any sense though. I thought she had wanted Caleb all to herself. Why would she want me to sleep with him?

"Scarlett, come down here please!" I heard my dad shout from downstairs.

Oops. He sounded peeved at me. I wonder what I did now. I clearly told him last night that I would be hanging out with Portia and staying at her house. Unless . . . he found out where I really was last night. But that was impossible. No one else knew where I was last night so I think I'm in the clear. At least, I hope I am.

"Sit down; I need to tell you something." He ordered when I reached the living room. I noticed Max lying on the couch so I pushed his feet over and took over one cushion for myself. He huffed about it, but I could care less what would make him more comfortable.

"Whoa sis, what happened to your shoulder?" Max asked me in shock.

I looked down and saw blood trickling down my arm. The source was a large hole with ragged looking edges just south of the joint in my shoulder by my shoulder blade. How come it wasn't healing? Did Caleb bite me last night or something? But why would he do that if what happened clearly didn't make him angry? Well, I suppose I can't make that assumption considering I wasn't conscious at the time. But I certainly needed to take care of this if it wasn't healing on its own.

"Oh, I must have fallen last night when Portia and I were going to the movies. Can I quickly go and grab some gauze and tape for this dad before you start in on whatever it is you need to tell me?" I asked him politely.

He nodded but I could tell that his mind was elsewhere. I watched as his hand raked through his thinning hair in frustration. Whatever was bugging him was obviously a doosey. My dad almost never got this way unless it was something serious. I quickly ran to the upstairs bathroom, grabbed what I needed to bandage myself up, and brought it back downstairs where I previously was. I was cutting a patch of gauze when he began.

"I was delivering some paperwork to the police station this morning and I overheard Chief Martin talking to Mr. and Mrs. Johnson. Now I know it's not right to eavesdrop, but I know this will be all over the news in a matter of minutes so I might as well tell you first. Umm, it turns out that they found Alex Johnson's dead body by the south end of Jefferson River a few hours ago. I thought you two ought to know considering you were good friends with him."

My jaw literally dropped to the floor at that point. Max flew straight up and sat perfectly at attention. It wasn't every day you hear about one of your classmates being murdered let alone one of your good friends! I wonder if Portia heard anything about it yet? I wonder how she'll take the news about it all? She and Alex hadn't been dating but she cared about him nonetheless just like the rest of us. Oh, I wonder if Griffon knows? Aww, poor Griffon! That was his best friend.

I wonder if Max was thinking about his stupid little rivalry with Alex just then. Because I know if Daisy was murdered, I would be thinking about it for the rest of my life. Thinking if there was truly something I could have done to get along with her more. Especially considering Max and Alex never really talked let alone argued like Daisy and I did. Oh, I couldn't stay in my house right now. I had to go and find Portia and talk to her about this.

"M-may I please be excused?"

Before my dad had a chance to respond, I was out the door balling my eyes out within seconds. The run to Portia's house wasn't that long . . . but it seemed to take an eternity with the news I barred. Imagine being the one to break the news to your best friend that the guy who had a crush on her has just been murdered. But she was the only one I could talk to about anything and she also knew about Desiree. There was no doubt in my mind that Desiree was the one who killed Alex.

I didn't bother knocking on the door at Portia's house. No I more or less barged in and ran to Portia's room like my tail was on fire. Jocelyn and Andrew had called out their hellos to me from the kitchen when I had passed it, but I didn't spend time to stop and return the favor. I sailed past Kate's room where she was coloring in a coloring book on top of her bed.

I burst through Portia's bedroom door and expected to find her asleep in her bed, but that's not where she was. Far from it actually.

"Oh no! Oh, Portia you didn't . . . "

Sitting in the corner furthest away from the bed, shaking with so much power that it appeared to be her own personal earthquake and covered in blood was Portia. The red substance was smeared all over her face and hands with very large splotches on her Dolce and Gabbana sweater she had just bought not too long ago. Her eyes were wide and filled with tears, which made the blood stains mix with the black streaks. No matter what she had just done, I was still her best friend and she needed comfort right now. But I still have no idea what happened and needed to proceed with as much caution as I could. For all I know she could have went on a killing spree last night and could take my head off in one bite. So I walked calmly and slowly over to her, knelt down beside her and wrapped her in a tight hug.

"I d-didn't mean to," she wailed into my shoulder (the good one). "It was that stupid blood someone put in the punch. It smelled so good I couldn't stop drinking it. And he *had* to follow me! He couldn't just leave me alone! I told him . . . I begged him to go away and he wouldn't. I'm a murderer, Scarlett."

I held her close and reassured her that I knew she didn't mean to do it. "I understand," I told her. "Blood makes us do crazy things. No one will ever find out it was you and it's over now. Don't worry, Portia."

Now, if only I could convince myself no one would find out what Portia had done. I'd rather not have my best friend go to prison over something she had no control over. And there's just one question that lingered in my head after finding out it was actually Portia who killed Alex by accident. Who exactly did Desiree consume as her meal last night?

# Chapter 52

*N*O MATTER WHAT REALITY I am in, I've been to too many funerals for my lifetime. Nonetheless, I still had to attend Alex's because it was the right thing to do. Being one of his friends when he was alive and all. Plus, I kind of had to accompany Portia for moral support. All this week she's been depressed and convinced that it was completely her fault Alex was dead. There were plenty of other factors who could be blamed for this before her.

I was getting ready for the wake at Caleb's place. Emma and my mom wanted to drive with me to show their support to Mr. and Mrs. Johnson so I agreed to just go over there two hours before it started. I had just gotten out of the shower and threw a pair of Max's old sweatpants and a wife-beater tank top on while I put on make-up and such. The door to my bedroom flew open and in stepped Caleb wearing his dress slacks and nothing else. That boy really has to start wearing a shirt more.

"What can I help you with, Hon'?" I asked him.

He looked at me funny. Holding a mechanical razor in his hand, he stepped back and looked at me like I was insane. I know he had been avoiding me in school every day since his birthday, but I had just thought that it was because he didn't want to talk about what happened between the two of us. What if he really didn't remember? I've heard nothing in his thoughts about the two of us after all. It's been all the usual stuff; school, food, cars, girls, and sleep. You know; normal boy brain stuff.

"OK, anyways," he shook his head and stepped further into my room. "I was wondering if you could clean me up before the funeral. I desperately need a trim and now's the perfect time."

"Yeah fine, let's get this over with," I answered him a bit snippy.

I pulled up a chair from my vanity and set it in the middle of the room. I also gave him the towel I used to wrap around his shoulders to keep the hair from falling on his slacks. He had set the razor on two and I began to go to work. Now, it wasn't the first time I've done this. Max and Holden used to shave their heads all the time. My mom taught me to do it for them so she didn't have to so often. I still hated to do this though.

It was nice having the opportunity to touch Caleb again. Even though it wasn't in an intimate manner or anything. I just hate the fact that I haven't had the nerve to bring up the events that happened the other night between us. Maybe this is the perfect opportunity to casually mention it? I could probably work it in somehow that he and I had sex in the back of his truck bed. I have no idea how, but it's possible.

"Caleb, can I ask you something?" I tried to talk over the sound of the buzzing razor.

"Sure," he replied.

I let out a breath and started the best way I knew how. "What exactly happens to a werewolf during a full moon?"

There was a long pause between us. Caleb was probably trying to think of a way to let me down easy or something. Who knows, maybe he would actually answer the question for a change. It would be nice to get a straight answer instead of a cryptic and twisted mystery. But I'm not getting my hopes up for such a miracle. The entire time I've been in Willow Creek—alternate reality or not—people absolutely LOVE to keep things a secret from me and avoid questioning altogether.

Not that I'm bitter about it or anything. But how would you like it if you were the one left in the dark for just about everything. Let me tell you, it's not a pleasant thing. Especially if you're the one on the receiving end of the secret. That hasn't occurred many times to me, but when it has it sure hasn't been in my favor at all. I just hope that when Caleb does finally speak, it's nothing to do with me and he'll tell me why he wanted me to stay away from his birthday.

I'd like to believe that there's an attraction between the two of us. But it's been one sided for so long I don't know what to believe anymore.

'OK, I have to tell her.' Caleb's voice said in my head.

He repositioned himself in the chair which almost made me knick his ear. Not that it would have been permanent, but I don't want him messing up my work as well. So I grabbed both sides of his face and turned his head back to its original position while commanding for him to sit still.

"Werewolves tend to break more rules when there's a full moon. They aren't in control of their bodies and there's a certain call that they can't really ignore."

"What about their mindset? I heard that one usually can't remember what happened to them the next day." I asked before I could stop myself.

"Umm, usually there's this big block inside of their heads, yes. The human part of them can't see or even hear what they're doing while there's a full moon and then the mischief starts. You don't want to be by a werewolf during a full moon, trust me. It's very dangerous."

OK, I have to get him to tell me better than this. Like, he still doesn't know that I know he's a werewolf. Maybe I should come out and just say it? There must not be too much harm in saying you know that one of your best friends is a werewolf. Well, I guess there's only one way to know for sure.

"Caleb . . . I know." I said bluntly.

"Know what?"

"I know that you're a werewolf."

He let out a huff and sort of half laughed at the same time. Well, I guess he wasn't in that much of shock. "Yeah well, you're a smart girl. I knew you'd probably figured it out a long time ago." He told me. Which was true. Sort of. Depending on how you look at it, of course.

"Well then why did you tell me to stay away at your birthday party then?" I took away the razor so I didn't do anything drastic. I couldn't trust myself with sharp objects around Caleb when I'm angry. He turned toward me with a guilty look on his face and a pleading look of forgiveness in his eyes. Oh, this sucker was in for it big time when he had finally explained.

"I couldn't have you around me when I changed, Red. I'm from a long line of alpha wolves and those are the most dangerous to be around when we get the call. And I know for a fact that my wolf would have taken a special interest in you and I didn't want you to be the one to be hurt by me. I'm sorry if I hurt your feelings." He finished.

Well, you can't really be mad at someone who was only looking out for your best tendencies. I suppose he thought he was doing me a favor not telling me the full extent of what he could do. But I highly doubt Caleb could ever hurt me even if he was under the influence of the call. Whatever that is.

And I'd like to point out that it doesn't surprise me one bit that Caleb is an alpha wolf. He already thinks he's the best at just about everything he does. So why not add the best wolf on top of that? I don't understand how him being the leader of the pack has to do with being the most dangerous either? Does he even have a pack to lead? I've never heard anything of werewolves in real life having packs yet. So how could I know for sure he's telling the truth? I think way too much into this kind of stuff, don't I?

That kind of answers my question of "does he remember what happened with us" then. I mean obviously he couldn't remember. Not when what he just said its impossible for him to. It just kind of sucks that he took my virginity and he doesn't even remember it. Wait a minute, technically it might *not* have happened. I mean, who's to say that I didn't just toss my clothes aside because I was too hot when I fell asleep after he had fallen asleep. He was going swimming in the nude after he transformed into the wolf. Who's to say he just didn't put his clothes back on? Honestly, I was so stupid not to think of this!

But, what about the sharp pain in between my legs when I woke up the morning before? There's no explaining that really. Unless I had spontaneously gotten hit there by him or something of equal force. Until I know otherwise, I'm just going to blame it on an unknown cause and call it a coincidence.

"Umm, Scar' I think I need to tell you something," he almost whispered when I have finished up and brushed him off.

I was a bit weary at first due to the way he had said it, but I still responded with, "OK, shoot." I had a feeling that whatever he was about to tell me, it won't be something I want to hear. Probably something like I'll never like you, you disgusting blood sucker. Ha, I have quite little hopes for myself. Let's hope that it's something a bit more clever than that, huh?

"Did umm . . . did you know that you're pregnant?"

OK, *way* more creative than I could ever come up with! Was this kid on crack or something? Not that I'm saying it's not a possibility that I am. But how on Earth would he know if I was right now? Did he have some special powers that can see who's pregnant and who's not? Oh . . . Oh God, I-I might be pregnant? That means that he and I *did* sleep together! And-And I'm going to be a mother. No, this can't be happening now! I'm still too young to be a mother! Maybe he was kidding? Maybe this was all just a joke? Maybe I should talk now?

"How do you know?" I asked quietly and in shock and horror.

"It's sort of a wolf thing. We have a very acute sense of smell and I can smell a baby growing inside of your stomach. It's also a werewolf baby, by the way. I know that for sure."

"How?!" I yelled. I was getting upset because he knew so much about my body that I didn't even know yet. "Does your super dog smelling powers smell another dog on me or something?"

"No." He simply said. "Do you see that mark on your shoulder there? Yeah, that's from the wolf. He was marking his territory and its how wolves mate. I just thought you ought to know that. So who's the lucky dad?"

I was too awestruck to speak. You would be too if someone just told you there was a kid growing inside of your stomach! Not to mention a kid who won't only be a vampire, but also part werewolf as well. Come on people, this just can't be possible! This must be a joke because there's no way that someone can smell a baby. Not when it's only a few days inside of you. No way!

What hurt the most about his little find was that he didn't even know it was his kid. I can accept the fact that I'm about to be a mother. I'm certainly not going to get rid of it no matter how young I am. Abortion has never and will never be an option for me. But I couldn't exactly tell Caleb, "Oh yeah, must be pregnant then. And if that's true . . . then you're the father." No, I couldn't do that to him when he's so young. It wasn't right to put him through that just yet. So I put on my mad face and did the best I possibly could throwing him out in a fit of rage. I even screamed "It's none of your business!" Before actually throwing him out. It was a top performance if I do say so myself. That is; until after he left, in which case I fell down on the bed and cried my eyes out.

I made a promise to myself to forget about the baby issues until after the funeral. Right now I had to deal with enough. When I drive home from this, I'll pick up a few pregnancy tests and follow the instructions on them. Hopefully Caleb was wrong. But something inside of me told me not to doubt him. As if my heart was screaming out to me that of course I was pregnant but my head was fighting back and had somewhat of a doubt.

Portia hadn't wanted to come to the funeral. I couldn't really blame her due to the fact that the police force is scouring the entire length of Montana in search for Alex's killer. When in reality, all they had to do was look not three feet in front of them at the sobbing brunette in a black Donna Karen. Everyone had pinned Portia's reaction on a secret relationship that supposedly developed between she and Alex. To tell you the truth, they did have somewhat of a relationship. They were there for each other when no one else was around. It seemed to me that Alex had fallen in love with her even though Portia was and will forever be devoted to my brother.

Speak of the devil; surprisingly he was sitting in one of the chairs in the back of the funeral home. He looked handsome in his black tuxedo with white button down. However, since the funeral was only a few months from homecoming, most of the men from my class just wore those. And I couldn't believe the audacity of Max; even at a funeral for one of our classmates and friends, he's off in the corner sulking about his own life. What was with him now?! I clucked my tongue against the roof of my mouth and excused myself from Portia's side briefly to talk to him.

"Max," I said as I sat down beside him. "What's wrong?"

I suppose it came out to him as more of a "let's get this over with" than an actual, genuine worry. But there's only so much of this pouting Max I can take. If he doesn't stop this behavior soon, I'm going to force him and Portia together and pray that that makes him happy. Who knows; maybe it will even get him to stop racing cars?

"Alex is dead," He coldly stated.

I tilted my head to get a better look at his eyes before replying, "Yes, there's his coffin right there." I pointed to the beautiful mahogany box fitted to the size of Alex Johnson.

"Can I tell you a secret?"

He looked up with the same bright blue eyes as I used to have, however with something hidden within the depths. His fingers raked through his deep red locks, disheveling it and making it stick up everywhere. I wanted to take the initiative and tell him that he's in a public place and that we were supposed to appear at our best. I refrained from flattening his hair myself and let him gather himself up for whatever he was about to tell me.

I've never seen Max in such fear before. Normally, Max wasn't afraid of anything as far as I knew. That's the thing I love about him most. He can stand guard and keep his cool in just about any situation. Except for when it comes to Portia. He seems to lose his top whenever she steps in the line of trouble or dances on his last nerve. Quite funny to watch I might add, but you should have seen it when the four of us were kicked out of McDonald's recently.

It was about a week or two ago when we were all sitting in the mansion's living area watching *Ultimate Fight Club* on the big screen plasma TV. Caleb and I took up almost the entire couch—me lying on one side while he was splayed on the other, our feet resting on each other innocently—while Max sat on the reclining chair with Portia resting her back against the foot of it. Now with the positions we were all in, you'd think we would be two couples chilling together on a Saturday night. But it was much, *much* more complicated than that.

"Anyone hungry?" Caleb sat up and asked us.

In the car on the way to the restaurant, the fighting began to ensue between Max and Portia. It started off with a simple argument about one sitting too close to the other in the back seat of Caleb's truck. After what had just been the arrangement in the mansion too! We even had to pull over so that Max and I could switch seats. It was quiet enough for the rest of the ride and well up until the parking lot. When we reached inside, on the other hand, the word chaos didn't even begin to describe it.

Apparently the fourteen year old, pimple ridden, bean pole of a boy at the cash register was hitting on Portia. In Max's eyes, saying "have a nice day" was only directed toward her and it had underlying meanings to it. We didn't even have time to blink before Max charged toward the counter, pulled the skinny kid up off his feet by the collar of the polyester tan and black shirt he was forced to wear, and stared him down.

"Don't you flirt with her!" He barked out. "You think you deserve someone like her? Keep dreamin' buddy because you are far from it!"

Caleb gripped my brother's shoulders and began to slowly pull him away from the counter but Max held fast. Yes, I am aware that Caleb is much, much stronger than Max probably ever will be—being a werewolf and all—but Caleb couldn't show him that. To everyone else, Max had looked like the stronger boy and that's how it needed to be portrayed to the world. So Max still had a death hold on the young boy with the nametag that read Marty on it. That is, until Portia stepped up to the plate to take a swing at him.

"Put. Him. Down. Maxwell." Portia bit out each word.

Max spun in her direction with Marty still firmly clutched in his vice grip. I knew that the only reason why Max had halted his efforts in assaulting the innocent young boy was because Portia had called him by his own geeky name. Now if she used his nickname (Maxi) I would have busted out in peals of laughter in the center of McDonald's no doubt.

Like the kid's shirt was on fire, Max dropped the kid and I noticed him hit his head on the counter pretty hard. I was about to ask the kid if he was alright, but I was too busy watching the hurt in Max's eyes intermingle with the fire in Portia's.

"But I . . . But he . . . . I was just . . . " He huffed in anger. "I was just trying to help, you know."

"How on Earth," she panted, "is scaring a fourteen year old kid witless for just doing his job helping?" Caleb had bumped my arm to signify that we couldn't let there be a scene between the two of them. How were we supposed to stop them though? The only way of getting the two of them to back out of the restaurant peacefully would be to drag them by the hair and I would much rather not have both of them redirect that feeling in my direction. I could, however, hear the plans going on in Caleb's head.

'If Portia lunges I could grab her by the waist and pick her up to carry her out. But she will be fighting back. I hope its Max that decided to make the first move. I can handle him. Hopefully he doesn't touch her though. I doubt anyone will be able to stop that fury.'

He had a point. If Max had touched Portia in any way; he would most likely have his arm ripped off in an instant. She wouldn't mind exposing the supernatural world if it meant attaching her greedy claws into Max's neck and squeezing until he got a clue. Heck, I wouldn't mind doing that myself half the time I'm around him. But nobody could get through to Max even if he was held at gunpoint and forced to make a decision about sharing his feelings.

Just then, a miraculous thing happened. Max's expression went from raging intense to calmly serene within seconds. He turned around to the cash register where Marty stood rubbing the top of his head and simply said, "sorry", in a very polite and respectful manner. It couldn't be . . . . could it? Portia nor I used our influencing powers on him because I would have felt it in the air. Did Max really just learn some manners . . . *and then execute them*?! The kicker was when he brushed past the three of us saying that he wasn't hungry and walked out of the door as if nothing had happened. Even Portia's mouth had been hanging open in shock. She looked at me with such curiosity that I could even read inside of her mind for once.

'Did that really just happen?' She asked me as well as herself. I just shrugged and continued to stare at Marty who was now chatting up a very pretty co-worker around his age about what had just happened; playing it off as if he was a bigger victim than he actually was.

"Well?" Max's voice brought me back to the present. At the funeral of an old, fallen friend.

Turning back to my brother I replied, "I'm listening."

There was that look in his eyes again. Not that it had completely gone away before, but I had been distracted. Now the rage and worry were burning brighter than a house fire. "I've done something unforgivable Scarlett," he began. "The night of the party I sort of . . . p-possibly could have . . . . I mean I—"

"Spit it out Max!" I demanded as quietly as I could.

"I killed Alex."

Now no one could really put into words how you feel when your brother tells you he killed a person. So many emotions go through you that it feels like you're about to explode. How could this be? He couldn't have killed Alex because Portia did, right? No, no this couldn't be right.

"I watched him dance with Portia that night too many times. She's mine and he can't touch her. I won't allow anyone but me to touch her. Not now, not ever again. I made sure of that."

The sadistic side of Max had finally caused him to snap. If my brother had really killed Alex then there was major damage done to not only his life, but everyone around him as well. What happened to Portia and who's blood was all over her after the party? Would the police find out and put Max in a Juvenile delinquent facility? If they did that what would happen to my family? In a way it's like a domino effect if what my brother is telling me really is right. But then again, he could just be insane and might have convinced himself that he murdered Alex just to make himself feel better. He *does* think it's his job to protect Portia even though she can clearly take care of herself; vampire powers or otherwise.

"How did you kill him, Max?"

"Poison."

"Poison? Why and how did you poison him?"

"I told you why. And it was the easiest way I think. After I saw the two of them dancing together I looked all around the house for something to hurt him with. By that point I just wanted to bash him up enough to make him stay away from her. But that was before I saw the cleaning supplies in the cabinet underneath the sink and I acted before I could think. I remember grabbing the bottle of Draino and the can of Pledge and pouring it into a cup of beer which I remember he was drinking and started walking outside."

My heart was racing and my palms were sweaty just thinking about what he had done. For some reason I could imagine myself doing the same thing. I know I never would try and kill another person, but part of me could just picture my brother's motivation even if it was the most horrible thing imaginable. Oh, why did he have to do this?

"D-Did he die instantly?" I asked out of curiosity's sake.

He glanced down and squinted his eyes as in confusion. "I don't know."

"You don't know?"

"Yeah I don't know. I was a few feet away from him and everything just went black. When I woke up I remember handing the drink to someone but the details were a bit fuzzy. I know it was him though. It had to have been. He talked to me and it sounded like Alex so it must have been."

Something didn't smell right about Max's story. I couldn't quite pinpoint it yet, but it hadn't yet set in. At that moment I couldn't look at him anymore. Thinking about what he had done to an innocent boy was just too much to take in. So I did what I thought was the proper thing to do and walked up to Alex's casket to take one last look at him. I walked up to the front of the room and for some reason I had begun to concentrate on how the material of my dressing was swaying. My eyes grazed down to the bottom of my dress and watched the hem twirl and swirl as my legs moved. When they moved from the hem up to my stomach my knees buckled for a split second and the sensation to cradle the slight bump that had mysteriously appeared was ignored. What was happening to me?

# Chapter 53

THE CASKET WAS OPEN, REVEALING a sickeningly white young boy killed in the prime of his life. The suit they had him in was just barely visible through the top. The black tuxedo complimented the silky white chiffon material lined in the interior of the casket. But there was something about the way his skin had paled against the blackness of the jacket that made me sick. In a way the skin was the same shade as . . . well, as my own.

It was a very powerful emotion that had swept over me and caused me to start tearing up when I stared into Alex's innocent face. I'm not too sure if it was seeing someone I knew personally dead or if it was slightly influenced by the beings inside of my stomach. Maybe it was both . . . because I actually believe I wouldn't have done such a thing in public, threatening to expose myself as a vampire to the whole town otherwise. It's weird to think that I am no longer alone in my own body.

"You were never alone baby."

Oh no. He's back. Just leave me alone Gunnar please. I'm not really in the mood today to deal with your sarcastic comments. Someone's hand rested on my shoulder, startling me and making me jump a little. I was hoping that it wasn't who I was expecting it to be but as I turned around my hopes were shattered.

"Long time no see Belwin." I said to the bigger, bulkier looking Gunnar beside me.

"Yeah well, I've been busy the last few months with things. I've always been around though." He responded.

"Don't remind me. You're looking healthy. Been working out or something?"

"Yup." He said with a smile as he flexed a bicep close to my face. "And it seems you've gained some weight too, Miss Scarlet. Maybe you should go on that special werewolf diet I've been hearing about. It's said that their blood is half the calories considering they are a worthless species with no courage."

"Shut up Gunnar! Leave me alone."

He walked away with that content little smirk he always has when he thinks he's won the battle. That boy is the lowest, most disrespectful dirtbag on the planet. I know he hates Caleb and has a right to hate him because he's the one that has my heart but it doesn't mean he needs to insult him at any opportune moment. Especially in front of me . . . the mother of Caleb's child. Ugh, I still can't get used to saying that I'm pregnant with his baby. It is the weirdest most foreign thing to hit my tongue ever. I'm having a baby. I'm having a baby. I'm having a real, live baby.

'And one of them is mine . . . '

*The funeral home had faded away. Night blanketed the whole room with only stars and a very bright full moon illuminating it. Trees sprouted up from the floorboards which were turning into dirt and moss and leaves. Instead of a dead boy's coffin in the front of the room a peaceful serene lake laid out. I was standing by the water alone and confused with the pain in between my legs once more, only not as painful.*

*I looked behind me to see Caleb's truck still crashed into the tree from before. I could barely hear snoring coming from the bed. Good, he was sleeping. That's a good sign. I'm at the end of the night after I blacked out. So what happened now that I'm having a vision about? I walked further to the water and sat down at the bank to look down to relax and pass time until whatever is going to happen will happen.*

*The reflection in the water, however, didn't resemble me at all. Yes I still had the same shiny auburn hair and the same facial features but my eyes were cornflower blue again. The eyes I was born with. My skin wasn't deathly pale either but a warm glowing tan color as if I had been a normal teenager at the beach all day. I was me again! No vampire in sight.*

*"Well, besides me." A voice said off to the side of me.*

287

*I turned and saw Gunnar standing by the bent tree just off the bank and an odd feeling stirred inside of me. A small piece of my brain was frightened of his new muscular frame and told me to run from him like always. But then the piece that usually feels repulsed by him instead felt more welcoming to him. Like I was actually happy he was there. Maybe that was a side effect of Desiree's stupid curse she put on me. It had to be because I would not ever be happy to see Gunnar even if he was about to save my life. Ok . . . . maybe then and only then but still you all get what I mean. I highly doubt he'd save me anyway.*

*"What are you doing here?" I asked.*

*"You know exactly why I'm here Scarlett . . . "*

*He began approaching me slowly and stopped a few inches in front of my face. His hand reached up and cupped my cheek, running his thumb across my skin in a loving way. In the next moment his lips were on mine and he was kissing me passionately. And I wasn't slapping him?! No, for some reason I just let it happen. I let him do whatever he wanted with his hands and lips sadly and never protested once. Caleb never woke up to save me either.*

My mom was standing near a couple of her friends from work no doubt gossiping about what could have happened to Alex. Everyone will be talking about this and making their own assumptions for a long time. The cops will never find out what truly happened after all which means this case will be wide open forever. I just feel bad for Alex's family mostly. Although the murder was an accident, it will never be justified. And they still have more than a right to know. Too bad they can't know and wouldn't believe if anyone told them the truth.

"Mom," I called out to her while I stood a few feet away from her next to the support beam, leaning on it really. Her eyes caught mine across the room and I believe she knew something was wrong. I saw concern lingering in her which wasn't a good thing always. My mom can read me like an open book after all. I just hope she can't tell already what I need from her.

She quickly excused herself from the mob of chattering women and walked over to where I was and immediately pulled me into a hug. Now I don't know if she was hugging me because of the whole Alex thing, but I'm not going to complain about it. I needed a hug after what I had just seen in that vision.

"Can we talk somewhere private?" I asked her pulling away. "I need to ask you something."

"Sure Sweetie." She replied.

We walked through the funeral parlor and out back into the yard where we both sat on the steps leading up. I didn't know if it was butterflies fluttering in my stomach because of nerves of if there was actually something growing inside. Because for some reason my brain was still in denial even though I knew it was most likely true. But I had to bring it up to her. She was the one person I could think of that could help me prove medically if there actually is a baby . . . or maybe even babies . . . in my stomach.

"Can I ask you something personal?"

She nodded even though I knew she was a bit wary to answer. And with the plan I had in mind she very well should be. See, there was no easing into this but I couldn't just come right out and flatly ask her to perform a pregnancy test on me. The best way I found was to just say, "How old were you when you lost your virginity?" Her eyes grew large as I suspected they would and her cheeks were tinting themselves pink with embarrassment. Now yes, maybe that was a *bit* too personal but come on when you are talking to your mom about potentially being pregnant all discretion goes out the window.

She gave me the full story about how she had been sixteen and her boyfriend—who was captain of the football team (yuck!)—had pressured her into it the night of prom and how he had dumped her right after. Cliché, right? Yeah well, not much you can expect from someone raised in the late seventies when everyone was experimenting already. I pictured a young boy with feathered hair and bellbottom pants looking cool in his popular polyester flower print tux. Doesn't say much about my mother's taste in men although look who she married and is about to divorce. But this was a good answer. The answer I wanted actually. It just wasn't a good feeling to know I embarrassed my mom like that.

"I'm not judging you. You should know by now that I would never ask you anything then judge you when you answer. You raised me better than that. Just like I don't expect you to judge me when I . . . when I ask you for a favor." I was about to just say it but I couldn't. I choked.

"What's your favor?" She asked when she noticed my uneasiness to say it.

"I . . . " Looking her in the face was the hardest thing to do for me at the moment. "I . . . " Knowing that once I tell her what I brought her down here for it might send her into a fit. She will most likely yell and scream at me not just for having sex with someone, but also because I had sex unprotected and it could have meant something much worse. Not to mention I didn't tell her about it after it had happened. "I . . . "

She was growing impatient and said, "Just spit it out honey," while rubbing my back with her hand. For some reason I was cowering at her touch. Thinking that at any moment she would turn that gentle motherly hand into a hard slap of punishment. But I couldn't avoid what she would most likely do just because it would hurt for a few minutes. No, I had to just come out and say it no matter what.

"I think I might be pregnant."

# Chapter 54

*Y*OU KNOW THAT MOMENT WHEN you are jumping off of a diving board, just as your feet leave the platform and you're soaring in the air and you think to yourself "What a rush!" The adrenaline has kicked in and has taken over your entire body and it's like you're flying in the air, weightless and free. Well that is completely the opposite feeling when you are a sixteen year old single, scared young girl hearing heartbeats from a monitor hooked up to your stomach for the first time. Oh, and not to mention there wasn't just one heartbeat—not even two! I heard three little heartbeats coming from inside me. The weird thing was, I was in no way frightened or upset about knowing.

Maybe it was because deep down I already knew the results? Who really knows. All I knew is what I was feeling at that moment. It was like I was drowning in a pool of deep, deep water. There was no ground underneath my feet for me to push up from and the lack of oxygen was crushing my lungs in my chest. The sinking couldn't be stopped even two month after I heard the little guys. And everyone knew I was pregnant then too. Not only because it's a small town and everyone talks, but also because my stomach grew so much beyond the normal rate that my mother was questioning how long I had been keeping this from her.

The only person that never once treated me like there was some alien that was going to pop out of my belly at any second was Portia. Not once did she even look at it unlike all of the stares I was getting from the entire population. Even little toddlers would stop in their tracks to see the girl with the big belly, only to be quickly pulled away and silently scolded by their parents. OK, so I know that I'm young and I'm pregnant but it's not like it's nothing they haven't seen before. Plenty of girls my age these days get knocked up.

'But they aren't a vampire and their babies aren't half werewolf.' The unknown voice said.

'Well yes, but they don't know that.' I quipped.

'Come on Scarlett you went from being one hundred and fifteen pounds one day and the next you added ten pounds of baby bump literally overnight. What do you expect them to think?'

'Not to mention they probably think I'm a whore.'

I've been thinking about that little tidbit of information for quite some time now. Actually sense people had first begun to notice. Portia had been quick to defend me to other people by saying that it was with the person I loved. But she didn't know the actual logistics of it all. Yes I do love Caleb, but that doesn't excuse the fact that we were both under the influence of something—he the moon and I the blood—not to mention I couldn't shake away what Gunnar had said about one being his. If that was even possible it means that my vision wasn't lying and Gunnar and I had indeed had sex not hours after Caleb and I had. That, in fact, does make me a whore.

'No it doesn't. Like you said you were under the influence of the blood. Plus I still think that Desiree lady did something to cloud your judgment that night. You know she cursed you so don't disregard that from everything.'

I repositioned myself on my bed to lay on my left side. I read in a baby book my mom gave me the other day that it's actually better not just for the babies but for myself because it puts less pressure on my organs that way.

'Three babies . . . '

'Yeah,' the voice replied. 'It's difficult for me to wrap my head around too. Are you ever going to tell Caleb they are his?'

'I can't!' I shouted in my head.

'I'm sorry, I'm sorry, I forgot that it's forbidden to let him know he's actually going to be a father! Good Lord Scarlett, what's going to happen when you need help huh? You can't even ask your own father for help now!'

That's true. When my father first found out I was pregnant he flipped and said that he was so disappointed in me that he didn't want to see me at that moment. That was about three weeks ago and I haven't even gotten a call from him since. You'd think that being a father and all he'd want to at least know that I'm healthy and everything is fine. I think that hearing my voice would just remind him of my condition and hurt him more. So for the past month I've been living with my mom and Jack in his mansion.

He's been . . . hospitable so to speak. Sure he doesn't approve of my being pregnant. Nobody does. But he's a lot more at ease then my actual father is.

'You sure about that?'

Shouting came from down the hall. Two male voices, one a bit older and louder than the other, were clearly fighting. But about what? They were coming closer to my room and I could hear Caleb trying to yell over his father to get his point. What they were fighting about I have no clue but I could make bets on it being about his future. College maybe? I'm not really sure but have no real enthusiasm to find out. I absolutely hate it when Jack berates him for having his own mind and making his own choices. However, no matter how much I tried to ignore the noise, I finally heard what they were saying.

"You are the future alpha of this pack! You need to be smarter than you are now about this! Do what needs to be done!"

"You're insane! You don't even know what you're talking about."

"Fine. If you can't own up to your own God Damn mistakes and take care of them the way they should be handled then I'll have to because I am sure as Hell not having this besmurchment on our family name. I've worked too damn hard and have given too much time and effort into making the perfect reputation for us to throw it away on some leach and her parasitic, half breed abominations!"

Footsteps stomped down the hallway and closer to my room after a door had loudly slammed shut. I heard Caleb yell, "Dad!" toward him and thought nothing of it at the time. I just assumed Jack was leaving the house or something. But boy was I wrong.

The door to my bedroom was swung wide open so roughly that it had actually tore it off of most of the hinges and it hung there loosely. It startled me so much that I had almost flew off of my bed and onto the floor. Standing there, still wearing his business suit and tie, panting loudly and looking at me with such hostility that it frightened me even more was Jack. This man wasn't a mere human like I could take down any other day. No he was a fully grown, experienced werewolf . . . an alpha no less. I couldn't even break one of his nails if I tried. But he could kill me and make it look effortless.

"You little bloodsucking demon!" He shouted at me.

What did I do?

"You are going to kill those things or else I'll kill you!"

"What?!"

Caleb had appeared behind his dad with his shackles raised so to speak. He was prepared to defend me no matter who the predator was even if it was his own father. "Dad," he spit. "Leave her alone now."

"Stay out of this Caleb. You've done enough." He replied in a rude manner.

Jack lunged at me and at the same time counteracted his son's attempts at grabbing him to hold him back. Instead, Jack's hands found my arms and gripped them so tight that if I had blood going through my body it would have stopped pumping through and they would have been blue. However, it just felt like a throbbing pain. I had thought I felt the slightest break in one of my bones but it's probably just my imagination. After all there was enough adrenaline pumping through the room I was bound to imagine just about everything at that point.

"Jack Darwin let go of my daughter this instant!"

I was the only one in the room that could see his brown eyes flash the brightest yellow. He was so close to me that I smelled his icky dog breath mixed with what I believe to be a bucket load of whiskey. Ahhh, so it had been alcohol influenced. Makes a bit more sense now I guess. Although he's always been this high maintenance though, becoming angry at just about anything and everything. Except at my mom of course. Hence why his eyes had just been glowing yellow for maybe two seconds.

He did as she ordered and dropped me like a sack of potatoes. I hadn't noticed I was lifted off of the ground until the mattress springs bounced me a ways up as I fell on them from a short height. My mom walked over to me and checked to see if I was OK but I just kept staring at Jack. I could not believe he had just blown up like that. For what purpose did he have to be angry at me? Nobody knew Caleb was the father not even him. So why the outburst?

"Get your stuff together Scar," my mom said. "We are leaving tonight."

A part of me didn't want to leave. I wanted to stay and wade everything out and I knew exactly why I felt that way. Being around Caleb made me feel more like he knew and we were happier even though I know it's not true. I'll miss him but there's only one question I had to ask before I brought my suitcase out.

"Where are we going to go?"

"Back home. To dad's . . . "

She looked at me for some kind of acknowledgement that it was the right decision but with the current circumstances with my father and me let alone her was something that could be a problem. We did have to leave, but was it really the best choice to show up at my dad's with luggage in hand and just expect him to forgive us both?

# Chapter 55

*I* HATE IT WHEN EVERYONE LEAVES me out in the dust. Not only was it alright with my dad that we came home, I guess it was his idea. You see my mom and he . . . well I guess for now I can pull out of first person and go into third because honestly I can't explain this without painting you a scene. Alright here goes nothing . . .

Jane was innocently walking through the supermarket looking for something to make for dinner that night. Jack had always been picky even back in high school and he carried it with him for life. He had been a fan of meat for some reason though. Every meat imaginable it didn't matter what kind or how she cooked it he would eat it. Although he was a man so it made sense. Ben, on the other hand, was much, much pickier than Jack is.

She shook her head clear of those thoughts like she always had. It was hard for her to think of her husband and not only remember the good times, but also the bad. Lord knows that there were just as many. She picked up a potato, giving it a once over before deciding to buy it, when she had felt someone's long, lean fingers brush against her ear and place the hair hanging over it behind. She wasn't frightened nor did she turn around and backhand the culprit behind her. A shiver, however, shot through her spine so fast it almost had knocked her over from the familiarity of the touch. Flashbacks of their wedding, smiling and dancing and being at ease, a year later when their first son was born how they were so euphorically happy she thought she'd just float away, and then, like a tidal wave, came rushing in the bad memories. Memories of Thanksgiving's or Christmas's spent alone with the kids because he was at the office or the nights spent shouting at each other for not spending enough time with each other. Screaming at him that she no longer loved him anymore and the pain she had felt when he had admitted the same thing.

The love never died on her end, but she wasn't going to let herself be treated like the poor loser in this situation. She backed away from him in the grocery aisle and kept on moving forward with the cart.

"Janie, talk to me . . . " that struck a cord on her heart strings.

"About what Ben? There is nothing to discuss."

She kept on walking hoping he'd just get bored and go away. That's what he had always done and that's what she was expecting. So when she had turned around she wasn't surprised that he wasn't there. Of course a tiny bit of anger bubbled up inside of her that he wasn't even going to try and make an effort to converse with her but that was his problem. So she went on shopping and just ignored their little run-in the best she could.

Jane had almost finished and was working on one last minute decision in frozen foods when she heard, "Janie come here."

Before she could protest again and just ignore him he grabbed a hold of her wrist and pulled her into the corner where no customers had been that moment. Jane couldn't get one word in edgewise before her husband's lips fastened themselves to her own. He gripped her by the waist and neck and pulled her so close to him that it was almost no longer two people. In her mind, he was just getting the last kiss in before the final goodbye. So she'd let him. Hell, who was she to fight a kiss from a man she had loved almost her whole life? Little did she know, although, that it was completely different for him.

He broke away from her mouth but still had a tight hold on her body. Ben didn't plan on letting her go the second time. He may have lost his way once but he found his way back and all he wants now is to just grow old with his beautiful wife.

"I was stupid Janie. I know that and I'm sorry for all that I've put you through. But I've changed, I can prove it to you."

Jane was skeptical of course. She pried herself off of him and looked straight in his eyes. "Why don't you start proving it to me by being a bit more respectful to our daughter."

That stung him hard. "She's pregnant Jane! What do you want me to do with that huh? She's a pregnant teenager who doesn't know what she's about to get herself into."

"She's also a pregnant teenager who cries at night because her father won't even talk to her. Jesus Ben, she needs us right now. And not just me, both of us. She needs her dad to help her and support her the most right now and you are just ignoring her. I know how it feels to be ignored by you Ben and let me tell you, our little girl doesn't deserve that kind of hurt. Especially not now. So get your act together," she spit out while jabbing him in the chest with her index finger. "Not for me, but for our daughter. Then we'll talk about 'proving to me' whatever you need to prove to me."

Jane started to walk away when Ben blurted out, "I know a way I can do both."

. . . And here we are. Seeing them kiss is still a bit too weird and disgusting to us still. But then again they are our parents and to see anyone's parents kissing is weird and disgusting. It is kind of nice though that my dad is making an effort to at least accept that I'm going to keep these babies. I'm going to need all the help I can get after all.

Sitting in the living room on my laptop with Angel nestled up next to me I began to think of names. It's sort of difficult to do it without knowing the sex of each baby but I tried. All that came to mind though was Simon and Buttercup. I probably shouldn't have watched so many cartoons as a little kid I guess. Caleb sure wouldn't like them if he had a say. As if on cue, Caleb's name lit up my cell phone. How does he do that?!

"Hello?" I answered.

Max and Holden stopped watching ESPN long enough to glance in my direction, acknowledge I was on the phone, and went right back to drooling over that hot chick who hosts that one show.

"I'm so sorry about tonight, Red. I don't know what his problem was."

"It's not your fault. Why are you apologizing?"

There was a pause and then, "I don't know. I just feel like it was my fault that he tweaked like that. I should have been the one to stop him but I froze."

"I doubt you could take on your dad Caleb. And I didn't expect you to. I'm fine and everything worked out. My parents are back together even."

"That's great."

He didn't sound too sincere with that comment, did he? Shouldn't everyone be as happy as me that my mom has finally stopped flirting with the rich scumbag? Especially him! Because what if my mom had actually been serious about Jack and they did get married that would mean we would have been step siblings. Maybe he wanted that? No, I know he didn't because I know he must have feelings for me more than platonic or familial. Subconsciously at least.

"Yeah, I guess. What were you and your dad even fighting about?" I asked as I penguin wobbled off the couch—pregnancy makes it impossible to get up normally apparently—and took it into another room.

He blew out a breath of air before warily saying, "My dad has it in his head that I am the one who got you pregnant. Insane right?"

"Yeah," I replied sarcastically. "Insane."

"Its-It's not me, right? I mean, you'd tell me if it was . . . wouldn't you?"

I had nodded my head before I remembered that he and I were on the phone and he couldn't hear a nod. "Yup." I lied to him. "I'd tell you if you had knocked me up. But it wasn't you so no harm done. Ha, man I'm an excellent liar! He believed every second of it at least. "I *do* have a question for you though. How long does a werewolf pregnancy usually last?"

"Around three to four months I'm told."

"Scarlett?"

Max and Holden were standing in the doorway to the kitchen just staring at me. I'm guessing they need to talk to me? Their faces matched each other perfectly as if they were the twins. Holden might have had a bit more concern to his look but they were both angry. If I know anyone in this world I know my brothers and I know what they are about to ask me. Well Hell!

Three Weeks Later

"What about this one?" Portia asked.

I nodded my head yes at the lacy, black, tu-tu looking thing. She and I were shopping for—get this—prom dresses. Let me tell you, a maternity style prom dress kind of looks trashy. That might be for the fact that teenage girls aren't supposed to already be pregnant at the prom. Either way I didn't want to buy one. The only reason I'm going to that stupid dance is because Portia got down on both knees and begged me to be her date. She didn't want another guy to take her and my brother still wasn't growing a brain so I'm her only option.

Lucky me, huh?

"I don't understand how popular chicks like Daisy—no matter how mean they are—still win Prom Princess. I mean, I'm not saying *I* want to be the bimbo up there accepting that plastic symbol of the fall of humanity but shouldn't it at least go to a girl with actual goals in life other than marry rich?"

I giggled through the dressing room door at Portia's ranting. She's upset because it was announced today that Daisy, of course, won the votes for Prom Princess. I would put my eternal life on a bet that says Daisy won by threatening people to doom them to unpopularity for the rest of their lives for her vote. And sadly people listened. Oh and guess who Prom Prince is? Yeah, you can all guess that one. The King and Queen will be announced at the actual dance.

"How do I look?"

She walked out in that black tu-tu thing. She didn't look have bad actually.

"Wow. Get it." I told her.

"You sure?" She asked insecurely smoothing out the dresses hem.

"Yeah, you look beautiful in it."

"And now for you . . . "

"Aw come on Portia! I'm not going to look good in a dress I told you this. Just leave it be. I don't want to go."

It was far too late though. She had already playfully skipped over to one of the racks labeled 'maternity' and started rifling through them as if her life depended on it. Can you imagine what I'm going to look like in one of those? My fat belly juts out far enough now that I can easily set a plate of food on it and let it go and it won't fall no matter what the angle. I should actually be giving birth to the little monsters pretty soon I think. So a dress . . . . yeah, not such a good idea.

"You are getting a dress and you will look amazing in it. Accept it and go try this on."

She handed me a light green, chiffon dress and I raised an eyebrow at her.

"You are going to kill me one of these days I swear it." I let out a huff and walked toward the dressing room like she asked. Oh the horror of having a best friend with power over you. Can't a girl catch a break here?

In my room that night, listening to Holden blast his heavy metal music, I had brought out the dress I had purchased and laid it on the bed. I kept feeling the chiffon material thinking how it would fit over my body. How on earth was I going to look pretty in this thing?

'You look beautiful no matter what you have on.'

At first I had to think about who was actually saying that, Gunnar or the unknown guy. Because I really hadn't been paying attention. Angel had jumped on top of my dresser and knocked over a glass candle I had sitting there which smashed all over the floor. What has gotten into that cat lately? He's been much more restless now and it's worrying me. Maybe I should take him to the vet. Angel's head turned in my direction and it was as if he was giving me a death stare. Well, no vet it is.

I went back to accessing the dress Portia made me buy today and picturing myself dancing in it. Being pregnant and so close to giving birth and all I wouldn't be able to dance much, but all I could think about was bouncing everywhere and knocking people over.

If someone had told me I would be pregnant this young I'd probably laugh in their face. I mean seriously! I guarantee if I hadn't snapped back from the vision before that I wouldn't be. Caleb and I would be dating and happy and in love and baby free. But now, I don't know if I actually *can* be with him. Not after I lied to his face and told him it wasn't his babies.

'God, I can't take this anymore!' A voice shouted in my head.

A blinding white light shot across my room from where Angel had been and bounced off all four of my walls. It knocked over several of my priceless items before settling on the hardwood floor, scaring me half to death. The only thing I could think of doing was clutching that old necklace I had still around my neck. I watched as the ball of white just laid there. What was I expecting it to do exactly?

Silly me, I made the decision to stand from my safe bed and move slowly over to it. Vampire powers aside I don't know what this thing is and what it could do to me. So I just stood in front of it and waited. Waited for the light to go out. Wait for it to explode on me. Wait for an alien being from another planet to pop out and sing the theme song for the WB . . . you know, the one the frog sings. Either way, none of that happened.

Nope, instead the ball disappeared. Just went away. Does that mean Angel is no longer my spirit animal? Without warning I felt a tear slide down my cheek. Angel was my pet, my friend. I don't want him to be gone. What did I do for him to just leave me like that?

"You didn't do anything." A familiar voice came from behind me.

I turned around as quickly as I could and saw something that should scare the wits out of me but didn't. There, sitting on my bed with a sullen look on his face, was the most beautiful stranger in the universe. He literally took my breath away. His white-blonde hair glowed just as bright as his whole body. It hung over the most amazing blue eyes I have ever seen. They were the color of the cold ocean but held all the warmth of the world in their depths. His features were even more flawless than a

301

vampire's and almost made him boyish save for the prominent jaw line he sported. He wore only a pair of white shorts with nothing on top but the most chiseled chest I've ever seen. It glistened so intensely that it was almost as if looking in the sun. But the one detail on him that stood out to be the most beautiful feature on him was of course the black angel wings sticking out of his back.

They weren't spread fully but I could only imagine how gorgeous they would look in flight. I could not stop staring at this man. He was perfect and I wanted to touch him to make sure he was real and I wasn't just having a fantastic dream.

"It's not a dream Scarlett. I'm really here." He said. It was the unknown voice inside my head. This was him. This was my guardian. He must be. But who was he and where did he come from?

"I'll give you a hint." He pretended to lick his hand and then rubbed it against his blonde hair as if a cat would do. A cat? How is that a hint in any . . .

"Angel?" I asked the stranger.

He looked up at me with sadness in those blue eyes and it made me break down and cry right at his feet. I grabbed his hands—which his skin was so soft it made baby's skin feel like sandpaper—and rubbed it against my cheek. I don't know why I did that really. Just a sensation I couldn't and didn't want to fight. Like I said I wanted to touch this perfect creature from the moment I saw him. And the fact that I've been with him all this time and didn't even know this was the real him actually felt OK to me.

"You should be mad." He said in that honey voice of his.

"But I'm not." I replied wrapping my arms around his neck and hugging him so tightly that I thought I'd kill him. Thankfully I didn't. But he did pry me off of him and pushed me slightly away from him. Now that hurt me.

"Scarlett, I'm an actual angel and I never told you. Be mad at me. Yell! Scream! Do something other than hug me and tell me you're alright with this because I know your not."

Even mad he sounded perfect.

"How could I be mad at someone who looks like you?" I simply replied.

And that made him furious. He stood up and started pacing like a caged animal with no way out. Truthfully I'm alright with him keeping me from this and I don't know why he's acting like this. I mean I didn't run and scream and I'm not about to shout at him for just being himself. He's the other love of my life so why would he be mad about this?

"Exactly!" He yelled out. "I'm the other love of your life. Do you know how hurtful it is to hear every day how much in love with another man you are?! How he completes you and how you don't want anyone else in your life ever? God, you never even thought about my voice in your head did you? I was just a friend for you. Well I'm sick of hearing about how Caleb is the only one for you. Come here!"

As if an invisible tether was tied to my waist I was being pulled (actually walking) toward Angel and I couldn't stop. He had mind powers, I could clearly feel them working against my own brain. He didn't have to force me though. I trusted him enough to know that he would never hurt me and I would listen to him until the day I die.

Inches in front of him he demanded, "Kiss me." And the next thing I knew that's exactly what I was doing. His lips felt like the most comfortable clouds and tasted like the most sinful chocolate and wrapped with all the passion in the universe. He was expecting the kiss to mean everything to me, which it did, for the most part. But I believe he also expected for it to mean that I would just forget about Caleb and go with him anywhere in the world or otherwise. I'm not going to.

He broke the kiss and looked at me in the eyes. All I could do was take the necklace in my hand once more and back away from him. I could feel everything he was feeling. Ripping out his heart was not something I was proud of. I felt like I had just killed and gutted a little baby kitten (irony aside) and I knew at that moment that how much he had really loved me. I wish things could have been different. And maybe in some other universe or time they could have been. But no matter how beautiful and perfect for me he is . . . I can't do it.

Right before my eyes the ball of light was back and flew quickly and loudly out the window. Angel was once again gone.

# Chapter 56

$\mathcal{P}$ROM NIGHT. SHOULD I BE more excited about this night? Maybe. Am I excited at all? Why would I be excited to wear a dress that makes me look even more pregnant than I already am, suffer hundreds of stares from my classmates, listening to them gossip everything to high heavens about me and be forced to eat crappy food? That's what I thought. The only thing I'm looking forward to seeing is Portia and Max walk in together arm-in-arm.

Yeah, you heard me correctly. Max finally asked Portia to prom. Shocking I know but hey, at least it happened for those two. Oh and Caleb and I are going together too. Now before any of you scream your heads off let me just inform you that we are going as friends. Since my date (Portia) found someone else, I needed someone to go with. And he was available I guess. Funny how he didn't even ask one girl to prom huh? He's basically the freaking king of the school! Any girl he asked would have said yes. So he wanted to be a loner? Doubtful.

Portia arrived at my house *eight hours* before the dance so we could get ready together. On average, does anyone know how long it takes to get a teenage girl ready for a dance? Add three hours to that and you have Portia's time.

Honestly, who spends four hours on their hair?!

Walking down the staircase wasn't the best part for me. My waddling motions from my giant belly didn't look all Grace Kelly-like. But I guess it was worth it to see my mom cry at the sight of me and to have my dad and everyone else tell me I look beautiful. Picture time was . . . entertaining, to say the least. Group shots, couple shots, and of course tons of single shots of just me. Portia had her camera as well which encouraged my mom to take even more. All in all it took about maybe an hour and a half to two hours taking photos. It was just about dusk before the limousine pulled up.

"Have fun kids." My dad said before shutting the door to the car.

"Be safe!" My mom yelled out while we were pulling away.

Little did I know how ironic her words would be for everyone that night. We had just barely pulled out of the drive-way when I had felt a sharp kick go through my stomach and made me double over. It was so intense that I couldn't focus on anyone asking me if I was alright or not. Then, all of a sudden, we all heard a woman scream coming from behind us. There, in the distance, was a fully grown white wolf the size of a fully grown grizzly bear dragging my mother by the shoulder with his teeth through the forest.

"Stop!" I yelled to the limo driver.

It was all happened in an instant really. As soon as the limo driver halted I threw myself out and tried to run in the direction of the forest. There, through the heavy exhaust of the limo and the foggy air through the trees, I could barely make out a large, lumpy shape with its shoulders slumped down. It was standing on its haunches and looked like it was about to attack. I couldn't make anything out of the grey mass but it looked to me the scariest looking animal I have ever seen.

I heard the sound of Caleb's door slam shut and the last thing I heard was a very familiar voice say, "I'm here to pick up my date now," in an eerily calm but sadistic voice.

I was then looking straight into the eerily green eyes of Gunnar.

I felt him grab my wrist, tearing into my rock hard skin breaking bone, and started to run at full speed, dragging me along behind him with his teeth. He ran faster than I ever could even with my vampire powers. Gunnar was now marveling speeds up to my own as I hit rock after rock with my skull. His teeth tore into my flesh and I felt every excruciating sliver of pain traveling through my wrist and down my arm.

Just like my mom I was being taken to the forest by some werewolf I did not know was a werewolf for reasons that were beyond me. All I could do was think really. Think about the alternate reality versus real life now. Think about the innocent babies in my womb whom I put in danger and might never be able to experience life. Think about Angel and what I had done to him. Think about Caleb who would potentially never know he was going to father children. So many things rushed around in my head that when we had stopped I hadn't really realized it. I was being tied to a tree and I hadn't been paying attention until someone said my name.

I turned my head to see Gunnar standing in the woods right in front of me. One of the babies had kicked my liver at the same time I had raised an eyebrow of confusion at him. What in the world?

"Gunnar? What's going on?" I asked him.

He just laughed instead of answering me. And the weirdest thing happened after that. He leapt off to the right and transformed back into the large grey wolf from before. I looked to my left to see my mom tied o a tree as well with tears running down her face. Her shoulder was torn open and obviously was going to need medical assistance soon otherwise there would be too much blood loss. Someone has got to help us.

"Help!" I shouted at the top of my lungs. "Help!"

"It's no use." My mom said beside me. "I've tried that. No one is coming."

She looked so sad and dismayed that I knew she was telling the truth at that moment. There was no hope for us. I should find that hard to believe after all there were plenty of people who saw what happened to us. But they were not going to come. Something deep inside of me told me so. And at the same moment of giving up a sharp stabbing pain went through my lower abdomen like it's never felt before. The babies weren't just kicking . . . they were coming!

"Mom, I think I'm in labor." I told her.

She turned to me and did the only thing she could do that moment. She looked at me in the eyes and said, "I'm sorry honey." All hope was lost at that particular moment.

"I told you to get rid of them." An unknown voice said from behind my mother's tree. No, it wasn't unknown. I knew that voice very well. I had just heard it scream and yell at me months ago. Jack. "I told you to get rid of them while you still could or I would be forced to take matters into my own hands. My son didn't believe me. He's not the smartest tool in the shed though. I know this much. But I smelled it. I smelled his scent on those babies from the very beginning." He pointed to my stomach. "Well, you have left me no choice."

"Why are you doing this?" My mom yelled at him.

"Oh didn't you know Jane?" he glanced at me and I sneered at him. "Your beloved daughter is a vampire."

You should have seen her face after he told her that. It was half way between impossibility and believableness. I could tell there was a part of her that couldn't believe it but logic tells her that it is quite possible and probable. She had to believe it eventually. Might as well be in this situation she is told the truth.

"And you see, we can't have a blending of the species. Especially with my alpha son. The werewolf gene will not be attached to a vampire's while I'm alive. So, of course you know Scarlett that this means I have to kill you right?" He flew up and planted his werewolf claws inside the bark of the tree around me so he wouldn't fall. Lifting one werewolf paw toward my face, he scraped a claw along my cheek and drew the slightest amount of blood and he said sinisterly, "I'll make it as painless as I possibly can. Although," He breathed very close to my neck, "I doubt that tearing off someone's head can be very pleasant. What do you think?"

He was mocking me. Oh well, bring on death I guess.

I braced myself for him to end my life as another shot of that searing pain made me let out a tiny whine. Give me a break it hurt! Nonetheless, I turned my head away from any sight of my mom, shut my eyes and bit down. Waiting. Waiting. Waiting? What was taking him so long? I opened my eyes and noticed that Jack was staring off into the distance with a shocked look on his face. Gunnar had begun to whine in his wolf form as if he was afraid of something. What were they looking at?

It didn't take long for the cavalry to answer my question. Two massive creatures had tackled Jack off of my tree and onto the cold ground with a very loud thud. The two creatures separated, giving me an opportunity to actually see what they were. The one who had taken a turn toward Gunnar was actually Max! He along with Portia was battling a werewolf without a second thought. Although his skin did seem paler for some odd reason . . . Oh my god! Portia turned my brother into a vampire! Finally.

The other that had stayed with Jack was of course Caleb. I already knew it was even without looking. I felt him. Father and son dueling it out supernaturally right in front of me. Jack took out a very hearty chunk of the Caleb's side and blood began to stream out. Caleb became angry and ripped off a very large piece of his dad's pointed ear. There was no quick healing after that. They were weaving in and out of trees and I could barely make them out now.

It was incredible how much adrenaline was still pumping through my body after how weak I had become. I felt like I just wanted to go to sleep and never wake up again. If I shut my eyes right now, that's probably exactly what would happen. I felt a strong hand on my shoulder just as I was drifting off and it started to pull on me. My eyes snapped open and I bucked up in defense. There was Max, clutching his bleeding side, right in front of me. A large chunk was missing from the bloody area. Gunnar had been particularly viscous with my brother. But there was someone else here. I could tell. I smelled chocolate which meant it was a human. I also smelled my dad's aftershave. Which I'm guessing Jack did too because once he turned to see my mom being untied he pulled away from Caleb's neck, roared in wolf form, Knocked Max clear to the other side of the forest, and ran in my dad's direction.

I screamed his name to warn him but he didn't hear me. Jack had pounced on him and bit down hard on his stomach. Hearing my dad scream and twist in pain, my mom shouted for him. It was one giant losing battle scene and I knew once Jack had hit vital organs that my dad was dead. Severally injured wasn't an option because there was no way we could get out of this in time to save him. Jack and Gunnar had returned to chewing on Caleb's body which had been lying off to the side the whole time.

I looked around to see Portia laying on the ground not moving. I didn't know if she was dead or not but I had made assumptions and none of them were good. My head snapped back to where Jack was, strangely Gunnar had disappeared somewhere else at the moment.

"Hey you filthy dog!" I yelled. "Get off of him!"

I knew it wouldn't help but I had to get him away. He had gotten angry at me and my plan had worked. Jack was averted away from Caleb alright. But now his attention was directed at me. He was running full force toward me with shackles raised and teeth bared. Snapping the chains off of me with his teeth like they were dental floss, he flung me forward so that I went hurtling into another tree. His sharp canines had slid past the spot on my wrist and sliced all the way down to the crease in my elbow. I wouldn't wish this sort of pain and horror on anyone I met. Anyone! It almost felt like he has cut my whole arm off instead of just tearing the skin. My body was up in flames and my vision blurred at the loss of blood to my brain.

He shoved me down and wouldn't let me up. He was certainly stronger than I was with no competition. He barred his teeth and let out a fierce growl as I lay there unable to move my limp body. The impact of the tree, however strong I claim to be, had done some pretty serious damage to my back and rib area. He snickered through his teeth when I moaned and whined in pain. He was happy with my suffering. This wasn't Jack Darwin anymore! This was a whole different person, or rather thing, that had taken over his body. For a short moment, he became a human (if that's what you could call him) and fisted a handful of my hair on the back of my head and pulled upward to meet his glare. I let out another moan of pain as he continued to smile sickeningly.

"That's right honey, beg for your life."

I was too weak to answer. He transformed into the beast again and grabbed me by the waist and picked me up so that I was directly at eye level with him. He wasn't the brightest but he definitely had enough hate in him right now to fuel some pretty sinister thoughts. I could see his eyes piercing my own with searing rage and I actually felt bad for him. I knew that I had brought this on myself when I had gotten pregnant with his son's kids. He saw my face soften into pity so he gritted his teeth and slammed my whole body into the tree trunk once more. He obviously didn't want to be pitied, especially by me.

I screamed in pain as the impact of the tree felt like it was killing me from the inside out. It probably was. I heard him laugh again through his massive canine teeth and he thought he had won the fight. I wasn't going to try and harm him in any way and he knew that. I couldn't!

He gripped my whole upper body with one large paw-like hand and held me to the tree with immense force while his other began to tear at my dress from the bottom. I felt like I was helpless. I gathered up all the sympathy I carried inside of me and used it in one simple pitiful tear as he had halted his actions for one brief second. Something in his eyes had changed. He was feeling guilt, I just knew it. I saw him consider it and the old Jack came back out. Only for a brief second. Maybe it was the sweet smell of revenge that had gotten to him but he wasn't going to give up. He had wrapped his massive paw around my face and thrust them away from his muzzle. He slammed my body against the tree one last time as I made another face of pain. I couldn't make him stop, I knew this, but I still had to try one last time.

"Jack . . . please!" I begged as my voice began to fade out. I didn't even recognize it as my own anymore. It was the voice of desperation.

There was a tiny ball of light that came out of nowhere and positioned itself in between me and the massive, dangerous werewolf holding me. I had heard Jack's jaws tighten and snap downward. Instead of biting and tearing my heart out, he had chomped out Angel's instead. He had gotten angry and threw the dead angel's body off of mine and it had slid into a mossy covered rock a slight distance away before hovering over me on all fours again.

He had killed everyone I loved. Everyone I held near and dear were dead now and I did nothing. I just sat up here in this damn tree looking while they died in front of my eyes. How could someone do that? How could someone be so evil that they kill not only their own son but everyone in his life? Rage had bubbled up so high in my blood stream that I had actually felt it boiling through my skin. A power had come over me that was so full of force that I knew what I had to do. It wasn't going to be pretty but it had to be done.

I threw my palms onto Jack's chest and shoved with all of my strength. And he went pretty far too. I stood up off the ground and brushed my torn dress off, let down my hair, and started to stomp toward what now seemed like only a tiny puppy dog to me after he had gone back to his wolf form. Seeing Caleb and everyone else lying on the ground not moving added more fuel to my fire.

I began to run at the wolf as he was weakly trying to stand up himself. I slammed my body into his own with one, thunder cracking blow. Jack's body flew back and slammed into a tree, causing it to snap in half. He threw back his head and howled an ear-piercing howl of pain and fury. Pushing the tree aside, he got up and charged me with his head ducked low. His skull hit me directly in the stomach and knocked the wind out of me for a brief moment. My teeth accidentally pierced the skin of his neck and I finally tasted that sweet vanilla flavor of his mutated blood. I quickly pulled out and tried to catch my breath and stop myself from sucking any more out. It might help but I didn't want him to die like that. It was too painfull even for the gross, disgusting thing he had become. He pulled away and clutched at his throat, bringing his hand back to view the white (no lie) blood that soaked his palm. My instincts kicked in at his moment of weakness and I wrapped one of my hands underneath his jawbone while the other gripped the opposite side of his snout. It was the only thing left for me to do. I tried not to think of the sweet face that I had once loved. It was just too hard not to, however. I twisted and there was a loud snapping sound coming from between my hands. I had snapped his neck! His body fell from my own and landed on top of me. I could feel his weight crushing against mine and it repulsed and saddened me at the same time.

I opened my eyes to see his body being lifted off. I shook off the dizzy feeling from the head rush that had just overcome me and sat up to see what was going on. Max picked me up from the ground and gently pushed me in the direction of the house.

"What happened?" I asked weakly.

"You kicked his butt to high heaven that's what happened." Max told me.

"Oh. What about dad? Is dad OK? He needs to get to the hospital now!" I shouted. My vision was still a bit blurry from the pain happening in my body so I couldn't see any of them.

"I'll take him." He said.

Finally my vision cleared. My brother Max was standing with Portia by his side, hand in hand mind you, and looking down at me. I stood and gave him a big hug not just for being alive but also holding Portia's hand. I had no other choice but to let him take dad to the hospital even though he was in no condition—bloodied up himself. Mom—who was actually the least hurt of us all—had went with him thankfully which had left just me and Portia to tend to Caleb's body.

She had bent down to feel for a pulse on his neck but I already knew nothing was there. Caleb was dead and that's that. Memories from the past had flooded my brain all of him. I was losing the only love of my life and watching him die in front of me brought me to full-fledged, shaking sobs.

A hand was being placed on my shoulder. "You can save him Scarlett."

"What?" I said shocked.

"Bite him." She said forcefully. "Bite him on the neck right now and he'll be as good as new."

There was no arguing with her. I had to try. I bent my head down toward his body, positioned my mouth at his neck, kissed the skin before I pierced it. He tasted too good I just couldn't stop. Drawing buckets and buckets of blood from his body. Something had hit my stomach from the inside at the same moment Caleb's face was turning blue. I hunched over further to ignore it but it was just too extreme. The babies were coming and they were coming now.

"Get them out of me!" I yelled. "They're going to die!"

Someone at the foot of my bed was placing my legs up in stirrups and probed my . . . private areas. Like my vision, the room was still blurry and the scene was all in tunnel vision. I could feel someone's hand intertwining with mine and I was squeezing the life out of it. Portia had been the brave one to be in the delivery room with me and thank the lucky stars it was her hand I was killing.

The doctor had pulled one baby out of me and he indeed had hair just like his daddy's and eyes like my own. I had thought up of just calling him baby A for now until I could think of a better one. Because I wasn't done. There was still two more to go and the second one was coming right now. I seized Portia's hand once more and gripped it for dear life as I had pushed out another baby boy. Baby B. Baby B looked exactly like his father. No hint of me in sight. Born with brown eyes and a slightly darker complexion, he definitely took after the werewolf gene. And then there was the last one. The girl . . .

I had asked Portia how Caleb was doing once everything was finished but she didn't have an answer for me. Did I do it right? That's all my mind could worry about at the moment. Especially once the doctor gave the babies the A-OK.

I had named the two boys Sonny and Hunter. Sonny being more of the vampire gene and Hunter having certainly a dog for a dad. And then there was the girl, Angel, well she seemed to glow when she was born so I found it appropriate to honor my old friend. There was something about her, however, that bothered me. She of course had light red hair coming out unlike her brothers and her eyes seemed a bit murkier than Sonny's. She was definitely more vampire . . . but was she even part werewolf?

My dad had woken up from surgery just in time to find that out with everyone else in my family. The only one who doesn't know yet would be the most important. And I'm starting to worry as every hour passes by that I hadn't bitten him properly and I killed him surely. Portia tells me he's fine and I did a beautiful job every time she can but I don't believe it. The only way I'll believe it is if I see him with my own two eyes breathing in front of me.

Two days in the hospital was Hell. I went to visit my babies through the nursery window but I want to take them home. I want this all to be over with and everything to go back to normal. I want Caleb to look at me and say he loves me. I want to tell him that he actually is the father of the triplets and I want him to forgive me for lying. I just want my life to be normal.

"You are a vampire who just had three half breed babies and is about to marry the werewolf father of those three creatures. Your life will never be normal."

I turned around from the glass to see Caleb standing there, a little battered and bruised but looking so much better already, smiling at me. He was alive!

"Yes, I'm alive and can hear your thoughts you know. So watch what you say little missy."

I was so ecstatically happy that I had just sat there and stared at him with a smile on my face not knowing what to do. Wait did he just say . . . ?

"Yes I did just say. I want to marry you. I love you and I want to spend the rest of eternity with you. Will you?" He asked still with me staring at him in disbelief.

I looked into his dark brown eyes that strangely didn't change when I had bitten them like they were supposed to and knew that it was where I belonged forever and always. "Of course!"

He handed me a blood red rose out of his pocket. I twirled the stem in my fingers and caressed the pedals. For some odd reason its smooth skin reminded me of my own.

"What did you do to this?" I asked him as he grabbed a chair and sat down next to me to watch our babies.

"What do you mean?"

"There is obviously something up with it . . . I mean its texture feels real but it's so cold. What's wrong with it?"

"I bit it." He said with a smile on his face. He was obviously content about accomplishing his first vampire task. He wasn't lying either. I saw two holes at the end of the stem from his newly required fangs.

"And exactly why did you bite it?" I placed the rose in my lap.

"Because I wanted to give you something to show you that your beauty is breathtaking, just like this flower, and I didn't want it to die on you a few days later so I decided to try and bite it to see if it would work. I think it's working so far so good. Do you hate it?"

"I could never hate anything that you give me! Not even if I tried." I replied while wiping a tear from my eye. I jumped on him and wrapped my arms around his neck. I never wanted to let go he made me so happy.

"It's going to take me a while to get used to being able to hear and respond to your thoughts." He said as he put me down on the floor.

"Don't worry babe," I nuzzled his nose with mine. "I'll spend the rest of my existence teaching you how to deal."

Now if only there was such a thing as happily ever after for the mythical world full of enemies!